HIGH AS THE
HORSES' BRIDLES

HIGH AS
THE HORSES'
BRIDLES

———— A NOVEL ————

SCOTT CHESHIRE

HENRY HOLT AND COMPANY

NEW YORK

Henry Holt and Company, LLC
Publishers since 1866
175 Fifth Avenue
New York, New York 10010
www.henryholt.com

Henry Holt® and 🅗® are registered trademarks of
Henry Holt and Company, LLC.

Library of Congress Cataloging-in-Publication Data
Cheshire, Scott, 1973–
  High as the horses' bridles : a novel / Scott Cheshire.—First edition.
    pages cm
  ISBN: 978-0-8050-9821-1 (hardcover)—ISBN: 978-0-8050-9822-8
(electronic book) 1. Faith—Fiction. 2. Fathers and sons—Fiction.
I. Title.
  PS3603.H4845H55 2014
  813'.6—dc23   2013031099

Henry Holt books are available for special promotions and
premiums. For details contact: Director, Special Markets.

First Edition 2014

Designed by Kelly S. Too

Printed in the United States of America
1 3 5 7 9 10 8 6 4 2

For Kate
before, now, and after

Apocalypse is our history.

—James Berger,
"Twentieth-Century Apocalypse:
Forecasts and Aftermaths,"
Twentieth Century Literature,
vol. 46, no. 4 (Winter 2000)

HIGH AS THE
HORSES' BRIDLES

WOE TO
THE LAND WHOSE
CHILD IS KING

They sit.

Below a painted ceiling looming high overhead, they sit and they wait. The ceiling yawns, stretching like one vast wing warming oh so many eggs.

See the stars, the affixed points of light, the glowing striated mists of silvery cloud. See the night clouds lolling, drifting above their heads across an expanse of blue plaster sky. Like vapors released, dust climbs blue-gray and upward like prayers.

Now, see the ceiling stretch outward and above the seated people, this for all of one hundred feet, over and above the lettered rows A through Z, double-A and onward—on and above, across the grand room of ceramic, marble, and wood. Heels click and rubber soles pat, the sounds bouncing off here, and there, up through open space like swimmers ascending for air. And above every head, the sky stretches on toward brassy balcony railings, sloping down from the armpit arch of the ceiling's rounded center. Steeping downward, over the balcony railing—not even one foot resting there—then, just as you'd expect, the tiered seating rises even higher. Their heads are closer to the ceiling up there, with hair well combed and slicked.

Clip-on ties by the hundreds, a few full Windsor knots and occasional spit-shined wingtips on the congregation elders, the men who drove their families. No buses, no trains, not ever. They are in the aisle seats, more leg room. The wives ask their husbands, "Are you comfortable?"

In the central seats, see the suit jackets and ill-fitting corduroy, all very tasteful and clean, but not new, not even close. There's no small amount of pride in their faces, and their hand-me-down clothing. The black kids from Jackson Heights, the Hispanic kids from Ozone Park, and the pink-faced Irish from Astoria will rush the aisles come intermission, and they'll say, "Excuse me," stepping on the elders' fancy shoes. They will parade the building halls and call to each other, cruising, and flirting, asking which church the cute boy goes to. And the Indian girls from Richmond Hill, the Korean boys from Flushing. Their parents will gather for lunch and then approach the elder men, and pay them proper respect. Mothers wear skirts that reach below their knees. Any shorter and they risk a talking-to.

But first they sit. They face the empty stage, awaiting the opening song and prayer, the first speaker of the day to take the stage.

Not just any stage beneath any painted sky. Up there, you'll find no less than the heavens of Venice. You want proof—the famed Rialto Bridge, one tenth of its original size, a reconstruction, spans the top width of the stage. The favorite bridge in a City of Bridges, burned once, twice fallen, and both times a crowd collapsed with it. Down they fell under the waters of Venice. Which means the audience, here, in the grand Queens Howard Theater, tucked on a wide city street between a mechanic's garage and a Mexican takeout, are assembled in something like a dry canal. More than four thousand worshippers sitting, and anxiously waiting for the day's first prayer for His Kingdom Come on Earth as It Will Be in Heaven, and the long falling rain of salvation, falling stars, blackened sun, and fiery burning rain, for the coming of His Holy War and Christ. They pray for Armageddon, End of Ends, Great Bringer of all meaning in Death. And the worshippers are both a sum and parts, a throng, a sea of people beneath a decorative replica of the real-world Rialto. But, sure as any day, you can walk this bridge spanning the Howard's stage, and some actually do, mostly maintenance men tending to the delicate bridge's woodwork. Like a painted crown it spans the stage beneath the stars of Venice, City of Bridges, of Water, of Light.

Howard Theater, Theater of Lights, every heavenly star is here.

What does all this say about us sitters? There is a kinship with the city itself, its ever-reconfigured paths, boatways, and alleyways, all searching out new ways of seeking, just the right place for New Venetians. Heirs of the city's favorite son, Marco Polo, poster boy for journeyers, brave and faithful seeker of unknown truths, seer of this world, and carrier of Holy Oil, gift giver of Christ to the yellow men. More than four thousand of his heirs, sitting here, beneath a faux Rialto, awaiting a description of this world. And the next.

Backstage, behind the hanging curtain, the boy is clearly nervous. Hungry and nervous. He can't keep still. He's done nothing like this before, and certainly not here. Worse, he needs to go to the restroom. Feet shuffling in place, had way too much orange juice, he tries to sneak a look toward the front rows where he saw his parents seated earlier this morning. They always sit up front at church, something Dad practically can't *not* do. Up front, as close as they can, Dad on the aisle, Mom beside. A pale vessel. Dad has even asked people to move before, said he can't concentrate sitting anywhere else. Sometimes lately he's been sitting, and then standing again, and then sitting. Standing. Like he can't help himself, trying to get his place relative to the stage just right. There they are: Mom with her long red curls, and Dad wearing a stern face, looking like he's in charge. But who's in charge anymore? Just this morning they had a fight and told Josiah to please leave the kitchen.

From the stage, the great room seems even bigger than it was this morning, how many stories tall, and the ceiling feels like a window into dark and never-ending space. How spaceships look from the inside, he figures. When he first walked in and his parents looked for their seats, and he stood there, looking up, the great sky opened above him. He imagined two suns, just like in *Star Wars*, and a butter-yellow moon between them. A rocket shooting like a star. But now the room is bigger, much bigger than what his brain can comprehend, because the place is full of people. The people make the ceiling seem higher. The lamp bulbs looming, glowing and alive with light, hot and actual. Like the roof has been blown, and here is this place filled with—Dad said the unthinkable number this morning, in the station wagon, on the way here. "Say it with me slowly, son: *four thousand people*." Of course, he's heard the number before, but not in any way like this, not seeing it made real, four thousand *bodies*. He's certainly never spoken to so many before. He goes cold as he peeks through the curtains. He sees the pastor, Elder Brother Kizowski, approach the microphone and check his wristwatch as he walks. The stragglers are taking to their seats.

Josiah remembers a blueberry muffin, is sure he saw a tray of them this morning, out there, somewhere, maybe by the food tables.

A quick run to the restroom, and maybe he can find that tray of muffins. Feet shuffling, he needs to get his father's attention. He needs permission to leave the stage, so he can go to the bathroom. He can never seem to hold his father's attention, not for very long anyway, and especially when it's not about worship. Even when his father does talk with Josiah about God, it's almost like the boy isn't there. At least this is how he feels, like his father is looking right through him, to some other place and some other time, like he's seeing someone else entirely. Josiah wants his father to see him. Twelve years old, light as twigs, he spreads the curtains and eases his head forward, onstage, the cloth falling around him like a robe. Josiah, the size of a full-breasted bird, of a sapling elm, made small by the height of the hanging curtains, fire tongues reaching up to darkness.

Brother Bob Pullsey approaches him.

Bob Pullsey is a tall man, tall as two Josiahs stacked. He has the face of the men Josiah has seen sitting alone on Forest Park benches. In his sixties, Pullsey is old for an assistant servant, not yet an elder, not one of the older men of distinction, the elder shepherds of this great fleshly flock. Today he's in charge of the onstage amplified sound.

"Brother Pullsey," Josiah says, a little bit loud.

He's seen before how this older man is set apart from the other older men. He's one of them, but also not one of them, and Josiah thinks he likes that. But Pullsey makes him uneasy, too. Josiah gets a queasy feeling in his stomach sometimes when he sees men not like the others. If God rewards those who worship him, why is the old man still handling microphones and helping elder brothers half his age? Josiah doesn't like math, but this seems like a bad equation, something doesn't add up. He knows that God is supposed to reward.

He calls to Brother Pullsey again. But Pullsey puts a finger to his lips—Shhh, I'll be right back—as he walks toward the pastor onstage.

The pastor, Elder Brother Thad Kizowski, is locally famous for his mid-sermon animated gestures. But his aren't the wild gesticulations you see on Sunday morning TV. He's not your

televangelist preacher who cries and wails in an Easter-colored
suit, the kind that reasons with the camera, a salesman for the
divine. A serious man, Brother Kizowski is especially serious
today. This is the inaugural morning worship of a half week's
convention here in a newly purchased theater. Every New York
congregation, even some from out of state, friends in Christ from
across the great ministerial map who have thicker wallets have
focused their prayers and financial efforts on this for going on five
years now. They have filled up donation boxes with children's
change, quarters, nickels, dimes, and spare adult dollar bills, and
sometimes paychecks *Pay to the Order of* . . . The Lord has seen
fit this year to provide them, for the first time, a place of their
own for large conventions. A place to congregate, and feel as one.
A new home.

Kizowski is a gray-haired Polish man who buried his father
not two weeks ago, a camp survivor undone by a bathtub slip and
fall. Kizowski's hands remain motionless and at his sides for much
of the time, except for when, like in karate, they cut the air to
punctuate a special point or phrase. Slice upward when you speak
of Heaven, to the side when you speak of Earth. Brother Kizowski,
in his dog-brown suit, straightens his back and lapel, and waits
for the bustle in the great room to settle. He welcomes the crowd
as Bob Pullsey walks onstage.

"Good morning, brothers and sisters!"

Kizowski waves to the audience with both hands and nods at
approaching Brother Pullsey. And at first they're all of them out
there wondering, even Josiah, what's this, why is Brother Pullsey
onstage with the pastor? Pullsey whispers something into the pastor's ear . . .

Kizowski booms: "What a special day on God's good Earth! Is
it not?"

But now it's clear, even kind of comic, why Pullsey is inter-
rupting the speaker. It's the microphone—the threaded grip has
loosened, and the mic is slowly shrinking down inside its metal

sleeve. With Kizowski's hands slicing out, the way he does, and with the mic stand lowering, Kizowski appears to be growing in stature, like he's levitating just above the floor. The mic continues to slide slowly down. A staggered laugh moves through the crowd, slightly checked but growing steadily. You never really know when to laugh in church. Especially when Kizowski's onstage.

He steps back from the microphone to let Pullsey have his way with the stand, and he gives the audience a cold sneer. Accidental maybe, annoyed at the timing, he's just gotten started for goodness' sake. He pulls exaggeratedly at his collar. "Really, I mean I'm standing here telling the truth, brothers and sisters, the life-giving waters are flowing. And maybe, just maybe I'm getting carried away." He looks up. "Is my time up already, Heavenly Father? Is this a message, the vaudeville hook? We haven't even had the morning song and prayer yet!" And the entire theater breaks into laughter, a hearty family-table peal of laughter, laughter of relief. Kizowski's just like us.

"But seriously, brothers and sisters. This is a very special day. Our first day in this new House of God." He's backed up considerably from the microphone now, hardly within its reach. Test those lungs, and talk to the cheap seats: "Can you all hear me out there?"

A throaty and high-pitched "Yes!" from the back row answers for all.

"Good," Kizowski says. "Because I just might save your life!" Some more hesitant laughter from the crowd as Bob Pullsey continues to wrestle with the mic stand. He takes a step back and stares at the mic as if willing it to stay put. It finally does.

"Thank you, Brother Pullsey. Do all of you know Brother Pullsey? No, I'm sure you don't. We have how many here? More than four thousand, I'm told, from all five New York boroughs. Even Kansas City! I met a sister who came all the way here from Kansas City! But state and borough lines don't matter in here, not even your ballot! Because we've cast our vote for Christ, for the one true God and His Heavenly Kingdom. Let it rule from Heaven over Earth, and over His ever faithful subjects. And are we not faithful? Are we not proud of our Lord God who has paved the way for an authentic service, a fine, clean worship just like our first-century brothers and sisters? And is our God not so generous to provide for us this beautiful house to congregate and have fellowship in these Last Days? A place for us to meet, and associate, and encourage. For today we sit within the House of God!" In a stretched, extended position, he appears to be mid-dive. His pants cuffs lift, revealing three inches of hairless pink ankle. "Are we not a cared-for people? A curious people in search of the unbound soul? Are we not explorers of a true metaphysic? And who else could lead this great expedition but our one true Heavenly Father? Now let us show an appreciation for the brothers and sisters who have worked so hard to get his house ready, brothers like our Brother Pullsey. Welcome to this year's convention, this year's New York chapter of Brothers and Sisters in the Lord!"

There is a thundering of applause, and Kizowski himself is clapping as Bob Pullsey bows to the crowd.

Up there, in the balcony, claps Sister Hilda Famosa. She claps for the pastor, and for his speech, but looking everywhere except the stage. She's looking around for her family. Where are her boys? The service is starting and her family is nowhere in sight. She doesn't need this kind of aggravation. Not to mention her vertigo. The seats are so high it's making her flushed.

No seats left on the main floor, so they had to sit in the balcony. Should've left the house at least an hour earlier, but nobody listens. And when you have to get two boys—no, wait, make it three because Havi brought his mejor amigo, little Issy, because *his* mother's all high again, who knows where his father is, and all of them fighting for the shower this morning, plus a husband who keeps giving her trouble. Like she doesn't have enough since Carlo Junior got his driver's license. She's never on time anymore. Why am I without my family? Havi and Issy said they were going to the bathroom, and that was twenty minutes ago. And so Carlo Senior went looking. You better go find mi revoltosos. And who knows where Carlo Junior is, lately chasing any rump that walks. And so their Bibles, and their jackets, and her snake-plastic purse all on the chairs beside her, so nobody tries to sit. She mumbles a prayer to herself, and wonders if this long suffering will make her a better bride for Christ.

And everyone here, in different ways, wonders the very same thing. Will they make a good partner for Christ? But not in one way or in one voice, because this is not a collective power, the funneled strength of a crowd. No, it's personal, a singular power, within each and every one where lives a now-blooming question: Does God know my name, and does He love me? Am I so lucky?

My name is Hilda, and I scrub the grout and bathroom tiles of accountants and lawyers and their wives. She mouths these words: You love me, I know You love me. But where are my boys? The pitch is pretty steep and getting steeper with each stair and the red velvet chairs feel like bird perches, this high up. Her vertigo is getting even worse. The stars above a long ladder's reach away. Her hands going pale as she grips the soft red armrest, the kind you find in old movie theaters. Well, that's what she heard some people say anyway, that this place used to be a movie theater. Tiene sentido, but *here*? Why sit up here? Why not come early and sit down front? Nobody listens. And a little boy sitting by himself right in front of me. ¿Dónde está tu madre? If I'm not careful, and he turns, the boy will see up my skirt.

The ceiling presses closer on the rows behind her, close, and coming down like a sandwich press meeting the way-back wall, stars and all, of the Queens Howard Theater. In any other theater in this world, a ticket taker dressed in cardinal red would stand up here with a handful of Playbills. But not here. Hilda has climbed to where the stairs stop, as far as you *can* go, where the ceiling *becomes* the wall. Where one of the maintenance men, Harold, from Brooklyn, fifty-six and round-faced, came all the way on the N train and walked how many blocks, has already lugged a gallon of paint from the first floor early this morning because some kid, probably not ten or twelve, a boy no doubt, stood up on his tiptoes and scratched away a star above BZ5. Where his father was forced to stoop, because like it or not the sky rushes down like a plaster-cast waterfall of stars. Be careful, or you just might crack your head.

From up here, the highest seat in his house, you can see it all, a crazy mixed perspective, where the clouds crawl high over the heads of husbands, wives, and children now settled in their seats. The applause has stopped. What sermon first? What song? Will there be talk of a new date? Because there's been rumor of a brand-new date. . . . These are End Days, the Last Days, and the signs of the times are real, everywhere, and it's so obvious. The earthquakes on the news. Russia killing all the God-fearing good men and women. Armageddon must be right around the corner. There has been talk among the congregations of a possible announcement, a date of divine prophecy revealed. The hour and the day made known, in honor of this new house of His worship. Since '75—five years ago, but feels like yesterday—when so many prayed for Armageddon, and the Holy Ghost spoke through the pages of Ezekiel, Daniel, and the ancient dreamer John of Revelation. All their numerical reckonings had been pointing toward a date just right around the corner: Come 1975, the End will be here! The date was wrong. How many subsequent defections from how many ministries? Some got lucky and found a family with these new Brothers in the Lord. Hilda wasn't around for all that drama, but she heard about it. She was new, and only started coming when someone gave her a pamphlet, "Don't Be Afraid of Death," two years ago on a subway. But of course the End didn't come in 1975, it wasn't time. But have you seen the TV news lately? The world is falling apart, with volcanoes, and they keep on talking about the Cold War, and how is war ever cold anyway? And the snatching up of the kids. Crack sold on street corners. Ay dios mio, what happens after Armageddon, then? Will the Holy Spirit talk to us today?

Hilda spots little Josiah opening a door by the stairs to the stage. Or maybe he's not so little after all. Almost the same age as Havi, but he's so much more mature. Josiah Laudermilk is special and Hilda knows it, too: special like her Havi can't ever be. He seems a little bit lost, and looking maybe for someone in the audience. Right there, in the front row, a man stands up and motions back to Josiah. It's the boy's father, Brother Gill Laudermilk. She doesn't talk with him too much at church, because he makes her uncomfortable. Muy intenso. Now he's waving at the boy, and excusing himself, making his way toward Josiah.

Kizowski is saying: "Let's open our songbooks to page number . . ."

Josiah walks toward his father, the door closing behind him.

The boy's father takes him by the shoulder and pushes him along and away toward the back of the hall, under the balcony, where Hilda can't see him no more. There is a yearning energy filling this place, a spirit she can't help but receive even as she's still feeling dizzy. It calms her even as it rises. She reaches one hand toward the stage, as if she expects to be taken, and lifted. But where are her boys?

Just like in junior high school, it's in the stairwells you find the kids. In the halls and every darkened corner. They ditch parents first chance they get, and the parents don't mind because inside is not the world outside. No crime, here, not in his house. No borough factions, or fights. Queens, Brooklyn, or Bronx. Best of all, no unbelievers. We're a clean people, have a good time with your brothers and sisters. But be in your seats before the service begins.

Havi and Issy stand by the water fountain and the restrooms at the top of the stairs. The doors to the balcony are closed, but Kizowski's voice booms through the walls. You can't get away from Kizowski. But with enough practice—and boy, do they have practice, church twice a week, sometimes more, for as long as they can remember—with enough practice you tune out the voices. Doesn't mean you don't get the message. These boys, thirteen and fourteen, they know it all by heart.

"Look at that," Havi says.

Issy looks. The girl is maybe thirteen, and coming out of the ladies' room, Dominican or maybe Puerto Rican, but it's also, like, she's a young woman. Not bodily—she weighs no more than what little girls weigh, it's like she weighs so perfect—but would you look at the way she walks. No time anymore for play dolls or boy crush magazines, she wears a yellow dress with a white stripe around her knees like icing. Issy feels a little dizzy, and he knows a soda will make him feel better, but he also likes the buzzy feeling when his body wants sweets. Right now he wants nothing more in the world than to know her name.

"Girl is fresh," Havi says.

Issy shoots him a look. Havi always gets the girls, but not this time. No way.

Havi says, "What I say?"

Issy watches the girl walk over to a man, probably her father, who talks with a fat Chinese brother sitting in a foldout chair. The Chinese brother is collecting donations in a tall wooden box with a handwritten sign taped to it: "Contributions for Furthering God's Good Work."

Havi whispers, "Bet his chair busts in like five minutes."

Is she looking? Issy's small heart hiccups. Nah, she's not looking . . .

Brother Laudermilk, Josiah's father, stands by the door. The door opens again, and hot moist air comes wafting out. The restrooms are enormous. "Like a house in there," says Havi. Urinals

line the wall, each one with a blue flush cake. The air in there
can't be helped, though. The Argentines, Dominicans, Filipinos,
Dutch. The Japanese, Ukrainians, Indians, Egyptians. The northern blacks, the southern blacks. Then every kind of white there
is. They all come to worship and they bring their neighborhood
smells, an invisible map of the world.

Havi says, "Jesus."

"Don't cuss," says Issy, looking away to the girl.

Then Issy looks at Brother Laudermilk, who now glances back
toward the boys, flattens his left lapel. Issy half waves, and says,
"Thas Josiah's father. You see Josiah around?"

Havi says, "Nah, I bet he's in the pisser."

Issy says, "Looks like he's waiting for Josiah."

"C'mon, les' go, b'."

"Hey, thas Josiah," says Issy. "Just look it."

The door closes behind the boy as he leaves the bathroom,
blowing his nose into a stiff paper towel.

Issy waves him over.

Josiah looks at the two boys. His father is chatting with the
large man, and with the father of the girl in the yellow dress,
and the girl, too. On the way to the restroom, Josiah and father
passed a lunch table stacked with heros. He showed his father,
and asked for one, please. But his father said, No, wait for lunch.
Food weighs you down. A spirit hungry for God is never satisfied.
Concentrate on your sermon, son.

Josiah throws away the paper towel and heads over to where
the boys are standing, but then hesitates. Should he talk to them?
Talk to Havi? He realizes he hasn't really talked to anyone his age
all day. He walks over.

Issy says, "Wassup, what you doing?"

Havi acts like he doesn't see Josiah.

Josiah nods his head, his father still busy talking. "I don't know.
I'm supposed to be somewhere. I have something to do." Figures
he better not mention his sermon because every time he gives

one at church, Havi makes fun of him after. Issy never does, though. Josiah used to think it was because of their parents, that he had two parents and they both went to church. Except then Havi's father started going to church, too, like his mother, and *still* he acts like a jerk. Issy's father's hardly ever around. His mom was, but not so much anymore. He's practically living at Havi's. One time, at church, when Issy's mother was there, she pushed Issy's head against a wall. Josiah was on his way to the restroom, saw it, and didn't know what to do. Issy's mom looked so mad, and she tried to keep her voice low as she smacked at Issy's head. Josiah went over and took Issy's hand. He had lied and said, My father wants to see you.

"You so weird, Josiah," Havi says, shaking his head.

"Shut up, Havi," says Issy.

"Why? He your boyfriend now? Yo, we should go get Shastas. Josiah, hey, you got fifty cents?" Havi pats at his pockets, like he swears he's got money somewhere.

Josiah shakes his head, no. "I like Royal Crown anyway."

"Your boyfriend doesn't even like Shasta. You know that girl, Josiah?" Havi likes talking at girls. He learned it from his older brother Carlo. Issy's more shy, and the girls like that about him, they like that he doesn't know he's handsome. Havi knows Issy's good-looking, but he'll never say it. Havi's in charge anyway.

Josiah says, "I don't know."

"You don't know nothing, man." Havi sucks at his teeth. "She's looking at me." Havi with his small chest pushed out, always ready, pre-confrontation. He learned this from his big brother, too, all five feet and five inches of bulldog Carlo. He checks himself in the silver backsplash of the water fountain.

Josiah surprises himself, and says, "Oh, yeah? Then why don't you go talk to her?"

Havi straightens up. "Say what?"

"Yeah," snaps Issy, laughing, a little bit anxious. "Thas a nice one!" He puts up his hand for a high five. Josiah looks at the hand, and then he looks at his own. Then he presses his hand against Issy's. He realizes he's never seen them outside of church before.

Havi says, "You two stupid." His face goes a little pale. "Why don't *you* go talk to her? Tell her how smart you are? Faggot."

Josiah wants to tell Havi to stop it already, teasing him hard for over a year. It's not like they were best friends ever, but Havi used to leave him alone. Until last summer, when Havi started dressing like his brother and wearing a thick gold necklace. The new clothes make him act like the biggest jerk Josiah's ever met. But sometimes the teasing is better than not talking with anyone at all.

Issy says, "I told you to leave him alone. Nobody's going to talk to her."

It's not like Josiah's timid, not at all. Sometimes he has a problem of saying too much. And face it, he knows it, he is more comfortable around adults. Other kids usually make him nervous. But who doesn't want friends? And Issy has always been good. Look how he's looking at the girl. Issy is in love. Josiah sees it, and it makes him smile. He draws a long breath and says: "Yeah, she's not for you anyway." He's nodding at Issy.

"Excuse me?" Havi scratches at his ear, puffs up.

Issy puts up his hand for another high five. "Havi got schooled," he sings.

Havi sucks at his teeth again. "Please." He flicks Josiah's ear.

Josiah flinches.

"You gonna tell your daddy?"

Josiah turns and looks at his father, who is still talking with the others.

"Huh?" says Havi. "You looking for your mommy, too?"

Maybe his father has forgotten he's here. He looks back at Havi, and suddenly wants to punch him in the face. He's never hit anyone before, and definitely not with a punch in the face. How would it feel? Would it hurt his hand? He thinks about this

morning, in the kitchen, when his parents were yelling again. His
father had said this time it was different. The Holy Spirit had
spoken directly to him. Josiah walked into the kitchen, and he
asked how it sounded. His father said, almost yelling, Would you
please leave the room while your mother and I . . . Josiah wondered, Why tell Mom? Not me? I'm the one giving a sermon . . .
He didn't like it when his father raised his voice to his mother.
Josiah's mind was racing. Did the Holy Spirit say, Not Josiah?
Anybody but him? Can the Spirit talk to anyone it wants?

In 1975, Josiah was only seven. Too young to remember, really,
but here his father was talking about 1975 again. About Armageddon. His father talked so much about Armageddon. Josiah
knew the scriptures, what the End was supposed to look like. Fire
in the sky, like a war. His father said it would happen maybe in
1980, maybe now. But he couldn't be sure, only that we have to
stay faithful. Look for signs. He heard his father say there was a
rumor an announcement would be made. Today. When Josiah
thinks of Armageddon, it makes him feel older, and bigger, stronger like his father.

Havi says, "You just gonna stand there?"

He steps up to Havi—right up. Makes a fist.

"Oh, shoot," says Havi. "Look it, stepping up like he's gonna
go ballistic. Please."

Josiah says a quick prayer and asks for the Lord God's blessing. And then, surprisingly, he relaxes his fist, but lifts his foot up
above Havi's sneaker. Because he wants to hurt Havi. He wants
to smash Havi's toes with the hard heel of his own dress shoe.

Issy shakes his head: Don't do it.

But they can't tune the voice out forever, and Kizowski is
coming on strong. His father crooks a finger—Get over here. We
have to get backstage.

The amplified voice speaks out: "You pretend to know the
mind of God? The hour? The day? There will come God's great

war, *Armageddon*!" And this word is like a wooden chair thrown against a concrete wall.

Issy says, "We should get back to our seats."

The voice surges through the halls like rushing dark water: "That Last Day will come like a thief in the night! Hear the psalmist! Who is there knowing the strength of His anger? His fury? You think His anger is like our Mount St. Helens?" A long pause . . . then, percussive, his lips closer to the mic, touching mesh: "Bah! A bee sting! A headache! For our God has come to prove to you that *His* fear will be before your faces." A laugh, expelling his breath: "The Lord God has shaped every mountain with His hands, and the heavens themselves. Little lady Helen is no different!"

Josiah unfreezes. Lets down his foot, away from Havi's. His brain swirls with the TV footage. The bursting of Mount St. Helens's rock face, the hellish smoke and flame spewing from the hole, the shower of black ash rain. He looks at his father, who looks back at him, tapping on his wristwatch. What was his father talking about with those brothers?

Josiah says, "I gotta go."

Havi says, "You so weird."

The speaker box says: "The insistence of this world is on hurtful things, on evil things. But our Lord God has no fear. You think God is only love? Don't you cherry-pick your scripture! Our Lord God is love, but also power! And fury! And that Last Day will be like none since the Flood. And God's army will come riding forth on horses, and the sinners' blood will run in the streets, thick and deep, high as a horse's bridle, and just as fast."

Issy says, "Nah, man, Josiah's cool." Issy swallows a gulp of air, his eyes still on the girl.

Josiah waves goodbye. He walks over to his father as the boys leave off. He sees Issy looking back as he runs, tripping on his way to the stairs. He nods hello to the girl in the yellow dress. But she looks through him, right past him, over and around, behind him. With every sense she follows Issy. Josiah wants to shout, "Hey Issy! She likes you, too!" But they're gone, the boys, like animals let off their leashes.

His father walks him down the aisle toward the stage, and alongside the audience. They enter the doorway that leads backstage. Soon they are alone. Josiah stops before going any farther, the muffled echo of sermon behind the concrete walls. "What were you and those brothers talking about?" he asks.

"Don't you worry," his father says. "You're young yet."

Josiah considers this, and does not like it.

Whenever his father doesn't want to involve him in a conversation at church, and sometimes it seems important, he says it's only for the older brothers. But Josiah knows so much scripture by heart, even more than some of the elders. He has displayed this scriptural knowledge in the past. As he gets older, the more he displays, the stronger he feels—at least here he does, in church, among believers. Even though he is powerless in school. Or around the block. Or in his neighborhood. Last week his father stopped a bully from stealing Josiah's bike.

"Were you talking about Armageddon?" he asks.

His father looks him up and down, smooths the face of Josiah's tie with his hand. "You're becoming a real young man. And you will get taller, I promise. But not today." It's an old joke between them. But Josiah doesn't smile.

He asks the question again. "Were you talking about Armageddon?"

His father touches the boy's cheek and says, "The first book of Corinthians, you remember? The faithful ask the Apostle Paul lots of questions. What about this, and what about that? But he doesn't answer them all. And why? Because not everyone was ready. Even to the faithful I give milk, he said, and not solid food, because you are not yet ready."

Josiah considers this.

"Isaiah, chapter three, verse four," he says. "And I will make the boys their leaders, and the children shall govern over them." He does not look away from his father.

Gill is silent.

What is a boy like this?

Can a father love his son and release him? Sacrifice him, and still love him? Is this not what God the Father did for the Christ? Jesus taught the Temple fathers when he was only twelve . . . And it seems like this has been the case ever since Josiah's third birthday, when he dropped his Dr. Seuss and picked up Genesis. Maybe even before, since his mother went underwater in a long white T-shirt and a modest black one-piece swimsuit. Baptized at thirty-five, her stomach was so swollen with Josiah, it took two men to get her underwater and rebirth her to the Lord. You were there, Josiah, she always says, my miracle boy inside me, and when I finally went under you dragged me down, so every last inch of my belly got saved. My belly button bobbed till you pulled me down, you keep my faith from drifting. I was thinking of 2 Kings, Gill always says, when you came up from the water. And I knew it then, this special boy would be nothing less than kingly. Born with a breath of God's power in his infant lungs. And your name would be Josiah, like the anointed boy-king of old. Only a child, but touched by God's great hands, the very thing we needed, the answer to our every prayer.

Josiah, Josiah, Josiah, hang on the boy's every word . . .

He kisses Josiah's head. "I'm proud of you," he says. "I love you. Your mother and I are very proud. You come from a long line of godly men. Got your notes?"

Satisfied, Josiah taps his jacket pocket, turns away, and heads for the backstage door.

His father never answered the question—and that kiss, what

was that kiss? He could have picked so many scriptures to show his father he wasn't a kid anymore. He turns back, and sees him. He takes the notes from his pocket, and raises them. He waves them and can't keep from smiling. Neither of them can. He opens the door to the stage. Takes two stairs at a time.

Josiah calls out, as Bob Pullsey walks right by him. The sound man rounds a temporary wall backstage. Puts up a finger, Just a minute.

By now Josiah is starving. Kizowski's been at it for nearly twenty-five minutes. It seems like he's finishing up, stopping for consenting applause after almost every line. That's the way to do it, but Josiah can't imagine being onstage for twenty-five minutes. Thank goodness he has only ten. He shouldn't have listened to his father, should've taken one of those heroes with him! Can't stand still; he walks over to Pullsey's wall. He looks up for the stars and the projected clouds, the night sky and ceiling lights, but he sees there instead the hanging ropes, the electrical cords, cabling, and catwalks that hang from the backstage ceiling.

He walks around the temporary wall, taking Brother Pullsey by surprise.

"What'd I say?" Pullsey raises his left hand, and it looks like he's actually going to swing at the boy, but he brings the butt of his fist down on a rusted pair of pliers. Tries to turn a stubborn nut, and says, "Nothing works like it should."

Josiah stops. He doesn't know how to react to this. Pullsey says, "I told you a minute. Now get back where you were until I say so." Pullsey keeps fiddling with the pliers.

Not Josiah's father, not his mother, not one person in his congregation, not even the elders talk to him like this. And Pullsey knows *exactly* who Josiah is, and why he's here—not sitting with his parents, but backstage, all on his own.

"Now," Pullsey says. The boy obeys, slowly walking back to

the curtains. He peeks between the curtains, to see if he might spot his mother.

There she is, in the front row, Ida, just like she promised. He needs her to see him.

But she doesn't see him, not yet.

Josiah's father, now returned to his seat, is nodding along with Kizowski's cadence. Ida Laudermilk scratches her head, looking from side to side, almost like she's bored. She looks his way—Josiah! She mouths his name, and her face blooms like a late morning glory. Josiah waves, his soul is enlivened, and this catches his father's attention. Gill Laudermilk squeezes Ida's right leg: None of that. Keeps a light, corrective grip on her thigh. He looks Josiah's way, nods approval, and then turns back to the pastor.

But Josiah keeps staring at his mother, and as he stares her face becomes suddenly estranged, the way a familiar word turns alien if you say it enough. A frightening vision forms there and grips him entirely: his mother sitting hairless, stifling a smile, her pale skull like a bulbous root pulled from the earth. He shakes his head, shudders, and she takes again the form of her old self. He is chilled from it, and watches her mouth move. She's saying, "Stop it, silly, you're getting me in trouble."

He looks at his father, who squeezes her leg again, and the shake of his father's shoulder tells Josiah this time the squeeze is more vigorous. Maybe even painful. He wonders whether his hands are large enough to squeeze his father's leg. Arm? Neck?

Gill looks at his boy, and then immediately away. Then he looks back just as fast. He cannot take his eyes from his son. Who is this boy? So unlike other boys his age. What does he know? What is he thinking? There is strength inside him, and Gill wonders where it comes from. Maybe Ida.

"So tell me, then." Pullsey's now behind the boy, arms at his sides like triangles. His face wears an expression of impatience, bottom lip over top, his mouth eating itself up.

Josiah says, "I thought you were over there."

"And now I'm here."

"I'm hungry."

"And?"

"I need something to eat. Is that part of your job? You know why I'm here."

"So you're hungry, wait until lunch."

"I can't."

A wave of applause echoes from beyond the curtains.

Pullsey lightly claps. "Brother Kizowski is a fine man, and a very good speaker. Big shoes, buster," he says.

"What?"

"To fill. Big shoes to fill. You're on in how many minutes?"

Josiah bites at a fingernail.

"Okay, okay, c'mere." Pullsey sits on a stool and waves the boy over like, Right here, kiddo, relax.

"What?"

"You're hungry, right?" He reaches under the stool and grabs hold of a gray metal lunchbox.

"What's that?"

"Lunch," Pullsey says, and hands him one of three sandwiches carefully wrapped in foil.

"My mother wraps them like this," Josiah says, biting into ham and yellow cheese. "Hey, what happened to your hands?"

"Chicken pox," Pullsey says. Rubs them together, cracking a knuckle. He puts the left hand in a pocket, the right behind his neck.

"I never noticed. Why'd you get chicken pox?"

"I was a kid. And kids get chicken pox."

Josiah wipes his mouth with the cuff of his jacket. "I didn't."

"Not yet."

Josiah chews. "Maybe God punished you with chicken pox."

Kizowski is booming, but it's muted some by the curtains. Pullsey and Josiah are surrounded by the lush cloth, a fiery red-orange. Ropes and sashes dangle from the backstage spotlights.

"Seventy years we live, brothers and sisters," Kizowski says. "In the case of special power, eighty. And the scriptures tell us it is *this* generation—not *that* generation, or *any other* generation, understand—but *this* generation will by no means pass away until the Day of the Coming of the Lord."

Clapping, clapping, and then it's quieter.

"Amen," says Brother Pullsey, offering a single quiet slap at his chest. He looks back at Josiah, and says, "Okay, that's enough." He brushes the boy off the stool.

"You hit me," Josiah says, not really believing it even as he says it.

"I didn't hit you. I just need my seat. And I'm sure you know what it is to be hit. Or maybe you don't, and you should." He looks to the stage. "Shh, he's almost done."

Pullsey walks back toward the curtains. Kizowski points two fingers at the crowd, then heavenward, raised above his head like goalposts.

"Are you an electrician? My uncle's an electrician," Josiah says from behind. "But I don't think he can do this kind of stuff. You must be a genius."

Pullsey turns, and boy is this guy grinning. "I know you since you're this big." He thumbs the top of his kneecap. "They've been spoon-feeding you forever." He turns away, and Josiah hears him mumble something about his mother's breasts—that she still feeds Josiah her breasts?

Josiah says, "I heard you cuss. What did you say?"

"I did not cuss," Pullsey says, and faces Josiah squarely. " 'Your breasts are like two young ones, like the twins of a female gazelle.' Read your Song of Solomon. The Bible's full of boobs. And," he leans forward, "I didn't hit you."

Josiah pulls back, not in fear, but in surprise. He walks back to the stool and he claims it. "So how come you're not an elder yet? Most of the old men are elders." He takes a bite of the sandwich and pushes at the temporary wall.

Pullsey almost takes the bait, but says a brief prayer instead. For patience. And a small prayer for Josiah, the twelve-year-old whiz kid from Richmond Hill who they say knows the Bible by heart. Exaggeration. "We all have our parts to play," he says. "And today, mine is making sure every word gets heard. You about ready?" He motions Josiah to please get off the stool, but the kid just doesn't give.

"Off the stool," Pullsey barks. "Now."

The boy drops his head like a corrected pup, and he moves.

"It's almost time," Pullsey says. "I'll walk you out there, buddy, and we'll get that mic just right."

Josiah looks up, defeated, but also half-smiling. Not so bad a feeling to be told what to do. He puts his hand in his right jacket pocket.

"What have you got?" Pullsey asks, not really interested.

Josiah turns away and takes out a *Star Wars* figure from inside his jacket. He carries one everywhere he goes. If his father knew, he'd be in big trouble. He likes how, with an action figure in his hand, the world around him becomes another world, a bigger world. Stones become mountains. Holes become bottomless pits. He makes like the figure is climbing his tie, swinging from a rope, and then he puts it back in his jacket.

"You're gonna be fine," Pullsey says. He squeezes the boy's shoulder, massages his bones. "Break a leg." He rubs at the boy's slender blades, and hears Kizowski declare from the stage: "Yes, brothers and sisters, please join me in welcoming our next and very special speaker."

"That's your cue," Pullsey says. And Josiah makes like he's ready, but Pullsey does not let go.

"Brothers and sisters, our young and gifted Brother Josiah Laudermilk."

The applause is especially long, as if the crowd is trying to coax the boy out from backstage where Pullsey holds on to his lamb-white neck. And Josiah can hear his father clapping. It's gotta be him, a deliberate, hard and hollow cupping of the palms. Loud, loud, loud. Clap, clap, clap. Not fifty feet from where he stands. This gives him strength. The boy looks up at the sound man, who now looks down at the boy. He's just a boy. Their eyes meet.

If you stay backstage, you'll stay a boy forever.

He steps out onto the stage.

"Be careful out there, big man. Knock 'em dead."

Carlo Senior tells them to shush it.

Issy whispers, "You hear that? You hear they said Josiah?"

Always angry before he got in the Lord, but now with church on the weekends and the family Bible study, Carlo Senior acts like a real man, and sometimes he's even so kind, never so pissed anymore. They call him Brother Famosa. Got church privileges, too. Brother Famosa's a greeter on Sundays, and maybe one day he'll be a servant brother like the other men who help out the church with their business. The microphone handling, the money boxes. Oh, and Sister Hilda Famosa just balloons when she sees him opening the door, and welcoming the congregation every Sunday morning. She wishes Carlo Junior would follow his lead, but his head is only in one place, all the chicas bonitas. And Havi—she's worried about Havi, how he looks up to his big brother. Issy does, too. She hands the boys thin spiral notebooks and five-color push pens, tells to them to write down a check mark whenever they hear the name Jesus.

Oh my God, here he goes.

Carlo Senior reaches across the empty seat beside him, and presses his finger to Havi's mouth like "Shhhhh." Smacks him on the back of the head. Issy inches forward and away, because he knows Havi's father will hit him, too. "You two be quiet," he says. "People are looking."

"Thas Josiah, Papi," says Havi.

"Like I don't know? Who you think watch the door when the elders had a meeting, stupid?" Carlo looks at his son like he's daring the boy to get this wrong. He lifts his chin like he's looking down his nose. "They even ask me to shake his hand. Because they know he needs to act like a man. You should be like Josiah, inmaduros."

Carlo leans straight as his wife rubs his back, Okay, okay, thas enough.

"Thas Josiah!" Issy whispers to Havi.

"I know, stupid. Thas why my father hit me."

Sister Hilda Famosa says, "Shhh."

So Issy pushes the red tab on his push pen, opens his spiral, and writes: "We should make him see us"

Havi takes the pen and writes: "Josiah's so weird"

Issy writes: "We should make him see us"

Issy waves.

He looks at Sister Famosa, and waves at Josiah again. She puts out her hand, You gimme that. She gives Issy a look that does more than any kind of slapping from her husband.

Gill watches his son step out from behind the curtains and slowly walk across the stage toward the podium. Kizowski waits with an open hand. Gill crosses his fingers, and then hides this small superstitious gesture beneath his legs. Earlier this morning, he told Josiah his best chance for success is to fast get the audience's attention, maybe start with a joke. Maybe start with a knock-knock joke. Up there you're a salesman! And so you have to sell yourself to the crowd. Gill should know, he's sold everything from aluminum siding to Simoniz. Advertise, Advertise the King and His Kingdom, born a Jehovah's Witness, he preached from door to door until the day he finally up and quit. They sang and they recited: "Stay Alive till '75." But they were wrong. So he took his wife and boy and he joined with the Brothers in the Lord. Look how lovingly Kizowski takes Josiah's hand, how he bends and whispers in the boy's ear. Five years now with this new family.

Gill thinks of family Bible studies at the dining room table, with warm bowls of popcorn on special nights when Mom's in a shiny good mood, Who wants butter on their popcorn? I'll melt it on the stove. Bible-study magazines spread on the table like treasure maps. My father, too, Gill has told them, and his father before him, how long we have waited! Four of the Laudermilk men, generations awaiting His return, and all in the blink of our Heavenly Father's eye. Who could've hoped for a son like this? Just look at him! So much more than his only child, as if Gill is ever lifting his son skyward, toward a burning sun going dark on the coming Great Day. The boy holds a promise of something extraordinary, a genuine love for the Lord, somehow an echo of authentic worship. Born with a belly full of Holy Spirit language, Josiah is their ticket home, a taste of the early time before the world forgot about the Good Book. Look at him! Up there! Onstage! So proud! My boy, clearing his throat! Gill's never been one for stages, that kind of pressure, never given sermons outside his home. But this? His boy onstage in front of thousands and delivering God's Good News? It's sort of like he's up there with him. Beside his son. The sermons *are* partly his. . . . Sometimes he forgets how young the boy is—"You can't spell 'theocracy'? Here, let me show you"—and then sometimes, oh boy, how his young son gets too big for his britches—his own father used to say it about Gill . . . —But this look, why this look? Why is Josiah just standing there, and not yet saying a word? Gill looks at Ida, who looks straight ahead and takes his hand (he uncrosses his fingers). She squeezes. But the Laudermilk calling is a prophetic one. No matter how close to fulfillment. Their calling is the searching itself. Dig out meaning from the pages.

Dig, boy, dig! And speak!

———

There is an air of apprehension in the hall, a buzz and mumble of concern as the audience sits and waits. But all the boy can do is look out at the smear of faces.

He's nervous and feels alone. He can no longer find his mother's face in the crowd.

So he offers up a small and unexpected prayer, a strange silent prayer, asking the Lord for his help and good guidance. He cups his hands together as if he were holding a scoop of river water, and blows lightly into his palms; this is his prayer. He tosses this prayer out into the wide space in front of him, beyond the microphone, off the stage, and into the sea of people. It's a gesture charged with an almost innocent significance, a naive grace. The audience is taken with this slow movement, reading in it all kinds of story. Some see Noah toss a dove above the tops of flood-buried trees, and others catch sight of John the Baptist, hands upturned, offering a life-giving dunk. Josiah sees only his own small hands, and then unexpectedly, and maybe not accidentally at all (because maybe this is, in fact, how prayers are answered), his mother's face in the void between his separating fingers.

Josiah turns slowly to his left, and then slowly to his right, like Kizowski does, both good moves to buy time. Then he turns back to his mother.

The boy says into the microphone: "Knock, knock."

Is this a joke? Is Josiah telling a joke? Issy can't look away. Havi is not paying attention, but something is going to happen, Issy knows it.

Josiah looks slowly from side to side, scanning the audience. And now Josiah is staring. Issy tries to see who he's looking at because the boy has stopped, is looking out straight ahead. At his family? Or maybe he's just scared shitless—if Carlo Senior caught Issy just *thinking* a word like "shitless," he'd definitely get smacked on the back of his head. Josiah's scared, and Issy sees it, but something is now on the verge. Issy senses it, even though he doesn't have the words, something like great years of light are coming from the boy onstage. Not real rays but something like a vision of what great light waits for Josiah. This is what a good future looks like, a mother, a father, and probably college, girlfriends and money and blessings from God because not everyone can be special. He knows Havi is jealous, always jealous of anyone who has more than him. But Issy is happy to not be jealous. So, again, he waves to his friend at church.

Hey, Josiah, look over here.

And the two boys have their moment. It's quick and definitive, like two cars passing, a flash of recognition. Or maybe like that ribbon flash of a setting sun that erases every last bit of foreground, like when your eyes adjust and the sun becomes a backlight, and the world is made knowable, and real—*this* is how Josiah comes to see his friend Issy, and how he comes to see the great crowd. Where's Issy's girlfriend in the yellow dress? His mother? There she is, and she beams like a momentary flash, a beacon. No more a color mass of pinks, and browns, yellows, and reds, and every fleshy color there is. No more a haze of many faces. This is how he sees Issy—and Issy's waving?

For a few stretched seconds Josiah is filled with a rushing desire to run, to run with Issy and all the other boys, off to who knows where. He rubs the toy figure in his pocket, and suddenly he is no longer hungry, like he'll never be hungry again. His mind settles. It slows. And he sees out there, all the faces, each one, every face, everyone a guest in His great house. He fills up inside with heat and with light. Puts a hand to his ear, miming to the crowd, and he actually says: "I can't hear you. I said, Knock, knock."

Feels pretty good, turns out.

Issy shouts back: "Who's there?"

Hilda lets it slide.

The boy is now abandoning his script: he has become an inspired riff, divinely played, and off the top of his head comes a loud and prophetic voice—because of growing talk among the

Brothers and Wives in the Lord, his father sometimes talking on the phone. The talk between his parents *just this morning*—there's been a whisper, slow-spreading like a fever, feels like all summer long. He hears the brothers talking here and there. The New Millennium is not so far away, a nice round number, and my God, wouldn't that make sense?

"Look!" Josiah yells, he can't help himself, a voice speaks through him: "For the Lord and His army come knocking!"

Excited, he lets his sermon notes slip and fall to the floor.

He looks down, pauses for what feels like minutes—and then he looks away to the back of the hall. He puts his hand to his brow as if saluting a brother in the way back row, as if guarding his eyes from the sun. "And there in the heavens, a door has opened!" Josiah's thin voice careens throughout the hall, even his mother is startled by its power. Kizowski stands from his chair backstage, and stumbles over to the curtain. Call him crazy, but he actually looks for a heavenly door. The kid's got something, all right. Without realizing, Kizowski, now side-stage, is resting his arm on Pullsey's shoulder. Trading glances, how old is the boy, again?

But Josiah is well beyond all this now. He sees every heavenly star within reach.

He sees every dream he will ever have, every way he will become, what he certainly must become: a receptacle, an empty bowl, a deep and lucky cup of God.

"The first voice!" he shouts out. "See the returning Christ riding on a great white horse, and here even now He comes riding!" He straightens his back, shouting, and believing every word as it comes to him: "The Lord God has said every star will fall, and the sun will turn black in the sky. And His voice speaks out like a trumpet!" Josiah sees the crowd see him, and their vision of him infuses him, informing him with a wholly new spirit. "And look!" He points to the ceiling. "The Lord God said, Come up here. And I will show you what waits for this world!"

HIGH AS THE HORSES' BRIDLES

Hundreds of heads, adoring and reverent, bent back now, looking upward.

Sister Hilda Famosa is swooning in her seat.

"And know this, while sitting in the house of Heaven." Arms spread wide, embracing every last hungry spirit in the audience, he says: "The Lord God said two thousand years must pass since the birth of the Son of Man. And then I will come, in the year two thousand, at the dawning of God's New Millennium! And in that last year the Messiah, our Lord Christ, will return!" His hands now reach, grabbing for invisible rungs. "And there I see myself standing as an elder before you! And then—only then—on *that* day—in *that* hour, a divine vindication, a great rain of tribulation and destruction, and the End will finally be here!

"At once," he shouts. "I am in the spirit!"

Overwhelmed, the crowd inhales, each one a child of God.

Lay focus on this boy, lay focus on me—O, look at me filling up with breath and divine voice, and seeing with the eyes of Heaven, because my Lord God opens a heavenly door, one that no man can ever shut. And He himself will enter. And He will sup with me, and I with Him, and He will set me on His throne until the End of Days. And He will write on me a brand-new name, and every soul, I swear, will hear it.

THE ENDS

EAST

1

FRIDAY, QUEENS, NEW YORK, 2005

The cabbie tore through a dead-red light and we took off for the expressway, away from the airport and heading for Richmond Hill. He was laughing, fast-talking into his ear clip phone. The sky outside was a cool blue David Hockney pool, but inside, the vinyl seat burned through my pants. I lowered the window. I'm guessing the language was Arabic. The ID card on the back of his seat gave his first name as Abdullah, and Abdullah let loose another howling and happy laugh. He saw me in his mirror and threw me a smiling nod. Pointed at his phone and looked at me like, this guy's really killing me.

We joined the traffic flow. The whirl of outside, the car horns and sirens, the screech and relentless machine din of city washed over the car like a wave. Everything sounded the same as the car dropped and bounced in jolts, over potholes and swellings all along the Grand Central Parkway. There was a roaring *whoosh* as a plane zeppelined overhead.

I was ecstatic to be free of the airplane, of its stale dry air, of the small soiled hallways of LaGuardia and those sad plastic baggage carousels. We rolled on solid ground beside the bay. I never liked flying, but I liked the world seen from way up there, the incoming skyline, the blunt slant of the Citigroup Center, and the sterling hubcaps and skyscraping needle of the Chrysler Building. I liked the shipwreck hulk of the Fifty-Ninth Street Bridge, and the concrete sprawl of Queens spreading out from the East River like some elaborate gunmetal carpet. What I didn't like was the turbulence, the need for airsickness bags. I didn't like the horror of hollow space between me and what was below, and that some five hundred people died in plane crashes every single year. I had checked before leaving. The odds are maybe not especially good, but actually quite good if it's your plane that spirals and explodes in the oily Hudson. Manhattan is an island, surrounded by water. People forget this. A sewer stink of sulfur wafted in through the window from the bay.

Abdullah shouted, "What a smell!" Then back to his conversation.

I was amazed by his fluid traversal between the two languages. I waited for him to pause and lean forward. "You're speaking Arabic, right?"

He said into the earpiece, "Wait a second." He asked me, "What, you speak Arabic?"

I said, "I'm just wondering if."

"Well because many of the businessmen speak Arabic." He lowered his window and slammed his hand against his car door, yelling, "Move, you fucker!"

It was Friday, nearly dusk, and I had only been here in New York for a few minutes but I found the city immediately overwhelming. Sunlight flashed between buildings as if some westward and strobe-bursting ambulance was keeping an exact parallel pace. There must have been a day, one specific day long ago, when I first looked up at the sun and asked out loud, what is that?

Abdullah laughed. "The traffic is starting! What can I do?"

I shrugged my shoulders.

He asked me, "Where are you coming from?"

"California. I moved there. But I'm from here." I was back, of course, to see my father. Sarah, the lovely ex-wife, she'd told me he was sick, said he sounded "strange" and something seemed "wrong," but she always exaggerated. I called him and he eventually relented. Really he was fine, just more tired than usual, and he missed Mom. But there was something about his voice.

Abdullah said, "California girls!"

A medium-sized bread truck blared its horn alongside us and briefly slowed, a car length ahead. It was then shot-put forward, barely missing a motorcycle. It screeched to a stop behind a red Buick Regal with T-tops. I imagined loaves of white and wheat, clear plastic packs of hot dog buns scattered between the bumps of back wheel wells.

"He has no patience!" Abdullah slapped his car door. "You're going to kill somebody! You want I should stay on the expressway? Too much traffic."

Flushing Meadows Park was under the overpass, and I saw the grassy lakes and rusting sci-fi ruins of the 1964 World's Fair. That version of the future dated pretty badly. Except for maybe the Unisphere (which I happened to like very much), a hollow steel globe tall as a ten-story building. Abdullah and I were emigrants flying through the Milky Way, our cab a slow yellow rocket, and the Earth was out there lonesome, spinning still in the distance. I played Wiffle ball here as a kid, on congregation picnics. So long ago I hardly remembered them, but still they came alive, flashes of light in my mind. Mom, Dad, and me on a yellow picnic sheet, cooking food on a metal grill sticking out of the ground, it smelling like chalk and smoke and soil. Our sheet always a bit removed from the others. A wooden table, a red-checked plastic tablecloth. Watermelon slices in a bowl. Mom talking macramé secrets with the wives, and a flash of Dad turning burgers. There was a picture somewhere among our family photo albums of a seagull, flying away, a stolen frankfurter limp in its beak. I thought of softball, my first game of softball. I was maybe nine or ten, at a church outing. Dad argued with the other dads; it was obvious we didn't know all the rules. We knew most of the rules, yes, because nobody grows up in Queens without playing Wiffle ball, or stickball, or some other street version of baseball in an empty lot or some neighbor's driveway. There was even throwball, without sticks. But these were bastard versions, fitted to whatever shitty equipment and how little space we had. We used to even change rules mid-game. Three bases sometimes, other times two. Balls hitting parked cars were fair or foul depending on who was playing. And balls that spun off cracks in the sidewalk were pretty much always played. Unless a hitter called out "Hindu!" Hindu? Where does something like that even come from? My father once told me they said it back when he was kid, too. It wasn't specific to my block, or to Queens. Dad grew up in Brooklyn, and so he knew how to play stickball, stoopball, skully. Street games. Kid games. But I don't think he ever graduated from them. No occasion. No need. He never played on a team, or had many friends that I could remember. Church was priority, a friendship with God. Except during that game of softball, we never played catch.

We tossed a ball back and forth, before I got up to bat. Mom had insisted we play because she thought it would be good for me, for us. In good weather, the congregation often organized activities: picnics, park hikes, and softball. But Dad usually said no. Or if we did say yes, it was with reservation, even with suspicion. We were both a part and not a part of the congregation. On the outskirts. Dad was suspicious of people with "too much time on their hands," like weekends—free time that could be better spent studying the Bible, or praying, or making a witness for the Lord. Why read the paper when there's scripture? Sometimes I just wanted to play *Star Wars*, and I'd hide out with action figures under the wooden table in our backyard. Why he allowed my

mother to buy them for me, I'm not sure; they were probably not
realistic enough to cause him concern. I used to hear the kids in
the next yard yelling or swimming in their aboveground pool, or
tossing a Frisbee, and I'd wonder why I shouldn't go join them.
What stopped me? I also at some point started wondering if I was
already too old for action figures. I also knew Mom wanted Dad
to just let me be a regular kid sometimes. She said it would be
healthy, more balanced. During the softball game, after I'd struck
out for a second time, Dad insisted I get another swing. He said it
was only right, and they should let me have another chance. The
other dads sort of froze. He encouraged me and said, Go on, go
ahead, and get ready to swing. The pitcher was a chubby and
pimply thirteen-year-old named Kermit and he was whining "But
I got him out . . ." Kermit looked around at the adults to see if
really he had to throw another pitch. I happily accepted defeat
and left the plate. Dad claimed the game was rigged. He threw
his mitt on the ground and kicked it so hard it soared over a high
fence surrounding sewage pipes. The mitt was borrowed. I don't
remember being embarrassed by all this. Not exactly. I sort of
liked that Dad and I were a team all our own, but I also remember the other boys in the field looking at me like I was some nut-
case, like I'd confirmed everything they'd already thought about
me. Weirdo. I do remember feeling like I was now seeing my
father more clearly, in a brand-new light, realizing that fathers
could actually be wrong, and, worse, not even know they're wrong.
I also remember faking that embarrassment, later on, as a teenager, about the very same game. Whenever I wanted to get the
man right between the eyes, I'd say something like "you don't
even know how to play baseball."

Of course nothing as silly as that had happened between us in
a long time, but even all the half memories accrue a sort of crust
that eventually feels real and whole. Like plaque on a white fake
tooth. We hold on to some memories for way too long. Still,
sometimes we bickered, father-and-full-grown-son stuff. Is that

surprising? I don't think so. We didn't *fight* much anymore. That'd ended years before. I guess the last actual argument we'd had, a real hot one, was after I'd moved to California. We had a shouting match over the phone. Because I think Dad believed I'd never fully go through with it. I'd pack my things, a week or so after I got there, and run back home fast as I could. I think he would've been happy to have me stay at home forever. Just us three—me, him, and Mom, one small team. But Mom never wanted that kind of life for me. She was thrilled when I left. Deep down, I think so. I hope so. Then again it's not like my father and I ever became best friends, either. There was a cooling-off period after the move, after the phone call. I would call and check on Mom, and if he answered he'd pass her the phone. But by the time I met Sarah, he and I had leveled off, and things were pretty good between us. We were cordial. He even asked questions about where I lived. Sarah pulled us closer together because he loved her. So did Mom. Either way, I hadn't been back to see him since Mom died, and no way was I letting the man get sick. If he *was* sick. It also seemed my one chance for redemption. Or maybe better to say redemption for all of us, because I was sure Dad was praying, still, for a late homecoming. Because if there was a Heaven—although I could never take the idea seriously—I figured Mom was looking down, and this would make her happy. I sat there in the cab entertaining fantastical thoughts of me swooping in, just in time. I would save my father.

"A shitty park," Abdullah said. "Used to be beautiful. You should see it Sunday mornings with all the garbage. I should stay in traffic, or go Queens Boulevard?"

"This used to be a kind of scary place."

"Safe now. Filthy, but safe."

A game of soccer was under way. Sub-bass music shook the back ends of SUVs in one of the parking lots.

"You know what, take me to Forest Park."

Not in such a hurry, after all.

Abdullah nodded. I saw his rusty rotting teeth in the mirror. He said, "They're trying to make this place beautiful again. Spanish families come every weekend. Music so loud the trees dance." Then he laughed into his phone. He put something in his mouth and chewed.

I said, "I want to drive through Forest Park for a while. And then we'll go to Richmond Hill." The house was waiting, and Dad was waiting. They weren't going anywhere anytime soon.

The cab dipped low and took to an off ramp.

When Mom first got sick, her dying was sort of unthinkable. Because I was so young? I don't know. Remission came and the cancer went, and the years passed by, but then she got sick again. I definitely knew this time where it was headed. Not *where*, exactly, but I knew what would likely happen, and still I have to say I had trouble grasping the endgame scenario. Even standing there right beside her bed, in the hospital. She was a ghost, surrounded by mint-green walls and silver bedpans, all the humming precision equipment. I was optimistic. And yet, here, in the cab, pretty sure Dad was doing relatively fine, I couldn't shake my uneasy feeling.

I looked at Abdullah. He put another piece in his mouth.

"What are you eating?"

"You want some?" He grinned. "Is betel nut. You chew the leaves and nut."

I frowned, making a face at him in the mirror like I have no idea.

"You chew it— What, I have a passenger. What do you mean? Who did?" He punched at the steering wheel. His laugh was all consuming, so great now it almost stole his voice. He wheezed, "Ah, my friend!" We traded glances in the mirror and he pointed at the phone, what'd I tell you about this guy?

A chatter blast of horns screamed out. A drill battering against a distant sidewalk.

He was digging through a plastic bag in the passenger seat

beside him. He reached back through the opening in his clear plastic pay box and handed me a small leather pouch. In the mirror he made small fingers at his mouth, a squirrel pawing a prize. "Like this, gives you a zing." The leaves were semitough, like wet bay leaves, and the nut slices looked peppery. I handed him back the pouch. "No, no. Keep it till we get there," he said. "We call it paan." Rhymed with "wan," and I was getting a little bit carsick.

"Tastes weird." It was like the tough skin of a new fruit, and the sensation was bitter, but pleasant. My tongue tingled and I looked up, catching his face in the mirror.

He nodded, grinning. "Keep chewing."

Ahead was Queens Boulevard.

Six wide lanes of stretch limos and smoke-belching buses racing past the strip joints and the pool halls, for the shopping malls and the nightclubs. My first girlfriend, from way back in high school. Her name. It was. Bhanu. Poor girl. We were young. She was so young. We went to a nearby school the size of a Texas prison, cut classes together, and hid in the stairwells. I remembered running from security officers in the Queens Center Mall, just a few blocks away, and how one time we found ourselves in the rug department at Macy's, on the very top floor, and how we pushed the rolling stairs between the itchy hanging carpets and sat up there for hours, undetected, in the dark, rug dander all in the air. We talked and pretended this was exactly where we wanted to be. I stopped sneezes by cupping my hands in front of my mouth. She covered her mouth so she wouldn't laugh out loud. It was all very sweet, like something out of a lesser John Hughes movie. We even etched the letters OMD into the wall behind the rugs, but then debated what the letters actually stood for. Bhanu.

Abdullah drove us by a hospital, and then by an old-folks' home for the near dead. The traffic here was infamous, the street far too wide. It was often called the Boulevard of Death. I gave Abdullah a hearty thumbs-up.

The betel nut was bitter, with a pleasant tongue buzz. The tires bounced, and they bounced. I was getting a little high, which was ridiculous. I was headed home. Had my father ever gotten high in his life? Before I was born? What a thought! The world is alive before we get here. The blacktop whisked by under my out-stretched arm.

Before I met Bhanu, cutting class was my way to spend the day, and such a lonely way! I often found myself just spending the time, as if I had so much of it, although I guess you really do when you're young. Sometimes I got as far as the front steps of school, only to turn around and get right back on a city bus. It was thrilling, an autonomous thing to do, a thing done outside, in the world, beyond the stricture of the Laudermilk home. I liked that my parents didn't know where I was, liked nobody knowing where I was. I liked being alone. And, yes, I sometimes exacer-bated that feeling with appropriately morose New Wave music. I had a pale blue Depeche Mode T-shirt, and I kept it hidden from my parents. Sometimes I stuffed it in my backpack before leav-ing. One time, I was maybe thirteen or fourteen, I took the bus back along Woodhaven Boulevard but went beyond my stop, where I usually got off, and I was fascinated to see the bus actu-ally kept on going. Inside me, somewhere, I already knew more existed, of course, but to see where it went, to go where it went, and see all the people on the bus come suddenly alive: it was exhilarating. I took it to the end of the line. Charles Park in How-ard Beach. Where it was empty, and desolate, and gray, and I saw what looked like a junkie girl, who I'm pretty sure was pregnant, or had an abnormally round and jutting belly, passed out on a stone park bench, and a little girl was sitting in the dirt beside her looking totally lost. I turned around and walked all the way home, I don't know how many miles, all along that same bus route, partly to see anything I might have missed, and partly to fill my time, to spend it, but also partly as punishment for cutting class and submitting myself so willingly to such a sad sight so early in the morning. I'd also recently heard—and when I say "recently," I mean with respect to visiting Dad, with respect to sitting with Mr. Abdullah in his cab, I'm not still talking school, here—I'd heard of Buddhist monks who could literally focus all of their energies, focus their blood flow and brain waves on any ailing organ of the body, harness and direct every cerebral effort. I saw it on the National Geographic channel. I've always loved this channel, the volcano documentaries and the earthquake specialists, the end-of-the-world scenarios and the survivalist shows. The idea of the monks, it stayed with me, it attracted me. I wanted control like that. Can you imagine? They even could slow their heart rates just short of death. Then again, who wants to get so close? I mean, who did these monks think they were? Lounging in their fancy saffron-colored robes. It's not like they were romantic figures for me, not at all. I'd never be comfortable in such loose swaddling, too much freedom. But I was becoming interested in what they did on the inside with all that off-spark, the like-lightning dancing around our skullcapped Tesla coils. How did they do it? Sarah always said to be wary of questions like this, they can be dangerous. She said those stories you hear of pilgrims who climb mountains in search of bearded gurus, those are about the lucky ones who made it back alive. The ones who saunter into town, hair mussed, unshaven and sexy, robe a little soiled, and they spend the remainder of their lazy days pondering the answer to their one very special question. But what about the ones who never make it back, the ones who fall? The ones who slip and break their legs, and die from starvation at the bottom of a gorge? What about the ones who die on the way back down, left to rot on the hard slanting rock? What about them . . . ? *Hmmm . . . ?*

I started recognizing the old neighborhoods. A corner Te Amo convenience store, where I used to play video games and tried stealing peeks at the girlie magazines. We were close.

"Good, right?" Abdullah pointed at his mouth. "The feeling."

"What?" I said. "Yeah." The park roads were empty and the way was smooth.

"It will never come again," he said. "Your head knows what it tastes like now." We turned off the boulevard, and took to the hilly asphalt interior roads of Forest Park.

"Now what?"

"Just drive," I said. "Is that okay? Don't worry about the meter. I have money."

"Everything is on the way to everything."

The green leaves and high bush were everywhere, thousands and thousands of trees among the pour and sway of concrete and blacktop surrounded by the pigeon-shitted rooftops of Queens, over five hundred acres of wood thickets and wilds in the middle of the New York City suburbs. There were rumors, when I was a kid, of families having picnics and going for long walks and vanishing forever among the towering oaks. There was talk of a child-killer living in a dried-up streambed. A lean-to in the sand. The taxi carriage floated some just before descending a large hill, and my heart did a light bird flutter. I thought of Sarah, wondered where she was and what she was having for lunch. I used to do all the cooking and was heartbroken to find out she was apparently eating just fine without me. And her new friend—was he a boyfriend by then? I'm not sure. . . . I like to think definitely, no. Regardless, he cooked. And the last time we'd talked, I interrupted dinner. She had told me she needed some time, and maybe we shouldn't talk anymore for a while. I said I called because I wanted to tell her I was going to New York, to see Dad. And I might be gone for a while.

"Good," she said.

Good?

"That's it?" I said. "That's all you have to say? We might never talk again."

I heard her friend in the background. He was Greek and every island-accented syllable from his mouth, no matter how banal, sounded like a serenade. I hated it.

"What do you want from me, Josie?"

I didn't answer. And I stayed quiet like that for a while, until she finally sang out: "I'm hanging up now. . . ."

I saw Abdullah's eyes in the mirror.

With my arm jutting through the open window, an upswell of cool air broke on my skin. It smacked at my face. It felt good. I stuck my head out the window and into the wind.

When I was twelve years old I had a vision. Even now saying that makes me uncomfortable. It feels strange, alien, like the memory of a scene from a film. An old and faded dream. What is a vision, anyway? I'm not sure I'm better suited to answer the question than anyone else. I'd even go so far as to say anybody who says they know is lying. Even the word "vision" is tricky, as if it names one of the natural senses. But you don't really *see* anything. I read up on the topic, years later, when I was trying to get a handle on the thing. Sarah helped, and gave me some books. She was a translator, mostly of Hebrew poetry, novels, but sometimes scripture, too, religious texts, and so she had a helpful take. Plus, the story appealed to her—the idea of me, onstage, as a kid. But she never fully got how it made me so uneasy. Still does. And how could she? How could anybody?

I did see something, though. But first, I heard something.

I definitely heard a voice. Not a "voicelike sound," and psychiatrists are careful to point out the difference, but a voice. Not that I've seen psychiatrists. I'm not crazy. But I did read books. Which is not to say you're crazy if you see a psychiatrist. Sarah went to one for years, her mother *was* one, and Sarah was fine. I probably should've seen one. I'm losing my point—I heard a voice, and it told me what to say, and so I said it. What did it sound like? If I'm honest, it sounded like me. Exactly like me. But it wasn't *me*. There's a scientific theory that says our belief in God comes from a voice like this one, that early humans were not fully conscious, not aware they "were," and so before we knew we were thinking, we simply heard a voice. That voice. The voice was not our own, and it told us what to do, and we did it. I think maybe something like this was happening to me. Which is not so strange, if you think about it. I've had a song or piece of music stuck in my head for hours at a time, days, and I swear I'm not the one who put it there. I hear it played inside the concert hall of my head, on repeat, in a loop, and I have no control over the noise whatsoever. What was it I heard back then? I can't remember, not precisely, but it was something like "Do it now."

I remember looking out past the audience and what did I see?

I saw what looked like a giant white horse. I then turned to my father. He was nodding, slow-motion-like, in a dream, and I heard it say again, "Do it now."

Like it was yesterday, I can see the horse, right out there in front of me, coming through the back wall of the theater. By the lobby doors and under the balcony; the rider wore a golden crown. I blinked, standing out there onstage. I shook my head, lowered my arms, and then I saw what it really was: a huge painted mural of a great white horse. I hadn't noticed it before—because it was too big? I don't know. But it was actually back there and beyond the audience, gallop-frozen, on a heavenly burst of cloud luster. I touched the action figure in my pocket, and thought of the tauntauns in *The Empire Strikes Back*, the large horselike creatures that walk reared back on their hind legs, and I pretended the horse was real. It was big, and beautiful, and painted so painstakingly, and its eyes were the glassy kind that stared right back and looked alive. The horse was looking right at me, and it would come hurtling through the wall at any moment. The plaster would crackle and shatter, gushing white powder on the carpet.

I heard it again: "Do it now." So I spoke.

My parents were sitting there in the front row, their mouths partly open, just looking, and wondering what in the world had come over their boy. The elders and the servant brothers were side-stage, now, and calling me over. But I couldn't hear them. I looked out at the faces, of friends, and family, and strangers mostly, and of Issy. I don't like to think about Issy anymore. Waving from his balcony seat, sort of haltingly.

Time slowed.

A cool and clear muffle of silence in the hall, and I could feel a sort of velvety veil about to be lifted. I looked at my notes. They had dropped to the floor. Were my parents angry? Was I in trouble? I saw them as if through thick glass, or deep water, and I couldn't hear or touch anything outside my head at all. I was standing at the edge of a high cliff, and I looked at my notes on the floor . . . Was I shouting just now? I think I was shouting. And then the audience exploded with applause. I heard everything, I saw everything, and I felt every texture in the hall for a long moment. I was every last body all at once, and I drank in the applause like it was a large cup of RC Cola. Mom and Dad stood from their seats, and they were clapping. All four thousand people, and they loved me—they loved me! I'd even dropped my notes on the floor, and they loved me. I couldn't remember what I was supposed to say next, and so I did what just came naturally: I recited scripture. And then I went off script completely, swept away in a rush of something new, some new *me*; maybe God did grant me sight, a revelation. A glimpse of what waits for this world.

He showed me a horse.

And I gave them what they wanted, what we all wanted: I gave them a date. I gave them what no one else would give them—or would they? I've often wondered, since then, if some other sermon had to be changed that day because of me and my big mouth. I gave them the day and the hour of the End. It would be twenty years more before I was wrong.

But at that moment I was the Josiah, king of the four thousand Christians, God's mouthpiece. It was like filling up with every bit of light and heat that had ever passed through my body. I was Blake's Great Revelation Angel, glorious and towering. Of course, I didn't think it at the time, only later on, like when I first saw that illustration in a coffee-table art book, but my God, that's just how I felt. I figured everything would be different. School would be different. And I figured if I bowed they would just keep on clapping. So with a small stiff arm at my waist, I bowed. The audience answered again! Another swell of applause! Which did what but just make me hungrier. I can still see that kid from way out here, through all this stuff we think of as time, the small and early spirit-hungry version of me—stepping out from behind the microphone and, boy, just look at him bow. No, he curtseys. Like it's his grand opening night, like it's his coronation. He curtseys, and the audience can't help themselves. Some people actually lose themselves in laughter, in appreciation, an ovation, and maybe some in their enthusiasm actually tarnish the dignity of the whole affair because let's not forget this is supposed to be worship, a serious business, God's business, but then again, who are we kidding: the kid is good. Curtseying, for crying out loud! Now raising a hand like No, thank *you*. Little me waves to the back, like some visiting ambassador. Remembering the scene sent me reeling, feeling every little thing all at once.

I thought of looking out there at my mother's face, the face of my lovely and still alive mother. Hands folded at her mouth, eyes teary with pride. My father nodding his head, My boy . . . The elder brothers from the side of the stage whispering: "Hey, psst, hey, time to leave the stage . . ."

I looked at Mom, and I took in a very deep breath. I concentrated on that small thing that lives way inside (I have tried this since and failed miserably): the tiny, invisible, indestructible point—but sometimes it fills up a room and touches its head to the ceiling; how big a horse would I need, if a heavenly horse came riding and rearing from back in the aisles? Come the final day, come Armageddon, the blood will flow and fill the streets, high as God's holy horses, the elder brothers waving me over . . .

Wait a second now: *Whose* blood?

I literally asked myself this question. This I remember more clearly than anything because it was the question that pulled me down to earth. I'd recited this scripture how many times without thinking? How many things are like this in life? *Whose blood?* My good mother would one day slip and swim through whose wet blood? The applause started dying away . . .

And then my mother nudged with her chin, a throw of her chin, like Go on, sweetie, go ahead. And Dad looking like, Hey, it's gotta end sometime . . .

I looked around the theater, one more time.

My mother would wade through a river of whose dead blood exactly? Red blood? Real blood? I looked up at the sky, at the cosmic ceiling, at the butter-yellow moon, and I don't know how I'd missed it! Even from way down there, onstage, I could plainly see it. Across the moon was a jagged line like a lightning bolt, a crack in the painted plaster probably not even wide enough for a finger. But if that moon were real, the crack would have been a canyon twenty miles wide. The ceiling was just a ceiling.

Does this make any kind of sense? Pictures of planets don't make planets, Josiah! The sky was painted prettily, yes. We were in a theater! In Queens! The trash bags were piled out front by the sidewalk, and the soda trucks were driving by in the street, and there was a whole world of warm-blooded people out there who had not an inkling of our blood-spilling talk inside. I actually played the phrase in my head several times in the following days: "The ceiling is really a ceiling."

I sat there in the back of Abdullah's cab, and thought of my father and how many different fathers we all have, of how many I'd had. All of them Gill, but different. There was the father I had when I was a kid, and I wanted nothing more than for him to be present with me in the world, for him to stop acting like I had something to give him, and to momentarily put aside his worship for a game of checkers. There was the father who argued with my mother, who soon insisted that church worship was no longer enough, and he wanted more worship at home. There was the father who eventually refused church altogether—but never God—when Mom got sick; and if already Dad was in a boat all his own—and he very much was—Mom's getting sick made him pull up the gangplank. There was the father who frightened me, who prayed for hours, on his knees, facing a wall, who I believe at least one time deliberately hurt himself; I was young and so I can't recall when for sure, but I remember finding him on his knees, in the garage, and slamming his thighs with a large yellow phone book, again, and again, and again; Mom rushed in, took me away, and shut the door behind us. There was my deliberate insomniac of a father, the man who paced, back and forth, in the kitchen, in the garage, on the sidewalk, who stayed up for days sometimes, refusing sleep, showing increasing signs of what I see now was temporary dementia. Mom would tell me not to worry and just leave him be. That my father was praying. One night, I was maybe nine or probably ten, it was three or four in the morning, I heard the early insects, and someone talking in our backyard. I went downstairs and looked out the kitchen window. I saw him pacing, talking to himself. I slowly opened the door, very slowly. I heard him repeating scripture like a mantra: "And he dreamed, and beheld, a ladder from the Earth, and the top of it reached up to Heaven, and the angels were climbing up and down. And he dreamed, and beheld, a ladder from Earth, and . . ." This made me afraid, and feel lost, unprotected. Except then I realized, as my eyes got used to the darkness, that my mother was sitting there in front of me, right at my feet, on the top porch step. She didn't turn around. She said, "Go to bed, love."

Most of that behavior, the more extreme kind, stopped the famous summer of my "vision," or whatever you want to call what happened. It seemed the very thing he'd been waiting for. And of course there was the father who tossed me aside when I left New York. Last of all, the father who lost my mother. I'd wondered how he'd go on. But he did. I wondered who he was now, without Mom. Was he different? How different? Without Sarah, I felt lost inside my own body, and she was alive and well.

I decided my favorite version of Dad was a young Gill Laudermilk, looking like an older Luke Skywalker, back when he and I assembled my first sermons in the garage, and I practiced speaking in the full-length mirror by his study desk, when he let me drive his station wagon, a brand-new Ford Country Squire, fire-engine red, in a nearby supermarket parking lot. My favorite mother was the great protector who once boxed the ears of a sixteen-year-old neighborhood bully because he had tripped me. A wide gash had opened in my bottom lip when my chin hit the sidewalk. Mom once said, "Never listen to what others say about your father, because your father is a man of God." She followed his every revelatory whim, every iteration. My favorite father drove up our street in his Country Squire like he was in a homecoming parade; he honked his horn and grinned from behind the windshield, saying, My son's gonna learn how to drive! Wheels crunching gravel in the driveway, he shouted: This old world, my boy, it's sinking! So if now's not the time to splurge, tell me when? Tell me when! . . . The porch of our house was a covered porch, yellow with white wooden columns, and you could see the newly built Sikh temple behind our yard, and around the corner its

pear-shaped rising roof, and my mother watching the workers
disassemble the scaffolding, saying, What happened to the Irish
and Italians, good churchgoers, this neighborhood is so brown . . .
From the porch, we watched lightning storms while sitting on
the sofa my father had found in a trash pile ten blocks away. It
smelled of basement wet and hot asphalt, and sat in front of the
living room window, opposite the sofa on the window's other side,
inside, where we watched old movies and ate peanuts from orange
plastic cups. Mom used to say, *Star Wars* makes me so nauseous.
I mean it's exciting, Josiah, it is, but the world can never get that
way because we won't last that long. Armageddon's right around
the corner . . . Sausages simmering in the Crock-Pot . . . . It's not
easy! she'd say. But not much longer before our Heavenly Father
comes home. And it's so, so sad that no one in the neighborhood
will ever see Heaven, because the Hindus don't know Jesus. These
statues of Ganesh, circus elephants sitting pretty with flowers in
their hands, this is God? Abomination!

And there was something about the way the Bible told them,
telling me, Sweetie, the monsters are real. A demon with six
hungry heads and the Wild Beast will come from the ocean, and
the Whore will ride on its slick, wet back, and that Last Day will
be like no other since the floodwaters covered this earth, wiping
away every evildoer. And the falling stars will blow like bombs,
and the poison mushroom clouds will bloom—

Goddamn! Dad shouts, I'm sorry for my language, but my
God, isn't it high time! Because this generation will not pass away
before the Day of the Coming of the Lord! So why not go ahead
and get us a brand-new car? Shiny and red like Golgotha's blood-
soaked mud! You heard it spoken by the brothers at church: You
were right, Josiah! It's coming! This is war, so stretch your legs!
And I bet everything we have in this life that this world will
crack in half, and stink like the dead egg it is! I will *not* be caught
unawares with my family running after buses packed with Catholics. I will not be dependent on Muslims, or Moonies, or anyone

but our provider who does not have a car, who does not need a car, but rides on the holiest of horses. And we will follow him to Heaven, to the sun if he takes us, this is not your mother's world, and this is not your world, so take this place and shove it down Gehenna's hungry throat. And, my son, when you are a full-grown man, and it's your time to steer, you will sit in the driver's seat and take us home in the fashion of real holy worship. And we will lift up ourselves and finally grow wings because this here round nest is done, say it with me, son, *"All the former things are passed away, all the former things . . ."*

I once saw my father's hands on my mother's neck, just once, on her shoulders. He was pushing her against the dining room wall. I was astonished. I thought they were hugging, but then they weren't hugging at all. When was this? Sometimes there were finger-thin bruises on her arms, but by the time I was a teenager the bruises had gone away. When I was about thirteen, I saw Dad limp and pale, as if he'd fainted, on the garage concrete floor. My mother was crying out, to me, him, to the ceiling: Your father's only sleeping, you wake up, honey, so what if they took the car. . . .

I looked away from the window, and toward Abdullah. A cigarette would have been nice. But the pack was in my bag, the bag was in the trunk, and I'd been quitting for years.

"To Richmond Hill, yes?"

I said, "Let me ask you something, are you Muslim?"

He looked at me in the mirror. "Why do you ask me this?"

"I'm just curious, because if you are, then wouldn't the betel nut be . . . well . . ."

He slung his elbow over the seat and he faced me. His eyes were then back on the road. "I am Abdullah. Almost too much as it is."

I laughed along with him.

"So where are we going?"

I told him the address.

A low tinny voice chirped from the cell phone's receiver. Abdullah shouted back in his language.

I looked out the window.

Why take the long way home? Why go out of my way?

A small boy swung from a fire escape on the first-floor front of a high-rise apartment building, and then the boy was gone, and then the building was gone, which was then replaced by other buildings, and storefronts with apartments in the floors above, and more tall buildings. I thought of how this place was vertical, and of beaches, and I actually had trouble imagining them. I'd walked on how many beaches, and I was seriously having trouble picturing them. The West Coast is all horizontal. No need to build upward there. Just bulldoze inland, to the foothills and the flatlands, head for the deserts. And now I was finding real comfort in the difference. I saw the brick buildings and flat roofs crowded with satellite dishes. I saw the pizza shops, and more pizza shops, the 99-cent stores and the sidewalk sales. We drove by myriads of splintering telephone poles shot at with staple guns, and the flapping flyers promising miracles of overnight weight loss.

The elevated trains over Jamaica Avenue rattled overhead.

The diners all along the boulevard.

The cars, so many goddamn cars, and the trees, the dirt squares surrounded by sidewalk, and the maples and towering oaks, four or five on every block, branches resting on saggy telephone wires.

The cars parked on streets, in the driveways. I counted the driveways until I stopped counting, and before long I recognized the store on the corner, "24/7 Milk Depot," they'd kept the name. Where I used to get bagels, and once I had to ask a tall pretty lady for help, to reach up and get the sanitary napkins that Mom had asked for, up on the highest shelf.

"We are here," he said. I paid and we stepped outside. He

handed me my duffel and winked. Trunk slam. The tires squealed as he pulled way.

I was back in the world.

The burned-out shell of a Volkswagen Beetle sat across the street, parked in front a vacant lot. It had no doors. A small girl played with a Barbie, her little legs splayed behind her on the sidewalk. The house, my father's house, our house, was looking really old. All of the houses were old, but ours seemed so very old. Which made me what, made my father what? The porch sagged, and leaned forward like it was easing into a recliner. The columns were slightly bowed, had arthritic elbows, and the house appeared to be in mid-exhalation. The chain-link fence was torn in places, rifts in the waffled steel. And the garage looked to have been unused for years. A large burn mark scarred the token front rectangle of browning grass. Weeds covered most of the front yards. I saw a mattress on a roof two doors down. A smell of fuel, gas, kerosene, something pungent was in the air. And the swoop of the Sikh temple's swooping roof, around the corner, was exactly where it should have been, rising behind and above my father's house. I am where I was made. I lugged my bag, opened the gate, and walked up the steps.

The porch sofa was gone and the windows were blocked by drapes. One window was broken and banded with silver duct tape, what looked like cardboard behind. I rang the bell, took a deep breath, and waited. I knocked, and rang again. Talk about déjà vu.

There was a rustling inside, a curtain moved slightly.

The door lock clicked.

Why not come home sooner?

The door moved barely away from the jamb, and a brass chain bridged the opening. Then it quickly shut.

"Dad?" I knocked again. "It's me."

"Who?"

"Josie."

"Josie?" His voice was weak. "Josiah?"

He forgot I was coming?

"It's me," I said. "I promise."

I heard the chain fall. He opened the door, and there he was, my father, barefoot and barely dressed, emaciated. Wearing nothing but a loincloth.

It was dark inside, and my nose quivered as I watched him shuffle up the hallway. A smell of wet rot and trash, a scuttling on the floor.

"Come in, come in," he was saying, and waving me on to follow.

I couldn't move in the hot stink of the foyer; it was a long hall, and it seemed even longer in the dark. The stairs leading upstairs on my left, the smooth wooden banister, and the living and dining rooms on my right. The bathroom was under the stairs. The hall ran between the stairs and the rooms on my right, like a dark alleyway leading on to the brownish glow of the kitchen, far away and half alive with dusk light. He stopped in that doorway, a pale golem shadow sipping from a glass of water.

My eyes were adjusting. I realized I was surrounded by plastic garbage bags. A month of trash, maybe more, in swollen stacks, piled on a broken chair, disemboweled and spilling on the stairs. My face flushed. I squinted.

"Not much food in those," he said. "Don't worry."

He disappeared into the kitchen.

My forehead was warm, not sickly warm but something else. I slapped at my temple. I squeezed the thin bone between my eyes. A fly buzzing at my lips, I blew it away. Breathed in, buckled some, and gagged. I was horrified. By the house. And, frankly, I was scared for my father. A family death can decimate a home, and here he was all alone and living with it.

"Get in here so I can get a look at you!"

I walked past the stairs and saw, beneath them, the door to the bathroom was shut. A faint red light was leaking out from beneath like a darkroom.

"Get in here!"

His back was to me. His white hair in a greasy straggle fell in the groove between sharp shoulder blades. It looked like he was wearing a diaper. Cat turds were scattered on the floor like cigar butts. He stood there in the warm bath of brown light and stretched up on his toes, skinny arms punching out slowly. He turned and faced me, yawning.

"Let me get a good look at you," he said.

Knots of soiled clothing and dinner plates caked with dry sauces on the kitchen table and counters. A few sofa cushions piled beside the fridge. Towers of torn, yellowing books, wet papers littered the floor and spilled from the pantry. A mustard-colored smear on the linoleum, and the rich bone-stink of food gone dry after too long in the air.

He said, "What?"

I was thinking.

"Close up your mouth," he said.

Thinking what.

"How about we have us a toast? Come on, Junior. Say something."

"A toast would be good, I guess."

"There's the spirit! I've been waiting!" A large white cat, with a gray belly swinging, rubbed its head against his shin. "I have cats now."

He turned to the refrigerator and with both hands he gripped and pulled the door half open. His elbows poked at the skin, and I thought of groceries falling through wet paper bags. He handed me an open bottle of beer. "I got them all ready, took off the caps."

I took the bottle.

On the refrigerator racks: a half-full bottle of red wine, no cork; a loaf of bread wrapped in plastic; half a stick of butter on a silver dish; and a clear pitcher of water. He let me close the door.

I followed him into the low-lit dining room to the same wooden table where we'd always had our Sunday family dinners. The table was mostly clear of clutter. And the bottle was cold in my hand, so cold it shocked in the dark warm sweat of the room. I wiped my forehead with my sleeve. He sat in a chair not so close to the table. They were heavy chairs. As a boy, I'd had trouble pulling them out from under the table so I could sit down for dinner. I pulled a chair closer to his. It hardly seemed the same room.

"I can explain," he said. "But first." He smiled, and there was a glimpse of younger Gill, a flash of resurrection in his eyes. I thought of how different it had been standing at Mom's sickbed, a year before, a vacuum between Dad and me, like a scooped-out hole in the universe. "This is a momentous thing," he said. "Never had a doubt, I knew you were coming." His lips were ashen, corners webbed with spit-milk. Even right here, in his presence, the man was somewhere else. Sarah was right. Something was wrong.

"So how's my little man doing?"

I wanted a smoke.

"To us!" he said. "Say something! Sit!" He raised his bottle chin high.

I sat, raised mine, and we brought the bottles together, but a lot slower than usual for a cheer. The bottles were collared with a limp silver foil and torn white paper, and they made no noise when they touched. No clink of glass, just a soft papery pat. The reality of the situation was settling on me. Something was very wrong. He had no idea. And I knew he would fight me if I said so.

"So," I said. "You look pretty good."

"*You* look good, taking care of yourself. How's the beautiful wife?"

"Not my wife anymore. You know that."

"Always your wife. Nonsense."

The window behind my father, I broke it once with a Wiffle ball.

"And I've never felt better," he said. "Despite—" He waved a hand. "Your mother, she used to clean."

So, he was partly aware. I said, "The house could use some attention."

"No one pays attention anymore."

My heartbeat, my pulse, and the stink, I was semiacclimating. I dried the back of my neck with my sleeve. "And you're feeling okay? How are you feeling?"

"Never better." He patted my arm and slowly stood. The hand was cold.

"You want to tell me what's going on?"

He left his bottle and shuffled to the opposite end of the table. He picked up a thin black notebook from a pile of back-to-school-sale spirals. Blue, red, yellow, green. He wrote something down with a pencil. "You always had a way, Junior, cutting right through the fat. Tell me now what's new. Talk to me."

I had no idea why he was calling me Junior.

He turned and yanked the pull chain of a small lamp on the other side of the table. The lamp cast a yellow cone over a thick open book. I saw his knotty spine. It zippered down from under his hair, and beneath the loincloth.

I said, "Are you eating? Please tell me you're eating enough."

"All I need." He turned the pages slowly and scratched some notes in the spiral. "Right on down to the meat of things."

Carefully, he set the book down, shuffled back, and pulled the chair farther from the table. I helped him some. He took hold of the back of the chair, and moved the chair slightly. Looked at it. Moved it again. Went back to the other side of the table and stood looking at his notebooks, shaking his head.

"Dad."

He took the spirals in a stack and squared them off, against the table, into a neat pile. Set them back down. Nudged them so they were flush with the table edge. Looked at them. Looked at the chair. He picked them up again, squared them off again. I didn't like seeing this sort of behavior. Compulsive.

"Dad," I said again.

He came back and sat beside me, and then he started to stand up again. I set my hand on his knee, and broke his concentration. He stayed, took his beer and sipped.

I said, "You look thin."

He looked at me, a sweet face really, which I didn't expect. He tucked his hair behind his ears, and I saw his eyes were green. He said, "I'm fine. Fine." A black cat jumped, landing on the far end of the table.

I took a long swig and thought of having a smoke, that maybe I could just step out back and have one, and wouldn't it be nice to come back inside and, like in a cheaply plotted movie, find everything up until now was a dream. I'd find Dad doing just fine, in a clean house, of sound mind, doing the weekend crossword in a brand-new blue Barcalounger. Or better—I'd find him a young man again, Mom healthy and alive. I'd had this kind of fantasy before but always cut it short knowing it would mean never having met Sarah.

"Sarah's worried," I said.

"No reason to worry." He gestured toward the hallway with his bottle. "Your mother was here, you missed her."

I wanted this to be true. Who wouldn't?

"She was here," I said.

He pointed to the hall. "You missed her."

What is it about a father's face?

I'd never given so much as a single deliberate thought to my father's eyes. I could talk of Sarah's pink and mottled cheeks, of the single errant eyebrow stand that poked out from between her eyes. But a father's face can be a frightening thing, a bridge between two voids. He was in me. I was in him. Where did that leave us? My mother's eyes were like light on glass, and flickering. Always anxious, and waiting. I used to think she was waiting for the end, like Dad was, a new beginning, whatever you want to call it. But now I realized—it hit me just like that—it was Dad who made her anxious.

"Mom's gone," I said.

He put a hand on my face. A minty aftershave mixed with every other smell, and it helped. "You think I'm crazy," he said. "And that's okay. We just don't know much, do we?"

I had questions. "Why are you calling me Junior?"

He was incredulous. "You're my Junior."

I looked at my lap. "What's my name?" I studied what was left in the bottle.

"Clever boy."

I tapped the bottle with a fingernail.

He touched my face. "I know who you are and who I am for the first time in my whole life." He grabbed hold of the back of my chair and stood again. "Good enough for you, Josiah? Hmm?" He pressed a hand to my shoulder, and with his eyes he seemed to say, This is what shoulders are for. "Gill Laudermilk," he said, "is a dead man and dying. I am a son of God, Yahweh's Junior. See me in my glory!" He raised both arms, and they fell back to his sides, just as fast. "Let me show you something."

I touched his side as he walked past, his naked skin. I squeezed lightly, partly to see if he was real, and he grimaced.

"I thought you were losing your balance."

"Follow me," he said.

His belly was hard, and starting to bloat.

"I gotta say you look really terrible."

"Never better in my life."

He led me to the living room where I used to watch TV with my mother. Where we ate ice cream from a shared wooden bowl. The carpet was the same dull gray, but now worn down and matted, balding in places. Outside light leaked in between creases, through rips in the cardboard covering the windows, but mostly the room was dark. An orange tabby beneath the glass coffee table, crouching, stared at me with silver eyes. A computer sat on the table. It was modern, thin-screened, and this was surprising, yes, but no more so than anything else. The sofa was covered by a white sheet, as if he were prepping to paint the walls. A pillow, a body-shaped impression. He'd been living in the living room and it stank of it.

"You can sleep here, or upstairs. I don't go upstairs much. I have trouble sleeping up there."

"So where?"

He pointed to the hallway, and waved his hand. "I know, I know, I know."

"We need to sit, and start from the beginning."

"You don't know the half of it!" He sat and turned on a lamp beside the computer, a replica of the lamp in the dining room. "My lifeline, Junior. Isn't she pretty?"

"You hate TV and you have this?" The sides of the computer were partly covered with yellow Post-it Notes.

"I still hate the TV! I keep two in the hall closet, never use them. But I hardly go out since your mother left."

"You said she was here."

"She's always here. And without this"—he touched the screen—"no legs. I'm exhausted."

We looked at each other, like we were both looking for the right words because how do you talk about this when you've never been here before? It was scary to see him like this. A laugh sprang from my insides. "You know what you look like? A baby. A filthy hairy baby."

Anxiety fell from his face, and he laughed back at me. "Ha! Now we're talking. I'm going back, Junior. Crawling back, diving in!" He rubbed his hands together. And then he looked at his hands, itched the back of his hands, one, and then the other. Rubbed, itched. Rubbed, itched . . .

"Dad."

The spell broke, and he seemed embarrassed. Put his hands under his legs.

I walked over to the window and took hold of the heavy drapery. I dug among the folds for the drawstring and pulled. Bent back the cardboard. An explosive swirl of dust motes and a long shaft of daylight washed in. I turned to his nasty look.

"Put it back," he said.

"It's good for you," I said, peeling away the cardboard.

"Let there be light!" he shouted, his arms half raised.

I laughed. He didn't.

He said, "I said put that back." He covered his eyes.

I walked over to him, and touched his shoulder. "Hey."

He slapped at my hand, and said: "This is not your house."

A white cat jumped into his lap and pressed its face against his arms. He stroked its back. "Good kitty." He looked at me. The cat jumped, as he stood. He walked away, hand pressing to his side.

"We'll talk more later," he said. "I promise. I'm tired."

I watched him walk away and this made me feel more alone than I'd ever felt. I had the terrible feeling that he would leave the room and I would never see him again. I folded the cardboard back in place, and heard the door of the bathroom slam

shut. I heard him fasten the lock. It all sounded like he wanted
me to hear it. I walked into the hall, and saw the red light spilling from under. I went back to the living room and dragged
at the curtains, covering the windows. The shaft of sunlight
drowned.

Time passed. An hour or so. I sat there in the dining room, at the table, and tried to get my thoughts together. I walked through the rooms, the kitchen, the living and dining rooms, and I was fascinated and moved by the most mundane things. The gilded frames on the living room wall, and how they'd been there for decades. They were now peeling and showing wood from beneath. I remembered my father buying them at a yard sale across the street, and hanging them on the wall just how he'd found them. They stayed empty for months. He eventually set a printed psalm within each.

I walked over to the bathroom door and called out his name. He didn't respond. I heard him snoring. I shook my head, totally befuddled, feeling uneasy, a little sick. I almost knocked, but went outside for a smoke instead. I felt helpless and dumb, even responsible for what was happening, whatever it was, and my fantasy of saving the day dissolved into nothing but anxiety and shame. Afraid the door would lock shut behind me, I picked up a piece of wood from the porch and wedged it between the door and the frame. The sun was gone. But still that stink of fuel. Across the street two boys played handball in the vacant lot against the side of a neighboring garage. I took out my phone and dialed Sarah.

It rang once, and I ended the call, regretting I had tried.

I dialed again, immediately ended that call, and decided I would never call her again.

I dialed one more time, and left a long and awkward voice mail, telling her where I was. That she was right about Dad, and I thought she should know.

Sitting on the porch step, I lightly stubbed my cigarette on the brick. I lit the tip again. The smoke wiped my busy brain clean. But there was also something in the spark of match to cigarette that I always loved, the simple act of setting fire to the paper's end. I liked the partial loss of me that came with every cigarette, the surrender, the abandon of will, the mindlessness of it all, like the emptiness you feel during a good long run. If I never turned my head, the house would disappear and take my father with it. I checked the digits on my phone. A blue rubber ball came rolling across the street.

One of the boys jogged over. He wore tube socks over his hands with holes cut for his fingers. The ball bounced against the curb, and the boy grabbed it. He threw it to me. I caught it, threw it back, and he jogged off. I wanted to get drunk. I wanted to stop myself from deciding what to do. I wanted to wait until morning to call someone about Dad. It seemed obvious. I had to call someone. But now? The man was sleeping. For sure, yes, a doctor, psychiatrist, someone would have to look at my father. They'd want to know everything. Where had I been, and how did this happen? How was I supposed to know? *Was* I supposed to know? I wanted to get drunk and not have to think about it and then drunkenly stew in the facts that my mother was no longer here anymore, not in this house, or on this earth, and it seemed a little unfair that he was stealing my attention away from her memory. But it was also totally unfair of me to think that way, because the man was obviously not doing well without her. I needed a drink, and one solid memory of my mother to cling to, before I could get myself together and attend to Dad. I figured I would look for the family album.

I also figured a fifty–fifty chance Sarah would return the call. But that was not a good bet.

I knew she wouldn't call. She shouldn't have. How is it we can love someone who refuses to love us back? A fucking teenager's question! But still . . . I mean, can you really love someone who's not really there? Not anymore? Which one of you is more of a ghost? Three thousand miles away, practically on the moon, and I was pining. Then again, so much of what I'd loved was already gone. Sarah. Mom. My business at the time, or what was left of it, was already swirling in the crapper. Now Dad was not looking especially good. There had to be a reason. Maybe that I hadn't been to church in over two decades. I mean if I really wanted to cut through the fat, like Dad said, so much fat, the question then was this: What exactly was the trajectory that followed from my brief career as a prophet? Scratch that: the failed prophet from Richmond Hill, Queens. Young Josiah Laudermilk, one of God's Great American (Would-be) Men. How did I get here? I'd been doing my best as an adult man to avoid the question. In fact, I had run from it, as far as I could.

I had run from east to western ocean, over mountains, and through deserts. Actually, I drove; I rented a green Jeep Cherokee because that vehicle made me feel like I was on a mission, and I never once looked in the rearview mirror. I ran through women, unabashedly, but ashamed, always shamed by needing someone, always someone, a woman, another woman, because love always ends, until I met Sarah. But then I ran from her after pretty much our first talk of children. I ran through cash, and professional success, and *away* from my livelihood. Thank God for my right-hand man, second in command, and closest friend, Mr. Amad Singh, who kept the great leaky boat afloat without me, minding the store way back in California. I ran from Mom, thinking death might be catching. And I ran from that stage, that damnable podium, practically as soon as I could leave the house (this house!), not realizing, of course, that I was headed right for the future—like all of us—headed for the year of prophecy 2000. (Not to mention the woeful and belatedly apocalyptic September that followed.) I ran from Dad. I ran from his insistence I was special, from his compulsive and overwhelming need to believe, from his very blood, which of course I couldn't get away from, no matter where I went. In fact, here I was sitting on the steps of his front porch.

Something else changed in me that summer. There was the "vision," yes, but also something else. I felt like I had grown up, which is ridiculous, I guess, because I was only twelve years old. Nonetheless. I felt different. Stronger. More assured. And less lonely—because of Issy, who all of a sudden started coming over to my house. Which brings us back to Issy, who for some reason remains entangled among my thoughts even to this day. Not every thought, no, but thoughts of family, of my parents, and the frightening and attractive idea of having a child.

Havi had apparently grown tired of him. It was bound to happen sooner or later. Yet our subsequent friendship was surprising to me. But also ennobling. Can I say that? Yes. Ennobling. Because he brought out something good in me, and so I was good to Issy. Or as good as a twelve-year-old can be, or be aware of. I was certainly aware that *he* was good, and not just to me. Just plain good. So when Havi got a girlfriend—who was *three years older* than him, by the way, which seems so wrong to me now (then again, his mustache had sprouted, on the sides of his lips mostly, a thin hint of a mustache, his mouth in a whisper of parentheses, so he did look older than he was), my point: Havi dropped Issy like a toy he got tired of. And it just so happened that around this time I was playing less and less with action figures, my *Star Wars* figures propped on shelves, like trophies from much younger days, and no longer climbing from my pockets. I swear it had something to do with that ceiling. Lost innocence? Too much? My point is simply that Issy's timing was good when one sunny day, after Sunday church, he asked to come over to my house.

This happened right around the same time Mom first got what she called body tired. "My whole body is tired. . . ." How could we know she was sick? She was tired.

I said, "Mom, you know Issy."

This was in the front hallway of the church, by a large pastoral painting. Mountains. Blue sky. Green grass. A lake. But no people. Not one person. The kind of painting you see in a thrift store, and wonder who painted such a big, boring, and unpeopled painting? And why such an elaborate wooden frame? What good is the view with no people? An Eden with nobody in it. Just waiting. We prayed daily for the end of the world, and here's what the world might have looked like before we got there.

Mom said, "Of course, sweetie, is your mother here?"

"No, she no here," Issy said.

I said, "Issy wants to come over."

"To hang out," he finished my thought.

It was plain that this tickled my mother, and she could hardly hold back her smile. I didn't have lots of friends, hardly any in my own neighborhood, which was only walking distance from Issy's, it turned out, and, especially since what had happened onstage. I was "weird." Even the kids at school had found out. Who told them? Mom didn't like to talk much about what had happened, and maybe this is why I especially felt so much love for her. Not that I loved Dad any less. It was complicated. Mom said my sermon had been lovely, even "inspiring" to the other kids in the congregation. But it had scared her. Dad scared her, too. How he then insisted that our family Bible study should happen twice or three times a week, from now on, not just once anymore, and how he would look at me, right into my eyes, like he might find some revealed secret there. He insisted I had a gift for communion. *Take this seriously.* A friend could only be a good thing.

She mussed Issy's hair. "No trouble at all. How about later today? We'll walk over and pick you up."

This amazed me. Confused me. How did she know where he lived? She somehow knew, and I didn't? What else did she know? She knew of whole blocks and neighborhoods, I soon found out, ones I'd never been to or heard of before. So we walked to Issy's house that afternoon, waved at his mother actually hiding in the window, who never did come out to meet us, and Issy came over. Not all mothers were the same, I knew this now. She stayed at that window and spied on us like we were stealing away her child. I saw scabs and cuts on her face. The house itself was a shambles. The front yard covered in large plastic toys, neon Big Wheels, basketballs, and broken bike parts, all at the feet of a powder-blue Blessed Mother Mary statue. As far as I knew, Issy had no brothers or sisters, and so we figured they weren't the only ones who lived there. Issy later told me the toys belonged to the other kids his father sometimes brought over, and that his mother always refused to talk to those children or cook them food or even come out of her room when they were in the house.

That day we walked back to my house, and my mother, I see now, was asking all sorts of questions to better understand Issy's situation. How long had he lived there? Did he like his block? Did he have lots of friends in the neighborhood? Did his mom have a job? And what was his favorite thing to eat, because maybe she could make it for him.

He and I went straight to the backyard, which wasn't so big a yard compared to some, but Issy just could not get over how huge. He said their landlord wouldn't let them use their backyard. We sat at the wooden table for a while and talked about Havi, probably because we had that in common, and about how he didn't call Issy anymore and ignored him at church. I remember more than anything else a small mouse in the grass, and Issy pointing at it. It was a dead mouse, curled up in the grass as if he'd been cupped in a palm and set there to sleep. Issy got up from the table, crouched down beside the mouse, and gently petted his finger along its rounded back. He sat there for a minute or so, and then looked up at me, his face like he wanted to say something, like he was disappointed. I could see he was about to cry, and he wiped his eyes and stared at me. Almost like he was daring me to laugh at him. I didn't.

I stood over Issy and said, "We have mice." I pointed at our house.

He smiled a big smile, and dug at the grass and dirt with his fingers and scooped out a hole in the earth and placed the mouse in it, moved it with a stick. We scoured the yard for what seemed like all day long, looking for the perfect rock to cover the hole. The mouse and the hole and the rock put us in the same world somehow, away from Havi, and all that came before. We never mentioned Havi again, and I realized I'd always wanted a brother.

It seems to me that Issy was somehow aware of death, or maybe just of sadness or maybe the harder parts of life, in way I wasn't, not yet. His life was more precarious than mine, less secure. My father was unorthodox, yes, but he was there. My mother didn't have marks and cuts on her face. This made me want to be a big brother to Issy. I probably never said it to myself or out loud, but that's what it was. And here he was a year older than me. But it wasn't just about wanting to protect him, if I could. There was something in him I recognized, something in myself, but also I was jealous of him. The Laudermilk house was a more secure place, absolutely, when compared with Issy's. But compared with the average family on our block, we were freaks. Daily life in the Laudermilk home was tricky—it was slippery—and even though I was dealing, always dealing with it, because I had to, it made me anxious. And here was Issy living a life lots more tricky then mine, in everyday ways, and yet he never once seemed anxious. If you could only have seen his face. He was untouched by it, or maybe he was just resigned and I'm romanticizing it all, or maybe he just never knew anything else. I wanted his peaceful way.

He came back that week, almost every day, and pretty much every weekday afternoon for the rest of the summer. Sometimes Saturdays. He occasionally joined us at church. One day, in our backyard, we talked about the girl in the yellow dress. We guessed at her name, and Issy decided to call her Ariel, after Princess Ariel from one of our favorite cartoons. How do I remember this? *Thundarr the Barbarian.* We loved that cartoon! We watched it, completely rapt, together in the living room, sprawled out on the floor in front of the TV, eating instant Jiffy muffins. I even remember the show's intro. A runaway cartoon planet flies by the earth and causes a global catastrophe in the future year of "1994." Just fourteen years away, at the time . . . Did I ever consider the coincidence, then? I don't think so. Six years off from my own "prediction." And in the year 3994, two thousand years later, Thundarr is born to save mankind. I even married Issy and Ariel, one day, the girl in the yellow dress played by a thin maple in my backyard.

Issy said, "You can do it because you're a priest."

Later that summer, Issy said we should go meet some girls. What girls? He knew girls? There were two girls that wanted to talk to us, he said. What do you talk about with girls? We spent hours, all morning long, learning how to use hair sprays and gels and trying to look as old as possible.

"You're supposed to use a hair dryer," he said. We were in the upstairs bathroom.

I looked in the closet where Mom kept the towels and the sheets and what looked like a tackle box filled with creams and makeup. I found the hair dryer.

"Here." He took it from me and plugged it in, and we blew our slick hair into deliberate cowlicks over our foreheads and sprayed.

We walked to Issy's school, and we walked into the school yard where the two girls should've been waiting for us. But they weren't. We sat on the monkey bars, and talked, and we joked, doing *Star Wars* impressions, and before long we forgot about the girls.

And then they were calling out for Issy.

"Issy! Issy!"

We looked all over, but we couldn't find them.

"Up here!"

We looked up and saw them standing on the roof of the school.

Issy said, "How'd you get up there?"

"The fence," one girl said. And she pointed at the fence, and how it extended alongside the school, up past a portico roof. "Climb from the roof," she said. "You afraid?"

Issy looked at me, and we read each other's thoughts: We must do this. Everything depends on us doing this. We ran for the fence and climbed like two chimps escaping from a cage, and found ourselves on the portico. We looked up and they were there, two Spanish-looking girls who knew Issy's name.

"Whas you name?" one of them said.

Me? I looked at Issy. I said, "Me?" And I looked back at them, at the hems of their skirts at their knees, and how did girls walk around in skirts? Climbing fences? In skirts? I was getting lost in thoughts of fences and skirts, and then both girls just started laughing. They said, "You can't get up here? We could do it!"

They disappeared from our view.

We froze. And then we scrambled.

"Here!" Issy said, "Look, a ladder on the wall." He was laughing, like how come we didn't see it? A black metal ladder bolted to the brick. We climbed it, and the upper edge of the building gave way to a view of the flat barren roof: broken soda bottles, cigarettes in piles, five-gallon cans filled with I don't know what like a janitor forgot they were there, a jellyfish pile of soaking-wet condoms, titillating and repulsive, and the girls. They were sitting on a brick rise that housed a large exhaust fan.

They were laughing and saying, "What took you so long?"

We walked over, and how did our hairdos look by now? More ridiculous? Less ridiculous?

The girls were playing cards.

"You want to play UNO?" one of them asked us, the same one who had asked my name. We sat down on the ground and joined them.

I don't know what I'd expected to happen, or what Issy had expected to happen, or for that matter what the girls had expected to happen. But whatever it may have been, no matter how grossly exaggerated, or poorly informed, no matter what kinds of kissing I'd dreamed could ever happen on a girl's mouth and cheek, it would have paled. And yet all we did was play cards. I saw their skirts, they were there, right there! The miracle of their knees. We played cards on a roof above the world.

Later that summer we pondered things other than love. We pondered big things like death, but in the same way we had mulled over love on the roof with those girls, wondering how it might feel. We got up close, and we looked, as close as we could without actually touching. Issy and I did what boys do. We secretly watched horror movies, and pretended to be unafraid. We imagined we were at war, in my backyard, and shot each other dead with rifle-shaped branches. We creatively killed a large insect we found under a stone. We looked at its carcass, amazed that it was here, still here, but also how it wasn't really here in the world anymore. Death had a hard shell, then, black and metallic. And then, one day—did we go too close?—my friend Issy disappeared.

Something hit me softly on the back. I turned and saw the small wedge of wood, and saw that Dad was now standing in the doorway. He was wearing pants—no shirt, but the pants were clean and white.

"What? You think I'd lock you out?" He laughed. "Get in here."

"So you're ready to see me, sir?"

He laughed again. "I was tired!"

"I was on the phone."

"With the pretty wife?"

"Not my wife."

"Baaah." He turned back into the house.

"Hold on." I followed him inside, glad to see him acting more alive. He looked better. I jogged after him, past the bags, past the bathroom door, past the red light, and back into the dining room. Again we sat at the table. The white cat jumped to his lap.

He took the last sip from his beer and said, "So, I should be gone pretty soon now."

Something caught in my throat, I coughed. "Stop. Don't talk like that."

"Tell me now what's new. I feel rested."

I said, "Well. I'm here. That's new."

"Ha!" He slapped my knee. "Isn't it?"

I said, "Are you in any pain? At all? You're too skinny, Dad."

"Every day I'm here is pain, Junior."

I looked at his side where the ribs were prominent. "Where?"

"Everywhere." He looked around the room.

So I looked around the room. I said, "You've got to take better care of yourself."

"I'm fine." He lifted the cat to his face and kissed the neck, his face in the fur. "I'm done taking care of things," he said. "Since your mother left, I'm tired."

"I know."

"What do you know?" he said.

"That she left. And you're tired."

"You don't know a thing hiding out there in Hollywood." He pressed his face against the cat's back. "Good kitty."

I put my hand on his knee and the cat swiped at my arm. It ran and hid beneath the table.

"Be careful with the cats." He made kiss noises, rubbing his fingertips below the table where the cat was.

"You were in the bathroom for a long time."

He waved it away. "Not what you think."

"What am I thinking?"

"That your old man is constipated."

I laughed.

"I'm fine. I think in there. It's comfortable."

"You're napping on the john and it's comfortable."

"You don't get to come here and tell me what's what."

"You're right." He was right. "Does anyone come over anymore? Friends from church?"

"Bah. Your mother had friends."

"So no church. Ever?"

"My dream last night." He rubbed at his mouth, smacked his lips. "Clouds opening up over church. This is not a church I've been to, but it was *church*, you know what I mean?"

I nodded.

"The clouds open up and there are these two big feet. You follow?"

"I follow."

"Tremendous feet, big as Cadillacs. And His robes are swaying there and He's facing me. But I can't see His face. He's way too tall. His head's up in Heaven. And He lowers himself just enough."

"Okay."

"He's hunkered there above the church."

"Okay."

"And He takes a king-size shit. Right through the roof." He looked at me, like what do you think of that? He said, "I've had that one before. Different, but the same. I don't go to church anymore." He peeled at the label on his bottle, looking not especially interested in our conversation. Then he looked at me like, you and I, we get each other now?

I laughed. "No, I guess you don't."

"It's all right here," he said, touching his chest.

I nodded again. Nodding seemed safe.

"There are so many things we got wrong." He leaned in closer. "You have to read it right." He lifted himself from his chair.

"Sit down. Please. I just got here and you're walking away from me again."

"I wanna show you something."

"You should sit."

He walked over to the book on the far end of the table.

I said, "You hungry? I can make us something to eat."

"Sonny boy, food is for the living."

I tried not to sound too worried. "You're ugly, I promise. But very much alive."

"You always were funny." He looked at me like he'd just remembered something, or maybe like he'd forgotten himself and he found it again. "Made your mother laugh all the time. You were a real stinker." He pointed at me.

I noticed his pants were painter's pants, hooks on the hips for hanging tools. He'd painted houses for a few years, and I'd completely forgotten.

"I saw your mother this morning." He flipped the pages of the book, looked up. "You still think I'm crazy."

"I think you've had a very hard year."

"Longer than a year."

"Mom's gone a year."

"I'm not talking about your mother."

I nodded. "Of course not."

"You know, she figured things out before she left."

What little daylight there was dimmed along the edges of the window shades.

I said, "I can get us a pizza."

"She's finally gone home, Josiah. Right where she should be. It's where she always was going. It's where she belongs."

I kept my mouth shut. "You should eat something."

"And I'm going home to see her."

Bite your lip.

What I wanted to say was, Dad, you got it all wrong. Death is not a home. Cancer is not a reward. When it comes knocking on your door, you should run. And if you don't run because for some reason you don't know any better, you should be taken up and protected. You should be lifted by your son, and slung over the shoulder if necessary, and hurried away to a hospital. Like it or not.

He made like he was coming toward me, but then he held fast to the chair.

"Don't you see, Junior? I'm on your side!" He pointed his finger again and it shook, a slight palsy. "We're finally talking here."

Then he poked at the book with his finger. "It's all right here, but you have to wrestle with it. I'm in the *Lord* because He is in *me*, you see? Always has been. You see?"

I stood and walked toward the book, which looked sort of like a Bible, the fragmentary prosy-poem look of scripture, chapter and verse, but it was different. I didn't recognize the names of the books. No Matthew, Mark, Luke, or John. No Genesis. "What is this?"

"It's scripture, what else?" He squeezed my hand and grabbed hold of the chair again quickly. His hair fell and covered his eyes.

I said, "Please. Let me go and get us some dinner."

"No, no, you go ahead. I'm gonna go lay down."

"You literally just got up." Or maybe he was right. He just needed rest. I didn't want to call someone and make too big a deal. He'd start acting like the Dad I knew, eventually, in the morning maybe. In the meantime, the house needed cleaning, and he needed a shower and shave.

"I'm tired and I take it when it comes," he said. "Tomorrow will be better, I promise."

I combed back his hair with my hands, so I could see his eyes. Still green.

He took a set of keys from his pocket. "So you don't get locked out." I followed him as he walked to the bathroom. He opened the door and the red light peeked from around like a fire. I tried to peer inside but he deliberately blocked my view.

"You're going to lie down?" I said.

The white cat snuck by and went in. He actually allowed this.

"Wish me good dreams," he said.

I let out a sigh. Relented. "Good dreams."

He took up my hand to his mouth and he kissed it. I don't think he'd ever done this before, kissed my adult hand. There was a pink swelling around his mouth, maybe from holding back a cry. His chin quivered. "I'm fine," he said. "I promise." He closed the door and he locked it. Shuffled about inside. There was a trickle, a scraping whine from the plumbing, and then a falling jet of bathwater. I figured he was taking a bath. Good for him. I needed to clear my head. A walk. A long walk, outside, in the open air. I opened the door, and whispered a brief prayer for the first time in years.

I walked back and forth on the sidewalk out front, around the corner, and all I could think about was Dad. And the cats. How were there so many cats? And what in God's name was going on here? Dad wasn't *sick*, as far as I could tell. But what did I know? Maybe he was. Even though he looked terrible, I didn't want to believe he was physically sick, and I was nervous and totally undecided on how to proceed. Plus all of a sudden, here in this house, I was thinking of Issy, and I didn't like to think about Issy. I thought of how that same year, in the fall, his father was sort of back in the picture when Issy disappeared, and his mother was getting herself straight, I think. Such a long time ago. I thought hard about it: a Sunday morning, and Issy went to get his dad a newspaper and a gallon of milk. But he never came back. On the news, the neighbors said they saw him come home, paper bag in his arms, and that he was last seen talking to a man in a pickup truck right in front of his house. Which does seem pretty memorable for Queens, because when did I ever see a pickup? But also an old woman from next door said she never left her porch, and she saw him leave that morning and never saw him again. What was it in the eighties? Kids were disappearing like it was some mini-Rapture. One minute they were here, and then *poof*. Ten years of grainy milk-carton photos and weeping mothers begging for the return of their kid on the local news.

Like it usually went, Issy's dad was a suspect at first, but he was cleared. I seem to remember this ruined what was left of that marriage. I definitely remember Mom sitting me down to tell me about Issy. She said she had some news to share with me, and that I needed to be a "young man" about it. She called me that, a young man. And this made such a powerful impression on me, because I'd been called a young man by the elder brothers in our congregation ever since I started giving sermons and scripture recitals at church. "*What a fine young man . . . A fine example for the other boys . . .*"

But, until Issy, I was just a boy to Mom.

He and his mother hadn't been to church that week, which wasn't so strange a thing because, like I said, sometimes he went with us, and sometimes his dad dropped him off and he went by himself. Sometimes he wouldn't go to church at all. But by the time Mom talked to me, the whole congregation was already whispering about his disappearance. It was on the local news, in the papers.

She said, "Young man, this world is sick and tired and broken, and one day our Heavenly Father will fix it. But until then, bad things happen. What you're hearing about Issy is one of those things, because no matter where he is, it's not where he wants to be, which is home and safe with his family. I want you to pray for him, okay?"

I remembered her makeup, and how much she seemed to have on while she talked to me, how there was a lot more on her face than usual, and how the ceiling fan in our foyer was spinning just above us. I came to know the word "foundation" around this time. Makeup fascinated me, because I figured I was supposed to like it on girls but I really didn't, the UNO girls on the roof wore no makeup, and wasn't it sort of like paint? This made me suspicious. I used to wonder what would happen if you kissed a girl who had a lot of makeup on. Would it get on your face and your hands? On your shirt? I thought girls mostly wore makeup to hide problems on their face. Issy's mom, for instance, wore lots of makeup to cover the pocks and marks. Mom, though, just looked so tired. I looked up at her and I considered the safety of ceiling fans, wondering whether the speed at which they spun was quick enough to take off somebody's head. I was confused.

Mom and I talked—I don't think I said much—and then Dad led me into the garage when she wasn't looking and asked me where Issy was.

"Tell me," he said.

I thought I was in trouble. "But I wasn't with him. How could I know?"

He asked me to concentrate, and said, "I don't mean know where he is like that." Dad asked me to think of Issy, only Issy, to try and reach up to God. He asked me to see if Issy was in Heaven.

He said, "You need to take this seriously."

"Commune," he said. "It's in your blood."

This only made me more confused. So I was relieved when Mom suddenly took me away by the hand. She glared back at Dad, and led me into the house. I couldn't know what that glare was about, not really, only it appeared Mom and Dad thought differently about some things. About me. They were different people. I don't think I really knew this before. From then on I wasn't surprised when they had opposite opinions, or when my mom got mad at Dad for whatever reason. I think it was then, when Dad told me to commune, and when I did try to do it, later, in my room—I seriously did—that I began to question what had happened onstage that summer. Maybe not in some clear way, but I certainly asked myself how what Dad called communing with God was different than praying to God. I prayed to God and I did ask Him to tell me where Issy was. So many times I asked this. I also recall hearing my own voice asking for an answer and I remember making a small sound. A kind of "Oh." My voice. I heard my voice, it was me. Dad asked me again, later that week, in a roundabout way, and I said I couldn't do what he wanted. I didn't know how, and I asked him to please not be mad at me. His face fell. We never talked about it again.

I want to say such sad and harrowing news of Issy made me cry, made me weep, but it didn't. Kids are too self-involved. Or I was, anyway, in the way that young kids can be: life will never end, and my parents will always be here. . . . But there was *something*. I didn't know what, a disturbance in my system of things, a first ripple in the unbothered water. Things did not add up. Where did he go? I asked myself that a lot. I prayed about it, thinking maybe I did have special access to God. But He never answered. One afternoon, I went out back and I cut at the one of the maples with a steak knife. I slashed at the tree. I threw the knife at the dirt at the base of the tree like I was throwing a hatchet. I pulled it from the dirt and I looked at the small hole I had made, and I punched the dirt as hard as I could. There was a small rock there and it cut the back of my hand, and like a bruised piece of fruit I now had a soft spot.

Weirdly, the church brothers started paying me even more attention. They sat me down in the back room and explained that Issy's disappearance was solid proof we were in the Final Days, and that he was my closest friend was proof of my gift. Satanic forces were actively working against me. Be careful. I must remain strong. And so it was time I give another sermon, perhaps at another local congregation.

I wanted nothing of the sort.

I looked around at the elder brothers. They were so tall.

"Where's my dad?"

There was a drop ceiling above us, rectangular foam tiles propped by metal ribbing, and I was filled with a sudden urge to push aside a tile and see what lay beyond there. Pipes? Electrical wiring? A dark empty space.

"Your father gave us his blessing," one of them said.

But I didn't want to give sermons anymore. Why? Because I was afraid it would happen again. I couldn't really put it into words, but it was the total loss of self onstage, in front of every-body—or is that the right way to put it? Maybe the opposite. I knew what I'd done up there was *special*, like nothing anybody there had ever seen. Certainly like nothing I'd ever seen, or done, and yet I'd been physically compelled to do it. It wasn't by choice, didn't feel like a choice. But I also knew very well what I had done, knew that it was me who had done it, even though I didn't exactly know what I was doing at the time. I imagine it like the way a child actor can't stay away from a camera the very first time he sees one, and he never knows explicitly why. An infant, and he's posing for pictures! All I knew was that getting onstage would mean doing that "thing" again, playing that part, and, frankly, it meant talking about God doing terrible things to fine people. How did I know who was or wasn't good? It meant talking about blood, and war, and vengeance, and getting nice people, as far as I could tell, to applaud for it. I could not have articulated this at the time, but I felt it inside my body. In my skin. And I was also a little afraid that it *wouldn't* happen—I'll admit that now: that I could never do it again. I was afraid to find out.

Plus the kids in church, they had already avoided me, but now, after Issy, they acted like I carried some kind of contagion. Get too close and disappear. Havi claimed he was Issy's best friend, probably for the attention, although by that time I knew it wasn't true. Some of the others, the older ones, closer to twenty, now started paying me attention. I was invited for after-church lunches. Let's go to a diner, and see a movie at the Woodhaven Boulevard Cinemas. I think they had some vague religious ambitions, and thought befriending me would improve their standing. I just

wanted to be alone. But soon it was settled. Again in the back
room, this time with Dad and the congregation elders. I would
give a short sermon at the end of October on the satanic evils of
Halloween. On devils, and witches, and ghosts, all abominations
in the eyes of the Lord.

The year before, a few neighborhood boys were seen trick-or-
treating dressed up like the rock band KISS. Obviously because
of a local demonic influence. Just look to the acronymic herald:
Kids In Satan's Service. It would be years before I got the unin-
tended irony, when I first heard "Rock and Roll All Nite," and
pretty much anything else from their totally benign catalogue.
Evil as Saturday morning cartoons. Nevertheless, my subject:
"The Satanic Dangers of Halloween, and the Everyday Demonic
Influences Around Us." Dad was enthused. Mom was not.

Was the timing appropriate? I mean, there was Issy to think
about, and *that* was what I should have been doing—as a family,
what *all* of us should have been doing. Praying for Issy.

She said, "I'm sorry, but I just don't like it."

This was in the living room, at the table. We were having our
weekly Bible study and she just came out with it.

Dad said, "Let's not argue in front of the boy."

That same week Mom went to the doctor, and told him how
tired she always was, whole-body tired, and it wasn't long after
that we found out she had cancer. I ran off into the backyard, and
sat myself again beside the maples Issy and I used to climb, and I
tried to not think about it at all. I slapped at the ground beside
me. It didn't hurt much and so I got on my knees and I punched
at the ground. Punched like I wanted to hurt it. And then I stood
up and I looked at one of the maples, imagining one of them was
me, and one was Issy, and I touched it with a knuckle to see how
hard it was. I cocked back my fist, such a small fist, and I punched
the tree. I scraped my knuckles on the bark. They bled. I punched
it again, squarely, and I heard my knuckle snap. I started crying,
and sat back down in the dirt. I prayed, cradling one hand in the

other. Where had he gone? Why had he gone anywhere at all?
And why *that* summer? I must have asked for this. Maybe I hadn't
talked with God himself, not had a conversation with him, not a
dialogue, but that didn't mean he didn't hear me. My God, what
had I done? I'd called out and asked for the End. I'd rolled out a
red welcome carpet, and, yes, I didn't know what this meant, not
then: that really this meant death. Real blood. Red blood. But
it was becoming clearer to me. It hadn't touched me yet, not
exactly, but nonlife, nonbeing, the hole in the air that Issy now
was, that *had* touched me, and I couldn't help but make a connec-
tion between the two. Here was the one kid who let me in, who
treated me like a kid, like I wanted to be treated, and so I acted like
a kid, the way I wished I could act with the other kids, or with my
father. Here was the kid who became my brother, who made me
feel less lonely, and now he was gone. My best friend, who never
once seemed anxious or afraid. I used to wonder whether Issy
somehow knew this would happen, that it was coming. Otherwise, why had we compressed what felt like years of friendship
into months, weeks into days, hours? I wondered if it was my fault,
whether God had simply answered my call. Issy was the first one
to go. And now maybe Mom would go next.

All this remembering took work, and walking up and down Dad's block, taking in the pungent nighttime neighborhood air, I got hungry. And thirsty, and I hoped to scare up some booze. I wanted to sit on the back porch and get tipsy. I wanted to look at the maples. Those same trees. Was it possible? The same dirt? I went back inside and stopped by the bathroom and listened there for Dad. He was talking in his sleep, mumbling. I said his name, quietly. Nothing. I heard his breath quicken and slow, quicken and slow, and I imagined his legs moving like how a dog's legs quiver when the dog dreams of a chase. I tried the doorknob. It was locked. I looked at the red light and walked away into the kitchen, opened the fridge and took out the butter. I rifled through drawers in search of a knife, found one, cut a thick slice of bread. I looked at the kitchen, at the cat turds, at the trash on so many surfaces. I took the bottle from the fridge. Uncorked, and nearly empty. I said to myself, If I don't move a muscle, then maybe the room will feel clean. I moved, and something crunched underfoot.

On the far wall, there was a simple wooden cross and beside it a decorative plate. I walked closer. These were new. Maybe not *new*, but I'd never seen them before. A gold Star of David was painted in the center of the dish. And burned into the wooden cross, on the horizontal piece were the words "Beth Sarim," and on the vertical, in smaller letters, "O. Laudermilk, 1930." I wondered who the "O." was. I knew my father's father was an Orville, and I think he shared the name with his father, my great-grandfather. But I could've been wrong. Probably my grandfather's. I had no idea who Beth Sarim was. Beside the cross was the backyard door. I pulled, but the door was stuck. The weather had done what it does, and the door felt grafted to the frame. I pulled, and again I pulled, until the door gave way, and stray leaves and string, paper cups and newspaper wads, all in an upswept pile against the door, tumbled into the kitchen. I jogged back to the counter. Grabbed the bread and the wine.

It was a quiet evening, and the kerosene smell seemed less everywhere now, and there were lights in the neighboring windows. In a back window of the house behind ours, a family was sitting around a table, and the father, or I assume it was the father, was talking lively with his hands. The backyard was smaller than I remembered. All overgrown with weeds and littered with beer cans and bottles, probably from neighborhood kids. Three bald rubber tires were stacked beside a pile of paint cans, and a twisted bike knotted like a ribbon sat on top of a red metal car hood. The Ford Country Squire! —No. And just as fast, I remembered that poor thing had been repossessed, not so long after Dad brought it home. Because the world in fact kept turning, and it turned out we couldn't afford the payments. At the back fence, like a V jutting from the ground, were the same two maples.

The evening breeze was slight. The leaves up top were flitting. I sat on the back porch steps.

The wine was cold and not bad at all and I watched evening come down behind the houses. The pearlike shadows of the Sikh temple domes darkened against the sky. I'm here, I'm right here, I thought to myself. And Dad's here, too, right there inside and asleep. He's alive. But the man should be in a bed. Were there beds anymore? Upstairs? I hadn't even been upstairs yet. More wine. Too many years had sloughed off this place, like paint peeling from a surface, all of it and everywhere else, the backyard and metal fence, the rusting wrought-iron porch railing, the blue mailboxes on the street corners, and the ice cream trucks, take-out delivery guys on bikes, and the next-door neighbors asleep in their beds or watching the nightly news in easy chairs, from all of this and everything, the years were sloughing off too fast. What happens next? We'd hug in the bright morning, avoiding all mirrors, and cheer flat beer until he finally gave up and died, "went home." I opened my phone and the digital green display lit up. I looked at the numbers.

I decided I would march through the house first thing in the morning, and tear every drape and shade from the windows, open every window wide. I wanted to light every bulb and start sweeping. I would wake the man up with a busy morning commotion, fresh coffee brewing in the kitchen. He'd come shouting from the bathroom, blocking the sunlight from his eyes, and see me in the hallway working a broom. The front door open, trash bags piled on the porch. And then he'd say, Thank you, Junior, thank you. He'd say, This is just what I needed, good light in here! Just can't get enough light! Then we'd go for a walk in the sun, me holding his hand, a giant hand, and my father a giant beside me. I drank. But part of me, I have to say, was also jealous of the man, of how he looked at the thing, unflinching. And yet a small part of me also disliked him for being so goddamn gullible about it all. Life is here. Now. God doesn't need your company. Leave Heaven be. I would save him after all.

I went back to the kitchen and foraged for more wine. I opened the refrigerator, dumbly, knowing there was no more left. I went through the cabinets, mostly empty; some were filled. One was lovingly stacked with newspapers, and another with pens and pencils bound by rubber bands. Another was stacked with empty wine bottles. One fell, I caught it in my hands, and this gave me hope.

The pantry.

It was a deep closet pantry with louvered doors. I'd hidden inside as a kid when my mother did the dishes, and also when she searched the rooms with a belt in her hands, anxious to give me a strapping for any disobedience. I don't like to remember this side of her. Plus that sort of thing only happened occasionally, and when I was very young. I saw a worn-down broom leaned against shelves stacked with dusty canned goods, and a stack of cardboard boxes. One had been opened, flaps nicely folded. Inside it, I saw two lamps messily wrapped in bubble packing, the same lamp I'd seen in both the dining room and the living room. Behind, there was a box with four bottles of red wine, screw-topped.

I chose a tall glass from the sink and rinsed it, dried it clean on my shirt.

Back outside, shouting came from a dimly lit basement window next door. Maybe Korean. The night sky in Queens had no stars, and the moon was somewhere up there dozing. It was a nonstop sky of dark blue and nothing. I thought, My mother is here, she's right here, and also she's not here at all. She's out there and nothing at all. And all of her was here when she was still here, even the yelling for my father, saying there's a spider in the bathroom, and the prayers before meals with a supplicant's napkin on her head whenever Dad was out of town, even the vein in her neck like the string on her red balloon face when she got angry. I let that memory go when it came. All of her was here when she was here, and nowhere else. I never thought of her name anymore. My father's name is Gill. I wanted to say his name out loud.

"Gill Laudermilk."

My glass raised, I said it louder. And I had a terrible feeling that there was more dead space between sons and fathers than all of the night air around me. Which version of Dad did I love? I loved mostly an invention, the best version of him I could think of.

"I am Gill Laudermilk's son!"

The moon peeked over the roofs, and I was tired. The lightning bugs were blinking, and I thought of the brief electric marks they make when getting snuffed.

I carefully closed the back door and took the wine bottle into the living room. And like rats after hours in a restaurant, the cats came out from the corners. They rubbed against my legs, flirting and following me with caution. I shook the sheet on the couch clean, shut off the lamp, and leaned back easy on the couch. Where was my bag? I pulled the phone from my pocket and tried to relax. The room was dark, very dark, and I set the phone green-lit and open on the table. I smelled the garbage in the hallway, but it was fainter. I was getting used to it. I deeply inhaled, filled my senses like I would in a Christmas kitchen. I drank in the stink and everything was going to be fine. The phone shined weakly and the numbers read "9:21." Things would be better tomorrow.

The white cat rubbed at my ankles.

I patted my lap: Come up here. Stroked her back. I wanted to ask her about the bathroom, what it looked like inside the red-lit room, and how it felt to be such a good kitty, to be trusted to see what was going on inside there, to be such a perfect fucking kitty. I stood up and, picking her up with both hands, I let her hang. Dangling there from my grip, the softly hissed. I let go one hand and lifted her higher, stretching my arm as far is it could go. She scratched at my forearms with her back feet. Was this the same vicious thing that had scratched my arm before? An itchy red line puffed up on my wrist. I took a gulp from my glass as the cat fought back. I squeezed my hand slightly, and actually moved the cat's ribs. I felt the shape of her rib cage, her interior, her tiny pink heart shaking there and sweating the closing rib walls between my fingers. The cage was closing in my grip. I put down my glass.

I pressed my fingers against one of the pink pads of her right front paw, and a single claw came curling like a sharp thin pinky finger. I kept pressure on the pad, keeping the claw extended, and I pressed a thumb against the claw. It poked against my skin and broke the skin of my finger but I pushed back more against the claw, bending it backward. She cried out, fighting my grip. I was afraid my father might hear. I squeezed hard on her ribs and reminded her that I actually had two hands. I pushed back on her claw and she cried and she fought.

She whimpered.

She stopped fighting, and let herself hang. I thought of wishbones, totally ashamed. I sat and placed the cat in my lap. She didn't run. She hopped off and just walked away, but not without stopping at the doorway and giving me a look of absolute disgust before leaving the room. The phone light had gone out. I closed the phone, opened it again, and left it there on the table, green-lit and glowing. I poured another glass and drank it down fast. It had been such a long first day. What would I find in the light of morning? I closed my eyes and the cats were slowly climbing up the couch, up my legs. They came out like shadows and covered me. I closed my eyes and prayed again. Again! I asked if I could please dream of Sarah, and I lay there for what seemed like only seconds before I fell into a deep heavy sleep, before falling into a long and semilucid dream.

WEST

2

SOUTHERN CALIFORNIA

It was a Sunday morning when Sarah first called to talk about Dad. I remember because I was standing on the treadmill she gave me. The TV was on, one of the news channels, and sometimes I looked at it, but mostly I just stood there staring at the dead odometer. I was fully dressed for the day, and sipping coffee. A glance here and there at the morning show. The power button on the treadmill totally untouched, no red numbers telling me how much time I had left. It should've been our eighth anniversary. A year already since the divorce, and things weren't getting any better. They *were* getting better, in that I no longer wanted to throw myself into the Pacific (in those fantasies, Sarah always came bounding down the beach, bikini clad, just in time . . .), but everything else was turning to shit. I still couldn't believe Mom was gone and all the world around me hardly noticed. This was *Mom*. We did talk, Sarah and I, occasionally, but not much. I felt like a stranger in my own life. The sound of her voice used to be mine, and now it was his. Nikos, the infamous Grecian usurper. I wanted to hate the man, but more I wanted to avoid what I really knew in my heart, the basic truth that she went with him because she was lonely, and because somewhere along the line, her loving husband had become an asshole. I'll say this: the phone call was unexpected. I took my cell from the holder on my belt.

Sarah 8:55.

"Well, hello, stranger," I said.

She said, "I can't really talk, not now."

"So talk."

"Okay. There is something up with Dad. Your dad. Something unkosher, I mean definitely. But I can't really talk right now. So call him."

"So nice to hear from you, too," I said.

"I'm serious," she said. "I'm coming," she said to someone else.

"What, is he sick? He told you he's sick? And who are you talking to?" I did not yet know about Nikos.

"It's not that," she said. "It's something else. There's a quiver in his voice, a kind of manic thing. It's depressing and a little bit scary. I can't talk."

"And yet here we are talking," I said.

"I'm coming," she said again to someone else. "Go see him. Just go see him."

"We should have dinner tonight."

Sarah and Dad had already been phoning each other for years, and this way before any talk of unhappiness, or separation, back when we were still giddy as pink pigs rolling in cool summer shit, and falling on each other every chance we got. Good God, I loved that woman. I should say actually it was Dad who phoned Sarah, and hardly the other way around. The man felt responsible for her soul.

"You should see him," she said. "Go visit him."

"Okay, stop. Dad and I are fine," I said.

"He tells me."

"And if he's sick, he hasn't said anything to me."

"Listen, I'll call you tomorrow, I promise," she said. "The man is talking to me about his dreams again, about your mother, and I'm not sure these are good dreams. Sadder than I've ever heard him before."

I said nothing.

"I'll call you tomorrow," she said. "I have to go. Maybe dinner tomorrow."

She hung up. I put the phone back on my belt.

"And happy anniversary," I said, because hey, you know what, who knows, maybe a post-anniversary dinner with Sarah. Some white wine, polite conversation. I'd been going through such a long and predictably depressing phase, typical divorce stuff. I'd been angry, and lethargic, then just sad, and generally unmotivated, afternoon bourbons poured to the brim of a water glass. But as of this morning, I decided, it was over, finished, finito. We were beyond the cliché of the broken warring couple. We were adults.

Beside the TV, on the far wall, there was an old picture of Sarah and me at the beach. Two silhouettes, the blaze of a setting sun. We'd lived there in the condo by the water for seven long years. I always liked beaches, but I never really liked the ocean. Too damn big. And that treadmill was tremendous, took three men to bring it up the stairs. She had given it to me the year before. Said it was her goodbye gift and, frankly, despite the fact that I did come to love the convenience, jogging a few mornings here and there, I was tired of seeing it every waking morning of my life. I wasn't exactly a runner when we met. Running for what? Toward what? I tried asking her this once. On our very first run. We'd been dating for a few weeks. I guess it was dating, but I also feel like I've never dated in my life. I feel like I meet a woman, or girl—this habit goes a long way back—and I completely surrender, all the way, I'm in love. Like it or not, it's all over. Maybe *they* were dating. But I certainly wasn't. We went on a run, Sarah and

I, which was probably a date for her, but for me was an expression of unbounded and obvious loving devotion.

This was not an easy run, especially for a beginner. Bogging down in the sand, I couldn't keep up. We went for a mile, maybe less, probably a lot less, before I was wondering how it was I'd never run on my own beach. *Baywatch* was popular at the time, and so I'd seen how beautiful running on the beach could be. It seemed to me I'd done something immoral, this not running. Sarah was ahead of me, her red-shorted bottom bouncing back and forth like a heart, upside down, buoyant, and persuasive. Keep running. But I was slowing, my heavy and also a little bit wet camouflage shorts weighing me down (I'd already tripped and stumbled into the water), and she was getting farther and farther away from me. I stopped running, and watched her go small, smaller and smaller, and then suddenly I started to panic. I felt like I had to prove myself; I was worthy. The last thing I wanted was for her to turn and see me just standing there, like I'd totally given up. So I bolted. I ran like I never had before, or ever have since. My calves on fire, the torn hems of my camo shorts chafing just above the knees. I ran for her, my tiny love getting small in the distance. No matter what, she would not turn and see me standing still or far behind. I willed it so. And so I ran. But then Sarah was getting bigger. Bigger and bigger with every passing second, because she had turned! I was powerless, and she had seen me for what I was, and she was getting bigger and closer and bigger and closer. Effortless for her, as far as I could tell. Then she was right there and slowing down and then she walked up to me, and said, hardly out of breath, "Hey, slowpoke."

She was careful to wipe her face of sweat with her forearms, and not her hands, I remember this, so she could take my face in her hands and kiss me. How do you describe a kiss without making it sound sentimental or different from any other kiss? I don't know. There was this—a piece of sand from her mouth went into my mouth, and that single grain tasted like salt and her sweat and

the whole Pacific Ocean. I didn't spit it out when she was finished
with me. I lightly bit it between my teeth, and I could not stop
smiling.

She said, "I like it when you smile. You should smile more."
She took my hand and we walked in the direction she'd been running. She said, "I don't like running alone anymore. . . ."

I stepped away from the treadmill, and told myself to stop
being sappy, and looked at the clock, nine a.m.

Already thirty minutes late for work.

But I also happened to be the boss, which came in handy since
work was seeming less and less a priority with each passing day.
Until today. This day.

I shut off the TV.

We ran a few more times together after, but never for very long.
I slowed her down, and I couldn't go very far, anyway. Eventually
I started running at the gym, by myself, and then on the treadmill at home. We took long walks together instead. She teased me
once and said my occasional morning jogs did not exactly make
me a "runner," not yet. At least not according to her, who was a
runner practically monkish in her devotion. Plus Sarah, with her
claustrophobia—and God forbid we call it that, because she
refused to admit she had a problem, "I just don't like low ceilings"—
she never ran inside. She preferred the freedom of a forest trail, the
wide beach path, the airy and open outdoors. At some point I
really should take my mileage outside, she'd said. She apparently
believed a treadmill in the bedroom by the window was supposed
to help get me there. Eventually. And she thought it would help
with the whole ugly common process of divorce, that it would
clear my head. On the other hand, I was convinced our problems
were not at all common. I bridled at the thought of being common. She often said, "But running can save your life, Josie."

The clock now read 9:04.

Amad was opening up the store, I was sure, and I expected
him to call any minute now, wondering where I was. I put the

mug on the windowsill and decided I would take the long way to work along the water, maybe give Dad a call. Have a chat. It would be three hours later in New York, about noon. A light spark of hungry angst fizzed in my belly.

I opened the window and looked out over the courtyard to the palm trees and the open back windows of all four buildings, curtain-sails ballooning with the morning breeze. I saw my neighbors' pull-blinds all gone wonky. The barbecue grills, and the folding chairs, the tikis propped in buckets of sand. I looked up over the roofs to where the birds were squawking. I was expecting seagulls, and a breeze carried over the salt-rot stink of the bait-and-tackle shop around the corner. Morning clouds were laundry white, slack, and sprawling over blue. What a day. I was very proud of this view. It wasn't cheap. And I remember there was a flood of blue sky that morning. I saw a shark's eye in water, a pale moon east of the morning sun because nighttime hadn't gone home just yet. I liked to think I wasn't one for omens. But Dad was maybe not entirely fine, and there I was way up with the clouds, fastening clothespins, and still needing a cigarette. I heard the water, the soft crash of ocean waves just across the street. I'd taken up smoking again, not sure why. This world works in circles, or maybe more like squashed, elongated ovals. I went downstairs and got a new pack from the freezer.

Keys, wallet, phone.

I took the path through the courtyard and around the garden I shared with my neighbors, where I never did much more than put out the occasional butt in the flowerpot soil. Bev, on the other hand, in the condo diagonally opposite, took great care with our little garden. She watered almost every morning. And Charlie, who lived right next door, often tended to a scaly potted tree, his favorite. The condo walls were so thin I sometimes heard Charlie talking to his parrots. He was a volatile man of sixty, fond of bicycles—the kind of guy who'd lived alone for a long time by the water.

Unkosher? I was already late for work. But I was heartened that Sarah and I would share an evening meal.

Sarah liked to think she was responsible for bringing Dad and me back together—and she was. But she also liked to think that, if not for her continual upkeep, he and I would forever lose touch. She was my wife (ex-wife), his daughter-in-law, yes. But she was also a stereotypical Jewish mother to us both. Make sure he's eating enough. Make sure *you're* eating enough. Would it kill you to pick up the phone? Whether she believed it or not, Dad was forever on the borders of my brain, practically stalking every thought since Mom died. He and I talked on the phone, but also he was right there on the perimeter of my thinking, all ghostlike and circling like a buzzard. Don't get me wrong. This is my father we're talking about. I felt nothing but love for the man but, like I said, it was complicated.

The palm trees out front by the street were spread up high like God's grabbing fingers. The fiery orange and midnight-blue birds-of-paradise bursting from the ground like frozen firework moments. And that fading neon pink bumper sticker on Bev's yellow Gremlin: "Live Each Day Like It's Your Last." That always seemed to me to be a terrible idea.

I walked toward the water and called Amad. I told him not to worry, said I was on my way.

He said, "You're late."

"I know. That's why I'm calling. To tell you I'm on my way, but I'm late."

He hung up on me. Very Amad.

I walked on and waved to Mrs. Dunbar, down the street, as she swept her driveway with a push broom. She waved back. I walked by, admiring the trees on her corner lot, the tall crepe myrtle with its brown-butter leaves, and her American persimmon in bloom with orange fruit hanging in orbit like succulent planets. We said a quick hello. Persimmon trees, at least the American ones, she'd told me once before, are naturally self-fertile. Feel free to draw your own conclusions from this, as I certainly had to on many a lonely night. . . . And the magnolias, Mrs. Dunbar loved her magnolias; she'd gone to great pains in the past pointing out to me the overt and subtle differences between the many types. The lily magnolia, the saucer, star, and pink star magnolias, all very beautiful and hung with those enormous and puffed-out

flowers, a black eye staring from the center of each. A cork tree
stood on the corner by the road. A wide monster of a thing, knotted, and tall as any tree I've ever seen. She'd also told me the cork
was not native to California, and yet this one had to be a hundred
years old at least. If that's not native, I don't know what is. I liked
pressing my fingers inside its soft and fleshy give-way bark.

I headed for work along the beach, wondering if my father
would answer his phone. Sometimes he flat-out refused even
though I paid his cellular bill.

I called, and it rang and rang and rang . . .

Of all things Californian, probably my least favorite thing was
the water. I liked the beach, yes, but you'd never catch me swimming. Water has no shape, and I like shape. I've had more than
one nightmare of me going over some mammoth and rushing
Niagara, on a spindly wooden raft, screaming my head off all the
way down, only to wake like a petrified dead man born to his bed
in the afterlife. I have to say I especially liked watching the sunset
from where my street dead-ended. All clichés are true, so I say
it's our job to refresh them. I liked looking out past the grassy rise
where the kids played Frisbee, and way out there beyond the
boardwalk. Past the deep stretch of sand and the lifeguard's tower
of rough, white wood, and beyond the tower, where the ocean
stretched out to the hazy silhouette of Catalina Island, where the
sun goes down to sleep. I stood at the waterline sometimes, at the
end of America, one of the ends anyway, and I imagined there was
nothing else at all.

Only days before, Amad and I made a wager that I wouldn't
actually show up this particular Sunday. He told me Teri, his
wife, had been asking questions lately: Seriously, how bad a shape
was the store in? Was business so bad? Should he start looking for
a new job? And what about the baby? (Teri was pregnant!) I mean,
if Josie can successfully close down three stores, why not a fourth?
Actually, Amad told me the bet was her idea. And I couldn't blame
her. The stakes were small—the loser bought breakfast burritos

and coffee—but I got the message. Otter Computer, right there on Main Street, was my first and eventually my only location. At one time there were four. Then three. Number two closed during the divorce. And finally just one left. I worked there a few days a week, but never ever on a weekend. Business wasn't great. Like I said, I was a bit unmotivated. But not the lovely Mister Amad Singh, my only remaining employee, and closest friend (also thirty-seven, such a complicated age). Amad was all things Otter Computer. He had been with me since the beginning. And I spent a good part of my days off avoiding his phone calls. The economy was tanking and he was worried about the business, with good reason. I always told him to calm down. I said I had a plan, and I knew what I was doing. Don't forget I built this place from nothing. Then again, I'd been saying that for a long while, and not very convincingly.

Nevertheless, I promised him that we would turn things around pretty soon now. Do your best and stay focused. I told him once how crazy he was for having kids and, I swear, he stopped just short of slapping me across the face. I agreed to start working on Sundays because the weekend business had been getting better. Sarah would have laughed out loud at the idea of me working on a weekend.

A buzzing at my waist; it was Dad.

"Hey, I was gonna call you again. I just called you."

"Hey yourself," he said. "I can't talk."

Another one in a rush. "Okay." I put on my talking-to-Dad voice. "So, tell me how you're feeling."

"I'm fine." He coughed. "I'm fine."

"Well, Sarah says you're not."

"Your wife is making up stories."

"Not my wife anymore," I said.

"Ridiculous. No divorce lawyers in Heaven." His attention must have been drifting, because his voice was getting lower, like he was talking to the room he was in and not to me.

"Well, maybe I should look at some plane tickets." Pause. "Dad . . ."

He coughed again. "I told you, I'm fine. Call me later. Sundays, I get a little busy."

"I'm headed to work."

"A little work and a little bit of wine. Good for the soul!" he laughed out. He was all of a sudden louder now, like he was shouting into the phone. "Hey! Maybe I can show you what I got going? You should come out and visit us!"

I didn't say anything.

"Josiah," he said.

"Like I said, I'll look for a ticket."

"Hey! Josiah?"

"Yeah."

"You eat yet?" he said. "I'm hungry. Tell your pretty wife you love her!"

"I'll call you later, okay?"

Since the divorce, I'd asked Dad more than once to please stop calling Sarah. But he couldn't sit back while I did apparently nothing. He'd say something like "Her blood will not be on my hands, but yours, Josiah, come the Final Reckoning." He still absolutely refused to call me Josie. And I'd say something like "I understand, Dad, and your heart's in the right place, I know that. But you should also know that Sarah is definitely not in agreement with this statement. And at least she's respectful enough not to tell you this. You do remember she's Jewish, right? Please tell me you remember she's actually Jewish."

"And what about you, do you think I'm wrong?"

I would then change the subject because I don't answer questions like this.

After Mom died, and then the divorce, Dad started calling Sarah even more. She'd told me, the last time we talked, really talked—this was weeks before, twenty-two days to be precise— that now he was calling her late at night and poetically describing

the weather back east. He was sharing his more recent and memorable dreams. I recall one of her favorites, Dad in a desert eating
the book of Daniel. Dipping the pages in a bowl of melted butter,
one by one. If Sarah and I had ever had children, I think, they
would have found her postdivorce friendship with Dad a little
confusing. I found it confusing. But for whatever reason he sometimes felt less comfortable talking to his own son about whatever
the two of them talked about. Whatever; we were fine. I think
Sarah pitied him, maybe even hoped in some weird way that if she
were generous with him it would be good for me by extension. Or
I liked to think so, anyway. When I reached Main Street, I stood
there at the beach end, where I came to the realization that I'd
never once, not once, explicitly thanked her for being so generous
with Dad, even after we split, and I felt very shitty for it.

Amad was standing in front of the store, on the sidewalk. He
was looking up and down the street, back and forth, probably
looking for me. There weren't many people about. Just before
the long pier that juts into the Pacific, I saw a family of five. Two
young girls and an even younger boy were having their picture
taken. The boy couldn't have been more than twelve or thirteen.
They were all standing by the iron statue of an otter balancing a
ball on its nose. The boy was trying to climb its smooth metal
back. He was probably about Issy's age, or Issy's age the last time
anyone had seen him, anyway. But I didn't think of him then,
watching that boy only now. Isn't that odd? Why not think of
him then? Why not think of him always? "We should all be thinking of Issy. . . ." I thought of Sarah instead, and of our possible
dinner, and made a dumb smile. I hoped the little boy wouldn't
fall off the statue and crack his front teeth, because I'd seen it how
many times before. I'd also seen ancient photos at swap meets
of nineteenth-century ladies in full-body bathing suits posing by
that very same statue. Nostalgia can sometimes be dangerous.
Otter was always a minor tourist draw, but tourists aren't really
people. They're all toe bouncers, invariably looking for some

manifest version of Heaven. Maybe tourism is a sort of sin, I think. Whereas Otter was the kind of benign sleepy town where kids leapt from the splintering docks, where locals fished in the big sun, leathering happily until they died.

Someone who looked like my neighbor Charlie came riding from the pier on a bicycle. A fishing pole balanced from under his arm and rested on the basket attached to his handlebars.

I waved and his middle finger rose, right on schedule.

Amad went back in the store.

Wooster's, beside the main beach lot and across from the clock tower, was teeming with hollering swimsuited kids. Sodas in hand, they ran off in a dispersive sprawl into burning sand. In the parking lot, surfboards stuck out from back windows of cars and trucks, like knife handles, and the voices of young women flittered, sliding my way on the hot breeze. I walked toward the water, toward the floral-printed bikini tops and torn jean shorts. Their young feet and candy-colored nails, pale between sunburned toes scampered over the hot white powder. The girls jumped, laughing, into the white, hand-blocked light of the blue sky, flip-flops dangling from fingers. I scrunched my eyes, and they all half dissolved in a sun-soaked vision of volleyball, flickering in the screaming radiant light. I had to catch my breath. And a throng of runners, immaculate, numbers pinned to their chests, came padding up the concrete path, and I wondered where on earth they were going. This was southern California, land of perpetual health. The religiously healthy nearly naked everywhere you looked. The roads like clogged arteries, but nobody seemed to give a shit, bouncing along beside each other, breathing smog and briny smoke blowing inland from the ocean. I was feeling hungry and thirsty. And tired, because I'd always been a light sleeper, suffered from scary colorful nightmares as far back as I could remember, and while I no longer prayed before sleep like I did as a child, to keep the nightmares at bay I did sometimes close my eyes and ask that I might dream of Sarah running.

I saw the taco line was way too long. I was sure Amad was steaming.

The grilled fish taco at Wooster's was not a thing for which I'd moved to California, but had I known the simple joy of it, I would have. Red cabbage slaw and a fresh corn tortilla. Hot peppers, radish, and a lime slice, squeeze your lime slices. Even for breakfast. This is among the most perfect things I've encountered on earth. On occasion, back east for business, I've even made pilgrimages to Brooklyn, the Bronx, and Queens in response to reverent whispers, rumors of a Latin authenticity, of, say, a short Dominican couple serving chimichurri in the back of an El Camino. I was always disappointed. I originally went west, I guess, because of the simple fact that it was about as far away from New York as I could get without leaving the States. I was a young man running. I chose Otter because of Main Street, which was really just so charming, but also for its rough beach and the eroding rocks along the shore. This was a humbling place, beaten down by water and wind. I was supposed to be here. A spot of such natural and open mystery that it let me fill up with wonder, and not have to give that wonder a name. New York had become a land of secret corners and dark side streets, all man-made. Everything we make seems to fall down anyway. And of course I went to California for the women. Who was I kidding? For the quivery dream of young women, the lusty blur that fills you just before waking. Pink mouth and breast, the unhinged leg hovering just above dream, still inside the still-asleep bubble. Until morning sun fills a gauzy window; then gone. Girls of my teenage American wet dreams. Barbie-doll drivers of classic cars laughing in the saltwater wind. Of course, I found no such thing. Sarah was nothing like that. She had freckles on her forehead. Really not so unlike some romantic runaway from a midwestern farm filled with dreams of a brand-new birth, placenta snail-trailing as you first cross Sunset Boulevard, fresh off the bus, I left under the oldest American spell of all: I ventured west to begin . . .

Another buzzing at my waist.

Amad 9:37.

I walked down Main Street, suddenly excited for work. I smelled the sun, and the salty Pacific stink. I would prove, today, this day, that Amad and Teri were wrong; this would be the start of the long-awaited resurrection of Otter Computer Incorporated. Of me. No more idle hands.

Then a buzzing, and a text from Amad.

"I've been watching you dawdling for the last five minutes. I can see you from here."

I watched Amad through the plate glass window. He was speaking with a large bald man in clam diggers, and he was wearing one of his ill-matched sweat suits. Clean white sweatpants rolled up high near his knees, and a bright poppy-red sweatshirt. He checked his watch and smiled, holding up an ergonomic keyboard. When Amad had first walked in the store, this was how many years before, after answering an ad I placed in the L.A. *Pennysaver*, I said, So, tell me about your work history. He crouched, started rummaging through motherboard stacks, and silently assembled a desktop system. Hardware and software, it ran Solitaire in twenty-five minutes. I knew my way around a computer, well enough, but really my reason for being in the business was happenstance. I was lucky. Then again, I was always good at selling. It was in my blood. My father was a born salesman, always selling me on the idea that I was special. I bought it, for a while anyway. I'd been giving sermons since I was seven because I had a knack for commanding attention, and I liked it. Even still, I can turn it on but rarely do. If I'd been born into a more practical family, I likely would have run for class president, or started a small business at twelve. The entrepreneur's toolbox is not so different from the preacher's. I say that with respect. And so I sold computers—processors, hard drives, and memory—and this turned out, at first, to be a lucrative and very special service. Inside the computer waits every future mapping of the world. Amad had tried to explain the inner workings to me many times. It's easy, he'd say, all very easy. I would stop him cold.

He looked up when he was finished, and said, "My name is Amad. This is how I work."

Then he said, "Forgive me, I wanted to kill the ugly man that was driving right behind me, but now I feel much better. Praise to all that is." I remember him nodding and making a sweeping-away gesture.

I once said to him, "I want to be more like you. You've got it all figured out."

He said, "I have no idea what you're talking about."

"The big stuff, I mean."

"Big stuff doesn't interest me. What big stuff?"

That first week we opened, a customer referred to him as Gandhi. He said, "You mistake me for someone else. Please, my name is Amad," and he put out his hand.

I said, "You are an unacknowledged master, a crackerjack Sufi. You help me recognize the world."

He called me a "foking tommy."

He said, "I'll kick you right in your balls if you don't stop that bullshit. I'm hungry and I'm going to lunch." Three hours later, I found him across the freeway, getting drunk on Budweiser. He raised a glass as tall as a nightstick and said, "Back home I was a rocket scientist." Then he belched. "It's not a joke." A few years later, he named his dog Little Josie so that I would have a role model. This also wasn't a joke, and when I look back I see the good sense it made. Little Josie loved every day, no depressions! If I'd paid more attention to the pup it probably wouldn't have taken me so long to snap out of my stupor.

I knocked on the plate glass window.

I watched the bald man leave as I entered the store. I waved, and Amad nodded back: So, you're actually here. He walked over to a display table sparsely stacked with boxes for external tape drives, cabling, wireless mice. The boxes were empty, and a pale ray of light painted a band across the table.

"Here I am," I said. "I told you."

He turned and walked to the back counter, obviously displeased. "And you're late. I thought you were going to watch the bikini girls all day."

A short, squat woman in wraparound sunglasses walked in and quietly waited. Her wide waist was cinched in a pleated denim grip. One size fits all.

"Guess what, I talked to Sarah today."

He raised a finger to his lips and walked toward the woman.

I saw my reflection in the mirror behind the counter, and the digital numbers, the red reversed clock numbers on the shelf behind me. . . .

"Please make yourself useful." He was suddenly beside me holding a clipboard. "Josie."

I shook away and took the checklist.

He said, "Inventory. Please."

Behind me, the woman said, "My husband says our old computer is fine. I'm not even sure what I'm doing here." I turned. She wore a baby-blue sun visor, crowned with explosible rust-colored curls, and they fought the visor's hold like blood boiling over.

"You are here," Amad said, "because you know that your husband, he is dead wrong."

I watched her for any signs of customer discomfort. She took off her sunglasses.

"Mr. Amad," she said, "why do you say that?"

"This is not a joke." He put one hand flat on the counter. "For your husband to privilege the old computer simply because it has worked in the past, simply because it is dependable, it is to take it lying down. It is to die."

A bit persistent.

He said, "It is we who change, not the world."

"My daughter," she said. "Her cell phone's more like a pace-maker. I don't think she's ever seen a typewriter. I say, learn all we can. Let me run next door and tell her where I am." She patted his hand like, you just wait right here.

I watched her leave, and said, "That was really something. The hard sell."

He picked up a fallen cable from beside my foot. "You're late. You dawdled. And somebody has to make the money here. What can I say?"

"But I'm here. You owe me a breakfast burrito. And a coffee."

"You mean Teri does."

"Teri isn't here."

"She will be. And if you want to ask her yourself, feel free. Myself, I'd be very afraid."

I laughed, and said, "Today's supposed to be our anniversary, and guess who calls."

"How is she?"

"We're having dinner tomorrow. Maybe." I gave him a look like, is this a dumb idea? Please tell me it's not a dumb idea.

"You are what they call a necrophile. You love what is dead. And my very pregnant wife is fine, thank you for returning the favor and asking about her."

"Oh, stop. How is she?"

"Too late."

"Seriously?"

"Seriously. You are way too late. And she's fine, giving me acid in my stomach. Do you know how expensive a preschool is?"

"I told you it would be crazy."

"What did you tell me? You told me nothing. You have noth-ing to tell me. Do me a favor and put on a chicken suit, and stand out front. We need customers. Unless of course you would like to make an effort here." He motioned toward the door.

The woman had returned and now she was dragging her daughter along. The girl was fifteen, maybe sixteen, gangling, and popping gum, a perfect picture of bulletproof teenage oblivion.

"This is my daughter, Alison, Mr. Amad. I'd like her to meet a person like yourself. And I'd like to buy her a portable computer for school. Like we talked about."

"Hello, Alison." Amad extended his hand.

But the girl just looked at it.

"Take his hand, young lady."

The girl reluctantly extended one hand, cell phone snug in the free palm.

Amad said, "This is Josie. My boss who is very late."

I set the clipboard on the counter. "I'll be right outside."

All three of them gave me similar looks of disapproval.

Sitting on the bus stop bench out front, I lit another cigarette and watched the tourists walk by lapping ice cream. I thought I saw Sarah drive by in a red Honda. Lately I was seeing her face in lots of places. Because there are several ends to every love, and good God, we mourn its death in many stages. I saw her in supermarket lines, in afternoon game show commercials, and in the face of pretty much every short female runner. Hairs glued in strands across her forehead, glasses forever fogged while she jogged, actually impairing her vision. A pink ribbon emblazoned on her T-shirt: "Race for a Breast Cancer Cure." She had a vast collection of souvenir shirts. "Let's Win the Race Against AIDS." Run for muscular dystrophy awareness, or heart disease, or some children's hospital. Actually, anything at all having to do with children. Personally, I'd never wanted to have kids. I had made this clear from the very beginning. I also said that if she wanted kids, well then, we should have kids. She sometimes accused me of contradicting myself.

I told her once how I heard a man tell his son—well, I assume

he was the boy's father, because they were walking along with
baseball equipment bulging from a duffel bag—this was a sunny
day and I watched this man proudly announce to his son, his chest
was all puffed up, he said, "Do you know it takes only *four minutes* for sunlight to reach the earth?" I figured no way this was
possible. I had to go home and look it up. It takes eight minutes,
it turns out. He was wrong. And I knew this was not the kind
of misinformation that would necessarily divert a child's healthy
trajectory, but all I could think of at that moment was when my
own imaginary son first asked me why the sky was blue, or where
babies came from. These are basic father-son exchanges, and was
I really going to tell my child, if we ever had one, that I had no
idea? I mean, I did of course, I do, but we all know where those
kinds of questions lead at some point—how did we get here, why
are we here, and what happens after we die?

I usually told Sarah the timing wasn't right.

She actually hit me once with a pasta spoon. This was not a
wooden pasta spoon. And this just because I told her that kids
would never keep us from dying. Can you imagine? I actually said
to my wife, No matter what you may have heard, you cannot live
through your children. Which was especially unfair, even mean,
because our life at home had become so constricting, the place felt
smaller every day. I knew that having somebody besides me—a
child, say—would have been a completely natural and welcome
and well-deserved change in our life. What can I say? The only
real family life I knew seemed distorted. What model would I
use? I told her once, toward the end, that a baby is no way to save
a marriage. I accused her of "polishing brass on the *Titanic*." I
believe she called me a motherfucker. Who was that guy? And
who was I now? I was a man who wanted to raise children with
his ex-wife. Ridiculous. I hardly recognize the old miserable me
anymore. I mean, there was a time when Sarah and I actually
clutched at the soil on a daily basis, and we would not let go. We

went mountain climbing. We drove cross-country and made love on desert floors. We bungee jumped over the Colorado River, and muled our backpacks down Grand Canyon paths. We took a hot-air-balloon ride in northern France and ate up the cold air in mouthfuls. We watched the ground fall away looking like a patchwork blanket, sweet earth sleeping beneath us.

I still loved her.

I considered calling Dad again, thought better of it, and watched the woman in the visor and her daughter leave the store.

They brushed right past me, as if we hadn't just met, a large plastic bag in the daughter's hands. The mother tapping the bag as they walked toward a gray-haired man sitting in an idling station wagon.

Amad was beside me, showing a receipt. He said, "Not a bad way to start the morning."

I said, "Today is the day, my friend. I can feel the tide is turning. I feel alive, Amad, I wish I could tell you." I followed him inside. He slipped the receipt into a black tin behind the counter. He snapped the tin shut.

I looked at him in the mirror, caught his eyes. "I may have to go to New York. See my dad."

"The walls are still standing, for now anyway." He patted my back. "But why are you having dinner with Sarah?"

I shook my head. "It's supposed to be our anniversary today, so it's funny, you have to admit. To have dinner tomorrow. But it should be fine, no big deal. Am I right?"

"Nothing is *supposed* to be anything and that is why you are always in a pickle. Nothing is supposed to be anything."

"One of your famous pep talks."

"Happy anniversary." He blew me a kiss, then opened the door to the storeroom and disappeared inside.

I laughed out, "Is that all you got? We need to vacuum this floor."

A muffled shout from the storeroom: "Teri is coming soon.
And if she sees you standing there and doing nothing she will ruin
our day."

"When do I get to be the boss again?" There was a lot of light
filling up the windows. "Tell me something," I said. "What are we
doing wrong here, exactly? And for how long already?"

"What are you talking about?"

"This, like a ghost town in here."

He came out from behind the counter. He took my hand in his
and he put it to his cheek. "My friend. If my wife left me, I would
shrivel up and die. So I'm sorry. I really am. And you are right,
this place will come back to life if we work together. Remember?
When I first met you I said to myself, this man knows how to make
money. Used to, anyway." He walked away. "On the other hand,
all of this did not happen overnight."

I rubbed my hands together.

He knew the story all too well; he was there for most of it.
How in the late nineties I'd backed a software developer after
reading a magazine article. It had claimed all the clocks would
stop come the New Millennium, 2000. My kind of language.

"Three million and change," I said.

"You see?" He was fully awake and alert now and kept looking
over my shoulder. "You were a millionaire. Maybe you still are,
I don't know."

"Not so much."

"You should come by for dinner this weekend and we can sit,
and we can talk about what we should do. Is that Teri? I think I
see her car."

"Tell her to make that chili."

"Come with me," he said.

We went outside. The sun was low and reddening through
clouds.

He said, "Look at them, all the tourists by the water. You see that? They always look for otters, and the otters have been gone for too many years already."

I nodded.

He jerked his head and looked away. "I thought it was her."

I said, "Do you think we can do this? I think we can do this."

"Look, you go and have your dinner tomorrow night, which if you want to talk about crazy, that is a little bit crazy. But be careful. I love Sarah, and I miss Sarah, but remember they call it a past for a reason. And this weekend we will have dinner at my home. And we will have Teri's chili, and we will have a beer, and we will knock our heads together until we figure out how we get this place shipshape. We are all in a funk, my friend. And soon I will have a son, or a daughter, either one would be fine with me, really, either one, as long as the baby is healthy, I promise, to put all the way through preschool. And then to college. And we will do what everyone else in the world is doing and that is having meals together and making a living and having a drink together and watching our little ones get grown up, and getting ready to retire so we can die a little bit happy, okay? What do you think?"

"I like it."

"A good plan?"

"Good plan," I said. "And what's the mission today?"

"I will take care of the front, if you do the inventory."

"No problem."

"This is not a small job. The storeroom is like a jungle. You'll be in there all day long."

Again with the buzzing at my waist, I hoped it was Sarah.
Dad 10:20.

I showed Amad the phone, and said, "Nothing excites me more right now than the idea of taking our inventory."

"Then we are halfway there." He put up his hands and went inside.

"Dad," I said.

"You called me before," he said.

"Yeah. And then you called me back."

"What?"

"You called me back."

He said, "Don't treat me like I'm crazy. You called me."

"Okay," I said. "Are you all right?"

"What?"

"I said are you all right?"

He coughed. "Your mother," he said. "She's here."

And then he hung up the phone.

Not long after Mom first got sick, I was maybe thirteen, Dad pulled me aside in the backyard. It was late morning. He asked me if we could talk, seriously, man to man. I nodded my head. The maples were in my peripheral vision, and some sort of family get-together was going on in the yard behind ours. I didn't recognize anyone there as a neighbor.

He said, "I've been praying for your mother. Have you been praying for your mother?"

We sat outside on the back porch steps. I was catching lightning bugs and letting them free. The day before I'd caught one and crushed it with my foot on the concrete and watched it glow briefly like the electric smear of a highlighter. And then I watched that yellow light dim and die out. I felt terrible, and guilty, and I asked for God's forgiveness.

I said, "Yeah, I pray for Mom."

"Good," he said. "It's working. And I'm going to tell you something that you can't tell anyone. Okay?"

I nodded my head: Yeah, okay.

He said, "I think our Heavenly Father is testing us. I think somewhere inside this horrible woe is a test, a reward. It's our job to find it. And I believe my good son has the gift of communion with our Heavenly Father."

I said nothing.

He said, "Don't you?"

I probably nodded.

He said, "I want you to commune with our Heavenly Father. Ask for his blessing on your mother, on this family, and I think even as much as we do this we *still* aren't doing enough. I want to *reach* him. I want to reach *out* to him. Will you make a sacrifice with me?"

This made me uncomfortable.

"Nothing would make me prouder," he said, "than to have my son beside me while I make a sacrifice. A burnt offering of thanks, a visible sign. Will you help me?"

I nodded.

I admit I was interested. What kid wouldn't be? I had visions of him buying a live chicken or a goat. From where? Maybe a large, live fish from the market. We went to the store to get groceries for dinner, and get charcoal, and Dad filled up a bag with fruits and vegetables. I saw the fish tanks all along the wall. I walked over to them, and heard Dad, behind me, raising his voice. I turned around. He was making a small scene with the produce woman.

"What kind of a produce section doesn't have pumpkins?" He must've wanted them for their dramatic size.

"But they're not in season," she said.

He asked her what the most expensive kind of produce was. The most precious. And she shrugged, pointing to a box of dried cherries, and Dad said, "Are those really considered produce?"

"They're in the aisle," she said, "so yeah. Ten dollars a box, which is a whole lot more per pound."

That first cancer was in Mom's left breast and I remembered how they cut out as much as they could without removing the breast entirely. Oncology has come a long way. I don't think Mom or the doctors would think twice about removing it now. She went through radiation therapy, and chemo, and the doctors said fatigue should be expected, but it would go away, eventually. Except she just got more tired. Mom had been working as a secretary for a large toy manufacturer back then (now out of business), and so the insurance was good. So were the people she worked with. They visited her in the hospital, and then they visited her at home, and they called her on weekdays while she lay in bed watching *Donahue*. Her boss was a friendly lady, I don't remember her name. I do remember Dad being rude to her, to all of them, and making a comment about the flowers they brought, that flowers always die and who brings flowers to a hospital? Who *doesn't* bring flowers to a hospital? Dad always seemed ill equipped for the world, or maybe he just lacked enough experience with it.

When Mom first found out she was shocked, yes, I think, definitely, reluctantly shocked and sort of confused. Dad was certainly confused. Baffled. Cancer was not in the plan. How does a family that gives itself all the way to God fall prey? But Mom turned stoic pretty quickly. She found a neutral and practical state of mind that played a good healthy balance to Dad's manic spirit and bent for abstraction. She would deal with this, and stare it right down. Therapy sessions were regular, and sometimes I went along. We took the bus when Dad was working. Mom didn't drive. I heard the doctor talk to Mom about "fractional kills," about the process of cancer therapy and the attempt to kill off the cancer, cell by cell, but that meant small good parts of her got killed, too. I tried to imagine what good parts of her, exactly, were getting killed, and because I couldn't quite imagine what a real adult woman's breast looked like (especially my mother's), I thought of her breast as maybe like a pear or some other piece of fruit, because that's what it looked like under a sweater or a dress or a shirt. A thin slice of that fruit got cut off at the hospital, every time.

She got depressed, and she prayed. Members of our congregation often visited the hospital and then the house, after she came home, and we all said prayers there together. Sometimes Dad would lead us in prayer, but then at other times some thoughtful visitor who clearly meant well would say something like "God works in mysterious ways," and Dad would get angry. Mom's cancer wasn't a mystery. It couldn't be. Impossible. To Dad it was absolutely obvious—she had done nothing wrong, probably never a wrong thing in her life, and so this couldn't be punishment. The only possibility was reward. Somehow, Mom's getting sick was a reward, a divinely inspired reward, and one that required a deep and considered interpretation lest we think otherwise, because to think otherwise would suggest a God with no plan at all, or at least one not so committed to protecting his devoted.

I only knew that something invisible was killing my mom, and that when I thought hard enough about it I found myself not wanting to talk about that thing at all. Or about anything. I for sure didn't want to talk from a pulpit. Yet Mom's sickness brought the elder brothers even closer.

Also, Mom slept a lot. I knew that, too.

She wanted to sleep, I think, because sleep made the hours pass along unfelt, and she could dream. She said she dreamed of paradise and Heaven. And the rest of 1980 seemed to pass like all of us were sleeping. I was in the throes of such adolescent intensities, some of which I can hardly now recall, and Dad was working nonstop and praying nonstop, blaming the world and life itself for Mom's misfortune—I guess, in a way, he was right—and Mom, a fast-graying and emaciating mamma bear in long hibernation, was always upstairs, losing more hair by the day. Dad slept mostly on the couch downstairs in the living room. Everything had changed. He was working two jobs, selling ad space in a local paper by day and working nights at a convenience store in Astoria. I was going to school, and coming straight home to sit with Mom, or to help Mom to the doctor, or do anything at all Mom needed. So church and Bible study fell off a bit to the wayside. But only for a little while because, this was about spring of 1981, the doctors said the chemo was finally working. They couldn't say how much exactly, but it was working.

Yet Mom was now more tired than ever. Dad was convinced we simply weren't doing enough.

Hence the backyard sacrifice.

We bought the dried cherries, and lots of other stuff, and we went home, and before making hamburgers on the backyard grill, the spring light still high in the sky and looking more like morning than night, Dad piled his produce on the metal grill grates. The box of cherries first, and everything else tumbled and piled on top. He squirted the stack with lighter fluid, and told me to not be afraid. He lit it. And the fire burned high and fast while he said a prayer out loud. Not as dramatic as a bloodletting, but it would do. It had to. The air smelled of sugars and charred fibrous vegetable skins and the cardboard box and brown paper bag it had all been brought home in. Dad raised his arms and his hands, and threw back his head in complete supplication, a desperate and sincere plea: Lord, please listen to my heart. His eyes were closed. But mine were open, because I couldn't look away from what I suddenly realized was a pretty girl in the backyard right behind ours. She was tossing her head back and forth to music I couldn't quite make out, coming from a boom box on the back porch. This was Bhanu. And I was changed. The answer to our prayers, and Dad was missing it.

Bhanu was Bangladeshi, and she and her family had moved in just days before. I didn't even know the family living there previously had left. There had been no children in that house, only an older Irish couple and the husband's aging parents. I didn't know their names. Bhanu became the only thing that could take my mind from Mom, and from Issy and the constant question of where he was. Things no longer made sense, and I could think of nothing but that. Plus, thinking of Issy made me not think of how sick Mom was. Bhanu changed all that. She was alive, and lovely, and from the very moment we met I would think of little else but her.

She saw our fire, Dad and me standing beside it.

Then Dad fell to his knees, and he tried to get me to fall down, too.

She approached the fence. She waved.

But I did not wave back.

Why not? Was I embarrassed? Absolutely. I was seeing myself and my father through someone else's eyes, and it was strange. We were strange. I knew this now. Then again, I was coming to know it more and more with every passing day in school, because strangeness can pass in grammar school, in fifth grade and sixth grade—but in junior high and high school? Not a chance. And they're made for that reason. Junior high and high school train a child and make him understand, follow the general social contract, et cetera. Strangeness of any kind, any deviance at all, will be amplified and shouted from the gymnasium rooftop and blared over the loudspeaker system. I was the Jesus Freak, the Preacher Kid, and this was the case because Havi—who I never spoke a word to ever again, and truly and shamefully wished cruel things upon throughout my teenage years—was in my school. He had nothing to do with the Brothers in the Lord anymore, and had decided the best way to make room for his hallway swagger was to tell everyone in the school who would listen, including teachers, deans, and the janitorial staff, that I was "Jesus crazy," and that I gave a sermon saying the world was going to end soon and that *his* best friend, Issy, would die even sooner. And remember that kid who disappeared, he would say? *That* was my best friend. Josiah's a freak.

At lunch, there were safety tables for all, every tribe and stripe. But not for the Jesus freaks. I became even more of a loner. It would be a long time before I understood how addictive and dangerous sadness can become, but at the time I reveled. My mother was ill, my father was a mystery to me, and I could not stop thinking about the unexplainable loss of my friend.

Regardless. I should have waved to Bhanu. I should have, because that one simple wave could have saved me years of trouble, of all that time trailing her like a sick dog on a very long leash. I followed her at school. I followed her in the neighborhood. I threw balls and Frisbees over the fence into her yard just to have a reason for climbing and standing on possibly the same spot where she had once stood. And I hoped to see into her window. I once braved walking right up to their house. I looked into a kitchen window just as her mother stuck out her head to hang a sheet from a clothesline. She didn't see me. I dove behind a small shed and froze for what seemed like hours. Until she shouted out to Bhanu to please go out back and roll up the water hose like she'd been asked to. I checked to see if she was looking—she'd ducked back inside—and I jumped the gate into their next-door neighbor's yard and ran for my life. I also once stood behind her at a corner deli, holding a small grape drink and praying she would not say hello to me. She bought a pack of black licorice—the only thing I found unattractive about her, which in itself made the licorice attractive, because clearly I was wrong—and an orange juice. She paid, and she turned and said: "Hi, Josie." Josie? I'd never heard the name before, and now I wanted to wear it like a suit of armor. After she shook her head, she said, "You're so weird." She left the store, and I stood there looking into the space she had just taken up, at the air itself, the dust in the air, like a cutout shape of her, until the woman behind the counter said, "You buy." Later, I bought black licorice and, just as I had expected, thought it horribly bad. One week after that, I bought black licorice and orange juice. I ate them together, in my mouth at the very same time, like two kinds of medicine at once; it was disgusting. But I finished it. I was in love.

Or what felt like love. Who knows what it is when you're young? I mean, real love has a long-burning fuse, but those first flares burn like hell. And they hurt, and snuff out all too soon. She would have nothing to do with me at all, I assumed. For years. But it didn't really matter. Because everything else fell away. School. Bullies. Issy. Even cancer. Love is a lot like faith, because you surrender yourself, fully, and with no expectations. There is hope, yes, but never expectation.

It was years before I finally opened my mouth and said hello back. This was in high school, and I found her smoking in the lower stairwells with the Goth girls and the metal girls, all lips painted black but hers. Christian Death and Slayer band patches on their denim jackets and backpacks. I was entranced. They all seemed so evil and romantic. I was fifteen.

Inspired, I said: "Hello."

She started laughing, and said, "Took you so long. He lives on my block!" she said to the girls. They could barely stop giggling.

One of the girls high-fived her, and said, "Isn't he that freak? Aren't you, like, a preacher?"

Another girl said, "No, he's the one with the mother. His mother has, like, cancer."

Bhanu said: "Shut up."

I sat with her at lunch that day. And we talked. This may have been the first time I actually talked with someone at lunch, or at least talked without worrying for my life, that some metalhead, or some jock, or some other misanthrope in hopes of scoring points with normals would trip me on the way to my table, or hit me with an empty milk carton, or ask me what I was looking at. It was glorious. In the fast-working ecosystem that is high school, here I was, a boy sitting with girl, a pretty girl, and having lunch. I wasn't such a freak after all. Things would get better. We walked home that day, and she said Goth was stupid, but Slayer was cool, and the girls were mostly smart and she liked them okay. We shared from a 25-cent bag of potato chips, and I tried to place her particular and lovely smell—and then one day, a long time later, this was years and years later, I was offered a coconut milk to drink, and I smelled it, and time caught me up like a trap. Here was Bhanu.

A few weeks on, my father spotted us walking home from school. He later asked me if I'd made a proper witness for the Lord. Did I tell her what I believed, and say why she should believe it, too? I must've betrayed myself and instead showed how it had never occurred to me once, not once, and I expected him to show some disappointment in me at the very least, say I should be ashamed, et cetera—but, surprise: grinning, my father said, "My little man is in love. Promise you won't tell your mother. Enough on her plate as it is."

He was all of a sudden full of surprises.

That same year, I'm guessing this was 1983, when there were commercials everywhere for what was being billed as a "Historic

Television Event." A made-for-TV movie called *The Day After*, coming soon, and it would air on a Sunday. A Sunday! American audiences would finally see what a real Armageddon will look like—a nuclear one, yes, and man-made, but who says God's above using such weapons? Why waste all that effort? There were stock-piles.

The whole congregation was in a tizzy.

We talked about it at home, over dinner, in the morning, for weeks before the movie ever started. What do you think it will look like? Do you think this is a sign of the times? Do you think the actors are aware that God is actually watching? And how could a young boy in love with *Star Wars* not want to see a movie like this? Special effects! Those two words echoed like a chant for me and every boy my age. The movie has special effects! My mother talked about the movie, but she stayed mostly quiet. It was Dad who said things like "This is ridiculous" and "We all know it's not coming for twenty years more, because of Josiah's vision." I would say nothing, and he would say, "The movie's bound to be wrong." But he also couldn't hide how excited he was. Taking my cereal box away from in front of me—I used to read every line of the ingredients list—he would eat dry Froot Loops with his hands, and said to the kitchen wall: "I wonder how much is actu-ally based on scripture?"

Sunday at church, one week before, an announcement was made from the stage.

Announcements were a big deal, and hardly ever good news, more like "So-and-So has been excommunicated and asked to leave the congregation," or "So-and-So is dead," or something fore-boding and starting with "It has recently come to our attention . . ." But this was about the movie. One of the elder brothers said to the hundred or so of us there: "There has been talk of a television film, I believe we all know what I'm referring to. *The Day After* promises to be not only an important film, but a relevant one, especially to our work here. Preparing ourselves for God's Holy War. And after much serious thought, we've decided to incorporate the film into our ministry. So we'll be viewing the film as a congregation. Next Sunday. In lieu of a sermon. And we'll talk afterward, as a congregation. Please feel free to invite your friends and neighbors. This will be a rare opportunity to make witness. And regarding the children, the film will be quite realistic from what I understand. And so children will not attend alone but with parents. Let us pray. . . ."

Dad didn't talk much on the way home.

That next day, a Monday morning, the mailman brought a letter regarding the kids of New York City's public schools, suggesting parents not let their kids see a certain upcoming television movie. That it would be age-inappropriate.

That next Sunday, church was packed. Extended family members, curious neighbors dressed in weekend shorts, and borderline stragglers who hadn't attended in years. Standing room only. I'd almost invited Bhanu, but, in the end, was so glad I didn't.

Four TVs had been brought in and set up for all of us to watch. We got there early, and sat up front by a TV as big as a sofa, encased in wood, with a turntable on top. A hefty thing, a real piece of furniture, it must've weighed a ton. I wondered how they ever got it in there.

The lights went low.

The microphones set up by the TV speakers crackled.

There was chatter, and shuffling in the seats.

I looked around and saw the faces of people I knew from the neighborhood, and the faces of strangers. Which was both exciting and upsetting. They had entered a place they didn't belong. They were dressed wrong. Talking, mumbling, when they should have been quiet. I saw the black man from the convenience store around the corner from church. He didn't seem to be with anyone standing in the back, by himself. He wore jeans, and a T-shirt, his usual white apron rolled up and tied around his waist. He wasn't looking at the TV, though. He was looking at the people in the room, the brothers and sisters. His face looked thoughtful, and bewildered. I realized he wasn't there for the service, as such, or for spiritual reasons of any kind. He was curious: What do they *do* in there? I watched him scan the room, until he looked at me. He gave me a neutral sort of acknowledgment, Yes, I have sold you Pop Rocks, given you change for Donkey Kong.

I looked away from him and toward the TV, the opening credits and then . . .

I've watched it at least one more time, some parts twice more, even read about it, and still I can't remember the plot; what was the plot? I remember the attack. A five-minute collage of mass death in Technicolor, the apocalyptic footage, fiery rain, the buildings blown to quick rubble and ashy voids, the rolling thunderheads of nuclear fire wiping out forests, livestock, and people, entire cities laid waste—and so much of this footage was real! Actual stock film clips of war and early atomic testing. All of this coupled with—how can I say it?—a cartoonish X-ray obliteration of people. A mother and her baby turn to the sky and *zizzzzzz*—dark bones in a flash, and they're gone . . . The infant's tiny skull . . . A man runs from his car for his life and *zizzzzzz*—his skeleton shows in a bloodred splash on electric white, and he's dust . . . A large group together and what are they doing? Walking? Standing? Sitting in church? *zizzzzzz*—X-ray fried, now invisible, and gone . . . I have to say, watching this again as a grown man froze my insides. It's too artful. Armageddon respects no bones. Only dust, instant dust . . . But to a boy, the scary stock footage within that film looked like news. I half expected to find the world outside our church destroyed when the movie was over. This was the End, factory manufactured, and yet the imagery was the same. This was not a biblical vindication, or God's fire raining down. This was man versus man. All the fault of bloodlust and earthly dispute. This strikes me as a great and disturbing irony.

Lights up.

There was some muttering. No applause.

How did we feel? How many different kinds of response? Was I the only one so frightened by what I saw?

An elder took the stage and calmly asked, "Any questions? Comments?" There were a few, but not many before the real event took place.

My father stood up and started speaking.

Dad never spoke in church. He said it wasn't his calling. So when this happened, Mom and I, we were dumbfounded. He stood, and stayed where he was, right beside his family, and said to the elder in a voice not quite loud enough: "I want to be a true believer, it's all I've ever wanted out of life." He turned and talked to the whole room now: "This means more like the Apostle Paul. More like our original first-century Christian brothers and sisters. Just a few decades from when our Savior walked this earth. Only miles from the places we read of. Galilee. Gethsemane."

I looked around and there were people nodding their heads, like usual, Yes, brother, say it.

A microphone came passed down the aisle, its rubber cabling falling on our feet. I looked at the mic, and wondered how many eyes were on me. Will he stand, too? Will the boy speak? Or maybe they weren't thinking of me at all. Dad looked at me. I couldn't read his face. I gave him the microphone.

"Thank you, son." Loud now, he was filling the room.

"Why such speculation?" he said. "Why doubt? We have living proof. Here. In the flesh, here, my son, who stood before you filled with God and gave a number. It's not for us to know how it'll look." He spoke to the back of the room. I turned with him. Mom kept looking straight ahead. She squeezed my hand. "But our Savior comes at the New Millennium. And *this*"—he gestured to the TV—"this *movie* has no place in here. All lies . . ."

"Brother Laudermilk," said the elder from the stage.

My father quieted him, his hands saying Now now now . . .

"Look at my boy," he said. "Josiah, stand up."

Mom squeezed my hand again. I didn't move.

"He's in shock. You see? You doubt him? A child? You doubt the Lord's Holy Spirit."

I still didn't move.

"And my wife. She wears a hat so you don't have to see her shining head. For you! You think this is sickness? This is God's work! All of it God's work! All of them signs we are living in the End Days, and you won't even see it. Look to the book of Matthew. In the Last Days. The Apostle Matthew says in the End Days one shall be taken, but the other left behind—"

"Gill." The elder was beside him now, his hand on my father's shoulder.

"You want to silence me? Make my wife an outcast? My son cast down like some false prophet for a TV show? In *here*? You bring *this*"—again the TV—"this Wild Beast. Mammon! Babylon the Great in here? Why not bring money changers? It's blasphemy!"

"Gill—" He tried taking the mic, but Dad wouldn't let him.

"Stop looking forward! It is here! In our presence! And we have to go back for it. Back! And return to original worship, to authentic faith. Have faith in the Word of God, in what God grants, a vision for his son, my son. A healing for my wife . . ." He fell back against the chair behind him. The brother sitting there caught him, held him up. "For my wife," Dad said. He seemed dazed.

I was heartbroken, for him. Confused.

"Thank you, Brother Laudermilk." The elder took the mic from Dad's hand. "Okay. So obviously—"

My father stood back up and shook his head, looked around the room. He wildly made for the stage, for the TV, and then he stopped himself. He turned back, and took my hand. He took my mother's hand and pushed his way along the aisle toward the exit. Some of the assistant servants followed, in case of a scene.

We went home.

That's when as a family we stopped going to the Brothers in the Lord. Or any church, really. Unexpectedly, I found myself actually going to church more, a weird rebellion against him. I sat there alone like Issy used to. Dad's display had sufficiently sullied what reputation I had, and whatever capacity I had for sermonizing or for visions had been supplanted by fears that I might have an unwelcome outburst onstage, like my father. I was now the son of the man who made a scene at church, and nothing more. That went on for about a month. And then it just stopped. Partly because I didn't know why I was doing it, and I would sit there for the duration of the service, hardly listening at all, trying to understand why I was there, and partly because I realized that not a soul there cared to speak to me.

I started telling Mom and Dad that I was going to church, but then I would go straight to Bhanu's house and watch weekend morning TV. We held hands under throw pillows. Mom hardly paid attention, anyway. Seems like Mom slept for years, all the while getting better according to the doctors, but sleeping away her every last earthly hour. She just slept and slept and slept. I became hungry for even more freedom.

Bhanu and I started cutting school together that fall. We hid deep in the woods of Forest Park, and watched truancy vans roam along the park roads. We kissed sometimes, and I wondered if God would one day open up the earth and drop me in for loving a pagan. While I knew Bhanu wasn't a Christian, I didn't really know what that meant. I didn't want to think about it, what it meant for her, or me, us, or for my family, and so I decided it was easier to not think about it at all. We only talked about it once, and I asked if she thought it was weird. We were trying cigarettes for the first time, stretched out on the cement floor of the Forest Park band shell.

We passed the cigarette back and forth like it was delicious, and she coughed. I didn't. I had a talent for them, and I liked how the nicotine made everything slow down and go foggy. I rolled my head to one side, and blew smoke in her face. She laughed and slapped at my leg.

I said, "Is it weird that we're different?"

She didn't understand. "You mean how you're *so so so so* white?"

Now I laughed. I said, "I mean my family. You're not Christian."

She looked at me like I was kidding. "You mean how you're not Hindu?"

I looked up at the sky, but there was no sky. Instead I saw the top-ridge lip of the clamshell and I thought of a giant clam. I said, "I guess so. Yeah."

She started to say, "I like you, Josie, even though you're not a Hindu—" But she lost control of her voice in a sudden coughing attack made worse by the fact that she could hardly stop laughing. I thought of the giant clam, and imagined we were lying prone on its tongue.

It was a long year, and much of what transpired at home with regard to Mom or Dad has fallen out of my head, forgotten. I spent that year with Bhanu, in and out of school, a place that no longer meant loneliness for me because I was with Bhanu, and her friends, who eventually accepted me, too. She was alive and love was all around me, and it felt like nothing else unfortunate could touch me.

Later that year, there was a high school field trip to Niagara Falls. I didn't tell my parents, and just went. Forged their signatures. It was the event of our year, and it would be all day long, with no real adult supervision, somewhere else entirely, outside of Richmond Hill, outside New York City. I bought a Ramones T-shirt from the Aqueduct Flea Market on Rockaway Boulevard even though I'd never heard one song. Bhanu mentioned them once and said they were cool and she was going to get their tapes. I never had the nerve to wear it. It looked too clean and too new.

On the bus ride upstate I told her all about Issy. I told her how much I missed Issy, and was that weird? We were sharing a tall black vinyl seat and it felt like nobody could see us, we were all on our own. She said, "You're weird, but that's not." I told her how I always wanted a brother, and she gave me a kiss on the cheek. What a shame kisses on the cheek never matter so much as you age.

She said, "Now you got me."

I floated.

We slept alongside each other there in the daylight, on warm black vinyl, until we got to Niagara.

The bus parked. We stepped off and felt the mist in the air, heard the rush and gushing of the falls. We walked toward one of the railings, and the great void in the center of the falls. We wiped water from our faces and stood there, spray raining upward and needling our foreheads. We clasped our hands together, and we were silent. We looked at the white implosive hole.

"It's so big," she said.

I said, "You can't even see where it ends."

"It's so deep," she said. "How deep do you think?"

"No idea."

She asked me if I'd ever read a short story called "The Wish." Bhanu loved to read. But I didn't read much, then, so I lied and said I'd heard of it. She said it was about a small boy who played make-believe and actually fell into one of his make-believe holes.

I thought twice before telling her a story this reminded me of. But then I told her about the biblical story of Korah, once a wise man of God, who bared his teeth, screaming for help, as the Good Lord punished him and turned the hard ground beneath him into a hole. A gaping and gorging mouth that swallowed him whole and all of his possessions, even his family. Bhanu asked me what he did to make God so angry. I said he rebelled against Moses (I asked, "Do you know who Moses is?" She said, "I've heard of him"), that Korah would not listen to God's appointed men. That he claimed he could speak directly with God. I told her how it took up two pages in my children's Bible storybook, accompanied by comic book–like illustrations, and that I'd seen it performed in full costume onstage at Bible conventions. At some point she'd stopped listening to me, and said, "That's a horrible story." She was letting her face get wet. Her mouth was open and the upward rain was on her tongue and teeth. I moved closer to her, my mouth closer to hers. The mere idea of a kiss! The possibility was so charged, I was surprised every time she let me.

We stood there and watched the rushing falls, and I imagined the observation deck collapsing and sucking us under, and I was okay with that. This was the asshole of the world, and I looked away toward the river, the Niagara River; who ever mentions the poor river? It came roaring at us like water spilled from a bottomless bucket, incoming nonstop across a long and winding table. I promised myself I would never let anything bad happen to Bhanu as we were both entirely overtaken by the drama of it all, and cued up our Walkmans accordingly.

The year I turned eighteen, Mom finally decided she was better. She sat up in bed one day, came marching down the stairs, and said she had to go for a special session at the hospital. Dad took her, and they came home with tremendous smiles on their faces; I don't know whose was bigger.

"Full remission," Mom said.

Dad took her face in his hands, and he kissed her. Never saw anything like that before. He kissed her so hard, she started pushing him off, and she was laughing, but he wouldn't let her go, she was laughing so much. Then he stopped, and picked her way up in his arms, and she was up there almost to the ceiling, and laughing, while he played biting at her belly. This is my most favorite memory. Not just because of how lovely, but because it woke me up to their lives in such an unexpected way. Like a bucket of cold water over my head. I'd been living peripherally, in my own home, walking along the walls like a mouse, following the same daily paths in hopes of avoiding direct contact with the people who owned this home.

But here they were, right in front of me. Mom was back, and

fully charged, and she swore she would set this house aright because this was a churchgoing family. I have to say there was a welcome sense of security in having her back and taking the lead, and we returned to church as a family. Dad was reluctant to go. He'd since taken to calling the Brothers in the Lord apostates. But he went anyway, for her. We all did, arrived just as service started, and left as it drew to a close. We spoke with no one. Mom also somehow managed to ignore the fact that I'd had a serious girlfriend for the last few years.

I'd thought I'd done a good job of obscuring the presence of Bhanu, even though she lived around the corner, but it wasn't like Mom was blind to it. She occasionally mentioned "the Indian girl around the block," and when she was really bugged at me, "the brown girl." When I think back on this behavior it seems so unlike her, uncharacteristic of her. She even claimed once that I chose Bhanu because she was Hindu. I remember being shaken by such a hateful accusation and not even bothering to respond. My parents began to unashamedly hanker aloud for the old neighborhood, because in the last few years Richmond Hill had become a haven for not just Bangladeshis, but Indians and Pakistanis, and there were rumors that the construction site around the corner was the future home of a Sikh temple. This was a new strain in my parents. I didn't like their new behavior. It appeared to be connected to Mom's remission: maybe she felt a debt to her Heavenly Savior and nothing less than the purest of worship would do. Mom and Dad were seeing eye to eye. They talked about the old days before the high trill of Hindi ragas, before the tap and pounding dance of tablas all of a sudden sang from car stereos all summer long. Before the teenage Hindi boys in shell-top Adidas made out with white girls on brick front porches. The corner store put up a sign in its window: "Fresh Goat Meat." And this absolutely horrified my parents because, What, now everybody's too good for hamburger? Dad turned hot dogs on our backyard grill, and the neighborhood barbecues smoked hot yellow curries.

The faces at church had changed, too. As many brown faces as there were pale, and I could practically see the gears of my parents' brains turning, trying to process this new information. Regardless, this was good news because the new faces probably didn't know of Dad's outburst. Or about me. So we got to arrive and sit and leave in relative peace. City congregations like this one are protean, always changing, just like the city. Picking a different congregation never even occurred to my parents, that I knew of. I spent most of those services thinking about everything but worship. I thought of school, and graduation, and leaving the house. I thought of Bhanu. I invited her a few times, but she'd always decline and then invite me to their temple, which I always politely declined. I told her there were people like her at our church now and she should try it just once. It wasn't like I was trying to convert her, I hardly paid attention anymore myself. It was more like there was this significant part of my life, and she had no idea of what it looked like, much less meant. I also wanted her to understand that I was going to church again for my mother.

One Sunday, when the minister onstage spoke of the doomed unbelievers, I couldn't help but think of Bhanu. That she was doomed. I'd avoided this for how long already, made excuses for me, and for her, for my parents, for God himself, but I could no longer cover my ears. The elder onstage said they were hiding in our homes and in our neighborhoods, the Devil-music listeners, and the adolescent masturbators, the false clergymen of neighboring churches, and closeted atheists, the New Agers and yoga practitioners, and even casual dabblers in the abominable Oriental religions. Hindus, Muslims, Sikhs. They would all be punished if they didn't open their hearts to the Lord. And then I saw Bhanu's lovely face. I thought of her mother's bindhi, the bloodred dot decorating her forehead like the center of a bull's-eye target—she who always had milk and jellied sweets waiting for us in their kitchen, ever since the first time I met the woman, in their kitchen, baskets of peppers hanging from the ceiling, when she took me into her arms and said with her lilting voice: "So this is the young man who has my daughter in a spell. Let me see you." She set me in front of her like a melon she was considering for purchase, and said, "Okay. Be good to my Bhanu and I will be good to you."

I sat there and looked at the minister speaking and I watched his mouth moving but I couldn't hear a thing. I imagined Bhanu's front porch collapsing in the swell of a blood-river wake produced by some warring millennial and messianic chariot. I thought of her sweet-smelling hair—coconut!—and I sort of swooned right there in my seat. I wanted to run out of church and do something totally dramatic, like yell into the sky and dare Him to touch one hair on her head.

That Sunday, because of that sermon, I started my long fight and flight from the angels.

Sarah asked me once when it was exactly I lost my faith. I told her there was simply no such singular time. No single moment when whatever hairline crack suddenly widened, opening up like a fissure. I don't even know what caused the crack to begin with. This was a slow and invisible process, practically geologic, but I do know that I didn't join my parents the following Sunday.

That next weekend, Dad asked if he could speak with me, alone. I assumed he meant without Mom around, and so I made like I was going to leave the room with him—but he stopped me.

"Can we talk?" he said.

Mom was sitting at the kitchen table. Crying, starting to wheeze. She was losing control and I was pretty sure it wasn't just about me not going to church.

"Shoot," I said.

He said, "Talk. Tell me what's going on."

I said, "I don't think I can talk about it."

"Try me."

Mom was recovering her composure.

Dad said, "Ida. Maybe you should leave."

She shook her shoulders, and wiped at her face. Makeup smeared. Without looking at me, she said, "Josiah."

I said nothing.

"Answer me this," she said. "Do you believe in God?"

Mom was on to me.

"You're angry," she said, "I know."

I expected to see judgment in her eyes, accusation, disappointment. I saw nothing of the kind. Only empathy, and her beaten soul.

"Me, too," she said, and stood up. She pushed past my father, briefly took my hand, and then let it fall away. She left the kitchen.

Dad said I'd grow out of it; it was just a phase. But I never did go back to church. Except then Mom stopped, too. She lost steam. And Dad was only going for her. Dad hardly looked my way anymore.

This made me bold enough to one day ask him—he was out back watering what grass we had surrounding the concrete patio—I walked right up to him as if I'd been dared to and I said: "Look at me, please, and tell me something."

He aimed the hose away, took his time. He looked at me.

"What about you," I said. "What's your testimony? Tell me. I have no idea how you feel. I come from you and so I'm a lot like you, but I'm also not like you at all."

He squeezed the hose with his hand and cinched it, so the water stopped and the hose looked like a snake swallowing its food. He was quiet for a few moments.

Then he said, "Your grandfather. This was a man of great faith. And he was wrong about some things, but he never lost his faith. I've been wrong, too, but I never lost my faith." He looked at me. "How strong will you be?"

We looked at each other for some time and then I turned and went back to the house. I heard the water jet from the hose and smack the pavement.

I'm not so sure faith is a thing that can ever be lost. Like every love we have, there's always remnants deep inside us, in our cells.

Mom and Dad did agree on one thing, though: that Mom would never get sick again. We'd been washed, a family washed by God's love and a chemical bath, and if we were to keep that death at bay, above all, we must remain clean. So morning and night we showered. "At rise and fall," Dad's words. And, yes, making something so personal the subject of our daily conversations, ritualizing, really, my morning and evening wash and toilet was discomfiting to say the least. It was odd. At first he asked if I'd fully washed myself, made reference to "our unclean fleshly vessels," which I supposed was my body. Before long, a new rule: he insisted I wash my vessel seven times, no less, the biblical number of perfection. I did this a few times until I no longer did, and Dad made a few passing comments about my skin not looking vigorously cleaned. I didn't exactly realize what this kind of behavior suggested, that Dad had other issues. Finally one day I had to put a stop to it.

He tried to open the bathroom door one morning while I was getting out of the shower. No knocking, nothing, he just entered. I threw myself at the door, and it closed on his arm.

He screamed. Slammed it open. I was naked.

He was wearing a small towel, barely covering him. His hair was wet, his skin wet and ruddy. Red marks on his arms and collarbones from what looked like a vicious scrub. "Seven times," he said, and turned, leaving the door open behind him. I moved to close it—he stopped me. He stopped the door. I grabbed his arm and I pulled him back into the bathroom. It was so easy, I remember thinking, He's so light!

I pushed him into the clothes hamper, and stood over him.

He was stunned.

He was naked now, his towel fallen to the floor. I wrapped a large bath towel around my own waist, covered myself, and left the room.

He passionately explained to me over dinner one night that *his* baptism, *my* baptism, and *Mom's* baptism—the original ones, mind you—were false, insufficient in the eyes of God.

"They lack commitment," he said.

We were sitting at the dining room table eating takeout Chinese food, passing the greasy cartons back and forth. Spooning onto our plates. Mom was quiet.

Dad said, "A sprinkling! Ha!" He was laughing; rice fell from his mouth as he talked. "Baby's getting baptized! Ha! And these grown-ups dunking their heads underwater. In a swimming pool! How very nice and casual. Ida?" he said. "What can I get for you?"

Mom shook her head: Nothing, thank you. Her head was wrapped in a floral silken cloth.

"This is how you were baptized," he said. "Josiah. You listening?"

I looked away from Mom, and said, "What?"

"Can you believe it?" He couldn't stop laughing. "We're supposed to take this seriously? You were baptized in a swimming pool. Above ground! I doubt you were underwater more than half a second."

I reached for a carton. Dad helped.

He went on to explain that the original baptismal command required full immersion. We *died* in that water, were buried underneath and not breathing, which took more than half a second, you bet. Only to be resurrected upon ascension from a symbolic and watery grave. He was positive this should be done every day.

"Every day," he said, "we live and die in the Lord."

Mom was hardly eating at all.

One Sunday, I watched her help him distribute pamphlets in our neighborhood, brightly colored Xeroxes announcing "The End Is Near," rolled into tight tubes piercing the diamond mesh of chain-link fences. She walked slowly, with a walking stick now. But when the overlarge drunk guy from three houses down cursed at Dad from his porch, when he rushed at Dad and pushed him

into the hedges, and when he then tried to put my father in a
headlock, it was Mom who hit him back. Hard. She scratched at
the big man's neck. She scratched and punched at the skin showing where his shirt pulled open, and she pulled my father away.
She swung her walking stick. It all happened so fast that when I
ran over to help, the big man had already fallen back on his yellowing grass. Dad's pamphlet was in a ball beside him. In the
kitchen, I watched her scrub blood from underneath her nails.
Nobody ever mentioned what happened.

Bhanu and I often talked about what we would do now that
we were out of high school. I wanted to move out as soon as possible, and so did she, but we both knew we were too young to get
married. And then in July of 1987, Bhanu went to her cousin's
house upstate for part of the summer. When she left she was
wearing jean shorts and a white T-shirt that said "Do You Want
New Wave or Do You Want the Truth?" And one day there,
while visiting neighbors, she dove into a swimming pool and she
hit her head on the hard concrete bottom. Either nobody else was
there, or nobody was watching, but either way, at nineteen, she
drowned and that was it.

I don't think I cried, not for a long time, anyway. I went to the
funeral. Mom and Dad supported this, it was too serious a thing
not to. Mom even sent me to get flowers, and told me to say they
were from them. I laid them there on a chair at the funeral home
without telling anyone who they were from. I walked up to the
front of the room, not really prepared for what was happening.
I'd never seen a body before. Bhanu was there, looking fast asleep,
and peaceful, and I was weirdly pleased just to see her there. I
kissed her mother's forehead, and saw after, in the restroom mirror, there was a red stain on my lips from her bindhi. I went home
and kissed my mother's cheek and I swore I could taste the dor-
mant death cells of her skin.

———

Bhanu's accident gave Dad a sense of hope, I think, about me. They had lost me to her, and the accident was a tragedy, yes, he said, "But this is an opportunity for the three of us to get back to how things used to be. We can regroup. As a family." We were at the dinner table, always at the dinner table, one of the few times of day Mom would leave her room. I don't remember what we were eating that night, probably takeout again.

Dad said, "I have an announcement to make."

My stomach tightened. I tried not to show any physical response. Mom said nothing.

He could hardly contain himself anymore. He was fidgeting in his seat.

"Well?" I said.

He said, "Not yet."

I looked at Mom. Her eyes didn't say much of anything. I looked back to Dad. "What do you mean, 'Not yet'?" He was practically bouncing in his seat.

"Wait," he said. He stood up, and walked over to where I was sitting, put his hands on my shoulders. Rubbed, squeezed. "Give me a second," he said.

He walked over to the window, looked out. Walked over to Mom, stood behind her. She stayed still. I'd been holding my fork in the air all this time. I set it down.

"What?" I said.

He started unraveling the cloth on Mom's head. She tried to stop him, took hold of him by the wrists. But he kept unraveling. He took off the cloth. She sat there, bald-headed. He grabbed her head, hands over her ears, and began kissing her head, here, there, everywhere, kissing her. He threw the cloth against the wall, laughing, "Haha!" He walked back to my side of the table, and then on into the living room, mumbling, and saying things louder. We couldn't understand what he was saying.

"We'll do it here. Right here," he kept saying. "Right here." He walked back into the dining room and tried to sit, could hardly

contain himself. He stood again, this time with a food carton in
his hands. He ate from it, pacing back and forth, dining room to
living room, in and out of the kitchen. Sometimes over to Mom,
to kiss her head, or grab her head and kiss it. She stayed still. Her
head cloth lay on the floor in a crumple. I watched it all as if I
weren't there, as if, if I stayed still enough, he wouldn't see me.
He paced, ate, and paced. Set the carton down. Picked it up again,
pacing back to the table.

"We'll do it here, do it here, do it here . . ." He was sweating.

At some point that evening I picked up Mom's head cloth and
gave it back to her. Dad's pacing and mumbling had moved to
other rooms. Upstairs. At one point, he stood in the bathroom
beneath the stairs and scrubbed at his face, looking in the mirror,
and calling out the numbers one through seven. Mom went to
bed. I started cleaning up the dinner table just as Dad sat back
down. He was saying, "Leave it, leave it, leave it . . ." He had a
notebook, and started writing in very small script. It looked like
he was making a list.

Dad had decided he was starting his own church, at home.
He'd received a revelation.

He said, "We'll invite everyone we knew from the Brothers in
the Lord congregation."

He was making a list of names.

"And the neighbors." He asked me to get him a glass of water.
I did. "And you'll give the very first sermon."

He probably assumed that if he could tell the old brothers and
sisters from church that I was giving the sermon they'd simply
have to attend. According to him, they had been eagerly awaiting
my return. I don't know where he got this information. The idea
seemed silly to me, even then.

He looked up at me, sipping water, his face glowing. "You'll
do it?"

I didn't answer. I think he took this for a yes. But it didn't
matter. Nobody came.

We sat there at the table next week, suit and tie. Mom in a dress. A stack of bagels. Cream cheese. He'd moved the table as far back to the wall and windows as he could, and set up a make-shift podium for me, a tall and slender chest of drawers he brought from his bedroom. He had called everybody, he said. Left messages. Told them it was "imperative" they attend.

We sat there for two hours. Silent. Until Dad suddenly left the room, the house. We heard the car start. Mom insisted she help me move back the furniture. We put the bagels in a paper bag.

Would I have spoken? I never thought about it, what I would do if anyone showed.

That night, at dinner, Dad informed us he'd received a brand-new revelation, a shower was no longer sufficient and I must swear to bathe myself, fully immerse my body underwater, at rise and fall, to keep the house and my mother's body clean. For me, this was too much to ask. The request was just too intimate. For the first time in my life, death was suddenly a worthy adversary, something worth fighting against, not something to be washed, or massaged, or colored with fear or fantasy.

A year went by before I could leave and afford an apartment of my own. I had a job at a Radio Shack and I finally cried for my girlfriend. A few years passed before I gave my savings to a coworker who had been developing what seemed a good idea for a video game. We got lucky. And before long, I was living in the future. When did that happen, exactly? Life was about what comes, and this was a frightening time for me because you cannot ever really know what is coming, no matter what, not the hour or the day. I was suddenly hanging out there like a leaf about to fall. But I was getting more and more okay with the idea of falling; everything that ever made me afraid started sloughing off like scales. One by one. Then I started picking them off.

I went to work one day at Radio Shack suddenly filled with the feeling that I was no longer a Laudermilk, which was thrilling and scary as hell. I gave my notice and decided to make a longish bet on my future. I would take my cash and move to California, where computer electronics meant more money, the magazines said, and because it seemed so far away.

Finally, one Sunday (always a Sunday!), I went home to say

goodbye. I found Mom sitting in the kitchen, at the table, and she was sipping Lipton tea with milk. Her hat on the table beside her. Her white head like a bright pearl doorknob. The blinds were louvered almost closed, the atmosphere of the room more like evening than the midday outside. She wore her blue slippers, her robe. I would be leaving New York in the morning.

She said, "Come over here."

I put my hand on her shoulder, picked at the pilling of her robe. The tea was half finished, so I turned and took the pot from the stove and poured more water in her cup. I said, "I'll be back soon to tell you all about it."

She patted my hand. It was on her shoulder again.

"And we'll talk on the phone," I said. "It's just a matter of making a living, and nothing else. You know that. This isn't the place for what I'm planning. California is the place for what I'm doing."

"You could just go to Florida, open a store. Not so far away. Or upstate," she said. I tried to respond, but she stopped me, and said, "I shouldn't say that. Don't listen."

"Josiah!" Dad shouted from upstairs. "Is that you?"

Mom looked up at me. She put both hands on my hand, and squeezed my hand. Her eyes were so very anxious. "You know that I want you to go, don't you? You know I am not your father."

"It's gonna be fine," I said. "I promise. And the moment you don't feel good, you call me. I'll jump right on a plane."

Dad's footsteps were on the stairs. "Josiah?"

Mom pulled at me weakly. I crouched down and we looked at each other face to face. My God, I came from *inside* this woman. Life was inside her, my life, and her life, and the very void I came from. Her cells would rise up and kill her, the second time around.

Dad's footsteps were in the hall. "Josiah?"

I took her face in my hands, pulled her close, and kissed her head.

"Up," she said. "Before your father—"

I shot up at the sound of his steps in the kitchen.

"So," he said. "A big day for the big shot."

A shadow, probably of some cloud, or of a passing plane, must have fallen over the house as the light gave way to dark through the blinds. The three of us stayed quiet, waiting for the daylight to right itself, because it always does. The next morning, I left for California, a brand-new millennium inching over the horizon.

It was high time for inventory: and what lovely things can I say of that storeroom? Not much. Then again, how was it that a room a third the size of all of Otter Computer contained so many things, more than the rest of the store combined? Boxes on shelves, on tables, on the floor—where was the floor? I could barely see it. I remembered painting the floor when we first moved in, a slate gray color, and we even tried to get fancy. We started painting decorative yellow caution lines around the shelves. They were tall shelves. But we abandoned the idea halfway. Who was ever back there, anyway, but us? Plus, business got busy so fast—back in the beginning, I mean—that we never got around to finishing. A good problem to have. But now we had plenty of time, a good thing, too, because it would take all day.

The storeroom was a mess. Rubber storage bins bursting with unwieldy spools of wiring, tools new and rusting, plastic tabs and drive plates removed from system cases, packages of nonscuff floor pads, of batteries and power cords. The cases themselves, desktops, large, small, and huge, arranged along the floor, against the wall, like VCRs tipped on their sides. And monitors! The

dinosaur parts of the '90s and early 2000s. Because they took up
so much space. Like a television showroom in there, but stacked
(of course, everything stacked), and precariously balanced on top
of one another, 13-inch, 15-inch, 20-inch screens. Some were
missing glass altogether, looking like cubbyholes for shoes.
Screens were cracked, even shattered, broken shards protruding
from the sides like teeth. My God, there was so much media, too.
Zip discs, floppies, and compact discs. Bags of magnetic tapes.
And the drives for each and every one, floppy drives and hard
drives, the all of a sudden everywhere CD-ROM. And of course
the boxes, so many boxes—of brand-new products, or broken
products, or wrong products waiting for RMA return authoriza-
tion stickers from distributors so we could hopefully, let us pray,
get our money back. Laptops piled like impenetrable textbooks.
Keyboards piled high like delicate rectangular plates. Green
translucent motherboards like slices of vegetative earth, freeze-
dried for science and posterity. And not just the current, but the
past, the long and recently dead stuff mercilessly mined for parts,
from manufacturers who had long ago disavowed their products.
It was overwhelming, gloomy, and cold.

Amad on the other hand was out front, with people—
customers, maybe. Warm sun coming through the windows.

I stepped on a screw; it went right through my sole and into
my foot. I cried out.

"Josie?"

"I'm fine!" I heard Amad coming closer, talking to someone,
maybe Teri.

"I'm fine," I said. "Stepped on something, but I'm good. Just
leave me alone and we're in business."

"Good!"

He walked away.

I saw in a far corner, by the back wall, a small clear space. By
the memory and CPUs. The central processing units, each no
bigger than a stamp. I went over there, with clipboard in hand,

and made sure my pen could write. I decided to start with the memory and the CPUs, which hold a special place for computer technicians, for someone like Amad, because without them you have no computer. Not so unlike a human, a computer can always do more, and know more, but only with respect to the capacity of memory and the CPU. The two hemispheres of a computer's brain. As for computer sellers, like me, the processors were special because they were expensive.

They were the only carefully ordered things in that room. Memory chips set in foam, in shut black cases. In neat rows like caviar tins. I read each label and made careful notes of what memory we actually had, what we thought we had, and before long my mind strayed away to other precious things.

I used to at one time actually believe Sarah had always been waiting for me in California. But tragedy generally works on us this way. We retrofit, like a prophecy in reverse. Sarah and I met in the Otter Beach Bookstore (also now out of business). I was standing there holding a large used King James Bible bound in soft leather, very old, and it fell open in my hands like a small animal dozing in my arms. Oversize and heavy, with a crimson silken bookmark hanging from the pages like the tongue of some serpent encased in a large block of yellowing cheese. I used to sometimes go to the bookstore in the middle of the day just to hold the massive thing in my hands. Never really read from it, except for the times I scanned for typos. I'd never once seen a typo in any Bible whatsoever and this had worried me for years. I wanted to look at it and hold it, open it and smell it, try to imbibe it in a way I'd not done before. To the point that I once tore a small corner piece from a page and let it soak on my tongue like a wafer. That was only the once, and I felt stupid afterward. It tasted the way old pillows smell. I was thirty-two when this happened.

Nathan Two Foot was the grumpy and vaguely Native American man who owned the bookstore. He would say something like, "Just take it already. From me to you."

And I would say, "But then I'd have no reason to come here and bother you."

And then I would usually leave, because my store needed me. Actually, at that point, my four stores needed me.

When I met Sarah, I guess I was something of a retail mogul, a respected businessman of the community. Amad and I led in points on the company's league bowling team. Here I was, a man with a 180 average and a custom red leather bowling glove. Team captain—a reluctant one, though. I liked being in charge, and part of me liked the attention. It came naturally to me, but it also made me feel uncomfortable. What I liked most was maintaining a cool and quiet presence at work, making random check-and-sees at the other locations. Employees looking up from a computer screen surprised to find me standing there and smiling. I never said much. But when we bowled or had a barbecue at Amad's or an employees' night at a local Chili's, I liked the opportunity to command. I would stand, and surprise them again. I would be charming, magnetic, if I wanted. But on most days, I didn't feel the need. I watched Sarah walk into the bookstore, not so much walk in as fall in, with her thin black running shorts, and her nearly sheer and wet-with-fresh-sweat T-shirt, aqua blue running bra showing beneath. The lenses of her glasses fogged. She came falling in with her hands on her knees, completely out of breath.

She said, "What's new, Nate?"

I had never once thought of calling him Nate, and was immediately filled with jealously for the level of intimacy Nathan Two Foot obviously had with this small woman, glistening there in a shaft of beach light.

Nathan looked up from his book and asked how much.

"Sixteen miles," she said. "Give or take."

He said, "There is something wrong with you. Who works themselves like this on a weekend?"

"You're working," she said.

"This isn't work." He looked back at his book and turned a page.

I must have looked ridiculous. My mouth open like in a cartoon, that tremendous book in my hands.

She walked over, ducked beneath the cover some, looked back up, and said, "If that's a King James: terrible translation." Her hair was a bit knotted up and back in a wet feathery bunch. Some frizzy wisps were dancing.

"My hair." She pointed at it. "Is it ridiculous? I was running and the wind is crazy."

I said, "A little bit. Yeah."

"Who buys a Bible?"

"I like to look at it." Her hair was in the hinge of her glasses. "Your hair." I put my hand near it.

"What."

"It's in the hinge."

"The *hinge*."

I laughed at how she said it.

She carefully took off her glasses and freed the red tangle. She looked at me and I could see she was straining. I moved in closer. Her eyes were hard at first, and then I swear we didn't speak for a long time. She just looked at me, trying to see me without any help.

She finally said, "For a second or two I can see you clearly without my glasses. Then you go blurry again."

I said, "I can see you clearly. Very clearly."

"Well, you got strange kind of quickly."

I said, "I don't feel so strange."

"Me neither. Maybe."

"What did you mean about the translation?"

She laughed. "Ah, you broke the spell."

She looked toward the front of the store, like she was waiting for someone. "It's beautiful, I'm kidding. Bad joke," she said. "I'm a translator, Hebrew," gesturing Blah, blah, it's boring.

We were still standing there.

I said, "And you're here for . . ."

"Catching my breath." She looked back to the front of the store again.

"You're waiting for someone."

"I get a little restless some places. But I like it here. And I like Nathan. You're waiting for someone?"

"Nope," I said. "Me neither."

"And I come here to run, a good path. Isn't that heavy?"

I put the book back on the shelf.

She walked toward the rear of the store. And I followed.

The door was wide open, and she was in the narrow restroom, washing her face. She threw water on her face and on her hair, and every time she lifted her arms the T-shirt lifted, too. Just enough. And, my God, is there anything in this world as intoxicating as that pink rise of hip skin all crimped from the elastic band on a pair of running shorts—has to be shorts—and peeking out from where you shouldn't see, like a rosy and puckered sun; I wanted to press my face against the skin of her hip—

"You're following me."

"What can I say, I think you're cute," I said. "And you're not waiting for anyone. And I'm not waiting for anyone. . . ."

She turned away from the mirror smoothing back her hair, smirking just barely. She was softening. "You think you're charming. When really you're just a weirdo who hangs out in a bookstore."

I laughed. "No, no, no. I run a store down the street. I just come in sometimes. At lunch." I cleared my throat. "You know, I actually have four stores." I showed four fingers, wiggled them. She laughed.

And then she tripped, walking out of the restroom.

I should've caught her, but I didn't, and she went flailing into the aisle. She stopped herself just short of smashing her chin on the floor. I rushed to help her up, and she let me.

Really I wanted to laugh, because people falling down always make me laugh, but she seemed so put together and maybe a little bit hard and serious. I decided in a split second that whether or not she laughed would determine everything else from now on. And then she cried out. Laughing like a shameless little kid, showing me her palms, scratched all bloody and littered with dust and grit and sand. She laughed and really she couldn't stop laughing. She covered her mouth and I fell for her, hard. Now I was also undeniably staring at her mouth, how her laugh was total and vulnerable and how she was fine with that, *I'd* never laughed like that, and how she bit her lip because she was starting to get nervous, and then I realized that I was the one making her nervous because I was also obviously imagining what she looked like in not so many clothes—but not in some lascivious or creepy way, but because I was totally overtaken by her skin and her hair and the small belly rise just above her shorts, and, my God, that glorious little crescent swath of skin—

"You're just staring at me like it's normal."

She studied me. She took her glasses back off and looked at me, her eyes scrunched and then open wide, trying to see more clearly. Then she grinned. It was a half grin, like I know exactly what you're thinking, mister. There we were beside the extraordinarily narrow restroom in the back of the store, beside the art books and the coffee-table books (where I first met Blake and his angels), and I wanted to put my mouth on the salty rise of her so slight belly.

"You work on this street?" She walked away from the restroom.

"I do."

"Prove it."

We walked over. I introduced her to Amad, and I think she was impressed, this also thanks to Amad who has never failed to make a good showing for me.

I offered to buy her lunch.

"Look at me," she said. "I'm a sweaty mess."

"Or a coffee."

We all walked outside.

"I do have a change of clothes in the car." She looked at Amad like, Can I trust this guy or what? He shrugged his shoulders.

"I can get us a seat outside." I pointed to the diner at the end of the street, across from the pier. "They have a mean breakfast burrito, and it might not be too late."

She looked at her watch and then walked away, yelling, "What about your store?"

I didn't answer.

She turned around and saw me watching her, laughed, and shook her head.

She changed in the diner restroom and then we sat outside on the deck, facing the water, where she relished every last bite of her burrito, which I found exhilarating. And watching this made me enjoy my omelette like no omelette I'd ever had before or have ever had since. She stretched back and yawned, reaching for the sun, and said, "I have nothing to do all day." Then she ordered a Bloody Mary and asked for a bottle of hot sauce.

I joined her.

And then we had another Bloody Mary.

And then we had a few petite margaritas each, and before you know it we were drunk in the middle of the day, fully alive in our liquor-dumb bodies. Just for the hell of it, we started acting like a couple very much in love, like we'd known each other for years. And then it kind of stuck and started to feel real, even though all the while our afternoon was abundant with the most wonderful of surprises, like her name, who she was, and where she came from, her parents, my parents, and at one point I apparently launched into a sermonic diatribe about God, the Devil, and the World and Everything in It. I'm told I instructed an entire deck full of people on the finer points of Armageddon and Y2K. We walked on the beach in the late afternoon, smashed on tequila and falling

on each other, acknowledging that what we were doing was ridiculous and we'd have to face the consequences in the morning.
I begged her, Please, just let me just kiss that pretty little ribbon
of skin on your hips, and she said What on earth are you talking
about?

"On your hips." I hiccupped.

"What." She started looking about herself. "*What?*"

"From your shorts." I pointed to the place, now safely cushioned by the hug of a gray sweatpant.

She folded down the pant at the waist one inch, and said,
"Here."

I knelt down in the sand and I lightly kissed her hip. She patted my head.

Then I vomited on the sand right beside her, not a lot, but
enough to cause her to start laughing, and kick sand over my
mess like a mother would or a girlfriend would, I imagined, and
she led me to the water where she sat me down. She leaned me
back and wet my hair and washed my soiled face in the lapping
tide. Drunk, too, she stroked my head, laughing out, and remembering to cover her mouth. I never went back to the giant King
James.

She moved in three months later, I insisted, and we threw
ourselves at each other whenever possible. And this wasn't just
sex, mind you, but face-petting and back-kneading on the beach
come sundown, and making out in restaurant bathrooms like we
were in high school. I liked to watch her eyes go wet with a kind
of boozy zip when we drank white wine. And then we'd fall on
each other in the stairwell. Sarah took to me much like one often
takes to a puppy, impetuously, absolutely, lovingly. In the beginning we were on fire, and I knew one thing: that I lived in the
world, and for the first time I was really living on Earth Time, my
feet firmly planted on the hard ground, here in this place of no
angels or demons, where clocks make sense and never go backward, only forward, and who knows what all awaits us when we

get there, and *how* we got here and *where* we come from makes no real difference at all. I believed myself worthy of that time with her. She was a woman who wanted to spend herself in love because, well, her rock-hard parents never let her spend love on them, and I was the kind of man, it turns out, who'd eat it all up, a cheapskate at a buffet stuffing his pockets with bread. I have to say here in the interest of fairness that I really did love her for this.

Sarah and I got married, quietly, on the beach, in the fall of 1997, on Otter Beach by the legs of the Main Street boardwalk. By a local judge. Just Sarah, and me, Amad and Teri. White flowers, flip-flops, and the crash of water in the surf. Tidal foam. It was lovely. I called my parents two days later to tell them. They'd known about Sarah, of course, and were happy to hear it, happy just to hear I was happy. That *we* were happy. So we flew out to see them as soon as possible. It was one of those rare times in life when happiness reigns; not that we became unrealistic or lived with rose-colored glasses on our noses—and I never did get that saying, actually, because I've worn real rose-colored glasses, orange-colored ones, too, and it's nothing less than wonderful, and in no way stops you from seeing the everyday ugliness that people are capable of; it merely changes the light, and I like light. It felt like we were wearing those white clothes, and holding those white flowers in our hands, for days.

We flew out to New York and took a cab to Richmond Hill. But I remember so little from the trip, and almost nothing from the experience of returning to the old neighborhood. I usually see and file away all I can, so I must have closed my eyes in the taxi. I do remember this: my father opening the door, and then something I never expected. The door opening wide, slamming open, really, and hitting the wall behind: and there he was, standing like a game-show host, in suit jacket and tie, with his arms out and open, saying loudly, "So, this is my daughter!"

Mom was behind him in a robe and one of her macramé hats, I think her hair was short and wispy, but finally growing some. Her face was pale because she mostly stayed inside. She was holding her robe together like I imagined a geisha girl would. She looked so proud of me, and of Sarah. In a low voice she kept saying, "Come in, come in, come in . . ."

Come to think of it, the house was already looking a little rough. Not dirty, necessarily, or terribly unkempt. But little things left undone were accumulating. Dust on every surface. A musty odor. Things were not put away. It appeared as if they'd been gone for months and had just returned for our visit, with no time to freshen up. Except for Dad. In his suit.

"You look so fancy," I said. We were standing now in the kitchen.

"Come on," he said, now arranging us, Sarah and me, like figurines on a wedding cake. Josie, like so, and Sarah, like so. "Okay, let me get a look at you," he said.

They stood there, Mom and he, looking at us, almost like they were willing us not to move, Just stay like that, because you look beautiful! I was really taken aback. But why should I be? These were my parents, and I was their son, and now I'd given them a daughter. I'd always figured Mom wanted a daughter; what mother doesn't want a daughter? She stood there looking almost shyly at Sarah, afraid to approach too close, like Sarah would skitter off into some other room. At the time I couldn't know or even consider the truth because I was too happy to wonder about its reasons, but now I see she was probably just afraid of what I might have said, of what horrible things I'd told Sarah about them. Not that I ever would, or did, or that Mom would seriously think I would do anything to hurt them, or that there were any horrible things to say to begin with. And yet this is something we do all the time with our boyfriends and girlfriends and husbands and wives, and our parents did it with theirs. We exaggerate and understate the family secrets, even lie, all in order to get more love. But I'd always been up-front and honest with Sarah, mostly.

"Look at you both!" His suit was too big in the shoulders, or he was getting thinner. Then again, he was already getting older, which is actually a silly thing to say because of course it's always true.

"Can we move now?" I asked, laughing.

Mom answered for all of us and ventured forward, her hands out and aimed for Sarah's face. "So beautiful," in her new low voice. "Look at her, with a mess like you," she said to me.

I laughed.

And she said to Sarah, "My boy knows I'm kidding, right?"

Sarah hadn't said a word yet, just kept smiling, our bags still hanging from our hands.

Dad said, "How about champagne?" He turned to the fridge, took out a bottle from the freezer, and started wrestling with the cork. "Leave your son alone, Ida. You're suffocating him." He wrapped the top of the bottle with a kitchen towel to get a better grip.

Mom pulled away from me, faking she was embarrassed. "I can't help it," she said.

Dad was pulling at the top of the bottle.

We set our bags down on the kitchen floor, and I said, "Get over here." I hugged Mom and watched Sarah walk over to Dad. She took the bottle from him, he let her, and she locked it between her knees, and turned the towel in her grip over the cork like she was unscrewing it. Dad watched, totally fascinated.

I watched, and Mom watched.

"What does she do for a living, again?" Dad was clearly talking to me, but still watching Sarah work the cork, the towel now tossed aside.

I said, "You're allowed to ask her yourself."

"Ahh!" Sarah said, aiming the cork away and *pop!* It hit the ceiling, foam easing out of the bottle.

Dad shouted, "I'll get glasses!"

Sarah offered me the bottle, and I took a swig, I was laughing, and handed it back to Sarah. She took a swig, she was laughing, and then she handed it to Mom, who refused, but Sarah insisted, pushing the bottle—Take it, just take it—while she wiped at her own mouth. Mom took it, and took a big swig. Dad shouted, "Aye! Wait for me!" He handed out glasses, took a swig of his own, and started pouring.

It was almost surreal. The new Laudermilk family.

I can see it now like a photograph, Mom, her head just above water, in a way. We had no idea she'd get so sick again. Dad in his Sunday suit. The two of them pleased in every way, almost overly so, trying so hard to get it right, because their son left once before, and this was the woman who brought him back and made them a family again.

Sarah said, "I'm a translator."

We all stopped, froze for a second, and then broke into such lovely and comfortable laughter because how strange was it that this was the first thing she'd said, that this was the first time they'd heard Sarah's voice, that we'd been in their home for five or ten minutes, and that all of the emotion welling up and spilling over was directly because of *her*, because she had softened me toward them and they knew it, and maybe "softened" is the wrong word, she made me better understand them and myself is what I mean to say, and the first thing she says sounds so unlike something one says in a room so emotional. And then said the second thing she'd ever said to them—a loving creative lie, and I loved her for it—she said: "So, Gill, or Dad—do I say Dad? *Dad*? Ah! All Josie talks about is you since I met him. Dad this, and Dad that, do you know?"

My father was always many things, contradictory things, but never a fool.

He took her face in his hands again. He kissed her cheeks, one and two, and he said, almost whispering: "Thank you." He wiped at his eyes. "Okay, enough of this blubbering. Ida, stop crowding your son."

"Oh shut up," Mom said, wiping her eyes, too. "You two take your stuff upstairs, and make yourselves cozy."

We went out to dinner that night, a local Chinese restaurant, where Dad ordered for everybody, and Mom and I talked all night about the neighborhood and how she was feeling, and I told her how good she looked—"What a stylish hat"—and she laughed. All the while Dad and Sarah talked, relentlessly talked. He wanted to know what it means to read, and reread, and translate scrip-ture, and not believe the words you're reading to be divinely inspired. How could that be? I heard Sarah tell him that she *did* think it was divinely inspired, but no more so than any other great book. This was like a different language for my father, and I think it was here, ultimately, at this very moment, at Yen Jing's Chinese restaurant, in Queens, Dad became so taken with Sarah. He was convinced they were reaching for the very same thing, only Sarah hadn't had the same opportunities, but the sensibility was there, and she would eventually see the truth he was trying to share with her. Sarah's heart was at ease, however—searching, but also at ease with itself. This was something he couldn't imagine. They were a pair that night, and it delighted both Mom and me. I can still see Dad, showing off, filling a spoon with hot Chinese mus-tard and swallowing it whole, his eyes tearing up, all of it a show for his new daughter. She couldn't stop encouraging him, daring him to do other things, while casting conspiratorial looks at me, and then at him, as she waved off my attempts at conversation: You leave us be.

The phone calls started the week we got back to California.

And yet she never saw them in person again until we saw Mom at the hospital, and then the funeral. I don't like to think about the funeral, though. But they spoke every week on the phone, sometimes several times. Sarah loved me whether I liked it or not, even when I was depressed; why was I so depressed? All of which of course made her one day stop loving me so much anymore, which makes perfect sense, now, when I think about it.

That's a cop-out.

I knew exactly why I was depressed. I knew why I was so miserable. And I'm sounding more and more like a hagiographer here. I nominate Sarah for sainthood! Instead of a somewhat sensible ex-husband who, believe it or not, has learned a thing or two about marriage and love, I have learned this: Nobody's perfect. Not even Sarah. Certainly not me. And more, it's unfair to paint such an unreal picture. Worse, it's not right, and plain inhuman to expect sainthood from someone you love.

Dad told her things he'd never told me, not once, for whatever reason—things about his own calling, even about his father. He hardly talked to me about his father, my grandfather. When I was a boy, I asked. It was natural. And he sidestepped every single time. As I got older, I got the feeling Dad felt like a disappointment to *his* dad. I could relate. Sarah said it had to do with what my father called my "calling." I'd heard the phrase plenty of times, but hearing it spoken from Sarah's mouth made it feel like a real thing in the world. No longer a family secret. Even though Dad was freely telling Sarah about his own calling, and that my grandfather had one, too, and I had no idea.

All of which eventually led to a much needed talk between Sarah and me.

This was just before 2000, and I wasn't doing very well. I used to think a small part of me, a very small part, a piece I thought I'd flushed, deep down, thought, Who knows, maybe Josiah was right after all. Who doesn't like to be right? And yes, there's the untidy technicality that Armageddon could be bad news for me (which is debatable because if I *had* been right, then technically I would've survived), and more, it would be very, very bad for Sarah. For the whole world, really, but at least there would be some order in everything.

The crux really was this: if Apocalypse never did come that

day, January 1—and of course I was sure that it wouldn't—if I was *wrong*, I had proof. I mean, if faith ever leaves you in a flash, then *this* would be that day. This scared me. The day was coming soon. Who would I be? What would I believe? And, most of all, what would this final disappointment do to my father? So we talked, Sarah and I, but I didn't tell her all of this. Not exactly. Rather I recounted what had happened on that stage. All of it. I told her about the moment, my reaching up for Heaven and receiving revelation from the Lord. I told her about the horse, and I told her none of it was real. Your husband is a failed child prophet, my dear.

She laughed, and said she wasn't too surprised.

And so I told her more, later on, the beach, which felt right, because so many important things happened to us on that beach. It felt good to be honest (although never entirely . . .). And she listened. Wives do this! I told her about it over dinner, and walking on the boardwalk. I talked more that week, and the next week, I talked a lot. At brunches, and over breakfasts before I went to work, until I think before long I was becoming unbearable because that year I went from hardly talking about it with her to talking about nothing else at all.

And then came the day, 2000.

Sarah and I stayed up that night, on the beach. A bottle of champagne. Takeout tacos. And we cheered at midnight to the great messianic no-show, and howled while the fireworks broke open like neon flowers over the Pacific. Sarah poured champagne on the sand, and said, "To a shitty year." We got very drunk that night, and convinced ourselves the new year would be new in every way imaginable.

It must have been the wine because I woke up that next morning, that first morning, and I was the same old me. No new me. I was disappointed.

We went for a walk.

It was a plainly beautiful day, brisk and bracing in that Californian January way.

"Talk," she said.

We watched a pregnant woman at the end of a nearby cul-de-sac sweep up New Year's confetti into a dustpan. I asked Sarah: If we had a kid, did she think I would pass on the "calling"? God forbid. I'd been wrong, and never wanted to be right. Even Dad had been wrong once. And I don't know what year Grandpa Laudermilk put his money on, but apparently he was wrong, too. This depressed me. We went home, and I've been told more than once that that day was the beginning for Sarah: from then on, I became increasingly "emotionally unavailable."

I hated the phrase.

We decided on a brief separation, a brief one, because the fighting became constant, about my moods, yes, but who doesn't have moods? But mostly about not having kids.

One year later, in September, the planes came.

What I'm about to say is not an easy thing for me to say, and it's the one and only real secret I've kept from Sarah, but when I first saw what was happening on the news, when the Big Shit buckled the fan and down came those poor toppling towers, for one brief dark moment in the basement of my soul I seriously thought the planes were proof. The prophet lives! I was only off by a year. Only one year, not so bad. I actually had this thought. Fleeting, yes, and fast like light, but that doesn't matter now. Because I didn't first think of their faces, and how every single one had a name, and I didn't think of the purple carpet on the Trade Center lobby floor. I didn't think of rubbing my shoe soles on the carpet when I was a kid, and shocking my dad's arm in the elevator on the way up.

That afternoon of the eleventh, Sarah came by the house to pick up some of her stuff, and I was drinking. She'd have a drink with me, a quick one, she said. She turned on the television and we watched the news, and then we turned it off. We were both feeling so sad and were dutifully polite to one another. We didn't really talk about anything. We just kept drinking. And then we fell on each other in the living room. She then hit me squarely in the face, and it hurt. I clearly heard the crack of her hand against my skin, and then the sound of her fingers tugging at the zipper on her jeans, even the *shush* of the silk ribbon line of her underwear just above her belt rubbing against the palm of my hand. I could've sworn I heard the blood rush all through my ears and my head, to my cheek where she hit me, thinking I could actually hear the skin going red. She hit me again. I grabbed at her wrists trying to stop her, and then thought better of it. She started hitting me in the chest like she was beating the steering wheel of a car that wouldn't start. She was crying, too. I wasn't, not yet, too overwhelmed by it all, by the pure and naked anger and the final remnants of our love and her frustration coming off her like sparks. Then she grabbed my face. I started to talk, and she said, "Shut up." She undid all of my belt and pants and whatnot, and then she undid hers, pressing herself against me. Then my back was against the cold hard floor, and she beat herself against me, again, and again, and again, with her hands and her haunches, until I pushed her off because I was going to start. So she let that happen. And then she pressed herself against me again, and again, and again. The floor went warm, and she pressed herself against me until it was almost unpleasant, I think, for us both. I was in one particular place in the whole of the world, knowing where I was and when I was, and then she fell back sprawling on my legs.

We lay there on the hard floor, legs crossed on top of each other for what seemed like a very long time. The room was quiet. She wasn't crying anymore. She patted my hand, because now, I think, I had started. She stood up and pulled on her jeans. She stuffed her underwear in her front pocket, and kicked mine within reach. She picked up a wadded sock from the floor and tossed it to me. I caught it. She allowed herself one more blurting cry, before stopping herself. Then she let out a cough of a laugh, and said, "That should not have happened." I'm sure at least a small part of her meant the last few years.

And thus my dear (ex-)wife, mid-separation, got pregnant. We did not keep it. Which ruined us and remained forever between us like a deep furrow in the dirt, which neither of us could cross.

Dad called me later that day. He wanted to know what I thought about the planes. I was in shock, stunned by the footage, and didn't have the appropriate language to express myself. I said something like, "I think it's scary as hell and it looks like the world is coming apart on TV and maybe it's symptomatic of a much bigger problem."

"What's that supposed to mean?"

I said, "I don't know, maybe we want God too much."

"We who?"

"People."

"What people?"

"Forget it," I said.

"Have you even seen the news?" he said. "You think this is really happening?"

I said, "I'm still processing. I can't even look—"

"Well, your mother is sick. She's sick again."

"What?" I said. "Say that one more time."

"Your mother."

"You went to the hospital?"

"She's been tired. We went six weeks ago."

"You've known about this for six weeks?"

"I didn't want to bother you."

It's very strange how it all works, how we get a handle on the darker things. "And you waited to tell me today. Something like this happens."

He was quiet.

"It's okay," I said, "forget it." I exhaled. Inhaled, exhaled. "At least I can process."

"This is what I'm saying," he said. "We can talk about it."

"Is she in pain?"

"Some."

"Same place?"

"Same place. And her liver. A little."

"A *little*?"

"That's the word the doctor used. A little."

"I'll look into flights—"

"You're not taking a plane."

"Shit. Are they even flying planes?" I said.

"I don't know."

"Shit, shit, shit. Can I talk to her?"

"She doesn't like the phone anymore. The radio waves, who knows . . ."

I didn't respond.

"Josiah?"

"Yeah." Biting my lip.

"You feel okay?"

"It's a lot at once. Jesus. I can see Mom's face, I swear, like she's right here in front of me."

"God is Giver of Tests. I've been saying this for years. We should not. Be here. I've been honing our worship."

"I'll tell Sarah about Mom. I'll call you back, and see about a plane. The doctors said how bad?"

"I told Sarah. She thought you should know immediately."

I held the phone away from me for a few moments, and then I put it back so I could hear.

"Josiah?" he said. "Your mother, she wants to go home, and her body knows it. But up here"—I pictured him pointing at his head—"she can't see it."

"Well, I don't want Mom going home. Or anywhere, but staying right here."

"You shouldn't be way out there," he said.

For Dad, the fact that Manifest Destiny had moved westward

meant that back east is, was, and forever would be the only real deal, God's One Manifest American Fingerprint. Everything after was blasphemy, half-ass imitation, poor and poorer servings of our Good Lord's perfect recipe. And L.A. County was the red swollen cherry on a shameful sinful sundae. He never did visit me.

"I'll look into flights," I said. "And I'll get there as soon as possible. No matter what it costs." Money wasn't a problem then. The paranoiac software bubble around Y2K had been actually good for business. But after the planes, business took an overwhelming nosedive. Plus the Internet. Amad told me we had to start embracing the Internet, and I was stupidly nonplussed. I got more depressed, and I convinced myself—which is not exactly true, is it, because it's not like we ever formally sit down and convince ourselves of anything, but my behavior certainly did speak of something out loud—I realized something: I felt guilt! Guilty about the planes. Which were in no way my fault, of course, but still I was racked with a personal guilt, like it was me sitting in the cockpit, as if they were only responding to my polite request for Armageddon decades before, and I felt more guilty, cripplingly so, about that brief but utterly corrupt and fleeting sense of satisfaction with regard to their belated-by-a-year but successful arrival. God forgive me. I even felt guilty about Mom, like I was the one who made her sick. Why did it take such a long time for me to see how self-centered all this was? Why was this the kind of lesson I'd always learn and forget, learn and forget? I was also feeling guilty for being so selfish with Sarah, for not being man enough to own my own destiny. Have a child, Josie, and bring some new joy into this world.

I eventually learned all this, and indeed I took it into my stupid heart, but not before the melodrama totally soured Sarah and me; and not before Sarah got pregnant; and not before we did not keep it; and not before all of this gave way to anger, so much displaced anger. And thus, hence, my "Mad Max" period, so called by Sarah, because I was mad at everything I saw and acted like the world was "nothing but dead bones and dust," her words (I wasn't the only one who could be dramatic). We fought fiercely about every fucking thing under the sun, except what mattered.

We split for good.

And then we tried again. Split. And tried again. We did this for years. We eventually divorced.

Then Mom died, a long and slow and eventual demise that felt more like she just went to sleep, and finally she never woke up. What she'd wanted all along. Losing Mom weirdly cushioned the divorce proceedings, probably because, well, the worst possible news certainly lessens the impact of just *bad* news, and also because I'd somehow gotten it into my head that if Sarah stayed in my life she would almost certainly die.

There is a sad and ironic sort of symmetry regarding Sarah's pregnancy, how after years of talking over the idea, it was only later on, after arguments and insults, and at least one assault with a kitchen utensil, that my seed took root in her womb as a result of what felt like goodbye-forever sex, both of us neck deep already in a trial separation, and that we didn't keep it, and how it was this whole distressing scenario that flung us back and forth at each other, for years afterward, until one day we realized our marriage had actually died long before. I'm told the procedure wasn't as physically painful or emotionally traumatic as it might have been if she had not decided and acted so quickly. I'm not so sure. I drove her home from the clinic.

My immediate response to hearing she was pregnant was the last thing she'd (or I'd) expected: "Let's keep it," I said. "Please." I look back at this now and, sure, I see how desperate I was. Maybe a baby would have fixed us. Sarah knew better than I did, so we wound up talking about it for hours and hours. I was also worried it might be my only chance, the Laudermilks' last chance for survival. I didn't mention this. The procedure took place inside of the first four weeks. And regardless of what the doctor said, and the pamphlets, and the websites, and what Sarah said, too, who promised it would all be fine, it was an awful morning all around. She spent the remainder of the day in the bathroom. She let me help her in, and prepare the water, get it warm, and hang a bath towel and a robe within reach.

She asked me to leave.

I stood there at the door for a long time, listening for signs of anything I could do that might be helpful. I talked to her some, too. But she wouldn't answer for a long time, and then she said, "I love you, Josie."

Stammering, I said it back. "I love you, too."

"But you have to leave me alone now. Okay? I'll know if you're by the door. Promise you'll leave for a while. Please."

I did. And then the doorbell rang.

"Go," she said.

I went into the bedroom, stepped over the treadmill, and looked out the window.

At first I didn't realize what I was seeing, and then I questioned whether or not I was guessing correctly. There were two young men standing at our door.

I looked at them, sort of in disbelief, at the timing mostly. I waited.

They rang the bell again.

They wore dark suits, flat shoulder bags propped between their feet. They didn't lift their heads. One had a Bible in his hands, the edges of its pages glistening in the afternoon sun. The other had a magazine rolled in his grip. It was clear: two Jehovah's Witnesses, my father's former brothers, and my ancestors in a way. I watched them moved on to Bev's door. They rang her bell, and waited. Knocked. And then they moved on to Charlie's door. I thought of Sarah who was not but two rooms away, and found myself suddenly offended by the intrusion. I wanted a smoke. But then, unexpectedly, a very small part of me also wanted to open the window and call down to them, ask the young men inside, and offer them water, a chair. It was like my past had come knocking and here I was looking at it.

I went over to the bathroom door, tapped gently. "I'm gonna step outside."

She didn't answer.

I went downstairs, opened the door to the courtyard, and said loudly, while lighting a cigarette, nonchalant, "Can I help you?"

The taller one turned, and said: "Good morning."

He walked over to me, and placed his shoulder bag on the ground. He was maybe nineteen, and had the delicate face of an adolescent with allergies. He motioned his partner over, and said, "My friend Gerard and I were in the neighborhood and we're sharing some good news for a change. Isn't this a fantastic day? Are you a Bible-reading man?" He opened his and flipped through its pages.

I turned and blew smoke behind me, but a breeze sent it back over my head like a hood. I started coughing.

He said, "If you're in no mood to talk, that's fine. Just one scripture, and we'll leave you be on this fine day."

I noticed a spot of unshaved whisker beneath the left side of his jaw. A pimple. The thinner end of his tie was hanging too long from behind, tucked inside his pants. I was still coughing. I cleared my throat. "What's your name?"

He closed the book. "Bart. And you, sir?" He put out his hand.

I took and vigorously shook it. "Josie," I said and looked up at the bedroom window. He looked up with me, followed my gaze.

"Forget something?"

"Bad day," I said.

"Even the bad days are a gift."

I looked at him. "I suppose." I looked up at the sky, and then back at him. I was starting to sweat. I wiped my forehead.

"Can we help at all?" he asked, looking at Gerard, at me.

This took me aback. "With what?"

"You tell us," Bart said. "You'd be surprised how much comfort the scriptures offer." He was kind of glorious there in the bright wash of morning, palm fronds painting low shadows on his sunlit suit. He said, "There's always a cause for sadness, right? It's the nature of an earthly life. But a spiritual life can be joyful, too. Our Heavenly Father loves me. He loves you. I know His love, and this"—he presented the world: trees, sky, and sun—"all of this was made for me."

Gerard said, "I have this knowledge, too."

This touched me. It really did, to really know something, to be so sure of something like this. I don't know what I'd expected from them, but it was nothing like this. Back in my younger and angrier years, whenever I saw the Witnesses, I felt either a great sadness, a pitiful and frustrated sadness for them, but also for myself because I was clearly projecting, or I felt a fast-abating fury, for lots of irrational reasons, one quick blast of invisible anger directed right at them, and also of course directed right at me. We don't like to see who we were, or who we still are in the places buried deep within us. But here they were at my door, and what did I feel? I was jealous! Jealous for their abiding assurance. Plus I was truly moved, I have to say, because I saw Bart really meant it. He wanted to comfort me. He wanted to help.

"My wife is ill," I said. "But thanks. And you guys," I was looking for the right words. "You're doing fine work. Just wanted to say hi, I guess." We were silent for a few awkward moments, our three heads warming in the sun.

Bart said, "We can just say hi. Like people." Gerard laughed.

There was a white dusting of what looked like doughnut powder on Bart's left lapel, and I saw Gerard was slightly paler than his partner. A thick blue vein ran along the length of his neck like a power cord. I backed up a few steps, and stopped. Stood there. They stood there, too. What was I waiting for? What did I expect? Time bent all around us, and I realized this easily could've been me—I could've been Bart. I *was* Bart. And he was me.

Bart looked at his watch. He said, "Well, we'll leave you to your wife. I hope she feels better. Maybe we'll stop by again sometime. And just talk. I might even use my Bible!" He laughed, putting his bag back on his shoulder. He patted Gerard's arm.

He said, "Josie, right? You know, the scriptures do make a promise. This life is not all there is. And I promised you a scripture." Then he recited: "And he will wipe out every tear from their eyes, and death will be no more. There be no more sorrow, and no crying, pain will be no more. The former things have passed away."

Memory washed over me like a slow wave. "Revelation," I said. "Chapter twenty-one."

Bart made a face—he was impressed.

"Your wife," he said. "I hope she feels better soon. And remember, one day, you won't have to worry about that anymore. That's what He says, anyway." His eyes looked skyward, and he put out his hand again.

I took it.

"You're not afraid of anything, are you?" I said. "Not even death."

We were still holding hands.

He said, "There are plenty of things worse than death."

I let go, and I stood there, looking at this young man, at the two of them, and I'm sure they were wondering, What's wrong with this guy? What's he standing around for? I thought of Sarah upstairs, all alone, and how I so wanted to be up there with her, right beside her, and I thought of the child, or not the child, exactly, but the idea of the child we might have had, and how it was only just that, an idea, a nothing, and not really here at all, and yet it was all I could think about so, in a way, it was right there in front of me. I actually started to cry. I wiped my face.

Bart said, "You want us to stay?"

"Funny," I said, "the strangest thing I just thought of. My father took me to a funeral, when I was a kid."

They were interested.

I said, "Not really a funeral, more like a wake for one of the neighborhood kids. About my age. He just disappeared one day. A year goes by and they figured we'd better have a service. Cleared the whole living room of furniture. No coffin."

Gerard said, "That's so sad."

Bart said, "There's no guarantee this side of Armageddon. But your little friend, he'll be on the other side. Waiting, and all made new."

I smiled at the thought, but I also realized, if this were in fact true, how strange it would be if he were raised still a child.

Sun splintered up there on the bedroom window, and I figured there had to be another kind of time, aside from what I imagined eternity is, or infinity is, and aside from our few years here on earth, a kind of time outside us, because I could pull a memory like fruit from a branch. I could reach for little Issy's face like an apple, and there he was.

Now Bart was talking about Armageddon, and how it would be good news for some.

I listened and was all of a sudden filled up with love for them both. I wanted to take them by the shoulders and shake them. I wanted to promise them a day would come when they would see the hard ground for the first time, really see it, and the sky, and the water, and if they were lucky, it would break their hearts. I wanted to promise them that on that day, your heads would fill up with fear, and with love, and that one day you'll get married, and you'll never guess how vicious things get in love, and if you're not careful, your wife will rightfully brain you with a pasta spoon, and talk of possible futures without you, and you will eventually come around, but it'll be way too late, and the floor will fall away from your feet. But who was I to promise such a thing? We were standing there, all quiet, and then I saw something: I saw fear in their eyes, I knew it, a natural human fear. I turned away from them. And looked up again. I faced the bedroom window, and closed my eyes, and I thought of Sarah and her claustrophobia, and I hoped she felt secure and safe and warm in her bath, but if someone ever asked if she was afraid of confined spaces, she would always answer, Absolutely not. This was a fear so ingrained, so embedded in her cells, that it only simply existed, was taken for granted, like the blood in her veins or the flesh on the soles of her feet. A fear like this is a hole, a blind spot, a negative space, and it makes itself knowable only by implication, by habit, by her choosing stairwells over elevators, by her avoidance of underwater tunnels whenever possible, and by her long lone runs into infinite space, no walls or ceilings anywhere. I opened my eyes, and saw her up there, my sweet wife, it was Sarah; how easy it is to forget how much and why we love who we love. She was standing at the bedroom window. A faint trace of a smile. She waved, just the barest suggestion of a wave, a slow and tired show of her palm, like she was saying goodbye. I turned, and the young men were gone.

Three hours I stayed in that storeroom. Three hours before coming out for air, and for lunch, and for something to drink because I was thirsty—and what did I find? Cold coffee, a crumpled brown paper bag, and a burrito half-congealed with cheese, poking out its head from a foil sleeping bag. All of this looking lonely on a cardboard box outside the storeroom door.

"What's this?"

"What?" Amad was plugging in the vacuum.

"This. Cold." I was sipping the coffee. "Totally cold. You couldn't tell me it was here? Where's Teri?"

"You missed her. Running errands." The vacuum turned on, *vroom*ing loud like a go-cart, and he pressed the thing with his foot so the top part with the bag unlocked from the sucking part and he pushed it around in front of him. "And you said to leave you alone!"

I shook my head. "I win fair and square. And cold."

He wasn't listening or couldn't hear me, just kept pushing the vacuum. Something small, hard, and metallic rattled up inside it.

I'd made some progress, planned an order, and filled a garbage bag with what we should have realized was garbage long ago. The floor was now showing through. I took a bite of the burrito. Delicious. And so I was a little annoyed that I could no longer be as annoyed as I had been with Amad for letting it get cold. What is it about California burritos? Why can't the other forty-nine states get it right? Or even close? Why can't they master a tortilla so it doesn't fall apart in your hands like a hot wet salad? And avocado everywhere. If you don't love avocado, then I pity your soul, and your soul's lack of green supple goodness. On every California plate like how New York puts parsley. It's generous. No pale ribbing of kale for a garnish. I mean, even the garnish was gorgeous, and it waited in a small plastic-covered cup at the bottom of the bag. But bring me hot sauce. Always hot sauce.

"No hot sauce?" I shouted over the *vroom*.

"What?" Amad shouted back, didn't turn around, and kept pushing.

I couldn't think straight it was so loud, so I grabbed the coffee and took my lunch outside, figuring I should try Dad again. I waved to Amad, pointing at my ears, "I can't hear you," and then to the door, "Be outside." I set the bag and burrito on the bench, sipped my coffee.

It was a lovely day, and the sky seemed a bit dark for so early. I called him. No answer. I called him again. No answer. It wasn't like he had a message service or a machine because God knows the man would never use one because he didn't care to, or he refused to learn how, or for some other irrational reason, and he'd say something like If I can talk, we'll talk. If I'm there, we'll talk. How can we talk if I'm not even there? This literalism always drove me nuts.

The vacuum stopped. I went back inside.

"My father's not answering the phone."

He gave me a curt nod.

"I talked to him before, doesn't sound good. Sarah said he sounds pretty bad. He was a little loopy."

"How loopy?" He was wrapping the cord around the vacuum neck.

"He said my mom was there."

"Where? There?"

My phone rang. "Dad?"

He sounded far away: "Why is my phone ringing so much?" Almost like he was on speakerphone and actually walking away from the phone while we talked. "I'm trying to sleep."

"I wanted to see how you're doing. I told you before I'd call."

"When?"

"Before. This morning."

"I have no idea what you're talking about." He was yelling now. I couldn't help but laugh. "Well, you're alive."

"Yes! I'm alive! Are you satisfied? I'm going to bed."

"It's like two o'clock. That's like four o'clock your time."

"I'm tired." He hung up.

I looked at Amad, shrugged my shoulder.

I went back in the storeroom, and I wanted a cigarette because now I was feeling anxious and I'd forgotten to smoke one outside. Plus there was no smoking in the storeroom, one of Amad's many rules. I'd smoke later on with another cup of coffee, but a *hot* cup of coffee. Planning cigarettes was almost always as pleasurable as smoking them. I'd never given real thought to who was taking care of my father at home since Mom died. Who was cooking? Was the man having hot meals? Then again, a burrito could be just as good cold. I organized and moved things. I swept. I picked up broken glass from things that fell from the top shelves and broke around me while I was cleaning up—we'd been on to something, after all, with those yellow lines—and before you know it Amad was standing in the doorway eating an apple, and saying "You're hired."

"I'm being serious," he said. "This inspires me. So clean!" He ran his finger along a shelf, held it up to the light, and even from where I was standing I could see the filthy smudge.

"Getting there," I said.

"Yes. And I'm going home now." He put out his hand. I shook it, exaggeratedly, like, You got a deal there, mister. I wiped what smudge came with it on my jeans.

"You close shop?" he asked me.

"It's been a long time."

"Yes."

"I'll close shop," I said, feeling very proud.

He waved as he walked away, and closed the door behind him.

I walked home along the water, and had my cigarette with a hot black coffee I got at the corner gas station. The smoke climbed up, the color of the moon's silver swirls. Obviously I had to go see Dad. As soon as possible. Maybe tomorrow. Tomorrow? Or was that too soon? But if I went tomorrow, it meant no dinner with Sarah . . . Which was an easy decision, yes, but also it felt important. I needed to recognize it. And then I looked out at the dark water and could've sworn I saw someone coming out of the ocean. A shadow of someone, probably just had a night swim, but then he bled away in the night.

I blinked my eyes, shook my head.

Dad was getting old, and I knew what comes next, what always comes next, and I wondered why I was smoking so much when I hardly liked the taste anymore. Plus dinner probably wouldn't have happened anyway. She and I were dead, long dead, and shamefully, forgive me, but a dying and not-quite-dead-yet part of me also used to sometimes stand by that water and watch the sun drop below the waterline at sunset, and I'd wish the great reddening ball would quash out, get doused, fall purple and cooling toward the bottom of the ocean. Take us all down with it. I put out my cigarette in the sand. I was getting morbid, and maudlin, and decided that what I really needed was to just get laid.

There was so much sand, and the ocean was rolling in and rolling out, and the waves were playing and toppling like animals wrestling. Water roiling and boiling in the dark. And then it happened again. I saw someone coming from the water. But this time it was two men, looking like two black liquid things walking from the water, except they stayed where they were, and were sort of suspended. One of the drilling rigs miles away on the water let out a booming signal, and it spooked me, so I took off running; then I stopped. I turned back and there they were, natural as night, two figures forming there in front of me. They were made of the water, and the dark light, and the night air. Just as fast, they disappeared. They rose up again from underwater, and then bled away in the darkness. It was all a trick of the light, or the no-light. I was tired, and I was seeing things, a grown man running from ghosts on a cool and lovely summer evening by the water. Things would be better in the morning.

EAST

3

The long *PINNNGGG* of a doorbell rudely pealed through the fog in my brain. My face all pressed up against the armrest of the couch, Dad's knees slowly went by. At some point in the night I'd apparently wrapped myself in the sheet. Cats were resting on my back. The doorbell pinged again. I wanted a tremendous orange juice. Voices in the front hall, feet shuffling, and then blurry sounds coming from the kitchen . . .

"Have a good day, Mr. Laudermilk."

Dad shouted: "It's a good morning, Junior, so let's take advantage!" The front door closed. "I made us some coffee!"

My face was mashed against the armrest and it felt just right until the part of my brain in charge of such things suddenly woke. The whole face hurt, pressure on every pore and wrinkle. I turned over, cats darting from the sofa. I stretched with a loud groan, causing an animal chain reaction where, beside the table, two fat cats, one first, then another, bowed up like stuffed feline stoles, stretching their spines. They yawned and fell back asleep.

I pulled aside the draping a bit, squinting at the outside day, and watched a deliveryman drop two garbage bags on the curb before hopping into a brown double-parked truck. Still in the head-melt of sleep, I saw an empty wine bottle on the table, a shallow bowl littered with cigarette stubs, and my phone, open, dead. The thought of smoking made me nauseated. I walked toward the kitchen and became aware, and weirdly okay with the fact, that I, too, was now walking barefoot, instinctively avoiding the cat turds and everything else. Dad was framed by a beige window shade behind him. He was wearing his loincloth and a white T-shirt. A large box lay on the table.

I pointed to the window shade. "Why not let some day in here?"

"Days are finished, Junior."

He was drinking coffee from an oversized mug emblazoned with a screaming image of Max Headroom. He sipped, Max all glaring teeth and white plastic shades. I had to look away.

He said, "I love a cup of coffee in the morning. One cup."

"Who was your visitor?"

"Delivery."

A haze and muffle between my ears.

"You found the wine." He pointed to yet another empty bottle on the counter.

"Jesus. Sorry."

"No, it's good. I'm glad."

"I'll be fine. I'm fine. What?" I was a palm-sized man climbing my own insides like a cave.

"What I say?"

"I thought you said something," I said.

"Not me," he said. "And I gotta say I'm glad you're not feeling so hot."

Another Max Headroom mug sat beside the coffeemaker. It

was already filled with coffee. "That's a terrible thing to say." I
picked it up. My right palm was pulsing; I switched hands and
took a sip.

"Means you're no professional, which makes me glad. Never
was either, myself. You hungry?"

"There is no food in this house."

"Bread and butter, Junior. Food of the gods." He looked toward
the counter where the bread, the butter semiwrapped in waxy
paper, and a knife lay. A pallid still life.

He stood, took the knife in his hand, and cut.

"What's in the box?"

He smiled like, Wouldn't you like to know, and handed me a
buttered slice.

"You're not eating?" I said.

"Hours before my time." Knife still in hand, he walked to the
box, bare feet hardly lifting from the floor.

"The old man keeps me in suspense. So when do you eat,
exactly?"

"Ha!" He cut the tape and pulled back the flap. Styrofoam
popcorn popped from the box. "I'm running low," he said, and
pulled from inside a ridiculously large pack of Post-it Notes. More
popcorn packing fell across the table like champagne from a glass.
"There's more," he said eagerly. He pulled out a pack of two toothbrushes. "I'm glad you're here, Junior." A three-pack of toothpaste,
and a carton of dry cat food.

"Me, too."

"Good."

The coffee was burning its way into my belly, a slight spike in
my bloodstream. I went all different directions inside. The coffee-
pot was empty.

"I need more."

He pointed to a green Thermos by the sink.

"Good thing I don't take milk."

"Milk's for babies."

I pulled at the loaf of bread. Balled up a piece and put it in my mouth.

"Eat all you want," he said.

He pulled two large loaves of bread from the box. He placed them on the counter, felt around inside the box, and pushed it aside. He pulled a chair from under the table, and there a second box lay, long and flat. He cut the clear tape seam and took from the box something wrapped in bubble wrap. Foam kernels on its surface; he wiped them away to the floor. He placed the object on the table and began to undo the bubbling, cutting it away with his knife. He took from the bubble wrap a thing, I don't know what, and held it up for me to see.

"See?"

It looked like a shield. "Is it a shield?"

"It is." He walked to the other end of the kitchen, by the back door, and held it to the wall. A small, decorative shield, an ornamental thing, not very elaborate. It couldn't haven been very heavy. The day before, he'd struggled with the fridge.

"What's it for?"

He ignored me and began feeling along the wall, all around the wooden cross, the plate painted with a Star of David. "Looking for a nail," he said.

I put down the mug and started over, but he stopped me with his palm. "Drink your coffee. Leave me be. I'm fine." He found one, pulled at the nail, and hung the shield from it. "Not the right kind, but she'll do."

I sipped my coffee. "The royal family crest?"

He wiped the surface clean.

He turned around and came closer, he was slow, but then he was standing right in front of me. Staring into my eyes. His face was so old. Too old-looking for his age.

"Do you believe in anything at all anymore?"

I rubbed my eyes, my temples.

He said, "Part of what makes people stop is because they

think He's invisible. Think we don't know what He looks like. He's not invisible."

"It's a bit early for me. . . ."

"Right there in black and white, and the world looks every-where but smack in front of their faces!" He placed his hand on the left side of his chest. "It's in our hearts! Telescopes looking over Mars and the moon. Microscopes looking in our blood . . ." He walked back to the table, across from me, and smiled like a man with a secret.

I said, "You know the heart is actually dead center in the middle of the chest." I pressed my finger there. "And not to the left."

"I know damn well where the heart is."

A shower or a cold bath would be perfect.

"Because this is where it feels." He prompted me to touch my own chest. "See?" He came closer again. "It feels like your heart's right here." He put his hand on my chest.

"Okay."

"Now hold on to your coffee mug, because what I'm gonna say next."

I couldn't help but love him talking like this. This was Dad, this I recognized. Maybe he was feeling better?

"The Psalmist sayeth, Junior, and I say it thus. Psalm 84:11." He turned and looked to the wall. " 'For your Lord God is a shield.' " He looked back at me. "In black and white."

There wasn't much sun coming through the windows, but enough, and it made my eyes pulse. I stepped back into the dark hall. "I'm listening. God is a shield. But I think actually the scrip-ture says he's a sun *and* a shield."

He shuffled into the dining room, looking like he might fall over at any moment. "The Hebrews used leather," he said, "and animal fat for shields. Painted red with blood." He paused. "Who wants something like that in the kitchen?" He threw up his hands, like, What are you gonna do.

I coughed into my hand. The tip of my thumb itched. There was a small puncture, and it was sore. I shook my head.

He looked at the only bare wall in the dining room; no pictures, no shelves. It seemed naked. "Some were bronze, a circle. But this is no circle. You saw." He sat down.

I needed more butter. "How are you feeling? You sleep okay?"

"I'm fine," he said.

"I was thinking last night."

"Good, sit." He tapped the chair beside him. "Look at you. I almost forgot what you look like. How's business? How many stores?"

I sat. "The stores are fine. Listen. I think we should see a doctor. Just to talk."

It wasn't quite a look of condescension, but his face definitely said, You don't know what you're talking about.

He said, "I saw your mother last night. And let's just say she disagrees."

"Ah! You dreamt of her, you mean."

"Of course." He looked at me sideways. "Sometimes I find her in the day." He stood. "I try to keep moving, keep the blood flowing. . . ." He padded into the dining room, and I wondered from where he got his loincloth, what websites he happened onto looking for a "modern loincloth."

"Dad."

"Yup."

"I need you to tell me." I followed him to the couch.

"What?"

"Tell me you're eating. I need you to tell me you're eating."

"Not hungry. Empty, fit as a fiddle."

"I mean are you eating at all."

He sat, pulled the lamp chain. "It's complicated."

"Talk."

He showed me his hand. "Stay there. I'm fine, and you're there."

"Talk."

He peered over the computer screen. "I promise I'm happy you're here."

"And I'm happy you're happy."

"We're okay, you and I."

"We are."

He hid behind the screen. "I take bread and wine on Sundays."

He showed me his hand again. "There are rules. And fasting is one of the rules."

Things were clearly not better. He was not better. And I saw how silly I'd been thinking that we'd wake up and everything would be fine. A soft lip of light lined the edge of the curtains. He said, "Sometimes I find your mother in the day. I go to sleep and I find her."

Ten o'clock in the morning, I was going through my things. Clearing some personal space for me around the sofa, trying not to get overly worried. What exactly should I do next about Dad? I decided on a shower. I would think in there. Plus Dad was in the bathroom again, the red light flaring from under the door. He said he'd been up since five.

I went to the second floor, and took each step up slowly.

Upstairs, the dark hallway was free of clutter and the four doors were closed and the long thick carpet runner lay on the slatted floor like a dead paisley tongue. No windows. The hall was dark and damp, and it smelled of soft wet wood, of mold, but there was also a welcome comfort in the stink.

The first door on the left led to the upstairs bathroom.

There was a shallow pool of browning water in the tub and a floating, speckled mass of bug. Dead flecks of fly and mosquito and gnat made a dark freckling shadow on the surface. A gauzy light came in through the clouded glass. No shower curtain or door, and a mass of moist towels lay on the floor. I opened the window, pulled away the drain stopper, and the water gurgled in a spinning fall. I turned on the light.

In the linen closet, I found sheets and pillowcases, washcloths and bath towels squarely folded and placed in flush columns on the wallpapered shelves. I was afraid to look at the toilet, but it was actually in pretty good shape. I turned on the shower and twisted the spray nozzle toward the wall so I wouldn't make too much of a mess. I gathered all the towels into one damp sop, stuffed them into a yellow pillowcase. The shower ran rivery lines along the grout between the tiles, and washed away what bug waste it could. The shower still running, I stepped back into the hall.

The second door was mine, or used to be mine, and this seemed way too easy, entering the room that used to be my room. I opened the door and saw light sluicing in ribbons through the louvered blinds and painting the wall with pale stripes. I saw the bedspread neatly tucked under the mattress, and I was sure this had to be my handiwork from twenty years prior. Impossible. I saw the empty closet. Clear tape in ripped fragments stuck to the walls and to the ghosts of *Star Wars* posters. Water bugs lay flat on their backs at the foot of a bed leg. A sticky mix of dust and oils skimmed the carpet like a hairpiece. I went back into the hall.

The next room was a large walk-in closet. And I often imagined, as a kid, that a demon lived among the board games on the highest shelf, and it could fit a small child in its mouth. This probably came from secretly watching *Poltergeist*, a definite no-no in the Laudermilk home, and from the subsequent nightmares of sinister closets opening up like demonic maws. I remembered telling my mother about the closet and she scolded me, said that was what I got for watching devil movies. She left me in the closet until I cried out for her. Then she came in, and we stood there in the dark holding hands. She said anytime you're scared call on me, or your Heavenly Father, and nothing bad can happen.

My parents' room was next, and I half expected to find my

mother in pajamas stretched out on the comforter. The door was sticking. The trick was to lift slightly, turn the knob, and push.

The room was dark, and a hot smother of air came pouring out. The bed was made, and a thin webbing of dust crawled the walls like ivy. The curtains were drawn. I saw the closet was full of clothing, mostly my mother's. There were also garbage bags on the floor, stuffed with what appeared to be her things. I bent down and found a yellow jacket. I put the jacket on a hanger, and hung it from the back of the door. I tried to imagine my mother, her arms filling the sleeves, her head. I took the jacket from the hanger, smelled it, and my stomach reeled. Stale and oppressive, it stank of age, of years and days and minutes of sloughing skin.

I flipped the light switch.

The quilted surface was scattered with short stacks of papers and more spiral notebooks. Barely noticeable at first, but they were in a sort of order, separate and organized. A pile of hand-written pages, scrawlings, and drawings. There were dated pages, like journal entries, and I recognized the uncanny logic and language of dreams. These were my father's dreams. He was writing out his nightly visions. Flying, teeth falling out, being swept from a hilltop by God's great palm, and taking heavenly tours. There were birth certificates and death certificates. Photo albums, and a pile of loose photos. I quickly flipped through the pictures. They were mostly old, ancient even, brown-and-whites, black-and-whites. There was the family photo album, but also albums I'd never seen before, pictures of people I didn't recognize. I saw one of two men standing in front of a Spanish-style house, I figured southern California. They stood beside a long and beautiful car, like a Rolls-Royce, their feet on the running board. They hooked their thumbs back, making like two lucky hitchhikers. On the back was a handwritten note, "C. Russell and O. Laudermilk, Beth Sarim, San Diego, 1930." The wooden cross in the kitchen. Beth Sarim. It seemed O. Laudermilk was the man at right in the photo, a youngish man about my age, his features partly blocked by the slanted brim of a dapper hat. Was this my grandfather? I'd never seen the photo before in my life.

I took the family album and the strange Laudermilk photo into the hall and set them on the floor by the bathroom door. I washed the wall and the tub. Stepping into the shower, I put my face in the cold rush of water. The spray and the water needling on my skin, I thought of rain, how different and dirty a falling rain on my body would feel. A barbed gray headache was starting.

Amad answered in just two rings.

"A big hello, my Josie! You did not call me yesterday. You forgot. What happened?"

"I miss you," I said. "Believe it or not."

"Where are you? You are in New York?"

"I'm standing here completely naked in my father's bathroom, right out of the shower."

Amad bit into what sounded like an apple. "The open-air lingam."

"You're eating an apple."

"I am."

"What's an open-air what?"

"You right now are an open-air lingam."

"My skinny business in the open air."

"Exactly. Like a stalagmite." Another bite. "Or stalactite, depending on your good mood, or bad mood. How long will you be staying?"

"Very nice," I said.

"So short-tempered."

"What's the weather like out there?" I poked through the linen closet and picked a clean white towel.

"Perfect. Like every day in California. My least favorite thing about this place, no bad days."

"How's business?" I said.

"What business?"

"Very funny."

"Very bad."

"I'll be back soon, and we'll have that dinner. I promise."

"My wife is not so impatient, but she wants to know what are we doing now. And I'm not sure what to tell her."

"Tell her the storeroom is glorious."

"How is your father?"

"I'm not sure."

"What do you mean?"

"What do you mean what do I mean? He says he's fine, and he's clearly not. I'm not sure of my role here. The man looks like he's been hiding away in the hills."

"It can be very nice in the hills."

"Not what I mean." I wiped at the mirror, clearing away the steam. "He says he's fine."

"I spent summers as a boy in the Zamuri hills, took my bath in the river. Wore only a light wrap at the waist. Turban. It was very pleasant."

I dried myself with the towel, cell phone wedged at my bent neck. "Anyway. He's fine, and he's not fine. I'm fine. Are you fine without me?"

"Tip-top." I heard something downstairs, Dad walking around; it made me think of a ghost and I wondered if people who believed in ghosts always believed in ghosts, or was it just something you *felt* one day and so you started believing.

I asked him, "What are you looking at right now, exactly?"

"A completely empty store."

"Numbskull. Go outside. What do you see?"

"Hold on. Wait. I'm walking. I'm going outside as we speak and, like I said, it's a beautiful day. Big deal. The pretty blond girl on her skateboard. Seagulls on the bench picking at a muffin."

"You need anything at all, you call me. I gotta go and dry my godly member. I'll call you."

"Be praiseworthy, Josie."

I wrapped my waist with the towel and walked back downstairs with the photo album under my arm. Litter grit stuck to my wet feet on every last step, and I saw my duffel bag was now with the garbage bags by the front door. I couldn't remember if I'd drunkenly left it there, or maybe Dad thought it wasn't worth keeping. I put the album on a step, opened my bag, and took out some undershorts. Towel around my waist, I tried pulling on the shorts but a large fly was buzzing around my face like a live wire. My foot got caught in the crotch of the shorts. I lost my balance, reached for the banister—

"What are you doing?"

My towel fell to the floor.

He was standing there, now wearing sandals and wide Bermuda shorts, which made his legs look storklike.

I pulled on my shorts. "Lost my balance."

He went back for the kitchen, shaking his head.

I was suddenly very annoyed, and everything I'd been thinking boiled over and out of me.

"Why are there dirty plates beside the door? And why is there a sponge"—I saw a sponge—"a disgusting sponge, is it milk? It looks like milk. Why is there a wet, milky sponge on the floor?" I put on pants as quickly as possible, socks and a T-shirt; where were my shoes? I cursed the fact that I hadn't brought sandals. Even he had sandals. I rubbed at my wet head and hair as I entered the kitchen, blinded by my hands, knocking against a wall. "You have nothing to say about this? The trash in this house? I mean, we haven't even talked about the trash in this house." I kept rubbing at my head. "It smells like a garbage strike in here." The headache was back, my bones were sore, and all the worry I'd been feeling was mixing with my frustration at his refusal or maybe his inability to see the desperate state he was in. I was overflowing with anger and confusion and a terrible sense of help-lessness, more than anything else, when I think about it, which masked itself as more anger and confusion.

I looked up—nobody there.

I pulled the window shade and it snapped up like a waking eyelid. The sunlight surprised me. I raised my arms against it and pulled the shade back down.

"There's a dead mouse on your windowsill. Just so you know."

I flipped the light switch. The bulb buzzed, it flickered. I crossed the kitchen and looked at the shield hanging on the wall. Nothing special, far as I could see.

I said, "And you have good water pressure!"

"I installed that shower!"

"So you can hear me." I walked to the dining room, draped my towel on the back of a chair. "Do you have any aspirin? I'm starv-ing. And it's pretty ridiculous that we're sitting around like there's nothing wrong. I'm supposed to be doing something! You know I am."

He was sitting at the computer. Lights out, drapes pulled shut, a bluish glow was painting him the colors of aquarium water. The light in the room lessened from dim and dimmer to dark, from kitchen, to dining room, then to living room. He was typing, one finger at a time.

"Dad."

My bedsheet was balled up under the sofa. I dove to my knees and snatched it, snapped it, shaking it wide and white. Crumbs dropped like sand on the coffee table. I folded it, neatly, and set it on the back of the sofa. A cat tried to sit and make it its bed, but I smacked at its fat crispy bottom.

"Dad. Please."

"What?"

"The house—look at me. This place is making you sick. I'm not kidding."

"Don't be mean to the cats. How was your shower?"

"Why?" I was going through my pockets; where were my cigarettes?

"They're on the dining table. You can smoke inside, you know."

"Oh, can I?" I came back lighting a cigarette, and from the side of my mouth, I said, "Because I don't want to make a mess and dirty up your beautiful home."

He looked up. "I don't remember you being this funny." He clapped his hands together. "I found it!"

I sat beside him in the marine light, the screen framed by yellow-going-green sticky notes.

"Read it," he said.

"What?"

"They have it." He pointed at what looked like an auction website. "Read it."

I read out loud, "*The Apocryphal Scripture.*" The word "apocryphal" was vaguely familiar.

"*Of the Old Testament.* By R. Charles." He beamed bluish in the light. "First edition, 1913."

"You're buying this."

"I'm trying. It's inscribed!"

This struck me as strange, from a man who refused to own an answering machine. But it also made sense that he'd be attracted to the book.

"I haven't done this yet," he said. "How do you do it? I order mostly groceries so far."

I tapped the ash on the rug, and I didn't give one shit about doing it. He looked at the white ash on the dark floor, and then at me. He gave me a cheeky smile, like he very much approved.

He said, "I haven't done this yet on the computer. You make an offer, I think."

"You've been looking for this book."

"Junior, the computer is a miracle. Look inside and find what you need. And don't worry, I know what else is in there, too."

"You've read this book?"

"I showed you." He pointed back to the dining room. "The big one on the table."

"You have it already." I was confused.

"But this is from 1913, the real deal first one. Inscribed! By Charles's own hand! Mine's brand-new; I ordered from a college bookstore."

"Since when does my father collect books? Or anything. Wine bottles, toothbrushes."

"This is scripture! God's Word, older than most of the Bible, bet you never knew." He looked at me. "If I could crawl inside and find this book and bring it back, I would."

Sarah had talked to me about this, and I had no idea at the time what she was talking about. I don't think she did, either. She was reporting whole sentences he'd said, telling me that he told her during one of his recent phone calls that he was no longer interested in "endings," only in "the first things," "beginnings." What first things? He said he was reading about Gnosticism, and Judaism, and he was intrigued, because what's a first thing if not Judaism, right? He wanted to know if she would help him facilitate some kind of understanding if not a full conversion to Judaism because he was sure she knew someone on the inside.

I stood up, and said: "No more. Enough! This house isn't good for you. It's bad for me, and I'm only here two days. We're going on a trip, a quick trip. And I'm gonna call up a doctor. I can't take this sitting around anymore." I was moving in small circles, not going anywhere. "What if you have symptoms and you don't even know? What if you're sick, if you have something? God forbid, but look at you! This is ridiculous. And I'm supposed to be taking care of you."

"I'm going the way of all flesh." He fell back down to the sofa.

I said, "This isn't normal."

"Physician, heal thyself!" He was very proud of this line.

I put out the cigarette on my shoe and threw it on the table.

He took the cigarette butt from the table and tossed it across the room. He grinned at me. "Hah!"

"What?"

"Let go, Junior!" He tried standing again. I helped him. "Just let go!"

"I need to make a call."

He was laughing. "You think I'm nuts. It's perfect, really, perfect!"

"What are you talking about?"

"I'm talking about Revelation!"

"I can't do this."

"If anyone can talk Revelation, it's my boy."

He was standing there, swaying as if a crosswind were blowing through the room. I thought he'd fall any second now. And I'm not sure if I said it to hurt him, or really just to get his attention, like slapping somebody in the wild throes of a breakdown. Either way, I just said it: "I was a kid. I made that shit up. And you know it."

He reached out for the computer screen, and steadied himself. He held fast to it, for support, and his chin fell into a tremor.

"I'm not stupid," he said, and waved me away. "Just tired."

I followed him to the bathroom, asking him, "Please, just please let me in." I tried to follow him inside. I wanted to help. He pushed me away. I threatened to remove the door from its hinges, to which he said: "I am still your father."

I sat at the kitchen table flipping through one of the photo albums. I saw pictures of our family at the park; on vacation; at church services and congregation barbecues. I saw school portraits of me from kindergarten on through high school, nearly every year, on two pages, my hair longer and less conservative from junior high on, a taxonomy of coiffured rebellion. There was one year, eleventh grade, when I briefly sported a meek attempt at a Mohawk, the sides not entirely shaved. I lacked nerve. The photographer had to tamp down the central tuft. This was soon repaired by way of Dad's electric clippers.

And there were pictures of my mother. I chose two, peeled them out from under the laminate, one of her in a high 1960s beehive, beaming like a supremely happy young woman in the passenger seat of a white convertible. She looked like a real lady of her day, ecstatic. Must've been taken before Dad. The other was a mom I knew, sitting in the sun with an arm around each of her boys, Dad and me, holding on to us like she'd never let go, no matter what, forcing a smile. I used to get the feeling that Mom wasn't afraid of anything at all, and that as long as she was here Dad and I would be well taken care of, that she kept us grounded. But really, I think Mom was afraid of something, of Dad's insatiable hunger for God, and if not for her and her fear I believe we all would have spun off into space and lost our minds already. It occurred to me that maybe Dad knew this, too.

I kept looking through the album, at the faces of people long gone, at cousins I'd never see again, at the faces of fellow congregants playing Frisbee at Bible-study picnics. And then I saw the face of little Issy. It sent a chill through me, literally. It was a class photo from elementary school, along with other class pictures of kids I knew from church. He was a boy, just a kid, seated next to an American flag respectfully draped over a globe, a golden curtain behind him. Of course I'd seen the photo before, but I'd completely forgotten about it, and somehow it was immediately the distillation of my every memory of him. This was Issy. His lips partially constricted, his hair a little mussed like he had just scratched at the back of his head. Everything about the face suggested a little boy, thoughtful and completely lost. Yet here he was. Right here. I peeled away the photo and put it with the others. I still wanted an aspirin.

I looked at the phone on the wall. It was avocado green and right where it should've been. This was the phone Mom answered when the school called saying I was absent. Yet again, your son isn't here. I used to wonder what made her angrier: that I was cutting school or that I was spending my time with the "Hindu girl." I wanted more bread and butter. The weary and wine-sugared brain cells were in need of funneling. I needed focus. So I poured a glass of cool water and took out the butter dish and bread.

I'm not a butter person, and yes there are what can be called butter people. French food, to this day, makes my stomach rumble. I know it's because of the butter. I don't like the slick it leaves in my mouth. Sarah used to say food is the truest mirror, and never trust the man reveling in Buffalo wings, with no regard for sauce on his fingers, with the pile of red-soaked Handi Wipes beside him as if emptied from an autopsy bin. I don't like things too rich. Yet I lavished the stiff bread with butter, knifed it on smooth and soft. I put a small pat in the freezer and let it harden. I ate the pat whole and started to feel a little bit better. Dark marbles of cat shit and white foam kernels of packing littered the floor like monstrous nodules of salt and pepper, and entire populations of cellular villages in my blood were running, ecstatic, as planes dropped boxes of butter from the sky. I opened the window shade as my father walked in.

"Good morning, sir. Again." I sipped from a glass of water. "You know it's nearly noon."

Hands at his eyes, and batting for the light switch, he said, "What's this?"

"It's called daylight. And as long as I'm here and you insist on living in a cave, I will have one room where I can go and live like a person."

"I was sleeping."

"I should have called a psychiatrist by now."

He rubbed at his eyes.

I held up my bread. "Can I please make you something to eat?"

He was considering something, looking up to the ceiling, bit-ing his lip. His shirt was wrinkled and situated oddly on his torso. His stomach peeked from under the hem, the skin shiny and stretched. And yet I swear he'd lost even more weight in the last two hours. He started forward. And he wavered there for a moment. What little color he had was draining from his face.

Then he fell over, catching himself on the counter.

"Hey. Whoa. Come here." I took him by an arm.

"I'm fine!"

I lifted him anyway, and brought him to a chair. I looked at him and wondered what my own kid would have looked like: part me, part Sarah, and, somewhere in the mix, partly this skinny old man. . . .

"Ankle's just tricky, I'm fine."

"You're not fine." I jogged to the living room, thinking now I would not take no for an answer. This was too urgent, and I would call for a doctor. On the floor beside a sofa leg, a cat was sniffing at my phone. I kicked at the cat and she cried out.

"Get in here," he called out. "Just follow me."

I found him pulling himself along the hallway. "You're like your mother. So protective, and when you get grumpy, every-body watch out." He was clutching the bathroom doorknob now. The red light was leaking from under.

He said, "You like eggs?"

How do you answer a question like this?

He pointed at my mouth, at something on my face. "You like butter, that's obvious, but do you like eggs?"

He opened the bathroom door.

It was dark inside, except for the plump red night-light plugged in above the sink. He nodded, prompting me to enter. It was very much like a darkroom. Negatives should've been dangling from clothespins affixed to the shower rod. And I have to say the red glow became spookily attractive pretty fast. The bathtub was full of water, clean and clear red water. A short cot, raised not six inches from the floor, was next to the tub. A thin mattress. A pillow. A black spiral notebook. He followed me into the red room and closed the door. I couldn't help but think of horror movies: I would now be bludgeoned. My father standing in the dark Martian light was shorter than I thought he should be. He was delicate and looked so fragile. I wanted to lift him and lay him on the cot. I wanted to pat his head with a wet cloth and read the man to sleep.

He perched himself on the side of the tub and said, "My head is the egg in here. I keep it warm and wait for dreams."

"You have dreams."

"I have dreams. And then I go looking for your mother."

He put out his hand, I took it, and he pulled himself to a

standing position. I wondered how much trouble he'd had before, having to lift himself, all by himself, from the cot. He opened the door and went back in the hallway. I stayed there for a moment, surrounded by the red walls of another man's insides, his stomach, his heart and lungs. I was foreign matter in my father's blood and I almost knew every secret, just this side of the blood–brain barrier. Somewhere just beyond the red walls, in who knows what other invisible place, I would find the dreaming brain of my father. I found him sitting at the dining room table.

He was looking away to the bare wall, coughing. He wiped at his mouth. "I don't care about church anymore. Not even the first church, first century. I wanna go back before that. I wanna go where we found God. And that's not here, I can promise you." He made a twirling with his fingers, and snorted.

"You're angry," I said.

"I've wasted too much time."

"You have not. Don't say that."

His face shone out all white: "This is not your body. Don't tell me what I've done."

I nodded.

"There are rules. Lay by a body of water. And the bath works out just fine." He shook his head like he was trying to stop himself from dozing off. "Pharaoh had dreams. Joseph read dreams. Daniel, Ezekiel, Enoch." He pointed toward the book on the table. I remembered our family Bible studies, and those names came at me like thrown ghosts. I practically had to duck. We'd spent almost an entire year, as a family, reading the books of Daniel and Ezekiel. At one point Dad had a large sketch pad set on a wooden easel—he'd bought these from a hobby shop— propped beside the dining room table. He drew childish drawings, stick figure versions of the visions found in these books, hoping they would make it all come more alive as he taught us. The Four Horsemen on stick figure horses. A throne looking like a geriatric shower chair for the elderly, floating over a typical cartoon cloud; everyone knows how to draw a cloud. I'd never heard of the book of Enoch.

"The first revelation," he said. "The very first, Enoch's dream in the apocryphal scripture. And that right there is the kernel." He hooked his thumb in the direction of the open book on the table. "This is hundreds of years before Revelation, before St. John comes along, before his blanket on Patmos beach."

"You need water? I need water." He waved, No.

I excused myself and went to the kitchen. And I knew he meant the kernel like in corn or a seed that grows, but I also thought of Amad, and how he'd be so proud of his little Josie for remembering his lessons over the years: a kernel is also the computing center, the core of any system, the small essential thing that remains in fixed memory forever. I breathed and went back to the table.

He took the water from my hand and he drank it.

He said, "John lay on a beach and he fasted. Another rule. No food, not a bite. So really I'm cheating on Sundays." He sipped again and handed back the glass. "And God gives John his revelation in a dream. But this is John's dream, it's not mine."

I drank from the water.

"Revelation, chapter twenty-two," he said. "Just before he's finished. 'If any man adds or takes away from these words then God will erase his name from the Book of Life.' Kaput. He's saying, Don't put words in my mouth. And don't go messing with my dream." He reached for the glass again. It was empty. I made to get up for more water and he gestured for me not to. He said, "What thou seest, write it down in a book. What thou hast seen, and what things there will be thereafter. You have to write it down."

"Okay."

He was looking at his lap now. "Tertullian fasted." He looked up at me, like it was time to finally say this, and we both knew it, so let's just go ahead and say it. "I understand why we don't—why you and I don't ever talk about some things."

"We're fine. You and I are fine."

"Why we are the way we are." He pushed down on the table and lifted himself. He said, "Have I embarrassed you? If I do, or I ever have, just be good enough to forgive me. Would you do that for me? I think every father does this to his son."

I had quick flashes of remembered moments that exactly fit the expression. Of course, I'd been embarrassed by my father, but what son can say this never happened? I knew no more about how to be a son than he did about being a father, and we'd had our respective jobs for the same amount of years. We'd had these idealized visions of each other that we loved, but they weren't us. I'd always loved Dad, but always a more palatable version of the man. *This* was embarrassing. I was the one who should've been embarrassed.

"I feel close to you," he said, and I saw his eyes change.

"I should've been here more," I said, "checking up on you."

"Oh, no, no. I give you a hard time, but look at you! I'm so proud of you making your way. Your own way. And on your own. You're way stronger than I ever was."

I never expected to hear something like this from him, never. How easily we forget how love works, that we love in the only way we know how. He was right there in front of me—but then he went gone in his eyes. It was the first time I saw this, and it frightened me.

I said, "Dad, you're so strong, it scares me. Even when you're wrong." I laughed.

The light suddenly came back alive, and he stood there steadily. He said: "I have walked in Heaven, and I have seen your mother. I saw her just this morning." His eyes were glassing over, and getting full. "I have been in the presence of the Lord because He walks in the halls of my head. He takes me up! I've seen everything there is, and whatever is left for me after." He touched my face. "Suicide is a terrible sin, but this is not the taking of a life. I swear it's not. I'm just giving it back."

He wiped at his eyes.

Leaving the room, and holding his side, he said, "I'll eat with you later, tonight, I promise. I think I'm done for today. Talk later tonight, okay? I'll get some sleep."

I licked my teeth.

"And tomorrow," he said. "You can call your doctor. I don't mean to scare you like this."

He opened the bathroom door, and then the door closed quietly.

I decided I needed a walk, and that I could not spend the remainder of the day indoors. He'd be sleeping anyway. I needed air and light. A low and dour rumbling in my stomach. I wanted to be far from that house, and so I headed for the train, walking as if my legs alone knew the destination, but my head had no idea.

The elevated train snaked along over the rooftops and the laundry lines strung between fire escapes, past the graffiti-covered houses and the wide-open top-floor windows, old women in pink scratchy hair curlers and soiled tank tops with their arms over sills, taking me to yet another train, and then to yet another which took me underground and way across town. I sat there looking at the photos of my mother, of a halfway anonymous O. Laudermilk mock-hitching a ride in old-time San Diego, and of Issy on grade school picture day.

I got off the train in Astoria.

I walked up the stairs to the sidewalk. Latin dance music played from the speakers of an old souped-up Toyota, the sound bigger than the car. On the corner a man served halal sandwiches from a large kitchen cart that looked like a freight elevator yanked from its shaft. I found myself staring at a Spanish bodega sandwiched between two Greek restaurants. Yellow awning, red letters. Posters on the windows for phone cards. I needed more coffee.

The woman behind the cash register had a round face. And behind the deli counter window was a stack of random deli meat nubs, elbow knots of ham wadded up in cellophane, a white dish presenting nothing but a mound of decorative green plastic garnish. I asked if she had any soy milk.

In a totally surprising and dragging Slavic drawl she said, "You are kidding, correct?"

"Yes. I'm kidding. Plain milk, no sugar. And a bagel."

She winked. "With butter?"

My stomach gurgled. "Absolutely not." I pointed to a packet of aspirin.

I sipped the coffee and swallowed the four aspirin, walked outside, and studied the building's exterior. It was a yellow brick four-story walk-up. Next door, a sign over a 99¢ store read "Poco Poco." A table out front was piled with plain white T-shirts and a tilting stack of pink and blue scrub sponges. From the open door blew a nimbus stink of chemical dyes.

Across the street was a small garage with a sign that read "Fix-a-Flat." On the oil-stained sidewalk in front of the garage a box radio on a torn leather recliner played fast English metal. High operatic vocals. An older man in a Motörhead T-shirt came out of the garage and saw me. He lowered the volume, and waved in a vague way. He looked a few years younger than Dad. I imagined he had just one child, a son about my age, and they shared an expensive set of custom tools, they lived on the block. They drank beer together and even came to blows once, ten years before, at a cousin's wedding. And now they worked in the same garage and were always arguing over the radio station. Dad shakes his head saying I don't care if they do come from Queens, it doesn't get any better than Motörhead. They never speak of God, of devils and demons, of Armageddon, they never speak of any life but this one, and never once have they figured that the mystery of love and hate, and war and peace, and sex and food and Motörhead should not be enough for us on Earth. It felt good to be out of the dark house, and to be out walking in the sun.

I looked at the photos again and felt that somehow they made for some weird metaphysical equation that resulted in my eventual going back. Then, one block away, there it was: the Queens Howard Theater. The mammoth overhang of the copper marquee shined like a billion flattened pennies. Spelled out in big block letters: "The Landmark Queens Howard Theater." I stood under it. A large bronze plaque between the two front doorways read, "Placed on the National Register of Historic Places." Beneath that, black letters on a shiny new gray-metal sign, "Tours Given." I got queasy as I remembered standing in that very same spot holding my mother's hand. She had a brand-new perm, and Dad wore dark maroon penny loafers. Sermon notes were folded in my suit coat pocket, a *Star Wars* figure somewhere on my person.

I opened the doors.

Inside, the place was old and stately, but crumbling, once majestic, like the foyer of some failing antebellum estate. The ceiling still arched high above and a chandelier gently rocked there like a cracked crystal palace above an empty marble fountain. A rusting sign beside the fountain pool read "The Looking Glass." At either side of the pool, alabaster columns stood at the base of opposing marble stairways that rounded outward and upward. They looked like a pair of smooth white bull's horns leading to the second floor. The foyer walls were separated into rectangular paneled sections, with an elaborate molded framing for each. Within each frame were fading murals, depictions of famous biblical scenes. *The Binding of Isaac. The Four Horsemen*, white, red, black, and pale. Some of the murals were cracked, some vandalized, others surrounded by scaffolding. A handful of people were on the scaffolding lightly brushing at the walls.

No one seemed to mind me taking the stairs.

At the top, I turned and saw the rigging that held the chandelier in place. I pulled the bagel from my pocket, unwrapped it from the napkin, and bit off a soft chewy lump. There were voices behind me.

A small group of ten or twelve people; about half were young children and teenagers. The kids looked bored and restless. Some wore headphones. A man in a light pink seersucker suit and over-sized horn-rimmed glasses was leading them. He said to me, "Did you want to join us? We've not yet seen the Great Room."

I made an embarrassing animal grunt, my mouth stuffed with bagel, and I nodded, Yes, please. Taking my place in the back, I puffed out my cheeks, making a funny face at a small boy who had a furrowed brow and wispy eyelashes. He turned away. Who was this kid?

"The chandelier weighs six hundred and fifty pounds," the guide said. "And if you wonder how in the world they do this kind of thing, the flowers and candle shapes, the entire piece is made of soda glass."

The small boy said, "What kind of soda?"

The guide went on as if he'd not heard the kid's question. "She'll be back in working order soon enough. The fancy parts all fixed. But it's a slow and very expensive process."

A freckled boy of about sixteen quickly took off his head-phones. "How much?"

"A lot."

"But how much? A million?"

I was sure at this moment that raising a teenager must be a hellish thing.

The guide brushed at the arms of his suit, facing away from the group. "The chandelier, I'm afraid, is a nagging question. It's not of Howard origin, and we're not sure where it comes from." He turned and faced us. "We're in the business of restoring the original state and spirit of a place." He waved us toward two doors in the center of a rounded wall. "And now we have the Great Room."

He opened the doors. And there it was. I swooned.

How many times in a life do we swoon? I can think of only a few, and this was one of those: a major swoon. I had to grab hold of the wall because my stomach was flipping and I thought I might vomit. Then it stopped. I realized it was also because of the stink. Burning hair.

I asked him, "What's that stink?"

"Sulfur. We're raising the foundation some. Found a pocket way below. Ladies and gentlemen, the Great Room. Feel free to move about the balcony."

This was beyond déjà vu. It was dream leakage and it physically moved me. I had to step back out into the hall for a second. And then I stepped back onto the balcony of the Great Room. And that same odd rush of memory and oversensation rivered all around me: the ceiling, the stage—I saw him clearly down there, little boy Josiah, little me. Behind the microphone, and standing still. The audience wondering if I'll finish. Is the boy finished? I watch him lower his arms and bow. A long second passes and it's clear: *It is finished, the boy is finished, and the audience explodes with applause, four thousand clapping their hands, and they raise their arms, clapping above their heads* . . .

"Sir?" The guide was standing next to me.

"I'm fine. I'm just—" I knocked on the door, inspecting its hinges. "Beautiful work." The headache reared up, reminding me it was still there.

Satisfied, he pressed his hands together in a prayer formation. He bowed. "We do our best." He approached the edge of the balcony and gripped the brass handrail. "The ceiling, of course, is why we're here. Note the surface."

We all looked up, fifteen or twenty feet above our heads, where the ceiling was a steely gray. It had really faded. Some roundish silver and white static stars like milk splashes decorated the surface, a chipping and powdery plaster shown in blanched swaths from underneath. Then the stars began to glimmer and glow. They shook with a slight and unstable radiance, and they went out.

The guide was waving a large flashlight at the ceiling.

He said, "Voilà! You get the general idea."

He turned and cast the light onto a greater expanse of the

ceiling, where it dissipated into an ecliptic glow. "Now imagine the entire ceiling all lit up with stars and planets and shooting stars. All semifunctional until about fifteen years ago. And by then the Skyrograph, our very wonderful projector, was already sixty years old. She is right now, even as we stand here, being restored off premises. One of very few in the world, and did basically, *very* basically, what I just did with this flashlight. Only more. Who sees the moon?" He pulled the pant fabric up from his knees, and crouched. He said in higher register to the small children, "Hmm? Who sees the moon?"

I asked him, "What about the bridge?"

"Well." He straightened. "It's a real bridge, a small-scale replica of a famous bridge, the Rialto in Venice. There were clouds." He pointed with the flashlight. "Usually there and over there."

A real bridge, the Rialto. All this time I had no idea.

The freckled boy asked, "Can we walk on it?"

"Insurance says not right now. But soon." Like the boy, I wanted to walk on it.

The guide continued, "The Howard has passed through many hands. The last owners being a church group who lovingly restored much of the interior and exterior, I have to say. And to whom we are much indebted."

I felt like some of them were eyeing me suspiciously. I thought of Dad; was he sleeping, was he awake?

"Unfortunately, said group was no longer able to afford the building and so they sold the Howard to the city. We wish them well. It should *also* be said the original murals downstairs in the foyer were summarily, and dare I say unnecessarily, painted over when said group purchased the property. Previously, the panels beautifully depicted scenes from classical mythologies. We have promotional literature from the original period with detailed pictures. And we're handling the issue as we speak. You saw the scaffolding, and so . . ." He motioned toward a tall scaffold erected in the Great Room over the seats.

I saw that the balcony was bookended by a pair of opposing red velvet ropes, blocking access to two closed doors.

"Now, prior to the Howard's previous owners, the site was primarily used for entertainment. Onstage theater, and of course"— he presented the stage with an outstretched hand; in that hand was a remote control—"they showed movies." On cue, a massive white screen descended from the ceiling above the bridge. "The last showing was in 1977, the fantabulous age of grindhouse." He paused, appeared to make some decision, and continued speaking. "Do we know the term 'grindhouse,' hmmm?"

I wanted to know everything, all of it, and I was sure the more I knew about this place the more I would know about me. I saw the bridge was hidden behind the screen.

He said, "The last showing was a typical double feature. Deodato's super-gruesome cannibal horror, *The Last Survivor*. And a sci-fi classic, *Logan's Run*."

The children looked at each other. There was visible interest in the word "cannibal." I edged away from the group, physically compelled to see the bridge.

"Who here has seen *Logan's Run*? Hmm? Anyone?"

I dropped to one knee behind a row of seats, and pretended to tie my shoe. I untied the laces for effect.

"Let's take a look from the main room floor, and we'll get the full picture from there."

There was a shuffling of feet. Busy noises from the foyer came in through the open doors as I played with my laces.

"Every last inch of copper has been hand buffed by toothbrush. . . ."

Heels clicked on the marble stairs.

I looked around, stood up after tying my shoe. I rushed to the right side, sidling behind the red velvet rope, where the way led into a narrow hall that ramped upward and curved leftward so I couldn't make out exactly where I was headed. The hall maybe went where I wanted, I was hoping, and I continued along the rise of the ramp in the narrow white hall and I kept on walking until I saw a great wash of whiteness: the movie screen.

It was enormous, a giant's bedsheet.

It dawned on me: I'm out there. *Now.* I'm standing on the bridge *right now.* I lightly stamped my feet. I leaned forward and looked down at the decorative wood, at the latticework.

Then there was a crash of loud static.

A pure static sound came flooding from everywhere and filling up the hall and the whole Great Room, and the white screen suddenly went gray. There were flecks of black and gray, dark, and some darker, all of them dancing on the screen. Then the lights in the Great Room went out. And what was maybe a thread, or a maybe stray hair on a film cel, lashed across my vision like a long whip or a black lightning bolt from above. And the screen filled up with a giant image: a tall cross inside a large circle at least two stories tall. The image joggled and it jerked. There was a loud clicking sound in the static. The cross was there in the circle, and then it was gone.

Then just as fast, the image next took the form of a number, the number 5, a monstrous and backward 5, looming there twenty feet tall.

Then there was a 4, a backward 4 . . .

3 . . .

2 . . .

I didn't look away. I extended my arm and stood on my toes. I slung a leg over the bridge. I reached out, trying to touch the screen, which now was just a few feet away and hanging from the ceiling. I stretched myself and saw the individual white nylon fibers. I stretched myself and touched the colossal on-screen image of the 1. The lights came on, showing everything, the bridge beneath my feet, and the countersunk screws holding all of this together, the formed wooden joists above my head. Right there, beyond the reach of my hand, on the very outer edge of the ceiling, where the ceiling abutted the wall, and not so far from a small

Saturn's wobbly faux rings, was the neatly scripted signature: *Harold Lowell, 1965*. One of the painters had signed his name. Then the screen slowly lifted until every seat below sneaked into view. And then I could see the rest of the ceiling, and every faded body of light, every last crack in the plaster, the scratches, bruises, and pockmarks that inevitably come with age.

I walked along the sidewalk sipping yet another coffee, wanting to share with someone the strange dreamy feeling I was having. I got her voice mail and didn't leave a message.

I walked for a long time through the neighborhoods, past the apartment buildings and the two-family walk-ups, the brick houses so close beside each other, a border space of six thin inches between, the pigeon shit in dry white drips staining the ribbed aluminum drainpipes. Past the cell-phone shops and the Laundromats, the overcrowded railroad apartments one flight up and overhead, and Stinking Lizaveta's Famous Best Russian Emporium. I walked by a large gated mosque, aqua-blue minaret and dome shining, and I remembered there was a Russian Orthodox church just a few blocks away.

As I walked by the church, the doors slowly opened and out came a mass of people, some laughing and cheering down the stairs. It was a wedding. I stopped and watched them for a while. The white flowers adorning the railing and the long limousine parked at the curb. Bells were ringing, and the bride and groom wore red ornate crowns on their heads and they were both quite serious and also just short of cracking up. The older ones were stoic and congratulatory and appropriately delighted, and the younger ones in dress shirts with no ties or jackets, collars open at the neck, carousing and acting so healthy and happy, so outwardly and openly, that the whole street came alive with new life. The trees tossed pale green and yellow flowers from their arms and the light breeze made my hair move. I walked on past the Irish bars and the Italian delis until I found myself under the elevated N train.

I stood there beneath the high-up tracks. Shadow planks on the street and sidewalk as the train rattled by overhead blocking the sun and letting the sun through intermittently between the railcars. I thought again of my father, and of how many different kinds of people there are in the world, and I felt terrible for enjoying being away from the house for so long. Across the street was an abattoir for chickens in an extra-wide two-car garage. Steel shutter doors were rolled down halfway. There were feathers in the hot air, limp floating on the exhaust fumes, spinning and darting about in the traffic gales. I smelled metal and blood, and heard the buzz of bone saws, but not the cluck of a single chicken.

There was a buzzing at my waist. It was Sarah, and I broke into a sweat.

I said, "Okay. First. Let me say I'm sorry, but it's been an emotional trip. And I keep calling and hanging up and calling again because I know I need to stop calling you. And I was going to leave a message—"

"Forget it. I'm calling because I want to know about your father."

"So far, a very odd trip." A tall, zaftig woman in peach velour crossed the street while nibbling on a hot dog. I was still hungry, and this made me think of a knish. I wanted a knish. And maybe another aspirin.

"So talk," she said.

A city bus bulleted beside me, only inches from the curb.

"Well, to begin with, he's sleeping in the bathroom."

"What does that even mean? You need to give me more information."

"Sorry, it's noisy. Hold on." I left from under the train and walked along the block. "He sleeps in a little red cave."

"I have no idea what you're talking about."

"Everything's gone to shit. And I mean shit. The house is, I don't know what." I took a breath. "A giant litter box, cat shit everywhere."

"He has cats?"

"He's become one of those cat ladies with crap and litter on the floor."

"What else?"

"The house is a wreck, I can't do it justice. He weighs fifty pounds. You were totally right. He's in a very bad way. Never goes upstairs, I don't think he even has the strength to go upstairs, and he's living in the downstairs bathroom. I know this sounds like, What am I talking about? Give me more information. But I don't have much more information. Are you there?"

"Okay, slow down, slow down. You okay? I don't want to worry about you, too."

"He sleeps on a cot in the bathroom. All day. With a cute red night-light so it's extra fucked. And he says he talks to God in his dreams. They have conversations. He sits in His lap. He sees my mother, and kisses my mother. He's sleeping all day. And it's not like I think he's crazy. I don't know what I think. And he's buying things on the Internet, I don't know what besides toothbrushes and wine and cat food, and I had an experience today like I've never had before, like I'm the one going crazy."

"Why the bathroom?"

"I don't know. There are rules. He fills up the tub. And this is why I called you, I mean, why the messages. I want a knish."

"Mmmm."

This is the secret for walking in cities against the oncoming crowd: look down and pay no attention to others. Walkers parted like the Red Sea in front of me.

I said, "What's amazing is I can go for days, weeks in Otter and not see as many people as I'm seeing right now. And I think he's in pain. He's not eating, not a bite since I got here."

"So what exactly is he doing?"

"He sits there next to the tub. He's talking to me about eggs. There are garbage bags in the hallway, full garbage bags."

A hot dog cart was on the corner. There was a radio, badly spray-painted white, blaring beneath the umbrella. A game announcer said, "Be sure the Babe is rolling in his grave." I walked over to an apartment building and sat on the stoop. "I think he's in pain. And I think I have to call an ambulance or force him to go see a doctor."

"Or the police."

"I'm not calling the police. There's no *crime*."

"I mean to help him. Or the hospital for help."

An elderly woman gave me the stink-eye as she walked by and into the building. "Talk to me about something else," I said. "Just for a second. What are you doing? What room are you in? Describe the room."

"I can't believe now I have to worry about you."

I said, "I've never seen your apartment."

"I'm in my kitchen, the lightbulb over the stove. I'm dipping, as we speak, a bread heel in tomato sauce."

"I'm starving. Tell me something else."

"I'm reading Revelation again. Because it's my job to read. It feels like a peek inside your brain. Every book in Hebrew is eaten by this book. It leaves nothing. I also happen to be translating a book of Hebrew poems, so I'm especially sensitive. I'm thinking of teaching it next semester."

"You're wasting your time with Revelation."

"William James, by the way, you should read him if you haven't. You'd love him. He says if you want to see the significance of a thing, you look at the exaggerations. The perversions of a thing. This is your book."

"It's not my book. What's your Greek's name?" Because I didn't yet know.

A pause. "His name is Nikos."

"That's ridiculous. Are you serious? Totally predictable."

"He's a colleague."

"Well, I hate Nikos."

"The book is fascistic. And fetishistic."

I held the phone away for a moment.

I said, "What'd you have for lunch?"

"I had a kiwi smoothie and this. A long run before my flight. We're going to see my parents."

"We."

Another pause.

I said, "*We* never went and saw your parents."

"I know."

Both of us were silent.

"But he's not there now," I said. "You're alone."

"All alone, just the way you like it."

"Why say things like that?"

"I happen to be having a very tough year. But why would you know anything about that? I called my father and told him I wanted to see him. I'm trying to replace your dad with my dad."

"He's an asshole, your father."

"I know."

"And your mother—"

"We're still fighting. And not to mention the book is kind of beautiful in its own terrible way. Like *Texas Chainsaw* is beautiful. The lighting is perfect."

I lit a cigarette, and a fat black pug came sniffing at my feet. She looked up at me, panting, tilting her head. The owner mouthed, "Sorry," and pulled her away.

"I heard the lighter. Stop smoking. Take this trip as an opportunity."

I said, "More about the book, please, if this is what keeps you on the phone."

"I quote, and when the End comes the blood will be as high as the horses' bridles, or something like that. Why horses?"

"God's army rides on horses."

"But why horses? Why not as high as tank treads, if this is supposed to impress me? Or as high as a Chevrolet's side mirrors, and for two thousand years the faithful are wondering, What's a side mirror? What's a Chevy?"

"I'm picturing you behind a pulpit."

"Think of all those futuristic movies in the sixties and seventies. Everyone's walking around in a toga like it's the Roman senate. What togas? Here we are forty years later in the future. Show me a toga. Just one toga."

"You're in a mood."

"It's my mother. Do you need some help down there? And don't think I'm offering my services."

"You mean out there."

"What out there?"

"Out there. You said down there like I'm in Mexico or Texas. I'm out here, to the right. Pretend you and your hairy boyfriend are facing a road map."

"Oh, my God." She hung up the phone.

I bought a knish at the hot dog stand and stood there looking up at the brown wide building, at the fire escapes that climbed and covered its face. I looked down at the food in my hands, a knish nestled in a moist napkin. I totally knew the joy of an artfully knotted potato cake baked by a bearded Orthodox on the Lower East Side, but this was a different thing entirely. Scorchingly hot on the inside, lukewarm chewy breading, a waterlogged wallet smeared with mustard. Perfectly imperfect. Just like marriage, I thought. Then I caught myself. You were an asshole. And so she hung up. I chewed, thinking of her, of her walking, talking on the phone, Sarah with a smoothie spill on the leg of her jeans, her glasses in one hand and rubbing at the bridge of her nose, Sarah in her tiny black socks and neon running shoes, her eyes going red from sad TV movies. Sarah rushing downstairs in an angry huff and slamming our front screen door. Sarah calling me a pitiful, selfish shit, and swinging a steel utensil hard against the back of my neck. I thought of how we hate and love everyone we love. And I thought of her all alone in her new apartment sitting there with her laptop, drinking coffee alone just fine without me, the Greek on his way over for some friendly consoling, and my heart broke open like a sugar bowl fallen from a shelf. I started crying, let it happen for a few seconds, and then I put a swift end to that.

I walked for blocks and watched the blur of passing cars and the people, the overwhelming spectacle of street sounds and color, and I felt not quite a part. Almost, but not quite. Swimming above the city noise somehow, I finished the knish. I stepped around a construction crew and a large black hole in the street. I watched the steel-on-rock stammer of the jackhammer, and the hop of the man's orange helmet as he broke through rock. A small Asian woman approached a hot dog cart. Shock-white bowl-cut hair. She wore purple sweatpants tucked into black leather cowboy boots and pressed a shoulder bag against her belly.

The vendor waved her off before she got to speak.

She came over to me, pulling something from her bag. She looked at me blankly. "DVD?"

"Excuse me?"

"Good quality."

I looked at the cover, at the plastic sheathing in her hand, and I saw running along the bottom like blunt baby teeth the tops of block letters spelling out the sentence NOT FOR RESALE. I stared at this until she lost patience.

"Five bucks." She showed me the palm of her hand.

I continued to look at the case until she snatched it back. She disappeared around a corner down the street.

I shook myself, and called Amad.

He said, "Where are you?"

"I'm sitting on a beige brick step at the foot of a tall apartment building in Queens, not so far from the airport, I think. There's a hot dog cart in front of me. Construction across the street. A large bug is stuck in the rut of a sidewalk square." Oily water from who knows where drained along the curb and toward the sewer grating.

"And what is on your mind, my friend?"

"A woman just tried to sell me a pirated DVD. I thought of you."

"She was Indian?"

"Chinese. I think."

"The immigrant makes you think of me. The shady newcomer. Very nice."

"The software, you idiot. How's today? Any better? I'm trying to be a better boss."

"I have a cousin on my mother's side, he disappeared ten years ago muling CPUs in his rectum from Eritrea. This woman with the DVDs, she could be screaming inside for help. Did you buy anything from her? Did you give her any money at all?"

"No."

"Good. I have regretted almost every purchase from these people. The quality is very often bad."

"I may be here a while."

"And I am here."

"My father's really sick."

"I had a feeling."

"And I really do need you. You know that, right?"

He said, "More than you ever could."

"Good."

We were quiet for a moment.

"Josie."

"Yeah."

"Are you okay?"

"Perfect."

We were quiet again.

I said, "Make sure you give Teri my love. Rub her belly for me."

"I'll do that."

"So I'll be here, then," I said.

"And I am here, my friend."

I crossed the street and walked by the construction workers, by the bright orange cones, the yellow tape. I looked at my phone: six o'clock. It was rush hour. Six o'clock? The day had gone by so fast! No way Dad was still sleeping. I headed toward the main avenue a few blocks away, toward the subway stair that opened like a hell's mouth down inside the sidewalk, and I saw the bobbing heads. The bobbing rise of people coming from the trains, and they just kept on coming. They were shoulder close and moving fast, on cell phones sharing with their spouses, and they were coming fast my way. I used to look down on them, people like this. I said they were already dead. I said, Let them walk along their walls like rats in search of scraps. But now I saw not some marching millipede, khaki-legged and gruesome—no, I saw the quivering, the miscellaneous, the crowded and alive, busy soul of humanity. They came at me, surrounding me and passing like a stream flows around a fallen tree. I stayed very still—actually, I was in the way, and I enjoyed every last muttered complaint they made. Every curse. Then I turned and joined them, I walked, and I would go wherever they led me. Not because this was the true way, or the right way, but because this was just one way among how many ways alongside other people right here on this planet and, my God, that sounds so dramatic but really it just felt nice. I couldn't remember the last time I was so fully alive. Everyone's head was bobbing, and I saw the front doors of every building, and the TVs through first-floor windows. I felt warm air on my skin, wafting up from the sidewalk grates. The sun was going down orange in the alleys. Evening was on its way, and I was suddenly filled with an overwhelming sense of dread. Six o'clock? Why was I out and about gallivanting? With a sick father at home? Who needed me, more than he knew, and was possibly looking for me, and calling out my name at this very moment? I hailed a taxi, and told the cabbie I was in a hurry.

The bathroom door was open and red light poured into the dark hall, the red pooling on the floor and seeping up the opposite wall. My father was on the cot, his arms limp like snapped wings, belly pressing upward like a boil. There was a bottle of wine beside him, an empty glass. He was breathing. It was labored and thin, but he was breathing. I lowered the toilet lid because open it seemed too portentous, too hungry. I sat. I touched his head and his fine hair. It was nearly seven. I told myself I would call an ambulance if he didn't wake in the next thirty seconds. I'd bought some groceries from the convenience store down the street: a frozen pizza, crackers and cheese, a soft apple. I put the groceries on the floor. I dialed 911 and asked for an ambulance. He opened his eyes.

"How you doing down there?"

He smiled. "You remember?" He stuttered a bit. "Preaching from door to door?"

"I do. Some."

"You were what?"

"Maybe seven."

"You were speaking the old language, and that only comes from one place. . . ."

"Hey, I called for an ambulance."

He closed his eyes.

I arranged his legs on the cot and folded the pillow under his head, raising his head.

He pressed his hand to his side. "The body doesn't want to go."

"Maybe you should listen to it."

"No reaching God in a monkey suit."

The red was all around us. Everything was suffused with dark light. He made a look of disgust, and said, "What's all this to me, anyway?"

"There's me."

He touched my knee. "Of course."

"Good dreams?"

He laughed. "I was standing right there," he said, pointing with his finger at the tiled wall, up in the corner by the ceiling. But he couldn't move his arm. "Right there was Rockaway Beach. You remember Rockaway Beach?"

"I do."

"We went with your mother."

"I remember. You threw me in the water."

"I didn't scare you?"

"Of course not. We were playing."

He pointed at the ceiling, and it seemed to take all his strength. "I was hot inside, and light in my belly, and a hand comes taking me to Heaven. Your mother's all light. And you're all light. And all your kids are light."

"I don't have any kids."

He said, "You were an old man standing next to them."

"And Sarah's where?"

"She was light."

I drank some wine from the bottle and held it up to the red

bulb to see how red, my father on the floor, at the bottom of a deep red gorge. I was supposed to save him, to stop anything like this from happening. I had failed.

He asked, "What time is it?"

"About seven."

"A few more hours till Sunday." He looked at my glass.

"You promised you'd eat."

"I will, come Sunday. At midnight."

"That's five more hours. The ambulance will be here by then."

He tried to sit up. "I'm not hungry. Not thirsty. And swallowing hurts."

"You need food and you need water." His face looked flushed. There was a dappling of purple spots along his arm. "I think you have a rash."

"Fine." His eyes were lazy, starting to loll in their sockets.

"You're not fine." The skin around his mouth was cracked.

"Okay," he said. "Go ahead. Get us some bread. And wine."

I helped him sit up. "I got groceries."

"Rip me a piece and bring water. Pour me wine."

"Not a good idea."

"You want me to fight when they get here?" He leaned against the side of the tub.

I brought the bread and the pitcher from the kitchen.

"Pour me a glass." He tried to tear off a piece of the bread. "You do it."

I poured the wine and tore off a piece of bread. I gave it to him. He took the bread in hand, raised it slightly, and said: "The Body of God." He tried to take a small bite, pulling at the bread with his jaw. He dipped the bread in water and sucked at it. He raised his glass of wine.

"You really shouldn't." I tried to take it from him, and the wine spilled some. I let go of his hand. He straightened with a brief surge of strength, and said: "You will not do that again."

He looked at the wine, and then he swallowed it all in one

gulp. Red streaming from the sides of his mouth, he coughed. His shoulders convulsed and he spat. Then he turned, retching into the tubful of water.

He wiped his mouth, and said, "Your grandfather. We used to stay in hotel rooms. He traveled."

I tried to give him the water.

He waved it away, and said, "Took us wherever he went. Every room a Bible." His face was glowing. "Said they came from angels. Angels wore suits, key rings big as hula hoops. A briefcase full of Bibles. Had keys to every room in the city." His head lolling back and forth. "Where are the wings? Got holes in their jackets?"

"You never talked about him."

A long pause. "Hotels give me nightmares."

I took a sip of the wine, and set the bottle on the tub.

"He's been a constant concern," he said. "Your grandfather distresses me."

He was looking at the cloudy bathwater.

"They promised him it was coming." He coughed. "Light from Heaven, and it's all over." He wiped his mouth. "And the faithful will be glorified!" He coughed again. "But then it's the bread truck. And the birds in the morning, and the milk bottles . . ."

I put the glass of water to his lips. He sipped from it, and the cot made a snapping-bone noise.

I realized I was crying, and I let it happen.

He was talking now hardly above a whisper. "You're the last one, a long line of God's men. American men. You're the lucky one. Your grandfather, and his father. And his. You should have a boy. He'll be lucky."

There are brief glimpses that take you outside, beyond. The last time I smoked marijuana, I was thirty-four and sitting with a good client, poor guy had leukemia. My world opened out like the night-black sky and went on forever, unknowable. There is that long sigh that scoops you out all empty inside from your bowels and all through your soul when you're standing at the edge of a thing like the Grand Canyon. You wonder at the marvel of a crack, a single crack that opens up turning into something like this, where the world below breaks open and has nothing to do with you, and knows not a thing of what goes on outside its own rocky moon-mountain insides. And your hand is holding someone else's. Truth comes at you like the floor of an elevator shaft. There are only two good reasons I can think of for God. There is the Good Lord as uncanny family inheritance, a strange great gift from the people who birthed you. Say your prayers before bedtime. Like Dad gave me his God, and his father his, and his father's father, et cetera. Ad infinitum, for all I know. And of course the Good Lord comes in handy when you first meet the creeping fear of anything unknown, the first time He takes someone away forever.

Dad dropped his legs over the side of the cot and readied his hand at the sink. He took the wine from my hands, and I let him. He drank it all down, in one slow and controlled swallow, and said: "The Blood of God."

I helped him pull himself up.

He pressed a hand to the tall red wall. His knees were quaking. He whispered, "We're nothing, you and I, and everyone. Two ways, son, only glory." He paused. "And frustration."

He let go of the wall, and he wavered.

"Glory has been patient." His voice was slurred.

And then he fell.

Everything moved slowly as I reached for him. His arms going around my neck like a lasso, and then it was his weight and my weight together. The pinkish clouds of wine in the water were shifting, and we fell now together, slowly, against the side of the tub. His hand struck the water and our weight knocked hard against the porcelain, and the wine bottle fell in the pool, splashing red water on the walls. A dark blood cloud poured from the bottle, unfurling, rolling, and swirling in the pink dusky storm in the bathwater. The whole sky, all of it, I saw it there like a rippling mirror as we fell back together on the low red floor. I became aware of real time moving around me and beyond me in echoing swirls. I felt we were outside the world somehow, fallen outside and deep inside some borderless moment. It was vast and it was exhilarating. I was aware of my skin, of the very space in my skull, of the infinite space in my skull, of the tidal rush and pull of the so many people we are and can be and ever once were. I was aware of my very own heart, aware in that same way I'd been so many times of my stomach: it was full. My heart was full. I held my father in my arms, and I didn't want to lose him, and I didn't want it to be too late, was I too late? I wanted to go back in time, but I couldn't. And so I became very afraid. Above us, red clouds were poised so still. Then they broke and fell like rain.

EAST AND WEST

4

Desire can be so exhausting, and has way too long a memory. It was early fall, and the leaves were turning papery and thinning on the trees. The afternoons were suffused with that sad and lovely melon glow, when everybody knows the days are getting shorter and those last hours of work and school take on a fresh purpose, letting out in a day already going dark. Halloween candy was falling off the drugstore shelves. I didn't want winter to come any sooner than it had to. It had been weeks since I last spoke to Sarah and told her that Dad was being taken to the hospital.

Part of me wanted to tell her about the nurses giving me nasty looks. I mean, What kind of son lets this happen to his father? How they had to feed him through tubes because a body can only take so much before it breaks down, before it starts eating itself. How my father could not, or would not speak. About how Dad and I shared milk shakes from the hospital cafeteria, and the nurses split them into two small cups, and we used thick plastic straws.

I sat there beside him watching the slow and steady rise and fall of his chest, and made plans for the move because I hoped to take him with me back to California.

I needed to clean the house and get it ready for sale, but so much of my time was spent at the hospital that I couldn't really get much done. I slept in the chair next to his bed and spent my mornings scanning the *Times* and the *Post*, and I thought about giving him a haircut because his hair had gotten so long. I read the magazines and movie guides for celebrity worship: what's she wearing; who is sleeping with who. They were everywhere you looked, on the windowsills, in waiting rooms, by the vending and coffee machines. And I fell in love daily with Latina soap stars on telenovelas. There was a TV affixed in the right upper corner of his room. I realized at some point that I'd not been with a woman for a very long time, and what a pity it was that I hardly ever thought about it anymore, but also that now I was thinking about it a lot, actually. Practically all the time.

I had been casually talking with one of the nurses—in the elevators, or smoking out front in the parking lot. Not my father's nurse, but one of those passing nurses, always swishing through the hallways in her mint-green scrubs. Her name was Leeann and she had a bright blond and glorious Afro, magnetic blue eyes. Skin so fair I could see veins in her cheeks. I'd spoken with her a few times. Always something like Hello, ma'am, overly polite, and she'd say something like Hello, yourself, before I finally realized we were flirting.

We wrestled in a maintenance closet at two o'clock in the morning, where she pressed me up against the wall like this was our last, last chance, and the world was falling apart outside.

The next day, feeling guilty, I wrote to Sarah.

I considered calling. She deserved to know more about Dad's health, but calling felt too easy, anyway. And when was the last time I actually wrote a letter? There was something deliberate and mature about it, or at least I thought so, maybe even romantic. I sent her a postcard of the New York skyline: "Dad's not doing well. Things don't look good. I need to sell the house, which is a mess. I thought you'd want to know."

She called me a week later. It seems Nikos had a conference at CUNY, and while she hadn't planned on joining him, maybe now she would. She could check in on Dad and say hello, if I was open to it.

By the time she arrived, I was no longer sure I wanted her around, which isn't to say I didn't. I did want her, very much. I wanted her there in the house and in the hospital sitting vigil with Dad. I wanted her back home in Otter. And I wanted her every morning after, beside me wrapped in a warm toss of bedsheets, from that day on forever forward. I opened the door and there she was, in her arms a bright white daisy explosion in a cheap glass vase.

She pushed them at me and said, "You're supposed to take them."

She walked past me into the hallway. "So how far away is the hospital?"

In that moment, it was finally over for me. Not just because we were finished, but because we were both revealed, each of us new to the other. I saw her in the light of her new love, and I was standing there in the slant space of my father's sickness, all of which hurt crushingly only for as long as it took me to turn and follow her inside. I asked her where they were staying.

"Downtown, with a friend."

"One of his."

"Yup. My friend, too, I guess."

"I'm happy to hear it." I told her some more about Dad, as she placed the flowers on the dining room table.

She looked around. "This is why I love your father. He is so sad and totally fascinating. Like one of those mystics in the desert. But it's Queens."

I think it was actually those silly flowers that finally let the old house breathe. Like I'd been holding my breath for weeks, I let go a long low sigh.

She said, "I don't see any cat shit. So there's that." She took a protein bar from her pocket, and pulled back the wrapping. Took a bite, and pulled a daisy from the vase, gave it to me. "How can I help?"

She said she wanted to help clean while I sat with Dad. Nikos was out and about working anyway. By the time I got back from the hospital, she'd scoured the kitchen floor, emptied out a closet, and started organizing some of Dad's things. She said she wasn't sure if she could come back the following day. But she did. And again said she could only stay for an hour or so. Nikos (I still find the name preposterous), he understood.

But she stayed all day long.

"He wants me to be happy," she said. "Anyway, he's busy with social functions. Meeting with colleagues. He's never been to New York."

The days got shorter as we filled the boxes with garbage and set them on the street. We rented a Dumpster and joyously threw bags from the upstairs bedroom windows. We kept an ongoing pile of possible saves—the more interesting-looking books, the cleaner clothing. A few tchotchkes, the figurines my mother favored, and a sun-bleached jawbone my father found upstate in 1987. He'd Sharpied the date at the gum line. The wooden cross. The plate. I packed the family albums, and we braved the attic and its noxious air, urine-colored fiberglass falling from the rafters in leprous chunks. We sopped up puddles in the basement, and tried to identify a blue spongy mold. We boxed up his spirals and his papers, because God forbid some garbage picker, some young and impressionable squatter find my father's dreams and exegeses and start a cult. We nudged the cats into the backyard. I carefully packed his mail-order shield in bubble wrapping, removed the red bulb.

Sarah asked if she could stay at the house for a couple of nights, because it was a waste of time going back and forth on the trains. It would just be for a day or two, because Nikos's conference was over; he had other business, but not much, left. I said of course. We'd pretend like it was normal and comfortable. I think it felt, for both of us, like a way to fully bury our past. She slept in my old room, on a bare mattress on the floor. I slept down-stairs, on the living room sofa where I'd been from the start. Sarah went and sat with Dad at the hospital, and he never said a word to her. He just lay there in his semiwakeful state, eyes closed, alpha waves ebbing on the EEG. I was happy to have a break from the hospital, because I don't like hospitals. There's nothing so strange about that. Amad told me he'd fainted at the hospital before even arriving at their inaugural Lamaze class. The doctor talked to me about refeeding syndrome, and the possibil-ity of cardiac arrest and coma. We had to sell the house.

That second day, we both stayed home and cleaned, staying out of each other's way, mostly, and not owing each other a thing. It was like living together again but without the relentless loan and debt of love, or even good conversation. And I finally made a clear and deliberate decision, one I was sure she'd made a long time ago about me. I decided it would be healthier for me if I just didn't want to want her anymore.

I was sitting beside Dad, one morning at the hospital, marveling at the mysterious thing an eye can become when it sees. I asked him if he could see me. He never answered or moved his head. He just looked. I was flipping through the channels, when I looked up and saw the ghostly face looking down at me. I jumped to my feet, approached the TV. It was Issy. I don't know how else to say it, but I saw his angelic baby face up there on the TV screen, his name in white graphic letters, Ismael "Issy" Demundo. I looked around for Sarah because I wanted someone else to see. *Does any-body see this?* But she was back at the house.

The anchor said that recent information had come to light regarding Issy's disappearance, maybe even a possible suspect, whose identity was still completely unknown. A bartender had come forward and described a conversation he'd overheard twenty-five years before. He said the man had a mustache and wore a dirty white T-shirt. The man talked about the missing little boy from Richmond Hill, said he was the one that took him. And all of this would probably not have gotten the attention of the news if not for the fact that the latest episode of a detective show called *Cold Capers* was based on Issy's story, on the resurrection of Issy's case, which had long gone cold but now had a fresh new lead. The photo was the same as the one from our family album. I noted the date and the time of the episode.

Later that afternoon, I read a piece in the *Daily News* on Issy's case, and the perceived epidemic of disappearing children in the 1980s. The article claimed it was most likely media coverage that had changed, and the proliferation of access to the coverage, but that things were no better and no worse, back then, before, or since.

That night, I watched the *Cold Capers* episode while Sarah was on the phone, on the porch. I decided I didn't want her to see Issy after all. I didn't need her to see his face to make it any more real than it was, and I wanted to be alone. The show was disappointing, anyway. They were trying to re-create and make visible his disappearance through interviews with the neighbors and his grade school teachers, and through a not very convincing portrayal of his mother. They tried to condense Issy's most essential earthly moments into fifty-nine minutes, including commercials. The show was followed by some local news coverage. The reporter showed Issy's block, interviewed the neighbors, even spoke with some childhood friends. No sign of Havi, though. Or me, come to think of it. The neighbors wanted details, to look at the ghost if they could, and to play a small part in the drama. Even I did, because the death you never see is your own, so we pay close attention to the others. Earlier that morning, I'd read a short piece on Issy's mother online, about how she'd spent the subsequent decade devoted to finding her boy, every last dollar, and in doing so tried to assimilate every last moment in scrapbooks. The cuts on her face had settled into scars. She had that conquered look of a junkie who'd finally stopped because she had a sadness even drugs couldn't fill. How was it I had no idea of her search? She had seventeen scrapbooks filled with photos, news articles, report cards, and the ripped pages of coloring books. I definitely understood the impulse and temptation to think every living moment deserves its own eschatology. But that's just no way to live.

That next evening, after a long day of cleaning, Sarah and I sat on the porch where it was cool in the shade of the roof, our legs and feet brilliant in the sun going down. Boys were playing handball across the street. We ordered Chinese and drank wine and I told her about growing up in the neighborhood. She asked if I was still running and I said yes, and that I dreaded the idea of ever stepping on a treadmill again.

She laughed.

And for one brief flash we glimpsed the old love for each other, but then we also felt a longing to be somewhere else, with someone else. I thought I saw in her face the suggestion of a playful smirk, but I knew it wasn't for me.

Half joking, I said, "We should go upstairs and see if we still got it."

She laughed, slapped my back, and went inside, leaving me alone.

That next morning the bell rang, and we both jumped, excited to allow another force into our brief afterlife together. It was two Jehovah's Witnesses, a man and a woman, and Sarah and I watched them through the curtains like we were hiding from a couple of trick-or-treaters. I thought vaguely of Bart and Gerard, and how it was not entirely impossible that I would see them again. Then the hospital called. Dad had finally opened his eyes. I asked Sarah to come with me. I insisted. Dad would love to see her.

She said no, better not. It felt like the right time to go, plus Nikos was waiting.

She got her bag together, gave me a long hug, and closed the front yard gate behind her. She waved goodbye. I watched her walk down the street, hoping she would turn back and wave.

A few days later, the doctors said Dad was as ready as he'd ever be. They'd forgo any psychological testing as long as he was released into my exclusive care and custody. The man still wasn't speaking. So we made plans for his eventual discharge from the hospital. I asked the nurses for advice on what kinds of serious problems I might encounter taking him home with me out west. And without them, I never would have given thought to all that sand. He'd need his own wheelchair but forget about taking him to the beach. I said goodbye to the lovely Leeann.

The real estate lady promised it was a one-stop-shop thing with her. She knew plumbers, electricians, whatever. She said definitely keep making repairs but focus on the front yard and porch because this is what sells a house, a porch, and the market was looking pretty strong.

The doctors said Dad showed plenty of promise, even though he hadn't said a word. The eyes were open, but he hardly moved, and they wanted to keep him just another day or so. So I should've been retouching the walls and scraping rust from the back porch railing, peeling paint flakes from the front porch columns. I should have been increasing our "curb appeal," and getting ready for his return so we could finally leave. But I was spending time at my father's computer. It radiated the same bluish glow that colored his face when he was rapt in his own daily online sessions, his hunt for I don't what exactly except that, hospital incapacitation aside, it might have never ended. I let the computer light paint my face, too. I listened to the hum it made when the moving parts got warm and the fan clicked on. I couldn't bring myself to wipe his fingerprints from the screen.

The search history was what you'd expect: Christian sites,

online biblical resources, a community blog for dream journaling, some vaguely conspiratorial religious message boards, even a few genealogy searches. Nothing especially fruitful. But then I stumbled onto a site he'd apparently visited a few times. There was an article there about a place called Beth Sarim (!). It felt like a small mystery was unfolding. I went and got the photo from the coffee table where it lay with the others: "C. Russell and O. Laudermilk." The article said "Beth Sarim," Hebrew for House of Princes, was the official name given a mansion in San Diego, built in 1930 by the Watch Tower Society (two separate words, back then). Beth Sarim was to be a welcoming-home place for "the return of the resurrected prophets and patriarchs of biblical antiquity, like Abraham, and Moses, David, and Isaiah." I was speechless. They'd built a house? An actual house? I sat back in my chair and thought about this. Architects were hired and blueprints were made. A hole was dug and the foundation poured because they were sure the End was just around the corner—and, lo, there would be a resurrection. So confident! Bold, really. I looked back at the screen, kept reading: "The End was to have come crashing by 1914, which would be followed by a resurrection of the faithful, and the Old Testament Princes would lead Mankind while God himself ruled over a new and Perfected Earth from His New Heavenly Kingdom and thus come the final disappearance of Death."

1914. My dear God. And when the Great War hit, they must have salivated. What did they do come 1915? '16? They built a house, for God's sake.

I kept reading: "It was then re-predicted that 1925 would ring out the first mortal blow of Armageddon. Beth Sarim would be Headquarters for the Earthly Princes in the End Times and Forever After."

1914. 1925. 1975. 2000.

What next? *When* next?

I looked at the Laudermilk in the photo, and it had to be my grandfather, young and handsome, with his whole life unexpectedly and aversely ahead of him. And yet nothing chilled me more than to read the final legacy of Beth Sarim. There on the screen, like an epitaph for that barren place as much as for my family: "Beth Sarim is privately owned now, adorned with tall palm trees, terra-cotta tile roofing, and a lush green lawn. It's registered with the city of San Diego as official Historical Landmark number 474."

The agent sold the house just two days after it was listed, to the Sikh temple right around the corner. They were expanding and would gladly pay the full price in cash if I would just please hurry up and leave, and to compensate for any emotional trauma I might experience after hearing their plans to immediately tear the old place down. They would do this as soon as I left the premises. I didn't really know how to respond except by nodding, sipping my cup of coffee. I called a company about a custom wheelchair. A social worker helped me arrange for Dad's release. I called Amad and told him I was coming home, that Dad was coming with me. I stood on that porch and watched the neighbors rake the red, orange, and yellowing leaves into small tidy piles.

It was still dark, before dawn, about a half mile down the beach from home, by the basketball courts. We'd been back in Otter for a week already, and I'd been rolling Dad around town in his fancy new chair, special-ordered, an all-terrain chair rigged for beaches. Large, white, with rubber pneumatic tires. Sky-blue seat cushion. It cost over two thousand dollars, and we were ready for just about anything nature might send our way. I wanted to watch daylight come on with my father.

Beaches are such a strange place in the dark, and so full of sounds, the rush and hush of water. I pushed the chair along on the concrete until we reached the courts. And when I pushed the chair onto the sand, it was exciting to see the wheels at work. The sand slowed us down, but not much, and we rolled along on the beach. We rolled over the sand to the courts, and we rolled over the courts and the painted lines to the short wall surrounding the concrete. I sat down and pulled the brake on the chair. In the center of the court, between the two poles, was a basketball, set in a recessed drain. There was a steel-wire trash bin filled with empty cans and bottles and partially deflated basketballs. A scrunched-up volleyball net spilled over the side. I centered my father in his seat, because he'd been slouching, his hair long and loose. His elbow was off the armrest, almost touching the fat wheel. I dried his mouth.

I said, "The water is right there ahead of us. It's hard to see, but you can hear it."

The sky was dark and deep, and a whole new day was waiting for us. I wiped saliva from his mouth. He wasn't speaking, not because his tongue or his brain had failed him, I think, but because he was exhausted.

I'd quit smoking for good when I got back. The tricky thing with smoking I figured is that you really *want* to smoke—as in, I really wanted to smoke. But then I just no longer wanted to. It happened when we got to California, on the shuttle bus to Otter. I'm not saying it's always this easy. I'm not saying I discovered some secret, I've figured out the cure for lung cancer: *Just stop wanting.* I'm saying I gave it a lot of thought.

I asked him if he was hungry. "Are you thirsty? Is it okay us sitting like this?"

I thought of that parable of houses built on sand. When the rains come falling and the floods come rushing, the houses on rock do fine. But the houses on sand are in for a shitload of trouble. Maybe that's why southern California seems forever destined for trouble, earthquake, fire, drought. I asked him if he remembered the parable.

I said, "Just look at all that water."

I stood up from the wall and walked toward the surf, where the ocean crawled along the horizon like a shadow you could see in the dark. It spat up and sloshed on the shore, coming up at me, and then falling back, like a tease. Think of a river, a long and meandering thin map line of a river, and its delta mouth fanning out and into the ocean. I was staring from the mouth of some great river, at the mouth of some vast unknowable and shapeless thing.

And then Dad called out: "Josiah."

I turned.

I wasn't sure if I was only hearing things in the wind maybe: a seagull, or someone else on the beach. I looked around. But then I saw his mouth move. He said again: "Josiah."

I jogged back over the sand, almost manic, tripping in the catch of the sand. I couldn't get to him fast enough, afraid he might never speak again. I didn't want to fail him.

He was slouching there like a skinny little boy on phone books, a blanket over his legs, getting smaller by the second. I said, "Look at you, you're alive."

He nodded once, affirmative.

"How you feeling? Are you cold?" I was shocked, and trying to work through my shock. I set him straight in his seat. The dune grasses rubbed and shushed in the breeze. There was singing in the distance. He looked over toward the singing.

"I hear it, too," I said. "You been ignoring me? Something tells me you've been hearing me fine all along."

He said, "You sleep well?"

I said, "I couldn't really sleep. How about you?"

"This chair is ridiculous."

I laughed. "I know, I know."

The singing was more than one voice. We saw a fire down the beach, a small fire, a flaring match head from where we sat. He asked me if I had dreams.

"As in last night or what do I want to do with my life?"

"Last night."

His voice was clear and firm, but low. He cleared his throat. He sounded like a man who'd been biding his time until he had something to say.

I said, "Last night, I don't remember. But I have dreams. Look at you, all talkative."

He breathed a great, big, wearisome sigh.

I said, "Sometimes I have nightmares, bad ones. But not as much as I used to."

He faced me as much as he could. "I'm sorry to hear about that."

"Not a big deal."

We listened to the singing and watched the match head bob down beach.

He said, "What about?"

I heard the voices of children. I said, "The usual. Death. Hell. Murder."

I laughed, and so did he.

I said, "I have this one, a recurring one like outer space. No light or stars. But there is this one light, a white pinprick of light. I think it's supposed to be me. And it gets bigger and whiter until it takes everything over. And there's a screaming happening the whole time. Not like a voice, more like a low-flying plane. And it's louder and louder until I can't hear or see anything else at all. And I'm gone. Then I wake up with a hard-on."

"That's terrifying." He laughed while he said it.

A small group was coming up the beach.

He said, "I think my heart is slowing down."

"What?"

"Every day gets a little slower."

"It's slowing down right now?"

He smiled, patted my hand.

They were out there now by the waterline, Boy Scouts in army-green shorts, red handkerchiefs around their necks. A dozen of them, ten or twelve years old. Their pack leader had a torch, and they moved slowly, probably looking for air bubbles and crabs hiding under the sand. They were singing and I knew the song, or at least I knew part of it. I knew the first verse, the chorus. They sang: "As I went walking that ribbon of highway, / And saw above me that endless skyway. . . ." It was lovely. I looked at my father. He wasn't quite asleep but it seemed he'd already fallen back inside himself.

"Dad?"

The group stayed by the water; they'd probably found a jelly-fish. Their singing was petering out, and attentions were else-where. But a few kept singing, and I wanted them to sing because I wanted to hear the rest of the verses. How did the rest of it go? I actually knew nothing about this song, and yet I must have heard it a hundred times.

One of the taller boys threw rocks at the water, and then ran up the beach away from the others. The pack leader called after him and lowered his torch to the sand. The boy ran even farther up the beach.

The sky was opening up some. I saw clouds. A subtle light sneaked up from behind us. There were different shades of blue in the morning.

Dad said, "Maybe it's a dream of Heaven."

"Of what? You okay?"

The light was back in his eyes. He said, "Your dream."

"Doesn't feel like Heaven."

"Heaven is a beautiful place."

"Well, the dream definitely is not beautiful. How do you feel?"

The sky grew lighter. The boys were crouched, poking at some-thing in the sand. The pack leader held the fire up high, looking out for the boy who'd run off. By now, the torch seemed super-fluous.

"What's the most beautiful thing you've ever seen?"

"I'm really glad you're talking."

I turned and looked at the court, at the ball in the drain. The basketball hoops were bare, no nets or chains. My father's eyes went blank again. I couldn't look at his face when his eyes went blank. A rosy mist was dawning in the sky. But the question was a good one. I'd driven cross-country and seen things that won't go away, like when Sarah and I stopped at Cadillac Ranch while driving through Texas. The cars half submerged out there in the desert ground like they'd been here a thousand American years. The headlights and front grilles buried in the sand, and I remember saying to her that the idea of an ostrich doing the same thing is ridiculous. If it were true at all, the ostrich would eventually die away and no longer exist as a species.

He said, "Where am I?"

"You're here with me in California. On the beach."

His eyes glazed dully and he looked at me like I was a stranger.

I said, "Once, we drove through the Redwood Empire coming back from Mendocino."

He looked straight ahead at the water.

"I don't know how many hundreds of feet, the sequoias. Green leaves up top like a beard. Three thousand years old. And all I could think was, Hey, I think this is actually their planet."

The kids were at the water, and the pack leader was looking around.

"Sometimes Heaven's like a house," he said. "But always different."

I tucked the blanket under his legs and said, "Tell me your favorite Heaven."

He wouldn't look my way. He said, "There's a front porch. Upstairs, and downstairs. I saw the room where stars are made."

The water was taking on the lighter colors of the sky.

I said, "I was driving I forget where and saw a mountain on the side of the road. A white mountain, I forget where. Out in the middle of nowhere, scrub brush, and there's this shining mountain of bright white sand."

"Heaven is all white with clouds," he said.

"Like a miracle out there. The full bottom half of an hourglass. I had to cover my eyes, it was so bright. I climbed as high as I could and I swear the mountain was singing and humming right there under my feet."

"Heaven sings." He reached out a hand in the air. "Everywhere, and you can feel Him on your skin, and His throne is like a sky-scraper." He opened his hand in the air. "You can feel the light with your fingers."

"And what else," I said. "I've never seen a volcano. I want to go to Hawaii and see the lava pouring out and sizzling in the ocean, the world remaking itself. I saw something once in Death Valley, or just Death Valley, leave it at that. Rocks in the Racetrack des-ert. One was the size of a Volkswagen. This is way below sea level, no water at all. The rock has a long trail behind it, moves hundreds of feet, and nobody knows why. Like I'm staring at the tree in the riddle. A tree falls in the forest blah, blah and nobody's there to hear it. I was staring right at the riddle."

He said, "Heaven gets dark. It gets dark, and I keep getting smaller."

I looked up, and that boy was coming right for us.

He waved, and his feet made slapping sounds on the concrete as he hurled himself at the ball waiting in the drain. He had trouble bouncing it with one hand, so he dribbled with both. He tossed it in the air, but he couldn't reach the backboard. Dad looked at the water. I stood and said hello to the boy.

His uniform was looking a little shoddy, sand grit falling from every crease. His red tie was turned backward. I put up my hands and he tossed the ball my way. I dribbled and threw it right back to him.

I realized it was the first time I'd bounced a ball on the court. I didn't think I could make a basket. This would be an embarrass-ing failure of adulthood and might ruin him, for all I knew.

The sun stepped over the foothills and over the houses, the pink terra-cotta tiles. There was a dreamy glow of light in the air; the morning mist was wavering and heading for the water. I won-dered how many suns there were: a sun for seagulls, and for Amad's Little Josie, even for the ticks on a stray dog's ass. A dog isn't so

selfish as to think it shines for him alone. I watched the boy
throw the ball and chase it, and throw it again. The boy didn't
know it, but he was me, and I was him, and maybe God didn't
know our names after all. If He did, He hardly said them aloud
anymore because of the thousand ways we daily do our loved ones
in. I figured that waiting for the End is the End. And I figured the
End was already here, always had been, and was happening over
and over and over again, every last one a blessing and revelation if
we'd only take a good hard look.

The boys at the water started singing again: "This land is
your land, / This land is my land, / From California to the New
York island, / From the Redwood Forest to the Gulf Stream
waters, / This land was made for you and me. . . ." Then for some
reason I started to wish they'd stop singing the goddamn song
already. I muttered this, and felt immediately bad about cursing
in front of the boy, because then the boy started cursing as he
bounced the ball. He kept saying "bastard," which sort of cracked
me up.

He said things like, "Our pack leader is a bastard," and, "Today
has been a real bastard." He threw the ball and got it nowhere near
the hoop.

I dribbled, and set myself at the three-point line. It was light
out now and I saw the hoop clearly. I couldn't use the dark for an
excuse. I dribbled, bent my knees like you're supposed to. I bobbed
there with the ball in my hands, and tossed it up in a high sailing
arc, when my father called out with a noise.

He was pointing out to the water.

I went over and knelt there in front of him, in the sand. His
eyes were lit from the inside. I said, "It's okay, Dad. What? I'm
here."

The waves rolled out like carpets plashing on the shore, and
the air was heavy with moisture. I could feel it with my fingers.
The water was deep and long; something forever about the water.
How it lay there how many millions of years already before I ever

came along, and it even let the otters stay until the last one got too old, and filled up with water, and fell through the water like a dark thick leaf dancing in air. The dawning light was on the Pacific like a yellow dust and the horizon had gone soft and disappeared. Dad was pointing and making that awful noise, trying to communicate to me what it was he was seeing.

I looked out again, and saw nothing—until I did.

Out there on the horizon where the morning light was going soft, I definitely saw something. There was this white and floating void quivering just above the water, and above it there was a dark and rising mass floating there in the air. I saw turrets and I saw towers. It was like the silhouette of an almost invisible city, and it hovered like a vision of the Heavenly Kingdom. It was there, *right* there, and I could see it. I bit my lip, hyperaware of how spooky all this was.

Then the boy came up beside us. "What are you looking at?"

Dad was still pointing.

The boy looked, and said, "What? Catalina?"

He started walking back to the group, and said back over his shoulder, "We take the ferry over and camp. Sometimes we stay the night in Avalon." He ran back to the others by the water.

Of course it was Catalina. But Dad looked on without blinking, his face practically radioactive with joy. I saw now the trick of light on the Catalina Island mountains, and the clouds, and the vapor mist along the horizon, and already the mass was changing shape, becoming something altogether different, but no less radiant.

I said, "Dad."

His eyes were blank.

I kissed my father's head, and we rolled back over the sand to the walkway, and I started pushing him home. We took our time. The oil derricks pumped behind chain-link fences beside the Pacific Coast Highway, and by the time we reached my street the morning sky was simply bright and blue and beautiful. I pushed

him up the front path to the courtyard. I rolled him alongside the
building and parked the chair. I touched his face. I unlocked the
front lock and propped the screen door open with a flowerpot. I
lifted him from his chair, and he was light, his long hair covering
his face. I decided it was time I cut it. I carried him, and we crossed
the threshold together.

Some of his things still needed unpacking. His books and
papers were in boxes beside the fridge. Resting on top of his boxes
was a blank red spiral I found myself unaccountably attracted to. I
swore one day I would fill it. The jawbone and a picture of my
young mother were on the coffee table where he could see. His
mail-order shield was on the wall beside the mirror. This was the
very first thing I attended to after unpacking his clothes. The
white cat napped on the back of the sofa. I could not in good conscience leave her behind. The plank flooring had a curved scratch
and groove from the door where it rubbed, and the radiator clicked,
and the stairwell was dark because the bulb had gone too dim. I
saw us in the mirror over the sofa, my father in my arms, and the
mirror caught a shard of sun from outside and flashed, filling up
the glass. I looked at us, a little bit afraid to look away. His head
was on my chest, and he turned away slightly. His long hair moved,
and a sleepy medicinal smell of bedclothes and of days long ago
home sick from school, and of that terminal air you find in waiting
rooms and clinics, and of my mother's soft and hairless campho-
rous head filled up my senses. I steadied myself and set him down
on the sofa. Even if I could get to know all the space in my own
skull, I'd never get inside of his. I combed back his hair and looked
at his face. This was not a gullible man, not at all. I saw a man who
was hungry and cunning in his own curious way, and was stub-
bornly still here, his lost and lank body afloat there on the mystery
of the world.

There are three kinds of time, as far as I can tell. There's God Time, infinity, which really isn't any time at all, but beyond time, and borderless, not in our purview. It's a scary thought, and I'm not so sure we ever come to really know it, whether we go out like space dust in death, like some manna from Earth, risen food for hungry angels, and fall back inside God, or if we fall forever forward, deep inside the advancing cosmos, pure expansion. And there's Earth Time, our time, great clock of the Holocene, and all of it somehow stuffed and stored inside a plastic pocket watch. It's the time of ends and there isn't a single speck of grace or evil outside of it; it's imperfect and enough in its broken wholeness. Then there's the Time of In-Between, outside of place, and inside of sex, of memory and dream, the time of saints, and of the dead we remember. It's the time of two times at once, of invention, of Beth Sarim and supernatural knowledge. It's the time of sticky nostalgic want, false memory, and cheap reminiscence, so be careful. It's the time of the world, and the world that we want. It's from where we pluck the saintly face of Issy. And it's where my father lives, the time of visions.

Look up and see there: the Great Room, the sky, and the ceiling. The boy sees the crack across a butter-yellow moon, and he doesn't know how he missed it. The ceiling is just a ceiling. I see the men and women dead a hundred years, dangling from strung-up leather pulleys, on ladders, and balanced on scaffolding, carefully painting suns and drawing the circles of planets. I see my Dad in that pacific place between disappointment and hope, filling with pride for his little guy standing up there in a nice clean suit. And Mom with long red hair curling over her shoulders, filling up with one day's portion of worry, honor, and delight. And I see Sister Hilda Famosa, frozen cross-legged forever in her balcony seat with her family, like she never got killed

one day because she forgot to look both ways and walked herself
in front of a speeding city bus on Queens Boulevard. I see the
little boy Issy running past me at lunchtime, crazy looking for
the girl in the yellow dress because now he's all in love, because
there is only one thought in all the world: what's her name, I forget her name, nothing matters like her name. Forget the killers,
remember the dead. Remember love and everybody's name. A
man with a paintbrush stands on the bridge above the stage. He
stretches for the ceiling, and signs his name on Heaven. The men
and women stand beneath a blank white ceiling before they drag
the heavens down to Earth, because they never once imagined in
a million years we'd ever get to go up there alive. See the ghost of
a small boy guiding his father's hand. He describes the great and
strange unreachable craters of the moon.

Last year, Amad told me the good news he'd heard about Sarah.
I didn't even know she'd gotten married, or that Nikos had been
out of the picture for so long. We were hanging up the sign for
store number two, two beaches south, in Huntington. Teri was
pleased. I have to say that good news about Sarah sent me down
a deep dark hole. In fact, Amad and I were supposed to celebrate
that night with dinner, but I excused myself and went home,
where I got very drunk with Dad. And when I say that, I mean I
got drunk while my poor Dad lay twisted in bed, not saying a
word and completely immobile. He'd been lying there for over a
year. He was here, but he wasn't here at all. Only his eyes were
alive, lit with that same anxious fire that showed on his face for
as long as I could remember. That final night he saw something,
I don't know what. If I were more romantic, I would say my
mother's ghost was there in the room, and that he saw her. Because
his face softened, and his eyes cooled, his heart was eased. A
peace descended upon him, a peace he'd been looking for his

whole life. I don't know what frightened me more, watching death slowly descend upon my father or how he seemed to welcome it body and soul. I kissed his still head. I sat with him for a very long time. And then I went outside. I walked, and then I ran over the sand, like a free beast, running alive into the night.

NO MORE
DOMINION

They come along the path out of the wood and rounding the tall tulip tree, all one hundred feet of sky-scratching smooth brown bark, the wide waxy green leaves growing in clusters. Past the coffee trees and thick leathery bean pods that dangle like bats from the branches. It's dusk and the air is rich with river smell, and with pig meal, and the char of the canebrake burning. Some come on horseback, but most come carriaging, gathered on wagons. Two wheels, four wheels. The clop and crack of hooves on limestone like splinters in the evening air. There is the buzzing chirp of katydids as bony hooves slap rock. And behind the farmhouse, brook water passes through tufted grass into a blanket of watermeal buds. Some of the wagoners ring handbells as they ride by in procession. The clappers knelling doleful as the sun goes low. The drivers click at their teeth, side-mouth, waving at the small boy as they ride by the farm.

Orr yells, "I don't know, Daddy. And there's more wagons up the way."

He pulls his hand from his pocket and opens his palm. His daddy's voice is low. Orr sees him, barely, through a cloud of smoke by the crackling canebrake high on fire. His father cutting a girdle in a hickory's bark by the riverside, says, "You steer clear. Just pick a pig. Go on now."

A baby shrew he found in the grass hugs blindly there at the boy's fingers, its whiskered and pointy snout sniffing at the air. A cashew, pink and soft. Orr nudges it some, and shakes his palm gently every time the shrew gets steady.

Another wagon rolls by.

The driver wears a hat whose brim hides his eyes. And the loping gait of the horses teases Orr with every rise and fall, just short of letting him see the driver's face. It's a long wagon with four wheels, plain, flat, and filled with children. He closes his fist over the shrew. A short boy waves at him, jumping and grabbing at a low branch passing overhead. One thing's sure, jumping boys haven't lost their mothers yet. That boy's too happy, must be his mama's back home alive. Another dizzy coming on; Orr is feeling poorly, maybe a fever.

"Orren Laudermilk, you get away from the road."

He turns to see his father coming up from the riverbed, the canebrake behind him burning alive with red fire. His father coughs as he walks, waving the smoke from his face. Jumping from the fence, Orr wipes at his pant legs and opens his palm. The pink ball of shrew uncurls itself. It sniffs, raising its head, sizing him up maybe. He rolls the tail softly between his fingers.

"What you got there?" His daddy brushes his fist with the hat.

"Nothing." He puts his hand in his pocket.

"You don't look no better, all ghost white." Orr's daddy presses his forehead with the back of his hand. "Warm as toast. Can't be pox. Can't be." His daddy feels the air for moisture with his fingers. "We need rain before our grass goes brown. And you can make yourself useful even when you're sickly." He points toward the hogs and pigs behind the fence, scattered about on their bellies and sides in the yard. Pink muddy mounds of belch and snore. "It'll be fall before long, and your time to kill. We'll do it together, I promise. But you need to pick the pig."

Orr nods some, Yessir.

"Look at me."

Orr looks.

"Your mother'd be in hearty agreement. No good reason to be afraid of killing." His father motions toward the yard.

"Yessir." He looks at the pigs, not sure what it will mean to pick a pig. Picking's not the same thing as killing, he knows that much. He nods toward the wagon up the road, and says, "Where they off to?" A sour spark fills him up, thinking what other kinds of places in the world there are.

"Oh, I can guess right, I bet." His father's face is broken with lines like tree bark. "You done the luck jars yet?" He yawns. "Put them with the soap. I filled a bag with every last bar. With any luck we'll sell all of it. Don't you leave it till morning. I'm leaving early and you're not well enough for travel."

"I never get to go into town."

"Plenty to do right here."

A wagon passes with a thin man in the driver's seat wearing bright red suspenders. The man nods.

Orr and his father keep their ground.

A young lady stands in the back of the wagon, her face shadowed by a bright yellow bonnet.

"Come on now," his father shouts at the wagon. "You all scaring my hogs!"

She walks toward the edge of the wagon, looking almost like she'll jump if she gets the chance. She says, "It's gonna be a glory day, and you all should join us tomorrow. We can dance with Him in His presence." She shakes herself like she's been doused with cold water. "You know about Heaven and hellfire, boy?"

Orr looks up at his Daddy, closing shut his hand in his pocket.
"We're not particular, and you don't talk to my son," his daddy
says as the lady in the wagon rides off. A bell makes a high, clean
racket in the evening. "Makes no odds," he says, looking at Orr.
"Put them luck jars in the wagon, could fetch as much as three
dollars apiece. Should be a good morning with all these folks
going up."

Some men on horseback come galloping. Orr moves closer to
the path. The horse legs work feverishly, tossing up dirt clods and
lime shards. He's not so scared and he blocks his face from the
dust as steam rises from the nostrils of the horses, their wet mucus
shining.

"Get over here," his father says. "Before you get yourself
walked on."

He turns back and stands beside his father as the men ride by.

Trees vein the blue dusk, and a sudden flutter like sheets of
rustling paper comes from the slow-burning cane. He looks back
that way, at the cave in the hill by the bank rocks, and the bats
come rushing out of it, spat from a sick mouth, almost eclipsing
the orange leaves of fire. The dizzy in his head drives the wet chill
on his skin.

"Fire's about done," his father says, walking back toward the
canebrake. "And you all keep moving now," he says louder.

Orr watches his father scoop up his hat from the river and
toss water at the fire. He pulls his hand from his pocket, opens it,
and he can barely see the shrew in the evening light. He pulls a
sharpened piece of cane wood from another pocket. He stares
until his eyes see better. Not so sure he can do it, kill a pig. He
turns toward the river, and his father pulling down the cane char.
The moon is out somewhere, making a cold glow over and through
the woods. He looks up, can't find it. He looks down where now
he sees the shrew nuzzling. He once watched his father sever the
head of a deer with a rusted saw. They never let him see his
mother's body. Already a year now without her. He pushes at the

shrew with the cane blade and looks back at his father hacking at the grasses. He stabs lightly at the shrew's belly, seeing how far he can push without breaking the soft pink skin.

"Get those jars in the wagon, Orr. I've got an early morning."

He wipes away a cold sweat from his warm face. It makes a dark spot on his sleeve. He presses the blade against the shrew's soft tail as it bustles on its back like an upturned bug. The shrew squeals. He turns away, his small body bucking with revulsion. Bitters from his stomach spit up into his throat. Sometimes he naps with the hogs. Pig bellies are round and tough like leather. He slaps at a fly on his neck, and again he pokes the tip of the blade into the soft belly of the shrew.

"Why you dawdling? You *need* to get in bed." His daddy comes up beside him again.

"I'm going, I'm going. There's still light left."

His father kicks a rock toward the path. "Dammit, Orr." He points at the hill beyond the path, where a large black sow, the oldest, freely grazes on the hill. "Get her in the yard. Now."

Orr rolls the cane back and forth between his fingers. Another wagon coming. "Why there so many wagons?"

His father bends and picks a stone from the grass. "Unneighborlies telling us all what's what. God don't play particular and neither should we." He throws the stone and hits the wagon broadside, the rider turns abruptly. "You're breaking up stones from my path!"

His daddy says, "They used to come around some, and knocking on your door. But I haven't seen them out this way since before your mother's gone. Must be a camp meeting up north some."

A lone rider approaches and slows, pulling up his reins, rubbing noises as they tighten around his gloves. He lets a rider go on beside him, and says, "You all should join us riverside tomorrow. A glory day and these years are glory years! We're living in the Lord's last century now!" He removes his hat and shows a smooth bald head. The man looks up. "These days are Last Days, and Heaven and Hell are hungry."

Orr looks back at his father.

His father says, "Get moving out of my land."

The rider smiles. "My scalp is clean like my conscience. And I'll see you tomorrow yet. No staying away, I hear. You best bring your boy when the Lord comes calling." He stands in his saddle and slaps at the neck of his horse, galloping off.

His daddy says, "Let's just hope these folks got dollars in their pockets. Ladies do like soap, all kinds."

"Where they all headed?"

His father studies him, and then says, "You see all around? Take a good look."

Orr looks.

"All the God we need and church, too." His father shows the wood, and the river. "All of this is mine. And yours. God's, too, if there is one. And it don't cost a penny from your pocket."

Orr nods his head: makes sense.

"Your inheritance, boy. Good land to work, and the character of your mother. May not be much, but it's yours." His father looks around the farm. "This is everything."

"Yessir."

"You remember the Montgomerys who moved back east? We had business."

"Yes sir." The youngest Montgomery boy had shown Orr how to whittle.

"They was like these but different. Catholics. Same thing, but different. At least they had enough sense to keep to themselves and never come knocking."

Orr's bones ache, and he thinks of dead pigs, and horses gone, and of his sleeping and buried mother. All of them in one place. He's warm and cold in all different parts of his body.

He says, "God's here, too?"

"All we need of Him."

Orr thinks on this. So He's somewhere else, too, where we don't need Him.

He looks at the pigs in the yard, his stomach weaseling up in his throat. Mamma's in a place where we don't need Him.

His daddy rubs his fingers together. "And I can't figure why God'd want my corn to dry anyway."

Orr opens his palm and watches the shrew crawl. His father snaps a broken branch from a hickory and walks off, saying, "Every few years they get together, particulars in bunches, swearing God is particular. All that sort of horse shit. Your mother, she wouldn't hear none of it."

The shrew's fine, just fine. Get the jars on the wagon pull, and bed the sow.

A blond woman passes along in the back of a flat wagon. She stares about, looking lost, misplaced. Her face is long and blank. She reaches out a hand toward Orr. She's reaching. He wants to take it, not sure why.

His father says, "Give me any tulip tree, a hundred feet high, and I'll bow down like any one of them." His father waves at the path. "Wave goodbye, Orr. They won't be back for a long while."

Orr waves. His father tosses a stone. The bats fly over, screeching, changing positions in the trees.

His father says, "Just like them, moving in bunches. What Kentucky needs is independent persons. You, me, and like your mother was."

A wagon stops and the driver tips his hat to the boy. The driver says, "Get on now." He smacks the resting horse's back. "I said get on!" But the horse stands still with his eyes bewildered, and looking backward, spying on Orr and what lies in his palm.

A thin switch snaps backward, comes down with a cleaving thwack. The driver shouts, "Get on!" And the horse snarls and buckles from the switch, rearing slightly, then falls forward into a reluctant trot.

Orr buckles, too, and is sure he smells the burning stripe on the horse's hide. His father's voice comes from behind him.

As the smell of cane char wafts from the river.

The black sow watches from the hill.

She's fat and she's proud, lifting up her gray snout, her black belly swaying as she moves. She's queenly there against the sky, the biggest of the lot. The oldest one of all. Her tail curls up in silhouette. A hot sick stirs in Orr's stomach. He shivers, heaves, and vomits. Not much, but it empties him. He wipes his mouth and spits. He cries some, but makes sure his daddy can't see. He dries his eyes, and opens up his palm. He presses the blade to his own soft neck, looking down there at the baby shrew. He presses hard, but does not break his own skin. It hurts. It's not that he's just afraid of killing, but also of what lies beyond the act, and he can't seem to figure it. He pulls the blade away, and puts it back in his pocket. He sets the shrew down in the grass. He walks across the path toward the black sow grazing in the dark.

It's early morning and a cold blue canopy stretches over the farm. The hogs are asleep in the yard. With a deep breath, Orr walks toward a large oak tree, dew dripping from the prickly browning tubers of a cancer root growing at the base. A dog barks, and Orr says, "Be quiet." A good sleep, but he's woken with a kindling in his chest, the kind of brittle breathing that comes with a slow-breaking fever. He snaps off a piece of the root and rubs it against his neck, at the same place he'd pressed with his blade last night. He walks toward the barn, itching at his heavy shirt and wiping sweat from his brow. "Wet morning," he says to the dog. "Think she'll rain?" He takes a piece of ham from his pocket, bites it, and throws the rest into the grass.

He hears the wooden clatter of a passing wagon but he refuses to look, afraid he might see the woman's face again. He reaches up and pulls at the heavy barn doors.

It's dark inside and the air is chilled and still. He walks along toward the back table, hay grass snapping underfoot. The black sow grunts and snorts, a few piglets asleep there at her teats. He looks away from her. A subtle light is bleeding through the clapboard slats, and the chickens are waking. Beside is the soap table. All empty now, every last bar for sale. The barrel beside it filled with ash for making lye. He takes hold of a long spade and pushes back open the doors. Morning coins of sun blink between the oak leaves and cast bright flashes as he walks toward the river. Horses are coming, but Orr won't look to the road.

He stabs at the earth by the bank rocks, digging, sweat gathering over his eyes until he strikes a hard surface. He presses the spade against the side until he can wedge the point beneath it. He presses with his slight weight until the object comes loose, breaking through the soil like a small coffin. His daddy's been gone for hours already. He never gets to leave the farm.

He pulls the old luck jar from the ground and wipes away the soil from its bellied surface. The molded shape of a man's bearded face stares back from the jar, his hard clay beard uncoiling, painted and covering one full side of the jar. A cork has been stuffed forcefully into the opening and seems almost fused to the jar. He studies it, turning the thing in his hands, and wiping the bearded face clean. He wonders how such a thing truly works. His father once told him they used to get made by witches. But not anymore. Anyone can make one, as long he believes, if he truly believes. Call it magic, luck, or religion, boy, it's God in a bottle and it works. The air still tastes some of chalky cane char. The bare and burnt stalks naked beside him. He sees clearly through the canebrake now. No place for hiding anymore. Their luck has been good since Mamma died, when the raiders came sneaking from behind the canebrake. They put a knife through her belly, left her lying on the bed. His daddy found her. He told Orr not to come any closer. His daddy pulling the petticoat back in place . . . You have to feed your luck, Daddy always says, like anything else alive. So they bury a new luck jar and get rid of the old one every time after burning the canebrake.

He tosses the jar into the river and watches it bob and jerk with the current, disappearing downstream, wishing the water good luck as it goes. Time to make and bury a new one.

He walks back around the barn to the doors.

The barn interior is more visible now with light stealing in between wallboards. Smoky with sunlight and brown shadow, flecked with swimming dust and yellow grit. He walks to the soap table and, kneeling, reaches under. Only four empties left. He picks the smallest of the four, an oblong jar with a greenish stain on the surface of the carved bearded face, wipes it clean of hay dust, and takes the fire tongs from a hook on the wall and sets them on the table. He looks around at the floor of the barn until he spies a mushroom lump of cow dung. With his blade he slices and lifts a small piece. Then he presses and maneuvers the piece into the open mouth of the jar, ridding his blade of cow dung like butter from a knife. He looks back and forth, side to side, in the barn.

Feathers.

He reaches over the chicken fence, takes hold of a hen, and pulls a grab of feathers from her back while she squawks and kicks out her feet. He drops the hen and bunches the feathers, slipping them easily in the mouth of the jar. The jar is warm in his hands and a plume of stink wafts upward, the dung cooking some on the bottom surface. He wipes sweat from his brow, spits into the jar, and sets it beside the tongs on the table.

A long wooden shelf hangs above.

He pulls over a crate and climbs up onto the table. From here the ceiling joists are that much closer. Chickens hop on the hard, packed dirt showing through a thinning layer of hay grass. Need to lay more hay grass. The black sow is asleep, her broad back rising in breath. The sun bursts between the roof boards, and he covers his eyes.

He takes a wooden box and a shallow clay bowl from the shelf, and climbs down.

The bowl is filled with calcified nail shavings, glass-sharp hoof cuttings, the remnants of a dead horse's tail. In the box are the remains of a King James Bible, a spilling bag of corks and bungs, and a pile of modest handmade crucifixes. The Montgomery boy showed him how to make them. He chooses one of the smaller ones, no taller than his thumb. A crude dying Christ hangs from the cross like a loose frayed ribbon. He opens the Bible at random, and points his finger on the page. He reads the verse out loud like his daddy taught him: "Be not righteous over much. Neither make thyself over wise. Why shouldest thou destroy thyself?"

He tears the page from the binding.

He spreads the page on the table and places the wooden Christ in its center. Chooses two large crescentlike hoof cuttings, and pulls a long black hair from the horse's tail. He scatters the cuttings over the Christ, folds the paper over its contents. He carefully ties the bundle with the hair strand. He then works the small bundle into the open mouth and drops it into the jar's clay belly. Chooses a leather cork, takes the fire tongs from the table, and leaves the barn.

Around back, he sets the jar on the ground and removes the top cover of a barrel. It's half full, and a cloud stink of urine opens upward, hot and metallic. The lean smell of cow piss rides on the rich rot of aged, wet wood, filling his nostrils with a sting and making him nauseated. He spits. The barrel's been full for weeks and the urine is dark, taking on the color of the wood like a whiskey. A crucifix floats there, sacralizing the urine aged and now turned to lant. He grabs the jar in the grip of the tongs, pressing the neck of the bottle up against the hinging pivot of the tongs, and he immerses it. The clay bearded face goes under. He pulls the jar from the barrel, made new, full and baptized in the sacred lant.

He stuffs the cork into the brimming mouth and it spits warm spume along the sides. He hammers the cork in with the butt of his fist, and then against the barrel. He wipes the sweat from his face and leans against the barn, feeling woozy. Walking back to the hole by the river, he allows himself some real satisfaction in his work, thinking of sitting down soon in the cool summer grass and the breeze drying his cold wet back, thinking of his mother, of the fine morning, and the good luck piss jars bring.

Orr takes a piece of hard bread and dips it in the ham grease his father left out for him. He stuffs his mouth, crumbs falling. It's well past noon, closer to evening, and his father should've been home by now. From outside there comes a nervous barking. It's the red dog on its belly. Beside the door, the fire in the pot stove shrivels inward, its blue leaves going cooler. Chewing on the bread, he goes outside and sees a wagon coming from the wood. He shushes the dog, kicks its haunches, and it runs. It's a large covered carriage, white-tented, and the horses are slowly moving. He picks up a stone from the ground, cocks back his arm. The dog darts toward the path, barking, yipping.

The wheels of the wagon are large and white, spokes blue and red. The finest wagon he's ever seen. He throws his body forward with the stone, but misses hitting the dog. He picks another from the grass. The wagon comes closer and the driver wears a hat tipped low, blocking his face. The horses have silver blinkers on their eyes, rebounding bursts of sunlight. Orr squints, walking closer to the dog. He throws the stone, and immediately wishes he hadn't. The dog cries out and turns toward Orr, tongue hanging, before running back to the river.

"Why'd you hurt your dog?" the driver shouts.

The wagon has pulled off the stone path, and moves quietly now in the grass. Not yet looking at the man, he stares at the wagon, at this rude turn. The horses are close now, slowing the rumble of their breathing, fume and spit fogging from their dark nostrils. On the side of the tent in large red and blue letters: "Langley's Daring Circus Show."

"Seems like a fine dog," the man says, a deep and croaking voice.

Orr looks up past the wagon wheels, past the horses' shoulders, their silver blinkers, to the dark man sitting in the seat.

"You're a negro," he says.

"And you're not blind at all."

The man climbs down from the seat and wipes his pant legs clean. He stands straight, stretches backward, and yawns. The biggest man Orr's ever seen. The man arches his back as he yawns. His thick and shining chestnut arms are raised and rearing.

Orr steps back. "Not my dog."

"Don't matter." The man's hairline is far back on his head, and his hair is round and cut short. He wears a black silk neck cloth and a silver ring on his pinky finger.

Orr says, "What do you want?"

The man bows some. "Your folks around? Maybe some water for my team?"

Orr looks back at the canebrake, how he can see right through it, no cover. "My daddy's right inside."

The man turns for the house. "Maybe you could you make us acquainted."

Orr picks up another stone, a larger one from the ground.

"I'm no dog, son. Put it down."

"My daddy's around. By the river."

"I think maybe we did this wrong." He loosens his neck cloth. "You know some negroes, don't you?"

"My daddy says you all are good workers even when you got no choice."

The man laughs. "True enough. You a hard worker?"

"I am." He calls to the red dog coming back from the river. "Come here, dog."

"Whose dog then?"

"Lots of dogs. Live all over, I guess. Some negroes live upriver in a small house. My daddy helped build it, and then he gave them a pig." He looks up. "Your face looks like a black cherry."

The man laughs. He looks at the back of his right hand and puts the hand behind his head. "Guess I do."

"I mean the color of cherries."

"I know what you mean."

"I've seen some look more dark."

"Well my daddy's the color of blackberries. And I just had me a handful back there, so no harm." He points back toward the wood, and then leans against the fence. "What's your daddy look like?"

"How do you mean?"

The man waves away his question. "What's your name?"

"Orr. Orren Laudermilk."

"That's a good name, Orr." The man puts out his hand. "I'm Cotten."

Orr throws the large stone toward the river. "My father looks like that." He points to a shagbark hickory, bark layers draped like hairy shingles, and a white ring cut in the flesh. "Can't get his face clean no matter what."

Cotten laughs and wipes the back of his neck. "And where am I, exactly?"

Orr takes a half step forward. "Woodford. Where'd you come from?"

"Back east. Headed for Lexington."

"You came too far west." Orr pulls at the shirt sticking on his fevered skin. "We can take your horses to the river."

"You're a good neighbor." Cotten begins unhitching the team. "You looking pale. You all right?"

"Just tired."

"All right."

Orr narrows his eyes, thinking on the man.

Cotten says, "I bet you're wondering what I'm doing out here. Fine wagon, no white folk."

"Ain't my business."

"That's true."

Orr touches a horse's head. "You whip your horses?"

"I have never whipped a horse in my life."

He looks at the man, his neck cloth hanging loose, and his smooth face. His eyes. Orr says, "I don't hate dogs."

"I know it," Cotten says, unhitching the team. He rubs the horses' heads.

"Soon as I threw it I wished I hadn't."

The big man looks at the dog. "Dogs don't lie. It's people you can't tell mean you harm." He pulls the team from the wagon, and they lead the horses to the river.

Back inside the house, Cotten points at the ham, and then to his own self. "I'm starving."

Orr says, "That's what it's for," and looks at the pot fire. He feels a surprising fearlessness with this stranger.

"Smells good. Ain't had a real meal all day." Cotten pulls a pink piece from the hock, chomps and swallows.

"You free?" Orr picks at the ham. "Out here alone, no white folk."

"We all free." Cotten wipes at his mouth with his sleeve. "Just most don't know it." Picks more at the ham.

Orr nods. "I guess."

"And most of us ain't free at all."

Orr chews slowly. "What's in Lexington?"

"Going to see a man named Clay. We write letters. I don't suppose your daddy keeps any whiskey."

"You particular about your whiskey?" He's proud to use the new word he learned.

"Can't say I ever been."

He turns his back to Cotten and walks behind the pot fire. "My father's not here. Not really."

Cotten lets out a hoarse snicker. "I know that by now, boy. You afraid I'm gonna take you and eat you all up? Put you in the oven? Come on now."

"My father keeps his whiskey on the window."

Cotten stands and rubs his hands on his pants. "Whew, too long on that wagon." He pushes aside the curtain and takes the bottle from behind. "All the way from South Carolina."

"Is that your wagon?"

"Man I work for." Cotten takes a pull from the bottle and his face contorts, his torso bends like from a blow to the ribs. "Lord!" He sets the bottle on the table. "Mister Bill Langley. I'm just renting." He takes another pull.

"My daddy says Kentucky did God's dirty work for him and made whiskey on the seventh day."

The man throws back his head, mouth full of whiskey and silent with laughter so as not to lose a drop. He wipes at his silk cloth, checking for a spill.

Orr comes out from behind the pot fire. "He let me taste it once." Just thinking about it makes his stomach wrinkle. "Most negroes around here ain't like you." Orr looks at the floor, and then back to Cotten. "You ever killed anything before?"

Cotten shakes his head. "What for?"

Orr shrugs his shoulders. "What's a circus?"

Cotten considers the question. "A place for making people happy."

There's a sound of quick breathing at the doorway, the red dog, half inside. Orr pulls a piece of ham from the hock, and throws it to the floor.

Cotten goes on, "We got horse shows and tricks." He takes another swig from the bottle.

Orr takes a piece of ham for himself. "You gonna work for a circus in Lexington?"

"No, sir." The bottle dangles from his fingers. He looks upward; Orr follows his gaze to the rafters, but sees nothing. "Can you read some?"

Orr nods. "My daddy teaches me from the Bible."

"That's a good book." Cotten clears his throat. "I guess you-all Christian, then?"

"My daddy says God ain't particular, and no one gets to tell you what's what."

"I like your daddy." Cotten takes another piece of ham. "I don't subscribe to nothing neither. Where'd your daddy go to?"

"North."

"What for?"

"Merchants. And for salt. He's selling luck jars and soap. Should be good with all them wagons going up."

"I seen all them. Got stuck in the middle of some taking up the road." He waves away all of what bothers him. He puts the cork in the bottle and sets it behind the curtain on the ledge. "Your father heading for a camp meeting?"

"What exactly is a camp meeting?"

"Like a big church meeting."

"You going to a camp meeting?"

"Never took." Cotten coughs. "Where's your ma at?"

Orr hesitates, not used to the question. "She's dead."

Cotten coughs again. "Well, I'm real sorry."

Orr fans the pot fire. Puts his hand by the heat until he can't take it no more. "Where you think a dead person goes to?"

Cotten shakes his head, and stands. "Can't say."

"That's what my daddy says." He barely touches the stove and pulls away his finger. "I saw my mother. On a wagon. Yesterday."

"Well, you never do know." Cotten sighs. "How far north your daddy go to?"

"Maybe two hours." Orr looks back through the doorway. "You know about Heaven?"

Cotten looks at the bottle on the window, then back to the boy. "How old are you?"

"Twelve and a half."

Cotten looks like he's either itching for another pull of whiskey, or maybe wishing he hadn't gotten started. Orr turns away from the doorway and looks back at Cotten, at his eyes paying close attention. Cotten says, "If people knew what free is, they'd live it. Not all slaves are slaves. And not all free are free."

The sky in the doorway is darker. Orr feels the blade in his back pocket. "I can show you how to get to Lexington."

Cotten tightens his neck cloth. "I'd appreciate it."

"Only one road. And I bet we pass my daddy on the way."

"Oh, I don't know about you coming. People see you alone with a strange nigger, we're bound to find trouble."

Orr pours water on the pot fire until it dies to embers.

"You're looking tired." Cotten touches his forehead. "And you warm."

"I'm fine."

Cotten laughs. "Betting you don't take no for an answer."

Orr waits for him to leave so he can follow behind, but Cotten excuses himself, nods, and extends his arm through the doorway, after you.

They gather the horses and lead them to the wagon. Cotten hitches the team.

Orr climbs into the seat, and feels again for the blade in his pocket. He watches the hogs and pigs sleeping in the yard as the wagon rolls on through the grass. The black sow's rump swings as she walks to the trough. Maybe that one. Seems right to pick out the oldest. Maybe not so afraid after all of the kill, of picking one, and having to kill.

———

An hour north along the river, Orr says he'll walk on no matter how far, and Cotten should just go east because he's bound to find his father on the road. But Cotten won't hear it. So they ride on along the path, over the limestone worn smooth by the herds of long-gone buffalo. They climb the crest of a tall wooded knob as a dumb white moon watches over them. They ride roughly over the grassy rise, the river going dark alongside them, until a field opens out below them surrounded by a wood. Fire lights smearing yellow trails in the distance. They ride closer to a wash of noise.

They ride through the field, as the night gets less dark in the lamplight out by the tree line. They ride past large rocks along the hill, where curious locals watch and bear witness to what appears to be a vast gathering filling up the field. Wagons in the field, littering the hill and the woods. There are voices, a rising din of shouts from the crowd lit up by a bonfire. The wash of noise grows, as they get closer, soon filling up the evening like the sound of a rushing waterfall. They see hundreds of horses standing there by the trees. On a short wooden stage, a tall thin man stalks back and forth before the crowd, hands flailing. The sound of the crowd is even louder in the corner of the field, where they make a strange wheat waving in the night breeze. Pink hands waving, and white hands, and the negroes in the back make a dark place, their forearms moving along in waves. They all move in the shadowed field, a spreading swath of smoke movement in the lamplight, the candlelight, and the bonfire beside the forest. Whiteheads fly to the tallest trees now dark in silhouette. The Appalachians hold sway in the east.

"That's my daddy's wagon!"

Cotten pulls on the reins. "You sure?"

Orr jumps down from his seat. "That right there. And that's our bag." He jogs over to a wagon and grabs at a bag, pulls out a bar of soap, and shows it like a prize.

They tie the team to a stump.

Cotten says, "Better stay close," as they venture into the crowd.

They walk by lean-tos and shelters made of bundled sticks, and by cloth tents pitched at woodside, by children sleeping in straw beds and infants feeding at breasts, napping in their woolen blankets. They walk in among the army of readying people, who press themselves ever closer.

Some sit still, consumed by a sober worship, but most move about, declaring aloud a commitment to the High Holy Spirit. They watch a youngster make exhortations from his father's shoulders, filled with the Spirit of the Lord, never too young for salvation. A magic maker performing tricks, dancing on eggs unbroken and telling futures. The leather-dressed men with rifles on their backs speak to all who might listen. An older woman, about his daddy's age, waves at Orr and Cotten, singing out "Glory, glory, Hallelujah! Glory, glory, Hallelujah! Sing with me, boy. I sing with God, and He says He likes my voice!" Orr can't help but smile. And other women sing prayers and poems, and listeners are bewitched by these women—by women! She swears she speaks to God direct! Orr sees the white preacher on the clapboard stage—the young man insisting on a truth, a new truth that you know in your heart was placed there by Christ, and your sinful nature needs his election, swearing, "You *will* hear my voice, because this mouth is God's mouth, and none other's. Never will you need the mouth of another to claim your stake in the Lord! God's eyes and ears hear *you*, see *you*, He knows *you* and your soiled soul." And the listeners cannot keep still. This blood is boiling over as they quiver and fill up with the Spirit, and they rock against Orr and Cotten. Cotten takes hold of Orr's hand.

"The Holy Fire is too hot for any standing still!" says the preacher onstage.

Orr watches the people shake and wave in the clearing. It frightens him.

There is a passing of the Spirit, unbounded by bodies. There is a heaving, a hurling from inside their souls in the torchlight. Retch any spirit that keeps you calm. Grab others by their collars, and fill yourself with overpour. Get drunk on the Spirit in this place, dance with the Spirit in this place, each one a name and a face before the one true God who grants salvation, the God who knows your every sin, your failings, and who forgives them, who grants mercy, and will be made glorified and will come down to this place soon enough—*to this place*—and set His feet on American soil. He will walk these hills, returning giant of Jesus Christ, oh Great Man of Original Liberty.

Orr and Cotten start away from the center of the crowd, toward the outer fringes of the great gathering, Cotten's big hand on the boy's slender shoulder. But the forest is no less spirited and filled with persons. The horses in half-light are tethered to the trees and their heads are lowered in shadow, drinking from water troughs and bowls. Orr and Cotten make for the back of the woods toward the river and away from the field. Still they are accosted, and handled, beseeched by other exhorters. "Won't you please show your love for the Lord?" The black folk among them see Orr walking with his negro.

Cotten says, "Stay close."

"Why they crying?"

"They don't wanna be here no more."

Orr sees mostly legs and bellies, so Cotten sets the small boy on his shoulders. "Look for your daddy, go on now!"

Orr taps Cotten's head. "I don't see him nowhere."

"What? Too loud. Keep looking."

They shoulder on toward the river, where the trees are darker and the chanting is lower behind them. Thinner trees shake in the wind and look alive. Orr swats at a low branch grabbing at him.

There is a loud cry, and Orr points that way. "Look!"

Waist deep in the river water and sloshing about is a wiry and
bare-chested man with a wild white beard, his black hat sliding
off the side of his head, almost falling; he's constantly pulling and
setting it straight. The man forces a struggling piglet partly under
the water. He laughs and belches. I baptize you in the name of
the Father and the Son and the Holy Roast! He wrestles with the
piglet and pushes the head fully under. The man's hat falls away
and rushes downriver. Some of the watchers cheer, raised whiskey bottles in their hands. But most point, and cry out Blasphemer!
as the man grapples with the kicking and pink suckling pig. It
slides some from his hands, front hoofs clacking.

Cotten says, "Let's get on now!"

Orr rests his chin on the man's soft hair, feeling unsure and
sick in his stomach.

Cotten shouts, "We shouldn't have come so far!"

"What?"

"From the crowd. We're too far from the crowd! No telling
what kind of people! See your daddy anywhere?"

Orr watches the woods unfold in the torch glow, as listeners
burst with exhortations right in front of his eyes, making speeches
like they'd done so all their lives, garbling words he's never heard
before. Cotten carries him past a small campfire. Clay jugs pass
among the fire watchers. An old man, his face red with cackling,
hot breath, reaches up to Orr, offers the boy a drink. The old man
says, Have a sip! Cotten just waves him aside. They move on further away from the crowd, to what looks like a white blur wavering back in the trees. It's too high, almost floating, it's a woman
with bright flowing hair. Her golden hair of sunlight hangs long
and ribboned with a white rope draped over her shoulders. She's
a ghost in a white gown looking like an angel. A crown of thistles
rests upon her head. In one hand she holds what looks like a wand,
a crooked stick like a witch's wand. She holds it high. And the
watchers yell out Harlot! whenever the stick falls to her side. The
other arm is tied with rope to a tree, her wrist going red.

Closer now, Orr sees a small stage and chair legs wobbling from under her gown.

Her hem has all gone muddy, and the watchers yell Harlot! Witch! while she cries out for help. Adulterous whore!

The white woman goes blurry in the trees, and goes smaller as they move away.

They head toward the crowd in the field. Orr looks for his father and sees that, now, inside the crowd, there isn't a crowd, but persons, faces, hands, and eyes. Each one a person, is a piece of the view from way back, high up on the knob. The poor folk and gentlemen, and the young ladies in silken wraps and gold finger rings muddy their finery as they move about and dance in the dirt. A snare drum pounds out a gallop. They raise their legs, dancing, walking and running in place, losing their bonnets and capes, fine hair loosening from pins and snapping back like whips, in enthusiasm for the Lord.

Orr doesn't know what to make of it all, and suddenly shouts: "There!"

They push through the crowd toward the stage behind a long wooden table, where sit baskets of bread and tin cups for communion, and the Christ blood in a fat leaden tumbler. The preacher onstage finishes with a flourish. The crowd responds with shouts of approval, as a new preacher takes to the stage.

"Right there! It's my daddy! Right there." Orr points to a man in the crowd. The man is shouldering a sack and can't seem to stop himself from laughing.

It is Gillon Dowse's first time onstage, this preacher of proud Ulster blood. He looks to the crowd, and the spirit in this crowd is fierce. So many exhorters in the field compete for listeners, speakers standing precariously on chairs. But there is a roar in these woods, and it comes booming from the lion mouth of Christ—This be all the spectacle we need. A bright torch blooms behind him. With hair long like a woman's, Dowse prays for the Holy Spirit, that this mouth speak only Truth, and that for Truth they will listen.

He spreads his arms out wide, black Bible in one hand, and the gesture fills him with boldness. "There is a heavenly scent in the air today. Who else among you can smell it? Can you smell the sweet Holy Spirit?" The listeners up front are swaying, their backs against the faithful sharing at the sacramental table. "This bounty is here and all for your taking, but only the pure in heart can sit. Dear God, I bless this table!"

Two tables, crossways, long wooden rough-cut slabs. The faithful take of the bread, and taste of the wine, their faces low and humbled under Heaven. The black folk take of less bread and of water, away at a farther table.

"Look this way!" he cries. "Because the Lord God knows your every secret and even now He knows your name." He demands: "I said look this way! Because this will be like no sermon before, a true American Gospel!" He can make out their mouths moving, the mumblings of prayer inaudible in the ruckus and racket of chant.

Only one man shows visible interest, standing off at the far side of the stage. A sack over one shoulder, the man is smiling, and Dowse assumes the smile is for his sermon, a great enthusiasm for the Gospel. The crowd around this man gathers, moving about, but those seated pay little attention. "Do you not smell the good clean air?" Dowse cries out. "This land made new in His spirit? His blood? I say, look this way!"

The heads finally look up from the table.

The backs of the others press up against them on the benches, jostling the cups in their hands. They all look his way, and their mouths fall open from shock. They rise—and see Gillon Dowse, in imitation of Christ. His arms extend in a crucifix gesture, Bible limp in his grip. Ankles crossed, he balances on one foot and drops his head to his chest.

He raises his head: "Now, won't you listen?"

There is a murmur of shocked hush at the tables. The smiling man with the sack, he whistles, he approves. "Take a look at him now," shouts the man.

Then another voice from the crowd: "Heresy!"

"Profane!"

"He claims to be the Christ!"

Dowse undoes his posture. "I claim nothing of the sort! But a recognition of His mercy, of His sacrifice and glory. I die for Him each day. Every day! And you die this day, too, for our Lord!"

The movement by the stage begins to drag, and the crowd calms even while the outlying listeners become one vast dancing witness. Here in Dowse's small assembly they start slowing, they set themselves apart. They still themselves and they listen. He hears the crying of a young boy, "Daddy! Daddy!"

He looks out among the crowd, at the man with the sack, and then to the other side of the stage where stands, not very far away, a very large nigger, held back by a crowd of what seem to be concerned white folk.

Whence comes the crying voice?

Dowse shouts, "For what reason do you throw yourselves? You dance in the woods like witches, when the Lord Himself walks these hills and you're too busy to see Him!" Dowse raises his hands in the air, shaping the world in his hands. "And our Heavenly Father sees us!"

The lull is widening now, as more of them stop and listen to the man onstage.

Dowse turns, and takes the torch from behind him. He holds it aloft out front. He is a fire breather and his mouth speaks Truth: "Do you see this face? See it? This is *my* face. *My* mouth. My soul stands before the Lord, and for it He knows my name!" His hair is dark wine pouring from a skull. "And He knows this heart inside my chest no less than He knows yours."

The crowd nods and murmurs.

The nigger is now holding back a boy, a small white boy, as the crowd wrestles with the nigger's thick wrists.

Dowse looks away, says, "And He knows my dreams no less than He knows yours."

A voice shouts back, "It's true!"

He walks back and forth across the stage. "For whom did the good Christ die on his cross? Tell me, who?"

Another shouts, "For me!"

"Yes! And no less for me, my Christ!" Dowse looks up to the night sky. "He is mine, I am His, and the Lord God knows my name. Now who among you in this land is not the child of God? Who among you?"

They all wave their arms, and nod, Yes, yes, yes. The man with the sack is awkwardly clapping, his hands still gripping the cloth of the sack.

Again, he whistles.

The circle of listeners grows in circumference, slowing outward like grass in a wind.

The boy is now yelling, and Dowse understands this was the crying he'd heard before, and yet he can hardly make out what the boy is saying, "My father, my father"? The boy is pointing at the clapping man, who now sets his sack down. But not on the ground—on the stage, on Dowse's stage. What presumption! Dowse ventures close, has half a mind to kick it off. But before he can, the man says boldly: "Why don't you just go ahead and make it rain, preacher? Make it rain!"

Torch in hand, Dowse says to the stranger. "I'm not the Christ, good brother. Never said I was. And I suggest you test not God, lest He answer harshly."

"No test for God, friend." The man laughs again. "It's a test for you. And I ain't your brother." He waves his hat at the gathering crowd. "Go on, we're farmers here, and it's a dry season so we could use a little miracle making. But we don't know much theater. So come on, let's see us some rain!"

A few laughs from the crowd, a few sniggers, and the faces look back and forth, wondering which of these two men will win.

Dowse places the torch on its stand. "Tell me, friend," he says, pulling his fingers through his hair. "What brings you if not a soul in need of a cure?" He looks at the crowd: Let us hear the man answer me this one! He sees the nigger talking to the white folk around him—where is the boy?—and the nigger is now getting smaller as the crowd walks him away toward the tree line. The boy is now struggling to free himself from the arms of a large white man who looks like a farmer. The boy is clearly yelling, "My father! My father!"

The man says to Dowse, "I'm here because I'm a man of luck, and good luck, I guarantee it!"

Dowse shakes his head and taps his palm against his Bible, chuckling. "Brother, only God guarantees."

"Then you must not be from around here, because out here we make our own luck. We got no choice!"

"I hear that," laughs a man in the crowd. "And with any luck we'll get rain."

The man now reaches inside the sack onstage. "Well, I ain't afraid of God, friend. He and I have no quibbling. Just with you and your clan here clamoring like roosters." He raises his head. "I'm a man of my own standing, and I make my own luck. Who else?" He pulls a large clay jar from his sack, a carved bearded face covering one side, and he says, "This'll keep you clean of his kind, or any other sour luck comes your way." He holds the jar above his head. "Who say'll give me three dollars for a good-luck jar?"

The crowd shouts back, some call him a heretic.

He shouts, "Good luck's all around you. Can't you smell it in the trees? And I've bottled all you need to take it home!"

A woman in a long coat shouts, "One dollar!" She shoves it at the man, taken in by his swagger, and tries to claim her purchase. The man holds the jar high, saying, "I make my own luck. Here's proof, a money-back guarantee! Show us proof, Fire-top! We need wheat before there's bread. Give us a miracle!"

"Here is a money changer dealing in the presence of God! And God alone makes miracles," says Dowse. "We give God no orders! We'd be in need of a new tongue just to whisper aloud His name!" Dowse shows the face of his Bible, and stamps his foot on the stage. Pacing. He is becoming excited.

Their applause takes them away from the newcomer. Hear, hear!

The lulled crowd awakens, as Dowse can no longer help himself. "Because freedom from a British king is no longer enough! The time has come for his Heavenly Kingdom on Earth!"

The crowd waves their hands and they move about in the clearing, nodding in assent. Dowse watches them stamp their feet and run in place, some in circles like horses.

The boy fights the farmer's hold.

"We do speak the same language, brother." He points to the boy's father, at the foot of the stage. "But what do you care for rain? I know what it is you seek," he says, swirling and grasping the torch, leaving fire trails in the air. "Liberty in body and soul! Our fathers, and our grandfathers, our brothers and sons all died for us, for this nation. I swear it was God gave us victory!"

The crowd cheers. They raise their knees and run in place, spending the Spirit that fills them too full.

"It was Captain Christ who gave us revolution!"

A birdcall echoes and the crowd shouts, Amen! Amen! Amen!

"He offers salvation in this world, and a salvation from it!"

The man stays beside the stage, tickled and pleased, even admiring. He is immersed in the great show.

"A constitution," Dowse shouts, "written by the heads of a Wild Beast! This is your land, yours! This place marked by His High Holy Spirit! Heal this place with me, and wait not for others. Heal thyself! Forsake the Pharisee help of doctors, and lawyers, of judges, and make of this land the Lord's backyard. Forsake earthly

princes and kings! For none of them know my name, and they
know not your name! What lay in my heart is sin, God knows,
but *that* He knows means He is within me. And I swear He knows
my name!" He leans toward the salesman smiling by the stage.
"You look at me good, now, brother."

"Oh, I'm looking." The man laughs.

"He knows your name, too, good stranger."

The boy shouts, "Daddy!"

Dowse looks, and sees the nigger is back, and now expertly
takes hold of the large farmer, squeezes him from behind as if
hugging him. The farmer's arms release the boy. The boy falls to
the ground and stumbles, slipping in the mud. The farmer looks
to be asleep in the dirt, and disappears as the crowd envelops
him. The boy is pushing his way through the crowd. Pushing his
way toward the stage. What tenacity, what strength, what faith,
this child.

Dowse turns to the man, and says: "You are but a child in His
eyes! And He knows every corner of your sinning soul, but *that*
He knows is good news. Be sure." He wags a flagging torch before
the gathering, and a thunder crack breaks above the hills. A flash
of lightning paints white light across the clearing—a brief and
moon-white glimpse of a hundred faces, a shock-still dance in the
glare. He extends an open hand to the laughing man. He laughs
along with him, a joyous yawp.

The man yells up to the preacher, openly admiring his show-
manship, and shouts, "You tricky son of a bitch!" The rain slaps
down on both of their faces.

The sky has opened up like a cataract, a down-pouring of rain.
The man stands at the front of the gathering, still some hundred
feet away, shaking hands with the preacher.

Cotten lowers the boy to the ground. "I'll go with you."

The rain falls in wet slicing sheets, as the field goes muddy.

The faithful are running in place in the rain. They dance, fueling themselves into a fervor. Cotten pulls back at the boy, his thick hand on Orr's thin wrist. The crowd lose themselves ecstatically in the shower. Their wet hands open and waiting.

Cotten shouts, holding the boy's wrist, "Don't get lost!"

The boy pulls away. "Let me go!"

The man is laughing along with the preacher.

But Orr knows his father's take on preachers, and still the man shakes hands with the preacher. Then comes a rush of onlookers in a wet wave of legs and bellies. Orr is caught between two strange women. His face is hot, the rain is cold, and he loses sight of his father.

"Ask and ye shall receive!" says the preacher.

The dancing is now at fever pitch, while some run in place and some in circles. The worshippers exhaust themselves, they empty themselves, and bells ring out in the rain.

Orr is pulled away. A woman on her knees pulls him closer.

Cotten's thick hand comes grabbing, but the wet palm slides down along Orr's arm, and the shaking crowd swallows Cotten whole. The woman on her knees is singing. Pale as death, she is old, and dank with rain. She sings a song Orr cannot understand. He sees through the wetness of her dress, and looks away. He's losing his breath, and the cold slapping water on his warm skin makes him go blurry inside. He looks between the moving bodies and the ribbons of rain for his father, Where's my daddy? The crowd pushes him closer to the stage. They push him as he shouts for his father. He falls and he rolls to the ground.

A strong thick hand reaches out for him.

Orr shouts out, "Let me go!"

Cotten lifts the boy. "You'll see better from my shoulders." But Orr wrestles against the big man as the white onlookers watch, Let me go.

"Let the boy go!"

Dowse looks for the boy.

Another voice, "Get your paws off that boy!"

Dowse sees the nigger make a path for the boy, and then squat low, his round head no longer heads high above the others, as he sidles off stealthily into the crowd. This pleases Dowse. God be with you, black. "See God's children sacralize this land with their worship!" he shouts. "Today is a day for our Lord and God, so give yourself to Christ and die this day. Kill off your old ways and come back born in His Spirit!"

Orr slips through the wet limbs and falls to the floor. Picks himself up and moves toward the front of the stage, can't see his daddy from here, and the fear is getting colder. He falls again just before the stage, face streaked with mud.

"And He comes with a great big stick! A brand-new Heaven and a brand-new Earth. Because the End is oh so near, I swear! And *this* time I know is the right time, the only time, for this generation will not pass before the Day of the Coming of the Lord! A revolution of God's own making, and no longer do we live in a time for waiting. And these years made holy are almost over, the Christ is finally come. See Him come even now in the hills, strolling like the walking sun, the trees like grass below His feet. For His head stays dry in the heavens, and His feet are wet in the Earth. Because Death has no sway on the Coming of the Lord. And Death will have no more dominion! Where is thy sting? Where is thy victory, O Death? See our Christ, He is come!"

Dowse drops to his knees.

There is a flash of lightning in the rain—then wait—wait for the buckshot of thunder.

Orr steps to the riser, Help me up.

He waves to his father, whose mouth is agape as he looks at the crowd.

What is happening to this great crowd? Then peripherally,

miraculously, most unexpectedly of all there manifests a young
boy who, to the man, looks like his son. What on earth are you
doing here, boy? Get you away from that stage!

The preacher, too, lifts his head. His eyes go wide, bearing
witness to yet another miracle.

Orr turns away from his father, and looks to the crowd. Slow
and strange, the world presses in on his skin. His forehead broils in
the cold rain, wet and cold, never been hot and so cold. Torches
spatter as an unlikely wave of flesh and human spirit falls away
from the stage; there is a slow heave and falling of people. They
turn sluggish, deathlike, and tired, a hundred souls or more. Mus-
cles relaxing, and down they go like husks falling from spent spir-
its; they exhaust themselves in exercise and enthusiasm for the
returning Lord. They fall. They all fall to the ground like one vast
body of so many parts, and fall into what looks like a slumber.
Mounds of mud and sleep; is this death? He's frightened by the
hundred fallen, the freshly threshed. They lie in the field like war
dead.

"But why, son? Will you not fall?" the preacher says to the
boy, at the far edge of the stage. "Spend yourself and be reborn,
awake in the Lord!"

"You're not my daddy," says Orr.

"You looking for your daddy, son?" The preacher extends his
hand, a fine fur on its back. "Come up here with me, and I will
show you."

Orr looks to his father, who is trudging in the mud for his son,
pushing others aside, saying to him "Get you away from that
stage!" Orr looks to the fallen covering the field, at the hundred
bodies prostrate on wet grass and rock.

His father coming closer: "You let go my son!"

Orr takes the preacher's hand. Lift me up.

Orr is lifted.

"You're all burning hot, boy." The preacher touches his forehead. "Now you look out there, and witness. These faithful will never have to go to the grave. Will never take a taste of death! Look at them asleep, and deep in dream. Heaven is the white sheet we sleep under. Where's your mamma? Is your mamma here?"

The raining sky and surrounding hills make for a febrile vision. Orr is scared and he looks at his father, who now holds out a hand to his son: Come down from there. And Orr feels shamed by his fear—I don't want it, and I don't want my daddy to see—but, look, there, out in the field is a stirring. See it? A handful of persons by the stage, they open their eyes. They awaken! Watch them kneel, and watch them rise. And there—in the field, waking up, is a beautiful woman. Reborn and refreshed, she looks just like her.

Shout for her? Run to her?

But he's too afraid of the dead, so he waves, the woman's face alight with resurrection.

"Is that your mamma, son?" Dowse asks. "She is a vision of Heaven."

His father says, "You come on down from that stage."

"Is that your daddy, son?"

He says, "I think that's my mamma,"

"Then go to your mamma, son. Go on."

Rising from the dirt and tangle of sleeping wet limbs this beautiful woman stands up. Is it her? She stands and stretches toward the stage.

"Mamma, I'm here! I'm right here!"

Deep within his heart, the vessel of his soul, he thanks the preacher and wants to say a prayer, his first prayer. Where does it come from? Not sure how, but the wish passes through him, up out the throat, and to his lips, these lips, where I say a wish out loud. Oh, take away the quiet creeping fear. With every passing syllable, the fear is further abated: Dear Lord, let it be her. And with enough luck, this woman waking up from the outside place, where there is no need for God, O God, please let it be her. Think on the black sow, how you won't have to kill her after all because Death, I swear, is beaten today. Death be now and forever undone. Amen.

ACKNOWLEDGMENTS

Books are only partly products of solitude, and so I must thank the following persons, places, and things:

Tom Cheshire, Jim Hanks, Joseph Salvatore, Matt DeBenedictis, Lauren Culley, Jason Tougaw, Duncan Faherty, John Weir, Carmiel Banasky, Bill Cheng, Alex Gilvarry, Kaitlyn Greenidge, Noa Jones, Tennessee Jones, Brianne Kennedy, Phil Klay, Liz Moore, Jessica Soffer, John Trotta, Sunil Yapa.

Jon Butler, Christine Heyrman, Paul Conkin.

True believers: O.G. Carrie Howland, plus all of Donadio and Olson (interns, too); and the deeply insightful Sarah Bowlin, along with the lovely people at Henry Holt.

Thanks to Jason Richman and the enthusiastic support of United Talent.

The Housing Works Bookstore Café; the dark and low-ceilinged stacks of the New York Society Library; the City University of New York; the Queens College English Department; and Hunter College, especially the Hunter MFA faculty.

Jon Butler's *Awash in a Sea of Faith: Christianizing the American People*; Christine Leigh Heyrman's *Southern Cross: The Beginnings*

of the Bible Belt; Paul Conkin's *Cane Ridge: America's Pentecost*;
Sonic Youth, *Silver Session for Jason Knuth*; Nels Cline and Devin
Sarno, *Edible Flowers*; Dirty Three, *Cinder*.

Mike Watt, at The Point, Atlanta, Georgia, 1997.

My family.

And best for last: my long-suffering lady, Kate.

ABOUT THE AUTHOR

SCOTT CHESHIRE earned his MFA from Hunter College. He is the interview editor at the *Tottenville Review* and teaches writing at the Sackett Street Writers' Workshop. His work has been published in *Slice, AGNI, Guernica, Narrative 4,* and the Picador anthology *The Book of Men*. He lives in New York City.